First Published in
ThunderPoin
Sum
4-5 Mi
Edi.
Scotland

Copyright © Ethyl Smith 2020

The moral right of the author has been asserted.

All rights reserved.

This book is a work of fiction. Names, places, characters and locations are used fictitiously and any resemblance to actual persons, living or dead, is purely coincidental and a product of the author's creativity.

Cover Image © Ethyl Smith
Cover Design © Huw Francis

ISBN: 978-1-910946-69-5 (Paperback)
ISBN: 978-1-910946-70-1 (eBook)
Printed and bound in Great Britain by Clays Ltd, Elcograf S.p.A

www.thunderpoint.scot

Acknowledgements

Those men and women who lived in 17th century Scotland and provided a history worth remembering.

Seonaid & Huw Francis of Thunderpoint Publishing for continued support and belief in my series about Covenanting times.

My family for support, patience and willingness to accompany me on research trips to strange places.

Dedication

Nathan, Rachael, Eryn, Skye
Luv frae yer Gran

This poem by Finola Scott perfectly sets the theme for 'Broken Times'

Finola is an acclaimed and widely published poet.

She is currently Makar for The Federation of Writers (Scotland)

Geese Turnin

In the shiverin derk we spy them skeinin oer winter-black loam.
We haislin them back tae clatter oan oor lochans.

In bricht simmer sun, in Enterkin Pass a bluidy skirmish.
Men slavery bound fir haudin tae their Lord, fir gainsayin
the king. Some, set free, return tae the lowe o beauty.

Sails crack, as oer the fame comes Renwick hame,
nae just a man noo. He returns chinged. A meenister
he gaithers aw, wi eens oot fir sojiers, bluid red coated.

Ahint it aw, the storm o Clavers, proud but nae Bonnie
mired in sae mony lives. Hauns an soul stained
Bluidy Clavers returns tae clink glasses amang his ain.

In springs bluid red dawn they're awa again. Lochs an muirs
ahint them. They tak tent o the breeze an slip awa north. Returnin.

Chapter One

'Hope is being able to see that there is light despite all the darkness' – Desmond Tutu

May 1683

Tobias Hawthorn stood on the steps of his kirk in Groningen and sighed as he watched two riders pick their way along the narrow, cobbled street then begin to cross the Grote Market. Early as it was, buying and selling was underway with all the noise of people bartering and arguing.

The riders soon disappeared among the brightly-coloured stalls and Tobias was left staring at the north-west corner of the square where the great Martini Tower loomed over everything. He frowned at the long dark shadow cast by the old grey tower and shivered, for it seemed like an omen.

Jonas Hawthorn and James Renwick rode in silence for several hours. Eventually Jonas pointed towards a small copse. "If ye dinna mind Maister Renwick, ah'd like tae stoap an gie they beasts a rest. We've a lang way yit an it's nae use wearin them oot sae early in oor journey."

James Renwick nodded and followed Jonas as he turned off the road.

Jonas jumped down as they reached the copse. "Aff ye git an wait. Thur's a wee stream ahint the trees an a patch o guid grass fur grazin. Aifter the horses are settled we'll hae a bite tae eat oorsels."

Renwick nodded again but said nothing.

Luks as if this is gonna be a richt cheery journey. Jonas sighed as he led the two horses away to enjoy a slow drink in the shallow stream then be loosely tethered beside the soft grass. When he turned back there was James Renwick, sitting against a tree trunk, eyes closed, lips moving as if in prayer.

He leant forward and tapped the still shoulder. "Much as ah appreciate yer devotions ah need tae interrupt ye. Ah'm famished an ma mither hus gied me a guid pack o ham, cheese, pickle an a wheen eggs alang wi a flagon o goats' milk. Will ye share it wi me?"

Renwick opened his eyes and smiled. "Wi pleasure." He took a slice of ham and a thick chunk of cheese and began to eat. "This is richt guid. Yer mither's done ye proud."

Jonas cut some bread and offered more cheese along with a hard-boiled egg. "Eat up. Ye'll need aw yer strength fur whit lies aheid. Frae whit ah've heard, them waitin in Scotland huv high expectations o ye."

Renwick sighed. "It'll be far frae easy but must be done. Since Richard Cameron was killed the will for resistance keeps slipping awa. Noo that I'm ordained I intend tae try and mak a difference tae the hopes o ma fellow man and lift them oot o despair."

"Soonds lik a richt task. John Steel spoke aboot meetin Richard Cameron. He found him a force tae be reckoned wi. A grand preacher but mibbe a tad radical."

Renwick frowned. "Cameron believed that the liberties o the kirk go hand in hand wi the liberties o the people. I haud the same opinion. Whit's wrang wi that?"

"Naethin. It's jist that John Steel seemed raither concerned aboot the way Cameron went aboot it."

Renwick's jaw tightened. "Cameron saw the way furrit, prayed aboot it and taen direction frae the Lord. Some folk didna agree wi whit he did or hoo he did it but trust me, it worked. The resistance grew. Kept on growing. If only he'd been allooed tae continue." Renwick stopped and stared into space. "If only."

"Weel," Jonas volunteered, "ma faither an maist o yer university professors seem tae believe ye're the man tae pick up whaur Cameron left aff."

"Their words encourage me but in truth this is naething new." Renwick smiled. "It's aye been there. Ye see ma mither lost three bairns afore I wis born. When I came alang and thrived she took it as a special sign and dedicated me tae the Lord. She often said I wis born for the Lord and wud die for the Lord. A while back I witnessed Cameron's supporter, the great Donald Cargill, mount the scaffold in Edinburgh's Grassmarket and it aw made sense. Everything aboot him, his demeanor, his willingness tae accept the ultimate sacrifice, his unswerving conviction."

Jonas's hand hesitated as he reached for another slice of ham.

They ate on in silence then Renwick asked, "Why dae ye feel the need tae mak this journey wi me?"

"It didna seem richt tae let ye travel alane. Nae unner the circumstances. Wi John leavin the way he did."

"Is it nae a bit mair than that?"

"Ay weel. Wi aw that's been said an aw that's happened ah want tae see fur masel whit the stramash is really aboot."

"And so ye will. But dare I ask why?"

"Ah trust whit ah've heard frae ma freend John Steel. Whit ye're sayin is somewhit different an ah find that raither disturbin."

"And somewhaur in atween micht lie the truth. Is that whit ye mean?"

Jonas flushed. "No jist that, it gies me the chance tae meet ma faither's folk fur the first time. Faither wis a young man when he arrived in Holland. He worked hard as a pastor, wis blessed wi a guid Dutch wife, an then thur wis me tae conseeder. Haurly surprisin that he's nivver been back hame. He writes regular an tells them aboot us an they write back but ah've often wunnered whit thur really like. They bide in the sooth o the country, amang the Lowther Hills. Ah've nivver seen richt hills."

"Dae ye ken whaur aboots? The village or toun?"

"Wanlockheid. It's a wee place. They say it's in a minin area."

"It is indeed and nae mony miles frae ma ain village o Monaive. There's a coincidence. Mibbe we'll get the chance tae gang there thegither."

"Mibbe." Jonas smiled but sounded less than enthusiastic.

When the two travellers reached the Scots College in Utrecht the evening meal was long past but the principal soon had them sitting in the refectory, being served with the best the kitchen could offer. However, he didn't stay to talk but made the excuse of much paperwork awaiting his attention. This seemed to hint at a coolness in the welcome compared to their earlier visit. Then the whole college had fussed over Renwick, seemed impressed by his reputation and had listened to every word as he related the sorry state of the cause back home.

This time caution seemed to haunt the air. Jonas wondered why. But if Renwick noticed he made no comment.

After their meal Renwick opted for bed and left Jonas to wander into the vast sitting room to join the tutors and students by the fire. Conversation hummed around him but few included him other than polite questions about his journey. This seemed to confirm his earlier suspicion that something was amiss, so he leant back and feigned sleep while trying to listen.

Renwick's name was mentioned, and not in the most complimentary tone. Jonas was tempted to open his eyes and confront the whisperers, then remembered he was a guest. Keep yer mooth shut. Ay. He began to guess what might be wrong, why this change in attitude from the very men who months before had been full of admiration. On the way up tae Groningen Renwick wis treated lik the best thing ivver. Thur's nane o it this time. An yit he's noo ordained an fully approved by as mony respectit professors an meenisters.

Gradually the room emptied, the fire grew low. Jonas admitted defeat and went to bed, weary in his body but his mind still wondering about their reception.

Next morning Renwick and Jonas arrived at the refectory to find a line of students waiting for them. After a polite greeting they conducted the two visitors in and stood alongside while morning prayers were said then led them to the top of the long trestle table and stood respectfully while they took their place. Every nicety was observed yet not one chose to join them for the meal but moved farther along the trestle table. Again, if Renwick noticed he gave no hint and remained his usual composed self.

The principal appeared as his visitors went into the hall to collect their bags and asked if he might accompany them to the stable and see them off.

"Of course, sir," Renwick nodded. "And please accept our grateful thanks for a fine meal, a comfortable bed, and much kindness for a second time."

The principal flushed. "Nae need for thanks. Ye're welcome here and I mean it sincerely even if there wisna the same fuss this time." He hesitated and looked embarrassed. "Dinna be surprised if ye dinna find a warm welcome when ye arrive in Rotterdam. I tak it that's whaur ye're heading. Mibbe ye dinna ken that twa students frae yer university are making it their business tae spread ill rumours aboot ye. Ane wis here last week. Whit he said challenged yer richt tae be ordained."

"Indeed?" Renwick stopped and stared at the principal.

"Tae put it bluntly, whit happened wi yer ordination has caused resentment, even a bit o jealousy, amang yer colleagues. Words against ye are being repeated. Some exiled Scots meenisters in Rotterdam seem tae agree and hae taen against ye."

Renwick stiffened. "Why shud my ordination cause ony jealousy or resentment? No one, least of all my fellow students, are in any doubt as to my calling, my determination to simply serve the Lord, obey his will, and dae richt for oor ailing country's spiritual future."

"Fine words sir and I believe ye but…"

Renwick held up his hand. "I'm prepared for all kinds of challenges and difficulties. Indeed I expect them. But rest assured the Lord will guide and support me for my honesty and willingness to tak furrit his cause in oor pair, beleaguered land."

"Ay weel. I'm reassured that ye ken it'll be a hard road aheid but ye shud also ken tae watch oot for enemies ye micht no expect. Trust me, they're waiting tae tackle ye afore ye even set sail for Scotland. When ye meet them ye'll understand, for they're likely tae bombard ye wi questions and accusations aboot yer premature ordination."

"It was done in the sight of God. Before that my theology and intent was rigorously tested. My professors were content itherwise there wud nivver hae been ony ordination."

"I dinna doubt it. But ye didna complete the specified course. It wis aw done in a short space o time. Richt or wrang this has raised mony a question and then there seems tae be concern ower the manner o yer ordination by Dutch meensiters."

"It wis done in the tradition o the Scottish Kirk. I insisted on that. Ivvery rule and nicety was adhered tae."

"To be sure. But some o yer critics are suggesting this affects yer competence and puts doubt on yer richt tae be accepted as a meenister."

Jonas cut in. "Sir, ah'm sure Maister Renwick appreciates yer concern and yer weel intended warnin but rest easy, he's mair than able tae field ony question or challenge regardin his richt tae dae the Lord's work."

"I hope so. The times we live in are difficult enough withoot dissent amang oorsels." The principal shook hands with them both. "God's speed and a safe journey hame. I luk furrit tae learning aboot yer success wi the cause. It's been sadly lacking since the loss o Richard Cameron."

James Renwick nodded, mounted his horse, and followed Jonas's angry back out of the stable-yard.

John Steel sat beside a yellow broom bush at the edge of the little birch wood above Westermains farm. Below him a full loyalist platoon was busy searching the house and outbuildings. As he watched two hen-house doors were flung open and terrified brown bodies shot out to run cackling and jumping in all directions.

John groaned. Pair things will be aff the lay fur days. Whit a cairry on tryin tae catch me oot. If only it cud aw be different. An aw done tae masel. Mibbe ah shud've turned an galloped awa when auld Airlie attacked me. Ma Juno's a fine beast, can ootrun ony o them. It wis her the greedy beggar wis aifter. When he didna git her he turned his wrath on me.

He thought about that moment in the battle of Bothwell Bridge when the Covenanting army was about to be overrun, when one of the greatest earls of the land had confronted him, expecting surrender and the prize of a fine horse. Instead John had retaliated by swinging his sword to cut the great charger's saddle traces then turned and escaped.

Mibbe ah got awa when the auld deil crashed tae the ground but ah stertit somethin that nivver seems tae end.

John watched the red-coated figures scurry here and there, poking into every corner, all the time egged on by their captain, the dreaded Crichton, who'd become a persistent hunter and enemy since John had managed to best him on several occasions.

Ane o they days, John promised himself. Ane o they days, Crichton. He shook his head and lay back on the wiry heather to stare up at the clouds drifting past. Instead of watching their gentle progress and allowing his mind to calm each one seemed like a reminder of each unfortunate incident he'd faced since that awful day at Bothwell. They kept on coming, so many he just wanted to close his eyes and shut everything out.

He took a deep breath. The sharp scent of heather bells brought another reminder. Git a grip. Stoap bein sic an eedjit. Stoap worryin aboot leavin James Renwick in Holland. God's sake, whit else cud ah dae aifter ah saw Robert Hamilton stickin his neb in?

Hoo Renwick sees onythin in a man lik yon ah'll nivver ken. An it's nae as if ah didna tell him braw plain aboot this so-cawed pillar o the kirk, struttin aboot as if he's a true supporter o the cause. Ah ken the opposite an ivvery word ah spoke wis the truth. No that it made ony difference. Renwick wisna fur chaingin his opeenion o the mealy-moothed rat.

So why am ah left feelin guilty? It maks nae difference. When ah got hame an tellt them as sponsored Renwick they wudna listen either. Ower taen up wi thur special young man's report an lukin furrit tae whit he micht dae nixt fur the cause.

John stiffened as he felt the ground shudder. He raised his head to peer over the tops of the heather bells and found a single line of troopers already half-way up the hill, galloping towards him.

Rolling onto his stomach he grabbed a low branch of broom and pulled himself snake-like under its trailing fronds as the first horse reached the edge of the little wood and stopped only yards beyond the broom bush.

There was Airlie himself pointing a gloved finger into the wood. "Three o ye. In there and check oot. Richt tae the back. Oor information says Steel is somewhaur aboot the farm. Maist likely he saw us coming and retreated up here." He turned and waved at the other troopers. "The rest o ye, oot across the moor. See if there's ony sign o movement. This cat and moose game has gone on lang enough. It's time for Steel tae be caught and hung."

John watched the three horses pick their way between the tightly-planted trees and into the darker shadows. The others trotted off to begin a wider sweep while their scowling master sat where he was.

John almost smiled. After Bothwell Airlie had chased him onto the moor and up to this same birch wood. John had known what to do, had known the very spot where he could drop through the thickest heather into a deep drainage runnel and disappear. The troopers had searched and searched while Airlie sat on his horse, only yards away from John's hiding place, scowling with the same frustrated looking face as he wore today.

This time John was less lucky. Airlie couldn't see behind the broom bush but if one of the troopers came out of the trees beyond it he'd pass the very spot.

One horse emerged almost beside the bush but on the other side.

The rider signalled all clear to his master and moved over to join him.

The second horse appeared almost level with Airlie. He also shook his head and called out all clear.

So far so good, till the third rider left the trees at the opposite end of the wood. John held his breath while the horse slowly approached. As it drew level the rider did look down. John looked up. Their eyes met. Neither blinked then the rider lifted his finger like a warning. Time seemed to pause before John heard, "Aw clear sir. Nae sign o Steel." The rider clicked his horse and continued along to join the waiting group.

"Richt." Airlie sounded disappointed. "We'll join the ithers on the moor. Mibbe a wider search will prove mair fruitful." He turned his horse and led his men down the long slope, away from the birch wood, across a field and onto the winding path towards the moor.

John sat up and watched till the troopers became tiny dots in the vast space. That wis Lieutenant McCann. Whit's he up tae? Yon time when Airlie wis aifter me an ah hid up cousin Bess's loft it wis McCann climbed in tae check. Even in the dark he musta kent ah wis there. An yit he said aw clear. He's done it again. Whit fur? Ah dinna even ken the man. Nowt as queer as folk.

He stood up and shook himself.

When John told Marion what had happened she looked alarmed then nodded. "McCann's been kind tae me mair than aince. He's nae lik the earl or yon awfy Crichton."

"But he's a military man, sworn tae obey orders."

"Ay weel. Jist be gled he did the opposite."

John gave her a hug. "Whitivver the reason, ah'm gratefu."

That night John lay awake for hours wondering why Lieutenant McCann had done him a favour. No answer came and gradually he wandered into the senselessness of the past few years. So much had happened, so much pain, so much cruelty, so many disappointments and setbacks for the cause. And yet preacher after preacher kept up the defiance. An they paid fur it. Huntit an harried till caught an tortured or executed. Mind ye, thur aye seems tae be anither yin ready an waitin. Ay. He sighed and shook his head. An this time it's James Renwick.

Chapter Two

Rotterdam was crowded with burghers, merchants, strangers, all determined on turning a coin. No one took any notice of two travellers guiding their horses through the narrow streets towards the harbour with the hope of finding a berth on a ship bound for Scotland.

Jonas knew where to go and headed for a particular inn which was popular with many a ship's captain. Here orders could be collected from shipping-line owners, messages dispatched, and of course a good meal along with fine ale and lively gossip completed the attraction.

The Fine Lady was well placed, close to the harbour edge, only a step from the great warehouses where anything in transit would temporarily lodge before moving on. Her impressive facade was pristine white, each mullioned window sparkling, every windowsill crammed with bright-red geraniums in matching pots, and above the well-polished mahogany front door swung a brightly-painted image of the lady herself.

Everything inside was designed to provide maximum comfort and the best of refreshment but only for clients with deep enough pockets to pay for such excellent service.

Jonas jumped down from his horse, tethered it to a long metal rail at the end of the building then signalled for Renwick to do the same. "Bide here while ah gang in an see whit's whit. Wi luck we'll hae a berth in nae time."

Within minutes he was back, looking pleased. "Thur's a ship leavin on the morning tide, straight for Leith. Luks lik ye'll be hame afore ye ken it. She's named the *Sweet Hope*. Soonds lik a guid omen. Ah've got directions whaur she's berthed."

They found the *Sweet Hope* beyond the customs house where lines of men were struggling up a long gangway at the far end of the ship to load the last open hold with bulging packets and barrels. An immaculately uniformed figure stood on the upper deck supervising the operation.

Jonas walked to the water's edge and waved up to the uniformed figure. After a few minutes the figure came over to the ship's rail. "Whit is it?"

Jonas called up, "Twa travellers seekin passage tae Scotland."

The figure nodded. "Up ye come."

Renwick made to step forward but Jonas grabbed his arm. "Leave the talkin tae me."

"I can speak perfectly weel for mysel."

"Nae doubt, but whit yon principal at the Scots College in Utrecht said strikes me as a warnin tae be carefu." Jonas hurried onto the nearest gangway and left Renwick to follow.

The uniformed figure was waiting by the focsle. "I'm Captain Fairbairn, master o this vessel. If ye're seeking passage there's only a double cabin left and ye need to be ready to leave by morning."

"Perfect," Jonas nodded.

"And I expect payment up front for steerage and meals throughout yer time aboard."

"Name yer price," Renwick cut in. "Time is o the essence."

"Is it indeed?" Captain Fairbairn's eyes narrowed. "What might be the reason for sic urgency?"

"The Lord's work."

The captain studied Renwick's sombre black jacket and breeches, the fine white stockings and silver buckled shoes then scanned the intense expression. "Ye certainly hae the look o somebody a tad serious for my liking. Mmm. Or maybe a preacher. A bit young though. But maybe no."

Renwick stiffened. "I am a minister. Whit's wrang wi that?"

"Nothing at all unless ye're one o they radicals as flaunt the laws and cause terrible trouble for our king and country."

Renwick seemed about to argue then hesitated as three well-dressed men and a very stout woman in an ornately embroidered brocade coat and feathered hat came along the deck.

The captain turned towards them. "These passengers satisfied me as to their intentions before I agreed to give them passage. Something tells me you two could be a problem. That I neither want nor seek. Back home each port is carefully watched and regulated these days, questions are asked about our business, where we've come from and what kind o cargo we carry. Each passenger is quizzed as well. Since my ship is heading for Scotland I must be doubly careful. We live in difficult times and the wrong answer can result in my ship being impounded, even myself arrested. If that happens nothing will be unloaded till the authorities check each piece against every last dot and comma in my cargo list. Such delays are bad for business so why would I take any chances?"

The four strangers joined the captain. Each held a metal tankard. Their red faces and unsteady step seemed to suggest that a quantity of ale had been downed.

Renwick glared at them but said nothing.

This seemed to infuriate the woman who stepped forward. "Hoity toity are we? Better than the likes of us, eh?" She turned to the captain. "Do you really think these two are the type of passengers you want on this boat? Look at them, that tight-lipped with dead-pan faces. A smile is beyond them, never mind any thought of fun. Whit kind of company is that?" She pointed a chubby finger at Renwick's stony face. "We're decent English travellers trying to return home only to discover the only boat available is heading for a Scottish port. A grave inconvenience so it is. But needs must. And we've paid good money for our passage. But sharing such limited space for days on end with these two. I don't think so." She stabbed a finger at Renwick again. "If he's not a God-fearing bible-thumper I'll eat my hat. He certainly looks suspicious." She leant forward and sniffed loudly. "He even smells suspicious. Go on Captain, test him. Ask if he'll take some ale and toast the king's health?"

Renwick stepped back as if stung.

"See?" The woman sounded triumphant. "Guilty."

Jonas grabbed Renwick's arm. "Apologies if wur giein the wrang impression. We've nae intention o imposin oorsels or causin ony offence tae onybody. Mibbe we best luk elsewhaur." He began to march Renwick towards the gangway.

Jeers and mocking laughter followed them down the gangway and back along the harbour till they were out of earshot.

Jonas released his grip on Renwick's arm. "Nixt time keep yer tongue atween yer teeth." He shook his head. "Ah'm no askin ye tae pretend ye're somethin ye're nae but fur God's sake man, it's time ye stepped intae the real world. They kinda folk are ivverywhaur."

Renwick didn't reply and they walked back to *The Fine Lady* in silence.

"Richt, bide here," Jonas ordered when they arrived at the inn door. "Dae naethin an speak tae naebody while ah gang in tae ask if thur's ither possibilities."

11

Hans Vrooman the moneylender had just finished his favourite supper of spiced meatballs and herb dumplings. Now he was sipping a long, slow glass of best French brandy.

Leaning back in his usual preferential chair by the fire he glanced round a room full of well-dressed customers and puffed with pride. Here ah am, as guid as ony burgher, a respectit customer o *The Fine Lady* hersel. A big chainge since ma days as Gaby the tinker back in Scotland.

Maybe it was this thought that had him opening up his memory, all the way to that other life where he'd earned his first silver merks by spying for the sheriff in the town of Lanark, repaying the kindness of John Steel's family by telling tales that had caused John's arrest, imprisonment and hefty fine.

When that happened he'd sense enough to disappear, then a stroke of luck had provided the opportunity of robbing a farmer of his savings while the man sat dead in his own kitchen. He'd gone in a poor tinker seeking a corner of the barn for the night and come out a man of substance.

An why no? He'd nae use fur it. Ah hud. That stertit me on the way tae real success as a man wi a new name an a pooch jinglin wi siller. Jist the thing tae impress the merchants in a busy toun lik Glesca.

Mind ye, if ah'd gone a bit further afield John Steel wudna huv caught up wi me. That wis a peety. When he cam on me ah tried tellin him ah wis somebody else. Aifter aw, ah wis dressed in ma finest. It made nae difference. He kent me fine an stertit accusin me o thievin aff an auld farmer. Hoo did he guess that, ah wunner?

Thank God ah hud ma wee knife jist handy tae slip it atween his ribs afore he said anither word. Ay. That stoaped him. No that ah hung aboot. Ah wis aff lik a whippet. An ah didna halt till ah reached Leith an paid ower the odds fur a berth tae onywhaur. It turned oot tae be Holland. An the best thing ah ivver did. Here ah wis wi plenty siller tae set up as a moneylender an mak mair. Folk here are as desperate fur loans as onywhaur an that means payin whitivver interest ah care tae ask.

Life wis guid. Better than guid.

And then Steel turns up lik the proverbial bad penny. Whit a shock that wis. Ah thocht ah'd left him for deid. He arrived alang wi a lad ah'd gied a loan tae a while back. Ane that wis aye complainin aboot the rate he wis payin. It wisna true. Onyway, naebody twistit his airm tae tak the loan.

God kens hoo they twa got thegither an God kens why John Steel wantit tae interfere on yon lad's behalf. They gied me the awfiest fricht, breakin intae ma hoose at nicht an threatenin me in ma ane bed, demandin ah free the lad frae his debt. Whit cud ah dae? In a pickle lik that ah'd nae option but write aff the lad's loan. Ah even promised tae chainge ma ways. Ah must huv soonded sincere fur they baith seemed tae believe me an let me be. That's the difference atween him an me an why ah'm a success.

This brought a smile and a self-satisfied nod.

That same smile vanished as a sharp pain tore across his chest. He coughed and doubled up. It happened again. This time he gasped, lurched forward and his brow hit the edge of the table. He remained still a moment, all his inner strength battling against a surge of overwhelming weakness. And then he was sliding from his seat, fingers clawing helplessly at the table leg before his face hit the wooden floor with a dull thump.

Eyes staring into beckoning darkness he became the child he'd once been, a terrified Gaby sitting in his father's cellar, alone for hours on end, hearing the sharp scratches on stone and glimpsing pairs of bright little eyes coming ever closer. Worst of all was the awful dampness that clung to his clothes and seeped into his skin till it became part of him.

His mouth opened. He tried to call out. No sound came only a trickle of saliva then nothing.

The moneylender's two minders sat in a nearby inglenook and watched the fur-clad figure fall to the floor. Their simple pie and jug of ale forgotten they moved as one to reach forward and grab their master's bulging deerskin satchel, the one that never left his side. A moment later they were across the room and out the door before anyone realised what had happened.

Jonas reached the inn door as it burst open. A heavy satchel banged against his chest. He stumbled back and almost fell as two big men pushed past then disappeared round the end of the building.

Renwick grabbed Jonas's arm and tried to steady him. "I ken

whit ye said but I'd best come in wi ye."

"Nae need." Jonas brushed Renwick's hand away.

"Ivvery need." Renwick was past him and in the door.

Tables were set, plates heaped with steaming food but no one was sitting at any table; they were all crowded at the far end of the room peering over one another's shoulders and studying something on the floor by the fire.

Jonas joined the outer row. "Whit's happening?" He craned forward as someone leant down to turn over a fur-cloaked body.

There was a face Jonas had last seen, late one night, staring up in terror from his bed while John Steel threatened him.

That night Jonas had heard a strange story about a poor tinker in Scotland who'd become a wealthy moneylender in Holland. The same one as had caused Jonas so much heartache over a loan.

Jonas stepped back and turned to Renwick. "Thur's been a sudden death. Ah think they twa men that run by us robbed the man. The law will need tae be sent fur. We best leave oor questions aboot anither berth on a ship till later."

"But I'm most anxious."

"Anither day will mak nae difference." Jonas headed for the door.

Renwick reluctantly followed him as he left the harbour and walked quickly up the first narrow street.

Renwick caught up with him. "Whaur are we going?"

"Tae find a bed fur the nicht. We've hud mair than enoch excitement fur ane day. As it happens ma faither's sister Jinty Brakel runs a wee inn at the tap o this street. It's naethin fancy lik *The Fine Lady* but it's clean an weel enoch laid oot, an she's a grand cook, an ah'm hungry. Aunt Jinty's fond o me. She'll mak space fur us."

The little inn was last in the long line of houses. The walls and woodwork were freshly painted and a small wooden sign above the narrow door announced *Jinty's Huis* in roughly-carved letters. Two trestle tables outside were occupied by men eating and arguing and laughing. It seemed a friendly kind of place.

Renwick smiled at the sign. "No Dutch I tak it?"

"Naw. Ma auntie's Scots lik ma faither. She's his younger sister. Ye've met the ither sister in Groningen, whaur ye stayed durin yer studies."

Renwick thought of his cheery landlady. "She fed me weel an gied me ivvery conseederation. I enjoyed my stay in her hoose."

"Jinty's jist the same. They baith cam tae Holland wi ma faither a lang time ago. The intention wis tae luk aifter him but Jinty nivver got ony further than Rotterdam. On the way ower she taen a shine tae the ship's captain an he tae her. They married soon aifter. Since then he sails the world then comes back tae her. While he's awa she's busy runnin her wee inn. They baith mak a guid livin an seem happy wi the arrangement."

In they went to find a smoky room crammed with more customers making a great deal of noise as they ate from bowls of steaming noodles. A tall woman in a starched apron and two young girls in similar dress were hurrying back and forward serving their hungry customers.

Jonas waved to the woman. She stopped, put down the heavy tray she was carrying and ducked between the tables till she reached him. "Jonas. Whit a surprise." She gave him a tight hug. "Guid tae see ye. Whit are ye dain here?"

Jonas freed himself and pulled Renwick forward. "This is Maister Renwick. Wur baith fur Scotland as soon as we can git a berth on a ship. He hus important work tae dae as a meenister."

"A meenister?"

"Ay. A new yin. Ah'm travellin wi him then goin on tae visit the family in Wanlockheid."

Jinty's eyes shone with excitement then she frowned. "An whit's yer mither sayin aboot this? Whit aboot yer faither?"

Jonas flushed. "Whit dae ye think?"

"Only tae be expectit." She gave him another hug. "Ye're an only son."

"Mibbe ye'd like tae reconsider," Renwick cut in. "Noo that we've reached the port there's naething tae prevent me going on by masel."

"Naw. Naw." Jonas glared at him. "Ah've stertit so ah'll feenish. Onyway, ah'm keen tae catch up wi John Steel again."

"I see." Renwick looked away.

Jinty blinked at the sudden change in tone. "Richt, come awa ben the back an ah'll show ye a couple o rooms. Ye can freshen up then huv a meal an a sit doon aifter yer lang journey." She bustled them through the crowded room and along a narrow hall. "Rooms are at the end ther. Ah'll leave ye tae it. Come thru when ye're ready." She gave Jonas a quick look and went back along the hall.

15

Renwick opened the door to the first room and walked in. "The very thing. Clean and comfortable. Yer auntie's being maist kind."

"Ay." Jonas stared at the straight, black-coated back. "Same as John Steel."

Renwick turned toward Jonas. "Ay. He's a guid freend. We can agree aboot that. Nae the best man tae cross tho. Him and I had words afore he left me at Groningen. I regret that."

Jonas nodded. "Ah ken aboot it. Robert Hamilton wis the problem. John canna staund the man. He tellt me hoo the coward ran awa at Bothwell Brig an kept goin till he wis safe in Holland. Maks ye wunner aboot his claim tae be cairryin the cause furrit."

Renwick stiffened. "I tried tae explain hoo a man can chainge and still dae guid things. But ye're richt. I shud hae been mair considerate and mair careful wi ma response."

"Mibbe ye can dae that the nixt time ye meet."

"I'll try, altho John can be raither difficult when his mind is made up. If I'm honest my attitude didna help. We'd been fine till he met Robert Hamilton again. Ower mony bad memories got in the way o reasoned judgement."

"Ah've nae problem wi his judgement. In fact ah wis gled o it." Jonas began to tell Renwick about Hans Vrooman the money-lender, who was really Gaby the tinker, how he'd tricked Jonas over a loan, and how John had put it right.

Renwick listened and gradually the tension that had travelled with them all the way from Groningen began to disappear.

Jinty was relieved to see two happier-looking faces come into her busy dining-room. Whitivver wis atween they twa seems settled. Jist as weel. They've a lang way tae go in ain anithers company. Aloud she said, "Sit yersels doon. Twa bowls o noodles wi chicken pieces comin up."

Jonas and James Renwick polished off a full bowl of noodles and chicken then a large slab of cake covered with sliced plums and soaked in honey. By the time they reached a final mug of ale Jinty was telling them she'd asked her customers to put the word out about two travellers seeking a berth for Scotland. "Ma customers are mair lik freends. They'll git the richt news fur ye. Micht tak a day or twa so jist be patient." She patted Jonas's shoulder. "In the meantime ah'll enjoy yer company. Mibbe ye'd even conseeder comin wi yer auld auntie tae the Scots Kirk on Sunday? Ah gang there in deference tae ma big brither."

"We'll baith come," Renwick smiled. "Indeed, I luk furrit tae it."

The Scots Kirk was an imposing building. Judging by the crowd waiting outside for the heavy wooden doors to open it was also well attended. Renwick seemed surprised to see so many.

Jinty explained, "We've a healthy congregation o Scots here. It fair increased aifter yon battle at Bothwell. Maist are still here."

"Will they nae conseeder gangin hame?" Renwick frowned. "Scotland needs them."

"Keepin thur heid on thur shooders seems mair important richt noo. Mibbe if things chainge."

Renwick sighed and followed her into the church where she led them towards a pew near the front. "We'll squeeze in here. Ah want tae hear Reverend Barclay as clear as ah can. He's weel worth listenin tae."

A tall, angular man, wearing a long black robe and a severe expression to match, appeared from a side-door and walked confidently towards the central pulpit. Everyone quietened and prepared to listen.

Now the centre of attention he wasted no time in welcoming his congregation before launching into a lengthy, detailed prayer. His voice was loud and clear and filled the great space as he invoked the Almighty to deal with all sinners. He then developed this theme with a carefully compiled and challenging sermon backed up by appropriate Bible readings.

Renwick was transfixed, listening intently. Jonas did try but couldn't concentrate. His journey since leaving home had been strange and unpredictable. His mind kept going over this, making him wonder what next. He wasn't sure if he'd like it.

The service finished with a well-sung psalm and a fierce benediction then Reverend Barclay bowed to his flock, climbed down from his pulpit and disappeared back through the side door.

A gentle hum of conversation rose as people prepared to leave. Renwick seemed content to sit on as if considering the words he'd just heard. Jinty shrugged and glanced at Jonas. "Sunday or no ah've mooths waitin tae be fed, so excuse me. Tak yer time. Thur's nae need tae hurry back. If ye git the chance try an huv a word wi the Reverend. Ah'm sure he'd be pleased tae meet Maister Renwick, him bein a meenister as weel." She edged out of the pew to join the slow-moving line of worshippers making their way towards the open door and out into the busy street.

Jonas and James Renwick were among the last to move. The kirk was almost empty when three black-robed figures strode along the wide centre aisle towards them. The leader was the tall, angular minister Renwick had listened to with such attention, the Reverend Barclay himself with a far from friendly expression directed at these two strangers still sitting in his kirk. Behind him came two younger men, red faced and clutching their robes to their chest as they almost ran to keep up with what seemed an angry figure.

Jonas took a deep breath.

Renwick simply smiled.

All three juddered to a halt alongside the pew where Jonas and Renwick sat. Renwick stood up and leant forward to offer his hand in greeting. "Sir, that was a grand sermon."

Reverend Barclay ignored Renwick's extended hand and glared at him. "Wud ye happen tae be James Renwick?"

"Indeed." Renwick hesitated before such aggression then turned towards Jonas. "May I introduce my freend, Jonas Hawthorn. Perhaps ye're acquaint wi his faither Tobias Hawthorn, meenister at the Scots Kirk in Groningen."

"Oh ay, Groningen." Barclay almost hissed the word then pointed a finger at Jonas. "Yer faither aye seemed a fine man wi a sensible heid on his shooders but recently he's been prone tae mak some serious mistakes. No jist that, his actions cud undermine oor Kirk's precious reputation."

Renwick frowned. "That sounds as harsh as it's untrue."

"Nae mair than needs saying Maister Renwick, since Tobias Hawthorn saw fit tae support the likes o yersel in joining the university at Groningen."

Renwick's frown darkened. "And I'm truly grateful for whit he did tae help me progress my endeavours."

"Whit age are ye Maister Renwick?"

"Whit has that tae dae wi onything?" Renwick blinked as if

18

confused by the sudden change of question. "If ye really want tae ken I reached twenty-one this year."

"And weel below the statutory age for entry tae the ministry. Twenty-five and above is the norm."

"But..."

Barclay held up his hand. "As if that wisna bad enough ye somehoo managed tae complete yer theological studies in four months. Sic a time scale is unheard o sir. Unheard o." Barclay took a deep breath. "And then we hear ye've been ordained as a meenister. Impossible, sir. Impossible."

Renwick stood very straight. "I wis ordained aifter proper and extensive testing in aw relevant areas. My professors shirked naething nor avoided onything. Ivvery aspect wis thoroughly covered. They decided I wis ready for ordination. I bowed tae their judgement and agreed tae the ceremony taking place. Noo that I'm ordained I hope tae continue the Lord's work as soon as I return tae Scotland."

"Hoo can ye?" Barclay's voice rose. "Ye've ben ordained by Dutch meenisters wi nae authority frae oor Kirk back hame in Scotland."

"Sir." Renwick sounded more weary than angry. "These Dutch meenisters had nae hesitation on the maitter, and nae hesitation in supporting me and my pair beleaguered country. They saw it as their Christian duty tae facilitate my ordination as a necessary contribution tae the church universal. They also did it at the behest o the Societies back hame. These men are guid Presbyterians, prepared tae keep on fighting against the terrible wrang that floods oor country. No jist that, they were committed enough tae send me here. They paid ma passage and upkeep. Let me assure ye that the ceremony itsel wis conducted according tae oor ain Kirk's rules and adherence."

"Wis it noo?" Barclay's voice rose further. "It still disna mak it richt. The hale thing is a farce frae beginning tae end. Whit maks ye think ye'll ivver be accepted as a validated, ordained meenister in ony pairt o Scotland?"

"Nae mair, sir. Ye've gone ower far." Jonas grabbed Renwick's arm and pushed his way past the three black-robed figures.

Renwick tried to free himself but Jonas tightened his grip. "Dinna gie that awfy man the pleisure o a response. Keep walkin an haud on tae yer dignity."

Behind them, Barclay called out. "I intend writing tae the university at Groningen in the strongest terms aboot this travesty."

Renwick half-turned but Jonas stopped him. "Ignore him. Ahint ye lies naethin but malice an spite. Ye need yer energy fur whit lies aheid."

"I dinna understand." Renwick's face was chalk white.

"Think aboot it," Jonas snapped. "Ye're willin tae tak the Word back hame. In fact ye canna wait. Barclay an his freends are sittin cosy an safe here, mouthin aboot theological niceties. Whit dae ye think they'd say if ah invited them tae come wi ye, back tae face real trouble and danger?"

Renwick didn't answer but his face grew even whiter.

Neither spoke after that.

As they walked back to *Jinty's Huis* Jonas kept glancing at Renwick's tight profile, remembering John Steel's earlier words about this young man. John wis richt. This yin's gonna end up his ain worst enemy.

Jinty was standing outside the front door of her inn talking to a little stout man in a tight-fitting uniform and a shiny peaked cap. She waved Jonas and Renwick over. "Guid news. This is Captain Edward Lowis. He's come in response tae yer request."

Renwick's face lit up and he hurried forward to shake hands with the little man. "Grand sir. We're keen tae set sail for Scotland as soon as possible."

Captain Lowis looked apologetic. "I've come to offer ye a berth but not for Leith like ye're hoping. I'm set for Dublin. Would that be near enough seeing as Mistress Jinty says ye're desperate to be on your way? There's plenty ships ply between Dublin for Glasgow. I'm acquainted wi a good few o the captains an could introduce ye to the right ones." He lowered his voice. "Since ye need to be extra careful."

Jonas frowned at his aunt. "Whit did ye tell him?"

"The truth." Jinty flapped her hand. "The last thing ah want is ye settin oot across the sea wi somebody as cud dae ye harm. Yer faither wud nivvver forgie me. Captain Lowis is nae quite o oor persuasion but near enoch. He'll see ye richt."

Captain Lowis nodded. "My family and myself belong to the Society o Friends. Most often we're named as Quakers. Our kind o folk are no looked on kindly by the king and church in England. A good few have been tortured or worse for refusing to give into his demands so I understand yer difficulties well enough. I don't usually carry passengers but I thought an exception this time might be helpful to a fellow sufferer."

Renwick turned to Jonas. "Whit dae ye think?"

Jonas shrugged. "Ah ken nocht aboot Quakers but a dae ken a kind offer when ah hear it. If the captain is willin tae tak us why no? Itherwise we micht wait lang enoch."

"If we accept when cud we leave?" Renwick turned back to the captain.

"Two days. Once my ship's loaded and the tide's right. The *Mary Rose* carries wood and bags o plaster for Dutch craftsmen working on some o the grand houses in Dublin. Their skill is greatly admired and sought after. I bring the raw material they need. On the way back I take barrels o Irish spirit so it works out well enough with a profitable load each way. My ship isn't the best-looking vessel in the fleet, nor the biggest, but I keep her in pristine order and she's more than able to weather any storm."

"See." Jinty smiled at the three men. "Problem solved."

"Is that oor ship?" Renwick stopped alongside a twin-masted brigantine anchored at the farthest end of a long loading bay.

"Luks like it." Jonas pointed to the prow decorated with an intricately-painted, many-petalled rose. "She seems bigger than ah thocht frae the captain's description."

"Hae ye sailed afore?" Renwick smiled at Jonas's tense expression. "Naething tae worry aboot. I had nae problem on the way here. And luk, I think that's the captain ower there." He pointed towards the open door of a huge warehouse. "By the pile o paper he's cairrying it seems lik he's been signing aff his cargo." He waved at the figure.

The captain saw him and called out. "Good timing gentlemen. Everything's in order. Cargo checked and in the hold. We just need the tide. Another hour should do it. Please, come aboard."

The captain waved them up the gangway and onto a pristine deck.

"Your cabin's in the focsle. A bit tight but you'll manage fine." He led them into a tiny dark corridor. "Leave your bags in there then come across to ma quarters. More space there to settle yourselves while I see about final preparations."

The captain's cabin at the far end of the upper deck was almost spacious with several heavily padded chairs and a large dining table. Close by a row of diamond mullioned windows another, bigger table was littered with what looked like navigational maps. A pile of rolled-up papers were stacked alongside. The walls were mahogany-panelled with a large candle-sconce at each corner. Along the topmost edge was a narrow frieze of intertwining leaves and roses. A comfortable yet workmanlike space.

Captain Lowis nodded towards the chairs then quickly left. Minutes later he could be heard barking out orders.

The *Mary Rose* slid smoothly down the river estuary and out into the North Sea. Jonas was now standing on the focsle. From here he could see all around, enjoying the view yet beginning to wonder when he'd see his homeland again,

The wind picked up. The mainsail and foresail flapped then filled and strained. The ship responded and almost leapt forward as if eager to be on her way. Ahead stretched an endless, undulating stretch of grey water. Jonas sighed and turned to look back. Minutes ago the coastline had been sharp and clear, now it was disappearing into the horizon.

One of the crew, a broad-shouldered and burly young man in an immaculate uniform stood at the helm, staring ahead as if he knew exactly where his fast-moving ship should go within this vast expanse of what seemed empty space.

After a few hours two of the crew came on deck carrying a large, steaming cooking pot. They headed for the captain's cabin and signalled for Renwick and Jonas to follow.

Once inside the pot was carefully hung on a solid looking metal stand beside the dining table. Cutlery and bowls were laid out alongside a complete cheese and a basket heaped with hunks of fresh bread.

Captain Lowis appeared and smiled at the two hungry expressions. "Time to eat gentlemen. Chicken stew, dumplings and a selection o mixed vegetables if my nose serves me right. The very thing after a busy day. Up to the table and enjoy our hospitality."

Jonas and Renwick quickly seated themselves then Renwick suggested, "Will I say Grace, sir?"

"Please," Captain Lowis nodded. "We need to be grateful."

Renwick looked pleased and bowed his head. Jonas did so more slowly as his nose twitched with the thought of what was to come.

Each bowl was filled with tender chunks of boiled chicken along with a good dollop of dumplings on top of mixed vegetables. The three men tucked in and not a word was said while the bowls were emptied.

Jonas took yet another hunk of bread to mop up the last of the gravy in his bowl and grinned at Captain Lowis. "That wis grand. Thank ye."

"Cheese and a tankard o ale to finish off?" The captain cut into the round cheese and signalled to one of his crew to fill each tankard. "No as fine as yer Aunt Jinty's cooking but we do our best. Make the best o it for if the weather grows rough it'll be cold fare and hard tack. We never take the chance o firing up the galley oven in the middle o a lurching, wooden ship."

Jonas looked anxious but said nothing.

Later that night he had cause to feel anxious. He woke up, aware that the rocking action had increased along with an extreme pitch and roll. He hung on to the edge of his blanket for a while then decided to investigate. He jumped down from his bunk, fell on the tilting floor and rolled over several times before managing to crawl out the cabin and along the tiny corridor to push open the outer door and peer outside.

Rain lashed the deck and water seemed to be flooding in on either side. Even in the dark he sensed that the sails were down yet the ship seemed to be racing on faster than ever.

Terrified, he hung onto a metal ring beside the little door and watched the storm take over. Around him the ship seemed alive, each plank creaking and groaning with the effort of hanging together. Little wonder, for time after time he could see the prow dip then plunge into a raging hollow of a wave, level out for a moment before sliding forward to begin the struggle of climbing all the way up the other side and into the white foaming crest waiting at the top. Above him he could hear the rigging screaming and squealing and rattling in useless protest against the howling wind.

Come daylight he could see more, realise how bad the situation really was and feel the shame of smelling his own fear. Now Captain Lowis was hunched at the wheel trying to wrestle back some control from the elements that seemed determined to defeat him. The ship had seemed so large and safe; now it was a mere toy, about to be swallowed or destroyed. But the captain hung on, never letting go of the wheel, desperate to steer the *Mary Rose* through this maelstrom.

Off to the left a faint coastline appeared but there was no attempt to try and edge towards it. This surprised Jonas, had him wondering why they battled on instead of seeking a chance of possible safety.

Renwick appeared beside him. Apart from his white face he seemed calm.

"This is worse than ma worst nichtmare." Jonas tightened his grip on the metal ring.

Renwick shook his head. "Wi the Lord's hand aroond us we hae naething tae fear."

"Ay richt," Jonas turned away to watch the spraying water again.

Chapter Three

Jonas crouched by the little door below the focsle, fingers gripping the round metal handle, clothes ever-more soaked, hair flattened against his head, limbs so cold he could hardly feel them. But he daren't move, daren't take his eyes off the captain still struggling with the ship's wheel. The first mate had joined his master, adding his strength in guiding the *Mary Rose* bow first into then through the breaking waves.

When the ship slid into the hollow of each surge a horizontal waterfall flew across the deck. The captain and first mate vanished behind this curtain and Jonas would hold his breath wondering if the rushing water had carried them away. When both men re-appeared, hands still locked on the wheel he'd breathe out then wait for the next onslaught. It happened over and over as if sea and ship were partners in some deadly dance accompanied by the screech and howl of the wind.

Day seemed like night; time was an alien concept. All that mattered was now.

Eventually, defeated by exhaustion Jonas was forced to turn away from this spectacle of nature's power, to force his hand away from the door handle and stumble along the little corridor into his cabin. Dripping wet and teeth rattling with fear he threw himself into his bunk.

Up till this moment terror and amazement had mesmerised him; now he grasped the wooden handrail of his tiny bed. Ma faither wis against this an here ah am payin the price fur ma defiance. Forgie me Lord. Please, in yer mercy, alloo this worthless servant tae see anither day.

Renwick lay in the bunk opposite, sound asleep. In spite of the rolling and juddering and creaking noises above and below he seemed at peace.

If he can dae it so can ah. Jonas closed his eyes and did fall asleep.

Hours later he woke with a start. The creaking and rumbling had more or less stopped. No sideways rocking, no tilting or bucking.

He glanced over to the bunk opposite. No Renwick.

He sat up and felt his wet clothes. Richt, aff wi these afore ah catch ma death o cauld. He swung his legs onto the floor. It felt steady. He stood up and didn't fall over as before.

He undid his bag, changed into dry clothes then made his way out to the deck where Renwick was standing by the ship's rail.

"Whit's happened?" Jonas hurried to join him.

Renwick turned and smiled. "Wi the help o the Lord, Captain Lowis managed tae steer us intae this estuary, oot o harm's way and intae a proper harbour. We've been at anchor for a guid half-hoor. The captain means tae bide here till the storm passes." He pointed further along the harbour. "See. He's doon there talking tae the customs men. Apparently the *Mary Rose* causes suspicion as she's come frae Holland. I think the cargo is tae be inspected. Mibbe we'll be asked aboot oor intentions."

"But whaur are we?" Jonas gaped out at a narrow harbour bounded by a neatly cobbled square with rows of narrow buildings, not unlike the Dutch in design except for strange wooden patterns on their frontage. Behind lay a huddle of red-tiled roofs and twisted chimney pots belching smoke up into a rain swept sky. Further back he could see an elegant church spire. "Ye still havena said whaur we are. Whit country are we in?"

"England. The port o Rye that borders the English Channel. I dinna ken hoo Captain Lowis managed tae steer his ship intae this estuary. We near cowped a few times when he tried tae steer against the waves."

"Ah'm sorry ah fell asleep an missed it. Ah must thank the man."

Renwick frowned. "It's guid tae be safely awa frae that storm but aw the same…"

"Aw the same whit?"

"I feel uneasy being in this parteeclar port."

"Whit way?"

"The English are nae exactly freendly towards us Scots these days. Whit if they customs men find oot us twa are Scots?"

"Ah'm mair Dutch than Scots. Onway, wur baith jist ordinary travellers heidin fur Dublin. It's nae oor fault that a storm forced us in here."

"Whit if they ask if we're Presbyterian?"

"Why wud they? Ah've nae intention o sayin onythin, an the captain's nae likely tae gie us awa. If they officials dae ask us questions we jist tak care afore we answer." Jonas emphasised the word *answer*.

Renwick flushed. "I'm mair than capable – "

"O gettin us intae bother. Whit aboot yon set tae wi they folk on the ship back in Rotterdam? Did ah no tell ye tae leave the talkin tae me?" Jonas grinned. "Ye didna. An luk whit happened."

Renwick's flush deepened but he said nothing.

Captain Lowis led the three customs officers up the gangway, showed them a list of the cargo, then took them below deck to see for themselves. Inspection complete he brought them over to where Renwick and Jonas were standing. "These are my only passengers, bound for Dublin."

The three officials nodded and simply asked the travellers if they were none the worse for their experience.

"Weel enoch." Jonas nodded his thanks for the concern. "An gratefu fur the captain's skill."

With that the three officers shook hands with Captain Lowis and went back down the gangway.

The captain watched the grey uniformed backs disappear into their office at the far end of the harbor then turned to Jonas and Renwick. "There's word about another plot against the King, whispering of possible invasion. All the ports are on high alert looking for spies. They say the plot was hatched in Holland so any ship coming from a Dutch port is suspect. Our unexpected arrival at sic a time might have been difficult had these men no been sympathetic to the likes o us."

Jonas and Renwick looked puzzled.

"They have relatives as are Quakers. A good few here belong to the Society o Friends. No that it's spoken about lest the government get wind. The law here has the same opinion o us as they do for ye Presbyterians."

"Hoo dae ye ken this?" Jonas asked.

"Rye is my home town. I brought the *Mary Rose* in here away from the storm for it's as safe an anchorage as ye can get." He rubbed his hands. "We should be safe here for a few days so rest easy."

Jonas leant over the ship's rail and studied the busy scene on the quayside below. People coming and going, girls gutting and packing fish while men in black aprons shouted and bargained with customers whose carts were lined up behind. Further along another ship was being unloaded with many men scurrying back and forward with loads on their shoulders. Loud voices mingled with bangs and clatters as metal rimmed wheels of the carts began rattling over rough cobbles to begin daily deliveries for neighbouring villages and towns. The noise seemed cheerful, in contrast to the sombre clothes of the people.

Behind the busy figures he could now make out a mix of warehouses, ships-chandlers, several alehouses and two prosperous looking inns with freshly painted signs swinging above their open doors.

"Where's your friend?" Captain Lowis appeared beside Jonas.

"Awa writin at yer big map table. Noo that aw's calm he's seizin the chance tae complete his report aboot his time in Holland. An thur's a wheen chapters o his Bible needin checked for the sermons he means tae gie when he's back hame. He likes tae be weel prepared."

"Indeed. He seems a most determined young man."

"Tell me aboot it. James Renwick's a man on a mission. Nivver lets up. Sometimes ah feel sorry fur him. Sometimes ah cud see him far enoch. No that he's likely tae chainge. Ah jist tell masel it's hoo he is an try tae pit up wi his ways." Jonas turned to the captain. "Ah wis wunnerin if ah cud leave the ship fur a wee walk roond?"

Captain Lowis shook his head. "I'd rather ye didn't. On yer own ye'd attract attention. And no the kind ye might want. Here in England talk o plots against king and country abound. The most recent one has everybody feeling uneasy and worrying about the nation's safety. This can make a stranger rather unwelcome. But—", he grinned, "— I could accompany ye. Alongside a well-known face ye'll hardly merit a second glance."

"Wud ye?"

Captain Lowis pulled out a large pocket watch from his waistcoat pocket and peered at it. "Give me half-an-hour to check out the day's orders."

"Soonds guid." Jonas hesitated. "But since ye belang here mibbe ye'd raither tak the chance o visitin yer family? Ah dinna want tae haud ye back."

The captain's face tightened. "I've no close relatives waiting for me to visit. It'll be ma pleasure to take a stroll through the town with you."

Half-an-hour later Jonas happily followed his guide down the ship's gangway and onto the solid stone harbour.

"We'll start across the Fishmarket then along the High Street. After that we'll turn down Market Road onto Cinqueports Street to see the town walls and the Ypres Tower. It was built a long time ago to defend us from the French and is an important part o the town's history. A short turn along there and up the Mint, back to the High Street, along Kenmaid Street to finish off with some refreshment at the Mermaid Inn."

Within minutes they were swallowed by a maze of busy streets where the upper storeys of buildings seemed to lean into the street with each level stepped out a little further than the one below. Some walls were whitewashed with wooden planks strapped across at varying angles, others were rough stone or plain brick.

"My, this is different," Jonas admitted.

Captain Lowis seemed amused. "Rather different to Holland?"

"Ay." Jonas followed the captain's broad back as he dodged through the crowd, nodding to one, having a quick word with another.

"Seems a freendly toun," Jonas remarked after yet another brief meeting.

The captain lowered his voice. "What you see isn't quite as it seems. There's a lot happening under the surface. But here, never mind about that, just enjoy your walk."

The streets were far from clean with a variety of smells which seemed captive within these narrow spaces. Jonas wrinkled his nose as he dodged between the filthy runnels on either side. "At hame wur mair parteeclar."

The captain grinned. "Each to their own. We all do things different."

By now they'd walked a fair distance. Jonas was relieved when the captain stopped outside an inn and pointed at the blue and silver sign of a smiling mermaid. "Oldest inn in Rye. Been here since the 12th century and still serving up good ale and the best hot-crust pie ye'll ever eat." He ducked under the low lintel and led Jonas through several tiny, dark rooms packed with little round tables, all occupied by loudly talking customers. Eventually, at the back, they found an inglenook with enough space for two.

Jonas sat down and waited while the captain spoke to a serving girl who quickly brought over two stone mugs of ale.

Captain Lowis took a long drink then leant back against the wooden back of his seat. "That's better." He drank some more then glanced at Jonas. "To your taste?"

"Best in a lang time," Jonas agreed.

The serving girl appeared with a loaded tray. Two large oval plates were placed on the little table in front of them. Each plate was piled with carrots, peas, turnip, and mashed potato set round a well-risen, golden, pastry pie. Jonas leant forward to sniff the meaty steam. "If it's as guid as – "

"It is." The captain thrust a knife into the pastry top. "Eat up."

After that both men concentrated on clearing their plates.

"Jist grand." Jonas wiped his lips. "Ye're richt, it wis ivvery bit as guid as aunt Jinty's pie an she's a guid baker."

The captain smiled. "A meal here never fails. Now another drink to wash it down before we walk back to the ship."

They sat a while in companionable silence unlike everyone else who seemed intent on making themselves heard above their neighbour.

Eventually Captain Lowis said, "Mind how I said I'd no close relatives around here?"

"Nane o ma business, sir." Jonas stiffened.

"No. But maybe it'll explain what I meant about a lot under the surface."

Jonas nodded politely and waited.

"We have a king set on changing this country into what he names as the Restoration. Before Charles Stuart we had a Protectorate with Oliver Cromwell in charge. He didn't approve o many things apart from work and clean living. Charles did away wi that."

"And?" Jonas looked confused.

"Cromwell closed all the churches. Charles had each one re-opened. The clergy got their parishes back, courts flourished to deal wi the changes in the law, schoolmasters, surgeons, and the like were allowed to apply for a license and given proper status again. Making money and then choosing how to spend it had approval. Ordinary folk could socialise as and when they wanted. New theatres were built, old ones re-opened, music rang out day and night."

"Is that nae a guid thing?"

"It would be except the moral backbone Cromwell taught us was abandoned. Ye see, the king has several mistresses, makes no secret about it, fusses over his illegitimate children and even gives them royal titles. He took the lead on how to behave and others are happy to follow. As for gambling, well that took over many a life. A good few estates have been lost at the throw o a dice or at backgammon."

"And?"

"My father and mother lived on an estate that was lost at the card table. They worked for Sir James Markham. Mother was the cook in the big house. Father managed one o the farms. The younger Sir James inherited his father's estate but was only interested in London high life, fashion, and indulging himself. One night, after a bucket o wine, he dared to bet the estate on a hand o cards, and lost.

The new owner, Louis Villiers, made things worse. He was a cruel, greedy man. Right from the start he cut his servants' wages by half then charged extra on the estate rents. My father took issue wi him but Villiers just laughed in his face and added another pound on the rent. Father dared to take his complaint to court. Villiers had a summons to appear. But before that could happen my father's cottage mysteriously burned down. My parents were rescued but badly burnt. A week later they both died."

"Whit aboot yersel?"

"I was at sea. Knew nothing about it till I came back."

"Dear God."

"No content wi that, Villiers put it about that my parents had been trouble-makers and critics against the king. He cited the fact that they were Quakers. The law seemed to agree. After that our meeting-house in town was shut down. Being a Quaker seemed reason enough to be condemned."

"When wis this?"

"Ten years ago. It's worse for us now."

"Soonds lik whit's happenin in Scotland."

"Indeed. And wi the same king. These days us Quakers meet secretly where and when we can. The Presbyterians have more in common wi us than they seem to think."

What Jonas heard took the pleasure out of his walk back to the *Mary Rose*.

Next morning the weather improved enough for James Renwick to ask the captain, "Will we be able tae set sail soon?"

"Wind's about right, sky's clearing nicely and the waves are running better. We could leave now but this is the Sabbath and I prefer to honour that."

"Of course." Renwick nodded. "I'm content tae spend time wi ma Bible and think aboot the sermons I'm planning." He glanced at Jonas. "Whit aboot yersel? Hoo aboot joining me in a reading and a prayer? Or mibbe there's a kirk here we cud attend?"

"Nothing to suit your beliefs, except – " Captain Lowis paused, "I was planning on going to a meeting this afternoon."

"A meeting?" Renwick frowned.

Jonas nodded. "He means a meetin o the Society o Freends. Huv ye forgotten aboot the captain bein a Quaker?"

Renwick continued to frown.

Captain Lowis smiled at Jonas. "Maybe ye'd like to come wi me? It's no a kirk, but none the less sincere."

Jonas nodded. "An dae me nae harm tae experience somethin a wee bit different."

"If ye'll excuse me I'd raither bide here." Renwick blinked and seemed displeased.

"Thanks for your company." Captain Lowis smiled at Jonas as they turned into Market Street.

"Pleasure." Jonas also smiled. "Even if ma freend disna approve. He's a mite set in his ways. Ma faither aye said the truth can arrive by mony a route so ah'm interested tae see hoo ye folk seek aifter it. Ah hope yer freends dinna mind a stranger comin amang them?"

"Not at all. Ye'll be made welcome." The captain slowed his walking. "The house for the meeting is just along here, next to *The Golden Fleece*. It's a popular inn with folk coming and going all the time. Who's to notice us two slipping into a nearby door?"

"But hoo dae ye ken whaur the meetin will be?"

"One o the men we spoke to on our walk about whispered the word."

The captain stopped by a tidy-looking, two-storey house with a small wooden porch out onto the street. "This is it. One knock and in we go."

"Then whit?"

"We sit round a table in a back room, away from the noisy street. We'll likely be about ten. We keep the numbers low to be discreet.

It means arranging meetings in other parts o the town as well but it's worth it. When we arrive just smile and nod, don't speak. We prefer to bide quiet and allow things to settle within ourselves. Now and again one o us might feel the urge to say something. If that happens just listen. Don't comment. It might no happen for sometimes nobody says a word."

"Is thur nae a sermon?"

"We learn by sitting quiet where we can engage wi the risen Lord directly through the Holy Spirit without the need for words from any minister or priest. We do share our thoughts and prayers though."

"Hoo dae ye ken when it's time tae stoap?"

"When the leader decides the meeting is complete he'll turn and shake hands with his neighbour. After that we all do it as a token o goodwill. We might then share a meal and talk a while but it depends on the situation and how safe we feel. But in ye come and see for yerself." Captain Lowis rattled a little brass knocker on the shiny black door, opened it and stepped into a long dark hall. He signalled for Jonas to follow him.

At the end of the hall they opened another door and entered a large room where several people were sitting round a highly-polished dining table.

Every person noted their arrival, smiled a welcome but remained silent. The only sound was the scrape of two heavy chairs as Jonas and the captain took their places.

After a few minutes two others came in to complete the group of five somberly dressed men and three women in almost identical grey dresses and lace caps.

Jonas lowered his head but continued to try and watch what next. No one moved. No one spoke. Each person seemed content to stay within their own thoughts, expressions contained and calm. The noise of the street seemed to become a distant hum. As he grew accustomed to this stillness Jonas felt his worries begin to lessen. Even the nightmare of the storm seemed to fade as he allowed himself to rest in the present. Ah cud git aised tae this. Dain mair guid than mony a sermon. And then he thought of his father, his insistence on listening to the Word, the importance of interpreting it, to try and grasp the truth, of working at proper understanding. Suddenly he felt guilty and became tense again.

A woman sitting opposite, older than the others, scraped back her chair, stood up and began to speak in a soft voice. She listed her blessings, her gratitude and asked for the will and strength to continue in the Lord's way. After that she sat down again.

The quiet was settling over the group again when a loud rap at the outside door had every eye open and every face tight and wary. The man at the end of the table rose, signalled for the others to stay put then hurried from the room.

When he returned he looked anxious. "It was a warning that the garrison commander has ordered a search o this street for possible spies. They've already started at the far end. Each house will be visited."

"Whit noo?" Jonas's heart began to pound. He looked at the captain for an answer.

The captain said nothing.

Neither did anyone else. Instead they all stood up, moved the chairs away from the table before pulling it further along the floor and clear of a finely-woven red carpet. This was quickly rolled up to reveal a double panel set in the wooden floor.

The man who'd answered the rap at the outside door took a small hook from his jacket pocket, knelt down and pushed it between the two panels to lift one.

Jonas stared. A trap door. Mibbe a way oot?

Once both panels were open he could see a narrow ladder. The man lit a candle and nodded to the three women who left the room. He then held the candle over the dark space.

Still silent, four men climbed down into the dark and disappeared. Jonas and the captain followed to sit on a low bench set against a rough stone wall. The candle hovered a moment, withdrew, the two doors dropped into place and the cellar became a black hole.

Above came the sound of the carpet being unrolled, the table being pulled back in place then heavy chairs thumped around it. This was followed by the rattle of plates and cutlery being set out before there was a whiff of roast beef with rich gravy drifting through the gaps in the floorboards.

Three loud raps at the outside door announced the troopers arrival then heavy boots tramped along the hall, finally arriving on the floor above the silent, hidden group of men.

An official-sounding voice barked, "We've had word about possible spies hiding in this area. Every corner o each house needs to be searched. Anyone considered suspicious will be arrested and taken into custody."

A polite voice replied, "Search away sirs. There's three other rooms upstairs. As ye can see my family is at dinner."

The feet retreated. When they returned the voice sounded disappointed. "Have ye had any strangers in here recently? Anything we should know about?"

"Only relatives and friends visiting as usual," came the polite reply.

Boots scraped as several heels turned and heavy boots tramped back down the hall. The outside door slammed shut. The brief invasion seemed to be over.

Jonas expected the trapdoor to open again, to be allowed to scramble out.

Nothing happened.

He was bursting to speak, to ask a question but didn't dare as he sat in the cold, black hole alongside silent strangers, listening to their soft, regular breathing. Way beyond he could still hear the faint sounds of the street. And then there was a scuffle, very slight like tiny claws scraping along hard stone. He stiffened, held his breath, strained his ears. It came again. Closer this time. He began to imagine a grey, furry body, wondered how large it might be, with a long string tail and a pair of enormous, clear eyes somehow able to probe this dense black. He longed to kick out, except no one else moved and their breathing remained as calm and regular as before. Toes curling inside his boots he tried to ignore the little scrape, scrape, tried to force himself to think about something else. Anything else. The more he tried to ignore the sound the more he seemed to hear it. And then commonsense won making him grin with embarrassment. Ay. Whit an eedjit. That hus tae be wee claws. Like enoch a gie wee moose. Naethin tae worry aboot. After that he switched his thoughts to willing the trapdoor to open again.

At first the air in this hidey-hole had seemed cold and fresh. Now it felt almost warm and the air was growing stale. Six bodies must be heating the little space, six noses sucking in air, using it up. Jonas's commonsense was beginning to slip away again when he heard the welcome sound of the table and carpet being moved.

The trapdoor opened. Everyone gulped in welcome air and blinked as a candle appeared to light their dark space.

The man holding the candle signalled for them to come up.

One after another the six men climbed the little ladder then helped close the trap door and replace the carpet and table. Finally they all shook hands.

The three women appeared, now wearing aprons, and offered each man a glass of water. Only then did the man who seemed to be the householder explain what had happened. "I think my wife and daughters helped convince the troopers that we were only having dinner and had nothing to hide. This is a warning though. We need to be even more careful."

"Is it safe tae leave?" Jonas could hold back no longer.

The man nodded. "The troopers will be further along the street by now. If ye're ready go through the kitchen, into the lane behind. Two steps further take ye into the backyard o the inn. Open the back door. It gives into a corridor that runs right through to the front. All you have to do is walk along and out the front door same as any other customer."

"Whit aboot the landlord?"

The householder stepped forward and touched Jonas's arm. "He understands our needs. Mind ye, a few coins now and again helps keep him sympathetic. It's how it is. I would have preferred a better introduction to our meeting but thank ye for coming. Now, on ye go young man and God bless."

Jonas and the captain followed the instructions and were soon walking down the busy street again.

"Ah cud hae done withoot that experience," Jonas admitted as they headed for the ship.

The captain glanced at him. "It was rather unfortunate but ye did well."

"Ye've been a lang while. I wis beginning tae wonder if something had gone wrang." James Renwick was waiting at the top of the ship's gangway.

"Dinna ask." Jonas turned back to the captain. "If that's whit it's like bein a fugitive it's nae fur me."

Captain Lowis shook his head. "That was only a taste o what's waiting for ye in Scotland."

Renwick looked at Jonas's white face then the captain's set expression and seemed to realise that something unpleasant must have happened.

"Right gentlemen. Time for dinner." The captain walked towards his quarters leaving Renwick still staring at Jonas.

"Lik ah said, dinna ask." Jonas wheeled round to follow the captain.

Later that night Renwick persuaded Jonas to tell him what had happened at the meeting. His expression grew more severe with every word. Finally he shook his head. "We step awa frae the true path at oor peril."

"Whit are ye on aboot?" Jonas gaped at Renwick,

"It pains me tae say this but Quakers and their misguided beliefs gie me cause for concern."

"Whit's wrang wi seein ither ways o dain things?"

"That's aw very weel but ony deviation must be approached wi care tae guard against ony wrang influence that micht bring harm."

"Dis that include the captain? The man whae gied us passage oot o sympathy fur oor beliefs? The same man whae somehoo managed tae steer his ship thru the worst o storms an intae a safe harbour. In case ye've forgotten we owe that man oor lives."

"That disna mak him ony the less misguided in his belief. Ye'd be better employed praying for his entry tae the richt fold raither than allooing him tae mibbe lead ye frae yer chosen path."

"Ah went tae yon meetin oot o curiosity an respectfu support fur a man whae's shown us naethin but kind conseederation. Ma conscience is clear on that score. In nae way did onybody at the meetin try tae influence me ither than gie me a welcome. Nor am ah makin ony judgement on hoo they folk choose tae worship ither than say they seem sincere. Ma faither aye tellt me tae luk intae ma hert afore condemnin onythin ah micht nae unnerstaund. Hae ye done that?"

Renwick's lips compressed into a tight thin line. "Ivvery day in ivvery way I seek the richt guidance and try tae follow it."

"Oh dae ye? Weel the words ye've jist uttered gie me real concern. Concern aboot yersel an ither things as weel. An naw. Ah'd raither nae hear yer answer." Jonas climbed into his bunk and faced the wall while Renwick was left to the silence of his own thoughts and opinions.

Chapter Four

Captain John Crichton hurried up the steep stairs to Sheriff Meiklejon's overheated room in Lanark garrison. As captain of John Graham of Claverhouse's mounted platoon he was one of the sheriff's temporary, if unwelcome guests, while they made further security sweeps across this unruly district.

He rapped at the tight-closed door, opened it without invitation and strode into the room to find his commander beside a roaring fire, enjoying a huge breakfast.

John Graham of Claverhouse didn't look up.

"Sir." Crichton stopped inches away from the food-laden table, clicked his heels and gave a smart salute. "The day's orders, sir?"

Clavers continued eating.

"The men are ready, sir."

Clavers looked up at his captain's rigid figure. "As it happens there's nae rush. I've decided on a chainge o plan. Hoo aboot a few hoors tae yersel and the men afore I send ye oot on a special nicht-time ride?"

"Whit huv ye in mind, sir?"

"A wee visit tae a certain farm by Lesmahagow, on the chance ye micht disturb an elusive gentleman."

Crichton stiffened.

"Ye ken whae I mean then?" Clavers sliced through a thick piece of sweet-smelling ham.

"He's a rebel an deservin a guid hangin."

"Ay weel, mibbe this wee sortie micht alloo it tae happen."

"The men will be mair than willin. As will masel."

"Nae doubt. Especially aifter the way John Steel has managed tae tweek yer tail mair than aince."

Crichton's face grew red but he said nothing.

Clavers laid down his fork and knife then delicately wiped his lips with a fine white napkin. "Och, calm yersel man. It's nae jist yersel he torments. Ma freend Airlie can testify tae that." Clavers sighed. "At the meenit the great earl's up at his estate in Strathmore. No that it's stopped him hassling me wi letters demanding whit progress is being made in capturing Steel. The need for revenge seems ivvery bit as bad as the day Maister Steel knocked the auld gowk aff his horse at Bothwell Brig. It's been a few years but the great earl's still obsessed wi the affront tae his dignity. He even regales the Privy Council aboot the problem at ivvery opportunity. A guid few o their lordships tell him he's lucky that's aw it wis, for Steel had the chance tae run him thru and didna. No that it maks ony difference. I'd be a happy man if we cud pit it aw ahint us and move on."

"Ay. Aifter Steel's caught and hung."

"Richt, awa and brief the men. Set oot aifter midnicht. By the time ye arrive at Lesmahagow maist folk shud be soond asleep. Gang quietly roond the edge o the village, cause nae disturbance as ye approach Westermains farm. Surprise is whit we're aifter. I had word that Steel's been seen aroond the place maist days but decided tae let him be in the hope he'll git ower confident and mibbe a tad careless. That way ye shud be coming back here in the morning wi a prisoner."

"Sir." Crichton saluted and hurried from the room.

Downstairs in the garrison kitchen Crichton warned the cook that an extra supper would be required before the platoon set out on their special mission. Out in the yard he gave the men the good news of a few hours respite before the unwelcome task of a night ride across rough country.

The garrison cook swore at the captain's disappearing back then returned to his floury board to pummel the dough he was preparing.

The kitchen door opened and Gus McPhail, the carrier, stuck his head in. "Mornin Sansom. Ah've brocht yer order. Whaur dae ye want it?"

Sansom turned towards McPhail. "In the cool room. Ah've a wheen loaves tae git ready afore ah deal wi onythin else."

Gus McPhail carried the pile of boxes to the cool room, stacked them carefully in a corner then went back to the kitchen to watch the flour fly as Sansom banged the dough back and forward on the table.

"Nae yer happy sel this mornin. Whit's wrang?"

"Clavers' platoon captain wis in here demandin an extra supper. Ye've nae idea whit they men eat at the best o times nivver mind expectin an extra supper. It'll pit the sheriff in a richt mood. He's nae pleased aboot huvin them here at aw. As fur whit they pack awa at each meal. The sooner they leave fur thur ain billet at Moffat the better."

"Why dae they need an extra supper?"

"Thur bein sent oot on a special nicht raid an need extra sustenance afore they go. In ma opeenion it's pure greed."

"A raid? Soonds excitin."

"Mair lik bunglin aboot in the dark. They've orders tae ride oot by Lesmahagow tae some farm whaur a rebel by the name o Steel seems tae be hidin. Whit a cairry on ower ane man."

"He must be special then?"

Sansom nodded. "Clavers an his freend the earl o Airlie huv been aifter this yin since Bothwell Brig. But somehoo he aye manages tae gie them the slip."

"Lik ah said, it soonds excitin but ah must git on." Gus McPhail laid his delivery note on the far corner of the table. "Guid luck wi the supper an yer extra work. Ah'll see ye at the end o the week."

Gus steered his cart through the garrison gate and onto Lanark High Street. Today he should be heading up the hill and across the bridge towards the Thankerton road. Naw. First things first. Ma freend John needs tae be tellt aboot a wheen unwelcome visitors comin his way the nicht. He clicked the reins and turned the horse's head to the left.

John Steel and his faithful dog Fly climbed the long path from Westermains farm towards the open moor. Tonight he'd be sleeping in his secret cave instead of a comfortable bed. Not that he minded. It was better to heed Gus's warning than take the risk he might be wrong.

He stopped at the edge of the little birch wood and turned to look back. From here he could make out every detail of Westermains, a solid, well-built stone house fronting a square courtyard of carefully arranged outbuildings which gave shelter from the weather and kept beasts and storage within easy reach. John smiled at the lazy curls of smoke spiralling from its tall kitchen chimney and remembered how much this layout owed to his clever father and the way he'd organised the place to benefit both man and beast.

Whaurivver ye are, ah'm gratefu. Withoot this farm God kens whit micht hae become o Marion an the bairns aifter yon grand earl chased them frae oor ain place.

As fur Crichton. Mibbe the less said the better, ither than ane o they days. Nae doubt he'll be gallopin up tae the farm wi his platoon expectin tae catch me oot durin the nicht an dangle me in front o ma pair wife lik some toy. Weel, nae this time. An aw thanks tae Gus McPhail jist happenin tae deliver at the garrison an hear the plans. Ay, he's a guid freend. Ane o the best.

Turning his back on the farm below John slipped in among the birches, weaving between slim silver trunks, ducking below delicately trailing branches and disturbing a variety of birds and tiny scuttling creatures.

On the other side of this wood he faced a trudge through open heather and fern all the way to the top of the first hill and then on to the next.

Soft clouds hung in the greying dusk as tendrils of moisture crept across the toes of his hard leather boots. Soon they'd rise, begin to swirl, take on a life of their own to wet his face and hold him within their silent curtain. Not that he minded. Day or night, rain or shine, wind or sun or mist he'd never lose his way. Since childhood he could as well feel his way across this moor as see it.

Fly growled and dropped down in the heather.

John stopped.

Striding towards him, out of the mist, came a tall, dark shape, a gangling apparition in a flapping cloak and grasping a stout stick.

The figure came closer. Now he could make out what seemed like wild hair, stuck out round a leather mask which completely hid a face. It was a scary sight but John smiled. Here was Alexander Peden, auld Sandy, one of the greatest wandering preachers who still defied the government law about no field preaching. "It's yersel, Maister Peden. Ah'm John Steel. We met a while back at Priesthill when ye wur visitin yer freend John Brown. Mibbe ye dinna mind me?"

The figure stopped and dipped his head to remove his mask. "Nae need for this disguise when I meet a freend." A bony hand stretched out. "Weel met Maister Steel. I mind hoo ye helped John hide mair than aince. It wis only a maitter o time tho afore the king's so-cawed law enforcers got haud o him ootside his ain hoose for adheerin tae the Lord in his ain way. Ay, and ye wur kind tae his pair widow when they did catch up wi him. He wis a sad loss.

But enoch o sic things, whaur are ye headin this evenin?"

"A secret cave tae avoid the same troopers for an hoor or twa. Whit aboot yersel?"

"On ma way tae Logan Hoose, seekin the whereaboots o the young preacher James Renwick. Ah'm keen tae meet him and hae a talk aboot his aims for the cause."

"He's nae here, sir. Nae even in Scotland. A couple o months ago he wis in Holland."

"Are ye shair?"

"Ah saw him ther masel."

"Nae point in goin ony further then."

"Why no join me? Ah've a wee cave in a safe gorge jist waitin tae shelter me fur the nicht. It's fine an dry an weel enoch hidden tae licht a fire an cook a couple o trout frae the burn."

The gaunt, eagle-like face crumpled into a smile. "And I accept wi pleasure. Lead on Maister Steel. Weel met indeed."

"This is richt fine. A secret gorge wi its ain burn runnin thru, bringin fresh watter tae drink and wee fish tae guddle. Whit mair can a man ask?" Sandy Peden sat by a crackling fire in John Steel's cave while two small trout sizzled on a stick at the edge of the flames. "I've walked this pairt o the moor mony a time and nivver guessed there wis onythin lik this nearby."

John nodded. "Ah found it by accident a lang time ago an hud the sense tae keep it tae masel. Jist as weel as it turns oot."

"Ay. These are difficult times." Sandy stared into the glowing flames for a few minutes then turned to John. "I dinna mean tae intrude on yer privacy but ye seem sair troubled aboot a lost freend. Ane ye lost a while back in a way that still haunts ye."

John stiffened and looked uncomfortable.

"Och, nivver mind me and ma words aboot things I can see in ma heid."

"Ay weel, ye're nae named Peden the Prophet fur naethin. Ah huvna forgotten yer warnin aboot pair John Brown bein shot ootside his ain door. An it came tae pass jist as ye said. But shairly cairryin they kinda things in yer heid is a burden ye'd raither be withoot?"

"Whiles. But I've gotten used tae it and believe that each and ivvery sign or warnin comes frae the Lord." He held his bony fingers close

42

to the fire. "It's richt and proper tae grieve but dinna blame yersel for whit happened tae yer freend. Indeed it wis maistly his ain dain. The meenit we met I cud see he wis his ain worst enemy."

John gaped at the old man. "If ye're referrin tae Lucas Brotherstone, hoo did ye meet?"

"On the moor. Nae lang aifter he wis flung oot his kirk for speakin against the government. It wis meant tae happen. Naethin surer. He tellt me aboot searchin for a Reverend Peden tae ask his advice aboot field preachin. When I said I wis Peden he didna seem tae believe me. Ma rough claes and lukin lik some mad, masked tinker wisna whit he expected. It taen a while afore he accepted this auld ragamuffin and agreed tae come wi me tae John Brown's farm at Priesthill. I wis there regular and kent that John wud welcome us baith wi a guid meal and a comfortable nicht's sleep in front o the fire.

While we were sittin by the fire Maister Brotherstone started on aboot his plans for field preachin. Much as I admired his intentions and his way wi words, whit he wis sayin cudna work, no wi a man as ill-suited tae life in the wild nivver mind a man in sic a fragile state o mind. I tried tae persuade him tae gie up on that idea and heid for a toun and try tae set up hoose meetins insteid o strugglin across open country he kent naethin aboot. He seemed tae listen and next mornin he set oot for Glesca wi Gus Mcphail. The last I saw o Maister Brotherstone he wis sittin in Mcphail's cairt lukin as miserable as the first meenit ah met him."

John seemed stunned. "Ah kent naethin aboot that. But ye're richt. He wis a difficult yin an gied me the awfiest bother. Mony a time ah cud hae seen him far enoch. But he didna deserve whit happened. Naebody deserved yon terrible endin."

"Ay, yon prison on the Bass Rock is an awfy place. Locked up and stranded in the middle o the Forth. Nae way oot nor in except by boat. Nae hope o escape. Mind ye, jumpin intae the waves seems mair lik madness than desperation."

"Hoo dae ye ken aboot that? Ah nivver said."

"Ye didna need tae." Sandy smiled again at John's shocked expression.

"Ye're certainly richt aboot it bein an awfy place. Ah managed tae visit it lukin fur Lucas but ah wis ower late. By then he wis deid."

Neither spoke for a several minutes then Sandy said, "As it so happens I spent a wheen years locked up on that same rock afore the Privy Council summoned me back tae the High Court in Edinburgh. I had hoped tae be released, tae be tellt I'd served my time. But naw. Insteid o offerin ony clemency their lordships wanted rid o me forivver and chainged ma sentence tae permanent banishment as a slave in the American plantations."

"But ye're here. Hoo come?"

"The Lord taks guid care o auld Sandy."

"So ye say."

"And he dis. I wis taen frae the court then marched wi sixty-six ithers doon tae the harbour at Leith and bundled intae the hold o the *Saint Michael*. Aince the hatches were shut ivverybody seemed tae gie up, even when I tellt them tae tak heart, that the Lord wud see us free afore lang. In fact they laughed at me.

When the ship left Leith it made for Gravesend tae meet up wi a London merchant. He'd paid guid money for us and wis expectin tae send us on tae Virginia. It taen nine lang days tae reach Gravesend, us shut up in the stinking dark, each shackled tae a post while the ship rolled and heaved and groaned. As for food or watter tae drink, there wis little o that. Nae the best journey. But lik I said, the Lord wis takin care in his ain way.

When the *Saint Michael* docked the merchant came aboard tae inspect his charges and wis astounded tae discover we werena real convicts but prisoners o conscience. The meenit he heard that he refused tae accept the contract and tellt the captain tae let us aw go. The captain and him argued for hoors, neither giein way, baith gettin angrier and angrier. Finally the captain taen a temper tantrum and flung the keys for the hold at the merchant and roars oot, "Please yersel. Ah want nae mair o this."

Within meenits the hold wis open, oor shackles unlocked, and we were up on the deck, thankin the merchant afore runnin doon the gangway as fast as we cud.

It wis a lang walk hame frae Gravesend and taen a while but we aw made it. And we didna forget tae thank the Lord for oor deliverance.

On the way back I stopped at a famous wall that runs richt across the north o England. It's named aifter Hadrian, the great Roman emperor. He hud it built tae keep the barbarians oot o his empire. When I stood there thinkin hoo us Scots are still conseedered as barbarians ma een filled wi tears at the injustice o it aw."

"Ah dare say." John blinked. "That's some story an maks ye an even mair surprisin man." He leant forward to carefully slide each cooked trout onto a thick dock leaf. "Here sir. Eat up. Ah've bannocks an cheese in ma bag as weel, an thur's a flagon o ale stored ahint ye on a stane shelf."

After their meal Sandy spoke about his wandering life with troopers often on his tail, all told with a mix of drama and humour which had them both laughing at some of his exploits.

Eventually they lay down on either side of the fading fire. Wrapped up in his great woollen cloak Sandy was soon snoring gently while John lay staring into the dark and thinking about all he'd heard from this strange old man.

Early next morning John and Sandy shared a thick hunk of cheese and some dry bread before a long drink of icy-water from the burn below the cave. Little was said as they ate and after they'd eaten they sat in companionable silence watching the mist rise and swirl above the gorge while down below remained clear, every detail of the tiny valley in sharp contrast to the grey ceiling above.

"It seems lik a glimpse o twa worlds at the same time," Sandy smiled. "And proves hoo the Lord moves in mysterious ways his wonders tae reveal." He stood up slowly. "And much as this has been a pleasure it's time I wis on ma way. Will ye guide me back up tae ma freendly mist?"

"Nae problem." John jumped to his feet. "Whaur will ye go noo?"
"I'll explain afore we pairt."
"Ah'm intrigued."
"Ye micht be." Sandy smiled.

John led Sandy up from the gorge and back to the spot where they'd met. "It wis guid tae spend some time wi ye, sir. Noo gang weel an tak care."

They shook hands then Sandy gave John another shock. "Last nicht I had a dream which tellt me aboot yer time in Holland wi James Renwick. Ye nivver said ye'd gone ower wi him and then fell oot sae bad that ye came awa and left him there. Can I jist say, he's on his way back tae Scotland, strugglin thru a terrible storm but safe enoch. A young man ye ken weel is travellin wi him."

"When…?" John stuttered.

"Soon enoch. And when it happens cud I ask a wee favour? If ye git the chance will ye tell Maister Renwick that if he's minded tae meet auld Sandy he'll find me in a wee cave, patiently waiting for a word wi him aboot oor precious cause? The cave is hidden by a willow tree, on the bank o the Lugar, close tae whaur it meets the Dipple Burn. If he maks his way tae Auchinleck Estate, tae ma brither Hugh's hoose at Ten Shillingside Farm, he'll pit him richt."

John could only nod then step back to watch the gangling figure disappear into the last few tendrils of the morning mist.

Dawn was breaking as John Graham stood in the middle of Lanark Garrison courtyard and listened to twenty-four sets of metal hooves clatter up the cobbled High Street. After the steep climb from Kirkfieldbank village they were reduced to a slow walking pace before reaching the main garrison gate which was tight shut.

Clavers could hear the snorting, the sounds of beasts sensing the end of their effort and the prospect of food and some rest. He turned and signalled for the guards to open the main gate then retreated to the steps of the sheriff's apartment.

In came the platoon, horses sweating after a rough ten miles from Lesmahagow, their exhausted riders suddenly ramrod straight at the sight of the commander's figure.

Clavers' sharp eyes could see no prisoner draped across any horse. No John Steel. He sighed, then in spite of his irritation he almost smiled as he waited for his captain to approach. "Whaur's the rebel then?"

Crichton snapped to attention and saluted. "He wisna there, sir. Yer information aboot Steel's movements must hae been wrang."

"Or walls aboot here huv ears and then repeat whit they hear. Steel must hae kent ye were coming. Whitivver. Tell me the worst."

"On approaching the farm we dismounted and went up by a field tae keep the noise doon. The men then surrounded the hoose while I rapped on the locked door. Mistress Steel let us in withoot ony argument and stood there in her nichtgoon, haudin a candle as calm as ye like while the place wis searched inside and oot, ivvery corner o the big byre, the stable, the oothooses, ivvery bale o straw, each henhoose, even the bairns lifted frae thur beds. There wis nae sign o Steel. It wis jist as if – "

"She kent ye were coming." Clavers sighed. "Naething shairer.

issue."

"On ma ain initiative I ordered Airlie's man McCann and ma sergeant tae bide at the farm for anither twa days and keep watch. That way he can report tae his maister hoo wur dain oor best. Their horses are stabled oot o sicht. If Steel appears he'll git nae warnin."

"Dinna kid yersel." Clavers gave a harsh laugh. "They rebels are far frae daft. They've warning signs in place we cudna even begin tae guess. Plain fact is we've missed him again. Waste o time but canna be helped. Richt. Dismiss the men, see the horses are rubbed doon and settled afore onybody has breakfast. Aifter that come upstairs till we hae anither word."

The sun rose with the promise of a fine day. Much like Sandy Peden the mist was gone as if it had never been. John Steel shook himself. Time tae check oot whit's happenin at hame.

An hour later he sat on the edge of the little birch wood and studied the farm below. The hens were out busily scraping and scuttling, the cows settled in the near field and the sheep clustered round their feeding trough. Just the normal routine.

Recently Marion had begun to insist on using special signs to warn of danger. Aware of this he waited where he was instead of hurrying down the little path to the house.

Marion appeared carrying a big wicker basket across the courtyard and out to the drying-green beyond as she did every day. He watched her hang up a full line of washing except for one item, the little patchwork quilt from the bairn's cradle. If it was missing John must stay away.

He turned to Fly lying beside him. "A nod's as guid as a wink. We canna gang hame yit. Hoo aboot an hoor or twa checkin the rabbit snares insteid o sittin here?"

Fly wagged his tail and followed his master through the little wood and onto the moor beyond.

John walked through the heather and ferns sniffing the fresh scent of the day and thinking about Sandy's parting words.

Renwick on his way back was no surprise even if he was coming sooner than expected. But what about the young man said to be with him? Last night Sandy had sounded impressive and convincing; more so after those last few words.

If he wis referrin tae Jonas Hawthorn why wud the likes o him want tae come here? He dis hae relatives at Wanlockheid. His faither's family. An he did mention them, said they'd nivver met. But wud that be enoch tae leave a guid life in a safe country and commit tae an uncertain sea journey for a land rife wi injustice and danger?

An argument one way then another bounced back and forward with every step. Finally John stopped and looked round in surprise to discover how far he'd walked.

Mibbe ah shud gang intae toun an ask Maister McAvoy if he'll alloo his twa spies tae keep an ee oot for ony unusual travellers arrivin by ship. Ay. Nae much passes the Jamieson brithers. An whit they dinna ken they soon find oot.

Suddenly he felt better.

Two days passed before John saw the sign for all clear, that it was safe to return home.

Once again seated at his own kitchen table he ate a good meal while Marion told him what had happened. "Crichton wis mad at missin ye, caused the awfiest fuss afore bein forced tae gie up an admit ye wurna there. He left McCann an a sergeant tae lie in wait fur ye comin hame." Marion laughed. "McCann kent fine it wis a waste o time, as much as said so. Mind ye, he wis polite an made sure the sergeant bid the same. It's funny hoo the men respond tae him withoot ony bother. Wi Crichton thur aye bristlin."

"Haurly surprisin. Crichton brings oot the worst in ivverybody. The vera opposite tae McCann. Luk at the way the lieutenant hus let me aff the hook mair than aince. Whitivver his reasons ah'm gratefu. When aw this is by wi ah micht git the chance tae ask him why he didna haund me ower tae his maister. Mibbe even thank him."

Marion laughed again. "An pigs micht flee."

"We'll see." John went on to tell her about his meeting with Sandy Peden. When she heard what he'd said she shook her head. "Ah dinna like the soond o this. An nae doubt ye'll want tae check it oot." She flapped her hands in frustration. "If auld Sandy's richt, things are aboot tae git worse. An here we are in the midst o it."

Chapter Five

A stiff breeze began to lift the foresail of the *Mary Rose*. Like any gracious lady she responded by almost skipping past lines of anchored ships, out of Rye's harbour to join the strong pull of the estuary towards the open sea.

Jonas Hawthorn stood on the main deck, listening to the flap of canvas and admiring the helmsman's skill as he steered his precious vessel along the centre of a narrow channel between green fields and stretches of marsh. On either side grazing cows seemed more interested in finding patches of sweet grass than watching what must have seemed a strange apparition pass by.

The helmsman smiled at the lowered heads. "Look at them. Not a care in the world. And here's us." He sighed. "Grateful as I was for shelter from yon terrible storm I'm glad to be on the move again. The whole town was full o suspicious folk, watching an whispering every time anybody left our ship. Coming from a Dutch port seems to be a crime these days. It's not a pleasant feeling being looked on as a spy or part o an invasion."

"Ah didna like it aither," Jonas agreed and turned to see the last of Rye's rooftops fade into the distance. Even the Ypres Tower, a formidable guardian built above the town, seemed like a child's toy with its tiny red and white Saint George's flag fluttering above the ramparts.

Captain Lowis appeared beside Jonas. "Cheer up young man. No need to worry. I'll see ye safe on the next stage o your journey."

Jonas nodded. "Why wud ah worry aifter the way ye saw us thru yon storm?"

"Ye could fool me. Ye've a face as if the cat's away wi the cream."

"Ah wis jist thinkin."

"And maybe worrying about the meetin we went to?"

"Ay. It's got me me wunnerin why ah'm heidin fur a country ah ken little aboot ither than it soonds dangerous."

"What happened at our meeting was only a taste. Trust me. But I thought ye were set on supporting yer friend?"

"Ah wis when we stertit oot but some o his ideas dinna sit ower weel noo."

"He certainly strikes me as a deep one and a mite unpredictable."

"An as thrawn as they come."

"For what it's worth, don't give up." Captain Lowis leant forward to grasp Jonas's arm. "A man like that can become his own worst enemy. That's when he needs as much help as he can get."

"Wi his nose in his Bible, or writin a sermon, or prayin fur hoors as weel as tryin tae pit me richt." Jonas sighed. "Ay. Nae worries ther."

Once in the English Channel the wind blew harder. The sails of the *Mary Rose* filled and tugged and she raced forward as if keen to make up for lost time.

Now the weather seemed to be seeking forgiveness for earlier behaviour, with no threat of sudden change, no looming storm. Skies remained clear most of the time with waves running well enough to maintain a steady speed towards far off Dublin.

After his near-death escape from the worst of storms followed by almost being arrested at a Quaker meeting Jonas found these uneventful days at sea long and almost wearisome.

As usual James Renwick was pre-occupied, spending most of his time in the captain's quarters, sitting at the end of the great map-table, taking notes from his Bible or writing yet another sermon in preparation for his task ahead. His self-absorption and lack of conversation irritated Jonas who was left to put up with long periods of silence. Occasional conversation with the crew or the captain became his only entertainment. By the time Dublin's skyline appeared he was beyond boredom. Only after the *Mary Rose* anchored and the gangway was hauled onto the harbour-side did his mood lift enough to permit a small smile.

"Is yer friend still busy?" Captain Lowis joined Jonas as he stood by the ship's rail studying the harbour activity.

Jonas nodded. "Nivver lifts his heid. Doubt if he even kens we've arrived in Dublin. Luks lik ah'll hae tae sort oot oor nixt move masel."

"Would ye like me to mak some enquiries? Ask if any ship might be leaving for the Clyde?"

"Wur beholden tae ye aready, sir. But ay, that wud help."

"Once the cargo's unloaded and the paperwork signed off I'll see if anything is on offer."

As soon as his work was done Captain Lowis set out for the

Harbour Master's office to ask what might be available for two travellers seeking onward passage to Glasgow.

Jonas and Renwick were eating a late supper when Captain Lowis returned. "Gentlemen, ye're in luck. The *Suzanna May* is due to leave for the Clyde in two days. I've spoken to her master and he's willing to take two passengers provided they prove acceptable. He insists on meeting ye first. I've arranged for him to come here in the morning."

Jonas glanced at Renwick. "Mind that last time. Weel, this time keep quiet an ah'll dae the talkin."

Captain Lowis looked from one set face to the other.

Jonas shrugged. "Ma freend has a habit o sayin the wrang thing at the wrang time. Him bein a meenister he canna help himsel."

Renwick pushed back his chair and stood up. "I am honest aboot my calling. Nae mair. Nae less."

"Ay. But it's hoo ye gang aboot it that's the problem."

Renwick sniffed and marched for the door without another word.

"See whit ah mean?" Jonas shrugged again.

Captain Lowis waited till the door closed then turned to Jonas. "I feel obliged to say this and I don't mean to offend ye or yer friend. One is as bad as the other. Here's a word o advice and kindly meant. If ye want passage on the *Suzanna May,* and I take it ye do, when the captain arrives listen to what he says. And when ye answer be careful with yer words."

Captain Ferguson from the *Suzanna May* appeared early next morning. Renwick and Jonas were still at breakfast. Both stood up, politely shook hands then offered their visitor a seat.

"Naw, naw. I've nae time. Ower muckle tae see tae an nae as mony hoors as I'd like afore we up the anchor." The captain stepped closer. "I unnerstaund ye twa are seekin passage on ma ship?"

They both nodded.

"Weel. I'm nae averse tae passengers but I need tae re-assure masel that I'm no agreein tae onythin as micht cause me or ma ship ony trouble."

"Neither o us wud wish that," Renwick replied.

"I dare say." The captain nodded. "But there's mibbe somethin ye dinna ken."

"We're aifter passage tae Glasgow. Ye seem tae hae space so whit else is tae ken?"

Captain Ferguson sighed. "I'm a guid Scotsman and law abidin and weel aware hoo we live in a difficult time. A time when ma government sees fit tae demand a list o ivverbody aboard a ship arrivin frae foreign pairts. Mibbe I shud remind ye that Ireland is conseedered tae be a foreign country. As for passengers, they must state their business. No jist that, inspections are made and questions asked afore ony passenger is allooed tae disembark."

Jonas said, "Ah'm on a visit tae meet ma faither's Scottish family fur the first time."

"In that case ye'll hae naethin tae hide, naethin the government micht tak issue wi." The captain now turned to Renwick. "Are ye visitin relatives as weel?"

"I'm on my way home after studying at a Dutch University."

"A scholar." Captain Ferguson's nose twitched as if sensing a problem. "And whit wur ye studyin?"

"Theology."

"Ah. That's a dangerous word tae hear these days. And Holland is weel kent for being a tad extreme wi its opinions on religious matters." Captain Ferguson peered at Renwick. "But mibbe ye're a faithful subject o King Charles, willin tae toast his health, and no refuse lik they radical Presbyterians?"

Renwick stiffened. "Whit has that tae dae wi onything?"

Captain Ferguson shook his head. "Ivverythin sir. Ivverythin. Tae be honest, yer attitude is beginnin tae worry me. There's ower muckle at stake for me tae tak ony chances wi somebody as micht turn oot tae be workin against the law."

Renwick's face went pale. "Please. It's imperative I reach Scotland as soon as possible. My life's work lies ahead in challenging the terrible wrongs that torture my beleaguered country."

"If that's the case ye're no travellin on ma ship. Maist like yer name's aready kent as a troublemaker. Yer freend's different. I see nae problem wi him. But there's nae space for yersel." With that the captain turned and left the cabin.

Renwick stared after the disappearing figure. "Luks as if I must bide and find anither way tae feenish ma journey."

"Jist wait." Jonas ran after Captain Ferguson and stopped him as he reached the gangway. "A meenit sir. Ah've a wee suggestion."

"Lik whit?" The captain looked surprised. "I've said ma piece."

"But suppose ye cud be persuaded tae chainge yer mind an alloo ma freend tae come, cud we no leave yer ship afore reachin Glesca? Mibbe git rowed ashore somewhaur private like. Whae's tae ken? And when yer ship finally docks oor names are naewhaur on yer list. Nae mention at aw. As if we'd nivver been on board."

Captain Ferguson's eyebrows rose. "My, but ye're a young man wi some interestin ideas."

"Think aboot it. This cud gie ye a heavier pooch fur little effort, nae bother frae the authorities, an twa gratefu travellers. Whit's nae tae like?"

"And hoo heavy micht ma pooch be? Hoo much wud ye be prepared tae pairt wi for sic a favour?"

"Whitivver the usual cost o the passage we'll pay double."

"Is that so." A rough hand grasped Jonas's arm.

"Thur's nae risk tae yersel. Nane at aw fur a pickle siller. An ye'd be dain twa travellers a richt guid turn."

The captain pursed his lips and gave Jonas a hard stare.

"We'll gie ye the money in Dutch guilders, worth a bit mair than Scots merks."

"Ye're a persuasive young man." The captain pursed his lips again. "Dublin tae Glesca usually costs twelve English shillings or the same in Scots merks. Mind ye, if ye're willin tae pay in guilders I'd still expect twenty-four o them, frae yersel and the same frae yer freend."

"Nae problem."

"I cud certainly dae wi a heavier pooch. And lik ye say, nae harm done. Richt young man, bring yersel and yer freend tae the *Suzanna May* later on the nicht. And mind I expect fu payment afore ye set foot on my deck."

Renwick gasped when Jonas repeated the deal he'd struck with Captain Ferguson. "Twenty-four guilders each? That's mair than we paid tae come frae Holland."

Captain Lowis nodded. "What I charged was a fair price but Ferguson is asking far too much for sic a short distance. Maybe I could have a word and see if he'll consider a bit less?"

"Maks nae difference," Renwick admitted. "We dinna hae that kinda money."

"Ah but we dae," Jonas cut in. "Ferguson's greed is oor only way furrit an fortunately ma faither provided weel fur me on this journey. Ah've guilders tae spare. If some o the money helps ye reach yer destination it'll be weel spent."

"But – "

"But naethin. Ah micht nae agree wi some o yer ideas but ma faither is impressed wi yer ability an believes in whit ye want fur yer country. He'd tell me tae pay up an git ye on yer way."

"But I can nivver repay this."

"Nae need. Conseeder it as a doon payment on yer future ministry. Mind ye, ah dae hae a wee request."

"Request?"

"Keep yer sermons ye're preparin fur yer congregations tae yersel an gie ma lugs a rest."

"Whit dae ye mean?"

Jonas grinned. "If ye dinna ken by noo ye shud."

Captain Lowis looked at them both and slowly shook his head.

Late that night Jonas and Renwick left the *Mary Rose* and followed Captain Lowis as he led them to the far side of the harbour.

Captain Ferguson appeared out of the shadows and came towards them. "*Suzanna May* awaits ye baith." He pointed towards the nearest ship. "But first – " He looked at Jonas.

"It's aw here." Jonas held out a small leather bag.

"Indeed." Captain Ferguson turned to Renwick and Captain Lowis. "If ye twa wud jist wait here." He signalled for Jonas to follow him.

Jonas obeyed and they both climbed the ship's gangway and disappeared.

"Whit's wrang?" Renwick asked. "I thocht it wis aw settled."

"Ferguson wants to see the colour o yer money," Captain Lowis replied. "It'll only take a minute."

Jonas appeared at the top of the gangway and waved to Renwick. "Ivverythin's fine. Up ye come. The captain says the tide's richt so wur aboot tae leave insteid o waitin till mornin."

Captain Lowis shook hands with Renwick. "Take care young man. Ye've a hard road in front o ye. Us Quakers understand that only too well. I realise ye dinna exactly approve o us but it makes no difference. I still wish ye success in yer ministry."

Renwick nodded, said nothing then hurried up the gangway to join Jonas.

"Did ye thank the man richt?" Jonas asked.

"I shook hands wi him."

"Is that aw?" Jonas pushed Renwick aside and went back down the gangway to Captain Lowis. "Ignore him, sir. He canna help it."

"Indeed." The captain smiled. "And no offence taken."

"Whit ye did fur us durin yon storm wis a near miracle. As fur yer patience wi ma freend; weel, thank ye indeed. Whaur dis the *Mary Rose* gang nixt?"

"Back to Rotterdam. Without any storm to contend wi I hope."

"Wud ye mibbe hae time tae pass word tae ma aunt Jinty? She'll mak shair faither kens."

"My pleasure." Captain Lowis took a sealed envelope from his pocket. "Could I ask a small favour in return?"

"Ask awa."

"I've a cousin in Scotland. Lives at Shawtonhill farm near the village o Glassford. I believe it's a few miles south o Glasgow. His name is John Hart. A Quaker lik myself. In fact I believe there's a few o them in that village. It's unlikely I'll ever manage a visit but I'd like him to know he's not forgotten. It's all in the letter. But mind, only if it's not an inconvenience."

"Rest assured it'll be delivered. Least ah can dae." Jonas pocketed the letter and gave the captain a firm handshake. "As they say, onwards an mibbe upwards."

"Indeed." Captain Lowis grasped Jonas's arm. "Just mind how ye go wi yer friend."

"That taen a while," Renwick said as Jonas clambered up the gangway.

"And?"

"Naething." Renwick bristled. "Follow me, I'll show ye oor cabin."

As he spoke two of the crew began to pull up the gangway.

Eight and a half hours later Jonas and Renwick stood on the deck of the *Suzanna May* while she skimmed through breaking day, approaching the first part of the Clyde Estuary. Morning mist drifted over the coastline, occasionally allowing brief glimpses of land.

The night had seemed long. They'd given up on their tiny, airless cabin where rest, far less comfort, was impossible and spent the cold hours on deck. Now Scotland lay ahead. They were both wondering how much farther before they must secretly disembark when Captain Ferguson appeared. "Prepare yersels gentlemen. Anither quarter hoor and ye'll be ower the side and awa. We've made a steady eight knots and done weel."

"Whaur are we?" Renwick asked.

"Approachin whit's kent as the Cloch Point, jist above Lunderston Bay and afore we're richt intae the estuary. Aince ye land yer best plan is tae climb the hill and heid across country for Greenock."

"Wud it nae be possible tae roond the point and gang intae the estuary itsel afore ye put us ashore? We'd appreciate having less distance tae travel."

"Nae way. It's ower risky. The less ony een micht see the better."

"But surely the mist wud hide us?" Renwick seemed inclined to argue.

"Yer freend and I agreed on a private spot tae land and that's whit's happenin."

Jonas and Renwick fetched their bags from the tiny focsle cabin and returned to the deck as the *Suzanna May* slowed her pace right down before the anchor clanked overboard to grip and hold the heavy ship in her tracks.

Captain Ferguson signalled for a tiny rowing boat to be lowered over the side then turned towards a crew member standing alongside. "Sam here will tak ye ashore. Ye'll be safe enoch. Nae muckle he disna ken aboot handlin a wee skiff. He'll keep ye richt. Jist dae as he says or ye micht git mair than yer feet wet."

Sam nodded to the two passengers, climbed over the side-rail and disappeared.

Jonas and Renwick hurried to the side and saw the burly figure almost slide down a rough rope ladder and into the bobbing dinghy. Another one of the crew took their bags, tied them to a rope and sent them down to the waiting Sam.

"Whae's nixt?" the man asked.

Renwick went first and had no problem sliding down as Sam had done. Aware of the ladder swinging against the ship's hull Jonas wasn't so happy and made his descent slowly, rung by rung.

"Sit at the back. Dinna move till ah tell ye." Sam began rowing away from the ship and into the swell where the tiny dinghy dipped into the trough of each wave then rose enough to cut through the breaking tip. Spray spattered over them as the boat rocked. Jonas gripped his seat and closed his eyes. Renwick seemed unconcerned and sat watching the steady rhythm of the oars as Sam pulled towards the misty shoreline.

Minutes later the grey veil lifted enough to show a rocky outcrop with a few skeleton trees dotted here and there. Further up came dense scrub then taller trees all the way to the top of what appeared to be a steep hillside. There was no sign of any building so the spot did seem private.

Sam lifted his oars and allowed the little boat to drift closer to the rocks. "Aince wur in a bit mair be ready tae staund up then fling yer bags as far as ye can an jump fur that big flat rock jist aheid. Wait till ah shout then dae it."

One after the other they made the jump, fell on their knees and felt a jarring knock but at least they'd landed on the rock and not in the water.

By the time they managed to struggle upright Sam was well away, rowing back to the *Suzanna May*.

Jonas looked up at the circling gulls who seemed to be laughing at the two humans and their antics. He frowned and waved at the fast-moving wings and beaks then turned his attention to the steep slope of the hill now facing them. "Jist suppose we cud flee, twa meenits wud dae it insteid o strugglin tae climb up there. Luk at it. Whit a challenge."

"The first o mony." Renwick nodded and began to pick his way across the rocks. He stepped into the heather and ferns which seemed to cover the lower part of the slope. Jonas followed and they soon came to lines of tightly-packed trees which made the route much slower and longer as they continued to climb towards the top.

They were both out of breath when they finally emerged onto a narrow path and a stretch of level ground.

The view behind them was breathtaking but neither was in the mood to look or enjoy any vista. Glad to sink down on the grass they rolled on their backs and lay still.

When they sat up Jonas asked, "Which way? Left or richt?"

"I think we want left." Renwick lifted his bag again and set off along the sandy path as a drizzle of rain began.

An hour later Renwick's determined stride was slowing down. Perhaps it was so many fine raindrops sticking to his eyelashes and blurring his vision. Perhaps the thought of where he was going had more to do with it. Whatever it was he seemed to be praying as he walked, as if seeking the reassurance he'd need for the days ahead.

Jonas followed closely behind, his eyes peering through the soft, wet mist with an expression that seemed to question the direction they'd taken. He said nothing but his face grew more miserable with every mile till the path joined another, much wider track, pitted with deep cartwheel runnels. This looked promising. He began to cheer up.

Eventually they came on a wooden signpost, its arrow pointing forward, the name Greenock cut into the weatherbeaten, moss-covered surface.

"Richt way aifter aw." Jonas sighed. "Ah wis beginnin tae wunner."

"Ay." Renwick nodded. "Me as weel."

Jonas stopped and looked at the scrubby landscape which stretched for miles around. "Disna luk much an disna keep ye happy as ye walk alang. By noo ma stomach's feelin as if ma throat's cut. This drizzlin rain hisna let up either. Ma jaicket's jist aboot soaked thru."

Renwick didn't answer and plodded on.

Jonas sighed again and followed him.

They reached Greenock before dusk. It had been more of a trek than they'd thought but their first glimpse of smoking chimneys spurred on their weary feet. Soon they were almost on the edge of the town. A few more fields before the rutted track became a cobbled street which hopefully would take them to an inn with a welcome and an innkeeper who asked few questions.

The first street became another, leading down a slope lined with tall narrow buildings of dull grey stone dotted with tiny windows that seemed to defy looking in or out. The town hummed with life with carts coming and going, shouts and conversation filling the air. It might be late in the day but people were still about their business. At the end of the longest street they saw the curving basin of a harbour, recently built by the look of it, and filled with a variety of small single-sail boats.

Renwick pointed. "Herring fleet. Common aboot here. Brings plenty work and a decent living."

Jonas shrugged. "Mair lik a hard life. Gie me dry land ivvery time."

"Each tae their ane." Renwick seemed about to say more then stopped. Just ahead was a swinging sign decorated with two silver fish jumping from a blue wave. "Luk. It says this is the *Silver Darlings Inn.*"

Jonas smiled. "Fish on the sign is fine but ah can smell roast beef. Perfect. Noo jist listen a meenit afore we gang inside, ah want ye tae haud yer tongue an let me dae the talkin." He pushed past Renwick, hurried up the three broad steps and disappeared inside the open door.

Renwick followed and remained silent as Jonas asked about a meal and a bed for the night.

A friendly-faced, grey-haired man in a pristine-starched apron shook his head. "Sorry gentlemen. Ye're ower late. Ivvery room's taen. As for a meal, I'm waitin for a wheen skippers tae arrive. They've had guid catches for mair than a month and want a wee celebration o their guid fortune."

"Can ye recommend somewhaur else?" Renwick cut in.

"Up the back o the toun. *Miss Nancy's Place* is mair oot the way. She micht be able tae help."

Disappointed, Jonas and Renwick retreated into the drizzle to trudge back up the cobbled street then off to the right, into a narrow vennel to find the suggested alternative.

This time their request met a nod from a small, stout woman with bright-red curly hair piled high on her head. "Ye're jist in time. I've ane room left that micht suit. Usually folk need tae book aheid for there's a lot happenin aroond here these days. Wud ye be aifter a meal as weel?"

"Please," Jonas nodded. "Whitivver ye huv."

"Meat and dumplings. Apple pie as weel if ye like. But first let me show ye the room on offer. See if it's acceptable." She ushered them both along a narrow corridor and opened the door to a tiny, spotless room crammed with two beds and nothing else.

"Suits me." Jonas leant in to lay his bag on the floor then stood aside for Renwick to do the same.

"Will ye be needin the room for ane nicht or mair?"

Renwick opened his mouth to reply but Jonas quickly said. "Jist ane. Ah'm here on a visit frae Holland lukin up some o ma Scottish relatives fur the first time. Ma freend here is showin me aroond, pointin me in the richt direction."

The red curls danced as the woman smiled at Renwick. "That's a kind gesture." She smiled again and peered at him. "Ye seem kinda familiar. Huv we met afore? Och, nivver mind me, it's nae maitter." She led them back along the corridor and into a noisy dining room where several customers were busy eating and talking. "These are ma regulars, a freendly enoch bunch. Ignore thur racket and sit yersels doon by the windae while I see tae yer meal."

Jonas and Renwick sat back and listened to the chatter and laughter around them. Warm and comfortable after their long trail through rain and rough country they were beginning to relax and close their eyes when a cheerful voice said, "James Renwick. Weel I nivver."

Renwick stiffened, opened his eyes then smiled with relief. "Wishart. Michael Wishart. Guid tae see ye." He stood up and shook hands with a red-haired young man. "I shud hae kent. The red hair."

The young man grinned. "Ay. Ye didna recognise mither but she wis sure she kent ye. When she said, I thocht I'd tak a luk. Gled I did. But tell me, whit are ye daing here? I heard ye were studying at a foreign university."

Renwick glanced at Jonas. "Michael and I were students thegither in Glasgow a while back."

"Ah see." Jonas looked tense.

Renwick turned back to Wishart. "I've been in Groningen University, preparing for the ministry. In fact I wis ordained there."

Wishart gaped. "Ye were aye determined aboot the Word, especially aifter ye saw Maister Cargill's demise on the gibbet at the Grassmarket. Soonds lik yer belief has taen ye a step further."

"Please, sit doon, join us till I explain."

Wishart sat down and Renwick turned to introduce Jonas who was glaring at him. "This is a freend, Jonas Hawthorn. He's worried aboot me speaking sae openly wi ye."

Wishart nodded to Jonas. "Nae worries. Honest."

Jonas said nothing but looked less annoyed.

Renwick turned back to Wishart. "Yon awfy day in Edinburgh brocht me a calling I cudna refuse. Noo I'm prepared and ready tae dae whit I can for oor pair beleaguered country's miserable existence under sic a misguided king."

Wishart frowned and lowered his voice. "I mind weel yer opeenions and aye respected hoo ye were pairt o the student protest against the Duke o York's visit tae Scotland a while back. The Privy Council took it ill and closed the university for weeks till oor parents or guardians paid bonds against oor future guid behaviour." He shook his head. "The situation is much worse noo. Mibbe ye dinna ken, but the Privy Council hae gotten haud o yer name and listed ye as a rebel wi 1000 merks on yer heid. I've seen a notice aboot ye posted on mair than ane wall. They seem tae believe ye were involved in committing a treasonable act at Lanark's Mercat Cross a wheen months ago. Some kinda declaration against the government and the king."

"That happened jist afore I left for Holland."

"If ye're on a wanted list ye're in real danger."

"It maks nae difference."

"Ye're a brave man then. Mibbe ane in need o some assistance?"

Renwick reached forward to touch Wishart's arm. "I'm keen tae reach the men whae sent me on my travels, tae report back and present masel ready for the work they expect me tae undertake."

Jonas stared at them both and thought about his recent experience in Rye.

"Yer dinner sirs." Mistress Wishart bustled in with a loaded tray of steaming food.

Wishart pushed back his chair and stood up. "I'll leave ye tae enjoy yer meal. We'll speak again later."

Jonas watched Michael Wishart and his mother leave the room. "Lucky thur wis nae room at yon ither inn an we ended up here."

Renwick smiled. "Jist proves hoo the Lord works in mysterious ways." He took his fork and pronged a gravy covered dumpling.

"Eat up. This smells guid."

Mistress Wishart cleared away the empty plates and whispered, "Follow me thru tae ma private quarters. I've a wee sittin-room whaur ye can speak private like tae ma son."

Michael Wishart looked anxious when he saw Jonas and Renwick and quickly closed the door of the little room. "There's been an unfortunate development. News o Colonel Dalzell himsel aboot tae arrive in the toun wi a fu platoon. It's no jist a visit. He intends making a thorough search o the hale place for possible spies or dissenters."

"Hoo dae ye ken?" Jonas asked.

"The toun garrison had word this aifternoon. Fortunately even thick walls hae ears. It's no hard tae ken whit's happening aboot here. We havena had an inspection lik this afore so something has triggered aff the great man's curiosity."

"Lik somebody whisperin in his ear." Jonas frowned. "Lik yon captain. Ay. Somethin wisna richt aboot the man. If he's let slip aboot us landin at the Cloch Point – weel Greenock's nae that far awa. Maks sense."

"Whitivver it wis we need tae mak shair ye're no here when the troopers arrive. That way Greenock remains innocent, her reputation intact as a respectable and law abiding toun."

Renwick stood up. "We must leave at once."

Wishart nodded. "It's aready arranged. Ye'll be sleeping in the back o a cart the nicht and nae in a comfortable bed. Hearing the news gied me an idea so I went roond tae Harry Benson, oor local carrier, and explained the problem. Dinna worry, Harry thinks as we dae and is mair than happy tae help ye on yer way. He'll be setting oot for the city as soon as he's loaded up. He often dis a nicht journey taking fish up for the early morning market. Naebody will think onything is amiss. It micht be a smelly trip but safe enoch. Ye shud reach the ootskirts o the city afore first licht. Harry will let ye aff, point ye in the richt direction then cairry on as normal. Hoo dis that soond?"

"Lik a guid idea," Jonas replied. "Thank ye."

"Least I can dae." Wishart smiled at Renwick. "It's been a brief meeting ma freend. Gang weel in yer work and tak care. Powerful forces are lined up against ye. Wi that in mind I'd advise ye tae pay attention tae yer companion. He seems mair practically inclined than yersel, if ye ken whit I mean. And nae offence meant, I only speak wi concern for yer welfare."

"Ay, weel." Renwick blinked and looked embarrassed.

"Richt. Gaither up yer bags and follow me." Wishart turned towards the door. "Benson shud be at the back door ony meenit."

Jonas and Renwick lay in the back of Harry Benson's high-sided cart, close to stacked barrels of prepared herrings. By now Greenock was dark and quiet, the only sound coming from the clip-clop of the horse, the creaking of a heavily-weighted cart, and metal-rimmed wheels lurching across uneven cobbles.

Once clear of the town the road seemed less rutted, the ground more level, enough for Harry to persuade the horse into a slow trot. A star appeared as clouds began to rise and part. A second joined it, then a third. Finally the moon sailed into view above the last few wispy trails.

Renwick watched the night sky grow lighter with even more stars. "This seems lik a guid omen."

"Ay richt." Jonas closed his eyes and turned away.

Chapter Six

Harry Benson's cart suddenly stopped. Jonas and Renwick woke with a start and sat up in the cold light of dawn to discover they were now in the city itself.

Benson hurried round to the back of the cart. "Richt ma freends, this is whaur we pairt company." He loosened the tail-bar and let down the heavy wooden board then stood back as Renwick and Jonas jumped down, glad to stretch their legs and move away from the strongly-smelling fish barrels.

Jonas gripped Benson's arm. "Wur baith gratefu."

"Gled tae be o help." Benson shook hands with them both. "Richt noo, ah'm fur alang the Broomielaw tae the mornin fish market. Ye tak the opposite. Gang richt ontae Clyde Street then aw the way alang tae the Saltmarket. Turn left ther and heid fur the High Street. Nae far alang on the richt is a wee lane intae Greendyke. Thur's a reliable stable there. Ye'll git a guid deal on a horse. The quicker ye move on the better." Benson paused then spoke directly to Renwick. "While ye've been awa studyin oor pair country hus slipped intae a worse state. Ye've a big hert takin on sic a challenge. Ah wish ye weel and pray for yer safety."

Jonas and Renwick stepped aside as the back-board was lifted again then waited till Benson climbed up on the front seat to click the horse forward.

"Benson's a guid man, even gied us directions thru the toun." Jonas watched the heavy cart trundle away and disappear into the half-light.

"If ye dinna mind I really want tae visit ane o ma freends." Renwick lifted his heavy bag and began to walk away. "He wis alang wi us at Lanark when we declared against the government. His hoose is nae far frae the Tron and no much oot oor way. He'll gie me news aboot the Societies whae sent me tae Holland. Mibbe tell me the best place tae meet up wi them."

Jonas frowned and began to follow Renwick. "Ah thocht ye said it wis near Lesmahagow."

"Only whiles. They move aboot for safety."

They walked on through the deserted street of a city still half-asleep till Renwick stopped by a narrow close-mouth. "I think it's thru here." He ducked into the dark, narrow space and signalled for Jonas to follow. At the end of the close they found a little courtyard bounded by the back walls of high tenements on two sides and a low, whitewashed cottage which seemed stuck in the farthest corner.

Renwick crossed the courtyard and knocked at the cottage door. No response.

"Wur awfy early," Jonas suggested.

Renwick waited then knocked again.

This time a pale face appeared at one of the tiny windows.

After a few minutes they heard a heavy bolt being pulled back. The sneck clicked. The door opened a crack and a young woman's anxious face peered out. "Whit is it?"

Renwick took off his cap and stepped forward. "I'm here tae see John Leslie. I'm a freend o his."

"Then ye'll ken he wis taen awa and pit in the Tolbooth a while back." The door clicked shut. The bolt slid back into place.

"Ah think things are worse than ye imagine," Jonas whispered.

Renwick frowned then turned to a low bench by the cottage door. "I need tae think." He sat down with a thump. Jonas shrugged and joined him.

They sat in the courtyard together, thinking their own thoughts but saying nothing to each other. After a while Renwick stood up. "I can hear the sound o carts and folk oot there in the street. It'll be easy tae blend in amang a crowd. Mibbe we shud mak oor way tae yon stable?"

"We need a bite tae eat first," Jonas said. "Ah saw an inn-sign back a wee bit. It must be aboot openin time by noo."

Once through the close they found the street was in full swing which meant pushing through the bustling crowd to find the inn again. This time the door was open. Jonas hurried inside. Renwick reluctantly followed him.

Captain John Crichton sat by a roaring fire in the back room of the *Crooked Man*, nursing a tankard of warmed, spiced ale, passing the time while his master John Graham conducted important business with Sir John Ross at the main city garrison. Ross was the official guardian of the city, a man of influence, and erstwhile colleague of the commander. Whatever he and Clavers had to say to each other was not deemed suitable for Crichton's ears. On arrival at the garrison the night before Clavers had been welcomed as an honoured guest and conducted up to the private quarters. Crichton had been ordered to see to the horses then dismissed to fend for himself within an unfamiliar garrison.

After the worst of suppers he'd slept on rough straw in the corner of a cold, draughty dormitory where every inmate seemed intent on snoring the night away. Cold, hungry and uncomfortable he rose early to seek a decent breakfast outwith the garrison.

He looked up as two men sat down at the next table. They were both young: one was well built and seemed able to handle himself, the other, slimmer, seemed more a studious, feeble type. Unlikely pair, Crichton thought and took another look. Both were simply dressed. Both carried a bulky bag as if on some journey. This interested him. He slid his chair round to watch and try to listen although neither seemed inclined to speak other than order a cooked breakfast then sit in silence till their meal would arrive.

The serious face of the slim stranger bothered Crichton. He'd seen it before. Wis it in the line o duty? He's certainly got ane o they prayin kind o faces. Did ah see him in court? Mibbe ah jist saw him in passin, but whitivver it is, ah've seen him afore.

As soon as plates of steaming food arrived both men ate quickly, paid, lifted their bags then left without a word.

In a hurry, Crichton decided. And no very happy wi ane anither. So whit are they dain thegither? More curious he rose and followed them.

Once outside it was difficult to follow the two heads as they disappeared then bobbed up again among the tight-packed throng hurrying in both directions at the same time, claiming the same space on the street.

He was so busy watching he didn't notice that someone else had noticed him.

Pete Jamieson sat in his favourite corner of his favourite howf *The Crooked Man*, sipping a glass of best port, and studying the arrangement on the large chessboard which took up most of the table in front of him. His brother Alex's bishop seemed poised to take advantage. How to counter it?

The Jamiesons had an ongoing battle on the chessboard. Day

after day. Week on week. Defeating each other was a passion. No quarter was given. But in the real world they thought and acted as one to make a formidable duo with a well-earned reputation.

The goldsmith James McAvoy was a well-respected, wealthy, astute businessman who relied on these two brothers to ferret out information from the darkest corners or apply force where required. They were good at it. Little passed through the city's underbelly without one or the other having a sniff or hearing a whisper.

Pete's hand reached for the pawn he could afford to lose as his brother appeared beside him.

"Mind yon platoon captain we hud tae deal wi a while back? The yin as taen a shot at John Steel?"

Pete hesitated. "Ay. He wis easy meat an deserved mair than he got."

"He's fit as a flee noo. Ah've jist seen him. By the luk o his antics he's up tae nae guid, jookin oot o sicht as he trails ahint a pair o strangers."

"Whit's it tae dae wi us? The maister hasna said ocht." Pete turned back to the chessboard.

"Mibbe no but yon captain's worth the watchin. Mibbe the maister will want tae ken. The twa strangers went intae Greendyke, heidin fur the stable or the smiddy."

"Ah suppose yer nose is tellin ye somethin's up." Pete downed his glass of port and stood up.

Greendyke Stable and the blacksmith shared the same long, two storey, grey-stone building at the end of a muddy lane. It was a well maintained, tidy place with a paved yard out front. The big double-door into the stable stood open as did the matching door of the smiddy where the furnace was sending out sparks and lighting patches of the dark interior.

"Luks promisin," Jonas said as he walked into the yard.

Renwick nodded. "I hope we can hire a horse. At least as far as Hamilton. Aifter that we can walk."

"Whaur tae?"

"Lesmahagow. We can cut across open country."

Jonas frowned. "Is that so. Weel, ah'd rather be ridin a horse. Dinna forget ah've a way tae go afore reachin ma relatives at Wanlockhied in the Lowther hills. Trust me, ah've nae intention o walkin ony further than ah need tae."

"Ye dinna unnerstaund. Whaur I'm going – the work I need tae undertake isna aye suitable for a horse."

"Hoo come?"

Renwick's voice rose and sharpened. "By it's very nature field-preaching taks place in lonely spots, way oot on the moors maist times, whaur a horse has tae pick its way wi care while a man on foot can stride thru the heather nae bother."

Jonas glared at him. "Luk here Renwick, if thur's a hauf decent beast fur sale in ther at a decent price ah'm huvin it."

"I still say we shud hire a horse as far as Hamilton and then see whit's best."

"Ye're nae listenin. Ah've aready said – "

Crichton stood a few feet away by the yard gate listening to every word. Field-preachin. Weel, weel, an it a hangin offence. Whit a pair o eedjits speakin that loud the world can hear thur plans. And that name Renwick. Somethin rings a bell. It'll come tae me in a meenit. Maist like he's a preacher. Ay. He smiled. Jist as weel ah followed ye. He pulled back his jacket and patted the heavy pistol nestling in his broad leather belt. Guid thing it's primed an ready. Ay. Ah'll enjoy this an git some credit at the same time.

The blacksmith was bent over, pumping a pair of bellows to raise the furnace heat. Long lengths of iron lying in the flames began to glow, almost ready to bend into shape for the fancy railings he was making for a wealthy town burgher's grand new house. Another two days and the full set would be finished.

He stopped, straightened up then stepped back from the searing heat to take a rest. Looking out from the dark interior he saw two figures outlined in the doorway. They seemed to be at odds with each other. He shook his head and was about to return to his work when he noticed another figure. A figure in a red, military jacket.

Whit's yon trooper dain hingin aboot here? He stiffened as the red-coated figure walked slowly towards the other two still arguing in the doorway. And then he saw the trooper's hand lift a heavy pistol from his belt. Dear God. He ran towards the open door. "Watch oot. Ahint ye."

Jonas spun round.

Crichton stopped then levelled his pistol.

Jonas grabbed Renwick, pulled him sideways and they both stumbled into the shadowy smiddy.

Crichton followed. "Richt ye twa. Ah'm arrestin ye as rebels. It's the garrison for ye baith and a cell for the nicht. Aifter that we'll see hoo high ye swing."

"Whit fur?" Jonas sounded defiant. "Ah'm nae rebel jist an honest traveller ower frae Holland tae visit relatives."

"Is that so?"

Jonas and Renwick took another step back as the muzzle of the pistol came closer.

On the other side of the smiddy the smith edged further into the dark shadows, his arm reaching for the workbench beside the furnace.

Crichton didn't seem to notice the big man in the leather apron. He stood there threatening his two potential captives, milking the moment, trying to resist the temptation to fire the pistol and do his worst.

And then out of the corner of his eye he caught a hint of a movement like a faint, quick warning then there was nothing as the metal head of the smith's long-handled hammer drove between his shoulder blades.

Eyes bulging the burly figure lurched forward then crashed to the flagstone floor, jerked twice then lay still. His trigger finger must have tightened. The pistol fired. There was a loud bang, smoke, then a sharp ping as a lead ball hit the metal anvil nearby then danced along the rough floor.

"Weel done, Ted." Pete Jamieson appeared in the doorway. "Ye huvna lost yer touch."

"Is he deid?" Jonas stared at Crichton's crumpled figure.

"Turn him ower till we see." Alex joined his brother. Together they tipped the heavy body over and studied the result of the hammer blow. Face drained of any colour Crichton lay there like a discarded, over-sized doll in a military outfit with the pattern of the stone-floor imprinted across his broad brow. His white breeches were wet and stained. One leg was twisted behind the other and one highly-polished riding boot had almost slid off. "Hoo the michty can fall," Alex whispered as he noted the bleeding lip and the child-like terror of the expression where minutes before it had been all confidence and sneers. One eye had closed. The other still stared as if seeing and not believing while the body seemed like an empty shell. He leant closer and caught a faint irregular gasp. "Hauf-deid ah'd say." He turned to Jonas and Renwick who seemed stunned. "Ye'll no git a chance lik this again. If it wisna fur Ted here – " He shook his head. "Ah hope ye're suitably gratefu. Noo, whaeivver ye are, dae us a favour. Git oot o here as quick as." He pointed at Crichton. "Dae ye ken him?"

"Nivver seen him afore." Jonas turned to Renwick. "Whit aboot ye?"

Renwick seemed speechless and shook his head.

Alex frowned. "Ah but we dae. Only too weel. He's bad news. Keen on chasin they Covenantin folk. Gits cairried awa wi his ain importance whiles. It's no the first time we've hud tae deal wi him."

"Whit noo?" Renwick finally spoke.

"Jist bide here a meenit." Alex ran out the smiddy and into the stable.

Alex came back with a stablelad. "Ah've asked this young yin aboot a horse an cairt tae git rid o oor freend."

"Whaur?" Jonas blinked.

"That's fur us tae ken an naebody else. The best ye can dae is pit distance atween yersels an here."

"We need a horse fur that."

The boy gaped at the group standing round Crichton's body and nodded. "Ah best fetch the maister."

The stable-master hurried into the smiddy, took one look at Crichton then stared at the two Jamiesons. "Ah want nae trouble here. Things are difficult enoch as it is."

"An ye'll huv nane," Alex replied. "A wee loan o a horse an cairt gits rid o ane problem. A wee sale o twa horses gits rid o anither." He winked at Jonas and Renwick then took the stablemaster by the arm and led the agitated man back to the stable.

Minutes later two brown horses, saddled and ready, were led out and a price was stated.

"Is this tae buy?" Jonas asked.

The stablemaster glanced at Alex Jamieson then gave a brief nod.

Jonas opened his travelling bag and held out a bulging leather pouch. "Ah've Dutch guilders here."

Jonas opened his pouch and found himself counting out more coins than he expected. Finally there was another brief nod and Jonas had the reins of both horses.

"Richt," Alex sounded impatient, "whaur are ye heidin?"

"Oot by Hamilton," Jonas replied.

"Aince on the High Street turn richt. Bide on it an dinna slacken aff till ye're weel clear o the toun. An mind, nae mention aboot whit's taen place. No if ye value yer skin. On ye go. An gang weel."

Jonas and Renwick mounted up and trotted out the stable yard.

Two brown horses almost galloped towards the city boundary and the open road. Even then the riders urged them on till the smokey urban haze had all but disappeared before easing the pace to a steady walk.

Jonas glanced at the set face riding alongside and gave a long sigh. "This is no whit ah expectit nor wantit. Nane o it. Hale thing's turnin intae a nichtmare."

"Naebody forced ye tae come," Renwick shrugged. "If I mind richt naebody even asked ye. As for whit happened back there – "

"The least said the better," Jonas snapped and clicked his horse forward again.

"That's an excitement ah cud dae withoot." The stablemaster pointed at Crichton's body then turned to the blacksmith. "Whit did ye dae that fur?"

"It wis him or – "

"Twa strangers. Naethin tae us. Whit wur ye thinkin aboot?"

"Ah dinna like they troopers nor whit they staund fur."

"Ted did the richt thing," Alex Jamieson joined in. "If he hudna ah wud. Man's a pest, pure and simple."

"Still disna justify," the stablemaster persisted.

"Ay it dis. We've hud tae deal wi him afore."

"So whit's the plan this time?"

Alex glared at the stablemaster. "Ah tellt ye aready. We git rid o him wi the len o a horse an cairt. Tak him tae the edge o Glesca Green an send him doon the bankin intae the Clyde."

"Ah'm nae sae shair – "

"Oh ye o little faith." Alex bent over Crichton, began to undo the top row of metal buttons and remove the fine red jacket. "We strip him so naebody kens he's frae the military. Aince he's in the watter he'll soon chainge oot o aw recognition. If onybody dis happen on his body an howks him oot the river it'll mean naethin."

"Ah suppose." The stablemaster bent down and began to pull off one polished riding boot. "They mak a fine pair."

"An thur baith fur the furnace." Alex tugged off the other boot, grabbed the one in the stablemaster's hand and gave them both to Ted. "Burn them alang wi the claes."

Ted turned and threw the beautiful boots into the centre of the furnace.

"An melt this doon." Alex loosened the dress sword, now lying under Crichton, and pushed it clear.

"Is that aw?" Ted began.

Alex was already rolling Crichton back and forward to try and reach the side-catch of the badly dented metal breastplate. "Here. This as weel." With a struggle he managed to pull the long pin up far enough to open the catch and lift off the shaped protector.

Ted took the two items and laid them beside the furnace then turned to lift the pistol still lying on the floor. "Is this tae go the same way?"

"Naw. Ah've a use for it."

"Somethin special fur yersel?"

Alex grabbed hold of the stablemaster's scrawny neck and propelled the man backwards against the wall. "Whit's that supposed tae mean?"

"Only jokin," came a croak. "Ye ken whit ah'm like."

"Only too weel." Alex released his grip, tightened it again then pushed the red-faced man towards the open door. "Git intae yer stable an fetch oot a horse an cairt while we feenish strippin oor freend here."

By the time Crichton was reduced to his underpants the cart was standing ready.

It was only a few minutes from Greendyke to Glasgow Green but Pete Jamieson took his time, driving the cart at a steady pace with his brother sitting beside him as if neither had a care in the world. Behind, under a tarpaulin, lay Crichton's body.

Once on the Green they followed a narrow track past lines of washing and women spreading out sheets to bleach on the grass while children played alongside. Gradually the track turned towards the river itself then followed the edge of the bank further along.

The cart kept going till it was well away from the women and children then slowed right down. Pete turned to his brother. "Climb intae the back an tak aff the cover while ah go in as close tae the edge as ah dare. When ah tell ye, lift up oor freend an shove him ower the side. As hard as ye can an he shud slide doon the bank intae the watter."

A few yards along Pete stood up and looked round. "Richt. Dae it noo."

Alex hauled the prone figure up and over the side of the cart, gave an extra push then watched Crichton's heavy weight hurtle down the steep bank then hit some low growing willows in the shallows.

"Christ," Pete gasped. "The bugger's stuck."

"Nae maitter. Drive on."

Pete frowned. "Shud we mibbe jump doon an push him in?"

"An draw attention? Naw. Drive on."

The big cart trundled on. In the distance the women continued to hang out their washing. The children still played. No one seemed aware of anything untoward.

Margaret Carlaw, oor Meg, was neither a Margaret nor did she belong to anyone. Her given name was Elizabeth, same as her mother, but the family found this too confusing and labelled her Meg, then oor Meg. Not that she minded. Having been born in a howf where customers paid little and demanded much she soon learned the art of appearing to accept whatever and always deliver with a ready smile. This had served her well enough although her independent spirit and obvious intelligence had done little to improve her status. She'd become a washerwoman, a hard-working one, as well as a good one. This had brought her work from the local garrison where the officers appreciated clean, fresh linen and were prepared to pay a decent price for it.

Each week Meg collected a pile of sheets and personal items, some in a sorry state, and each week they'd be returned smelling fresh, spotlessly clean, and crisply ironed.

The garrison commander considered her a treasure, not because of her good looks, pleasant manners or ability with laundry; he was grateful for quite another skill.

Self-taught, she'd garnered knowledge about plants and herbs that most folk simply ignored. Through time she'd learnt their properties and how and when to use them. For a few bawbees her comfrey ointment could relieve many an ache or help a broken bone to knit a little faster. Her fennel tincture made the best gripe water for miles and many a mother was grateful how it quietened down a colicky baby. Some of the city burghers also appreciated it and regularly bought bottles to counter the after-effects of too much rich food and fine wine. In winter she always had pink willow herb ready for those with coughs along with other remedies, less common and not discussed other than discreetly and in whispers.

Today Meg was in the middle of Glasgow Green spreading out the last of her sheets to bleach on the grass. Behind her line upon line of shirts and drawers and vests flapped noisily in a good drying wind. While all this was happening she could indulge in a wander to find some more of her favourite herbs. She took a net bag from her deep washing basket and headed for the river bank then stopped to turn and call back, "Ah'm awa tae git some feverfew. Ah saw some yesterday that's aboot ready for pickin."

The other women waved and went on with their work while Meg walked on, happy to be so far on with her chores so early in the day.

The feverfew was just at the right stage and she gathered handfuls of the daisy-like flowers. Her bag was half-full when she spotted a thicker clump further along.

As she drew close she noticed how some of the flowers were torn and the stems flattened. She leant over the edge of the bank and saw a long slithery mark through the grass and bent nettles, all the way to the white body of a man with his feet wedged in some low-growing willow branches.

Slowly she crawled down the steep slope and leant close till her ear was almost against the open mouth. Nae deid. But nae far aff. An a military man if ah'm nae mistaken.

She scrambled back up and ran towards the women shouting, "Thur's a man in his drawers lyin doon the bank wi his heid touchin the watter. He's nearly deid an needin help. Keep an ee on ma sheets till ah run up tae the garrison an tell them."

"Why the garrison?" one of the women looked puzzled. "Cud be onybody."

"His drawers are guid quality. Same as the officers wear. God sakes ah've washed them often enoch."

"On ye go." The woman laughed. "Ah'll luk aifter yer sheets."

Four troopers and a sergeant came with a handcart and followed Meg as she ran back to the spot on the bank.

She pointed. "Doon there."

The men quickly hauled up the man and laid him in the handcart.

"Ah dinna ken him." The sergeant looked doubtful.

"Nor me," said a trooper.

They both looked at Meg. "Are ye sure he's yin o oors?"

"Ay. His drawers are the same issue as yersels. Dinna staund ther arguin. Nae time tae lose if he's tae live."

The others nodded and began pushing the cart away from the river.

The garrison surgeon had been alerted. He was waiting by the hospital dormitory when the men arrived.

"Is it in here or the morgue?" the sergeant asked. "He luks deid tae me."

The surgeon bent over the cold body. "In here. But mibbe nae for long. He's far gone. Quick." He waved for an orderly. "Bring hot bricks and extra blankets till we see if we can warm the man up afore it's too late."

Next day when Meg brought the officers' laundry the garrison commander was waiting for her at the main gate. "The man ye found. He's a trooper richt enough an owes his life tae yer quick thinking. We've found oot whae he is, a platoon captain frae the Lanark garrison. He's richt poorly, touch and go, but getting the best o attention for his maister is nane ither than John Graham himsel."

"Somebody important then?"

"Indeed. Ane o the top men in the government and highly respected. He wis shocked tae discover that his man had lost ivverything, sword, pistol, breastplate, boots, claes, money, aw gone"

"No quite ivverythin. He still hud on his drawers. Jist as weel or ah'd nivver huv guessed he wis frae the military."

75

The garrison commander grinned and held out two shiny merks. "Commander Claverhoose left these for ye. Ah tellt him whit ye'd done and he wants ye tae ken he's gratefu. He said ane guid turn deserves anither."

Surprised and pleased Meg pocketed the two coins.

Once or twice during the next week Crichton's eyes flickered, otherwise he remained perfectly still. Not that he could do anything else, strapped up with a broken collarbone and several cracked ribs. That was bad enough but the surgeon was concerned how his patient seemed unable or unwilling to respond to any stimulus. Shock, he decided, does funny things to the mind.

By now he'd learnt who his patient was, heard of his reputation, and although he felt little sympathy he did wonder how the man could make a full recovery from such extensive injuries.

Eight days later John Graham was back in the city discussing the difficulties of patrolling the south of Scotland, seeking Lord Ross's support before the next Privy Council meeting where he suspected the Hamiltons, Douglases and old Dalyell might challenge his success in maintaining law and order.

Lord Ross was his usual enigmatic self, giving neither a yes nor a no, leaving Clavers frustrated and annoyed. Eventually the commander gave up, excused himself from an invitation to what would have been an excellent dinner and went to the garrison hospital to see if Crichton had made any progress.

When he asked the surgeon's opinion the man shook his head. "The patient is a little better. At least he seems to be, but still not moving even when we apply the special salve to help his bones knit. He has opened his eyes a few times. This morning he kept them open for a while, moving them as if trying to focus. We dinna ken for not a word has been uttered so far."

Clavers nodded. "I'll sit wi him a wee while and see for masel." He walked over to Crichton's bed, sat down and waited.

After a while Crichton's eyes opened as if he sensed Clavers was there beside him.

"Hoo are ye?" Clavers leant forward. "Better I hope."

Crichton's face muscles twitched. He closed his eyes again.

"Can ye hear me?" Clavers leant even closer.

The eyes opened again. The face twitched. The pale lips moved and Clavers heard a faint, "Ay."

"Weel done. But tak yer time, ye've been knocking at death's door these past few days." He waited a few moments then asked, "Whit happened? Wis it a robbery? Wis that why ye were attacked?"

Crichton's eyes opened again, seemed to be focusing on Clavers face. His lips moved. This time he said two words, "Field-preachin."

Clavers waited.

Crichton seemed to be struggling to speak again.

This time Clavers heard the name Renwick. He stiffened. "Renwick. Wis it James Renwick? Did ye see him? Tell ye whit. blink for ay. Shut yer een for no."

Crichton's eyes blinked several times.

Clavers stood up. "Weel done. Weel done indeed. This is important news. Leave it wi me." He squeezed Crichton's arm and hurried away.

Minutes later he was back in Lord Ross's ornate apartment at the back of the garrison.

Lord Ross looked shocked. "The Privy Council need tae be tellt."

"I agree," Clavers nodded. "The name Renwick's connected wi yon Lanark Declaration that caused as much bother a while back. In fact, we suspected he drew up the paper itsel. Aifter that he disappeared tae Holland but if he's back and meaning tae start up the field-preaching again – "

"He needs tae be found and stopped as soon as possible." Lord Ross's voice rose to a shout. "We must send a rider tae Edinburgh demanding a maist urgent meeting."

Chapter Seven

John Graham stood at the door of the lavishly furnished Holyrood apartment reserved for this sudden meeting of the Privy Council and studied the assembled lordships. Whit a bag o ferrets. Only ane man in the hale room I can trust. He caught the eye of Sir George Mackenzie, the Lord Advocate.

They both smiled as if sharing the same thought.

Queensberry, now a duke, was presiding over the Douglas clique like some self-important mother hen, talking and laughing with Lord Perth as if they were the best of friends.

As devious as they come. He nivver stops. But hoo did Queensberry manage tae git the likes o Perth appointed as Lord Chancellor? Whit's he up tae? Clavers' expression didn't change but his thoughts darkened. And here I am wi vital news aboot that rebel Renwick and whit micht happen if we dinna get haud o him. And they jist want tae waste time scheming amang themsels. Aw weel, it needs tae be said. He strode into the centre of the grand room and clapped his hands for attention.

One or two heads turned.

He raised his voice. "Yer Lordships, I bring ill news. News that we must act on wi the utmost haste."

"So I believe." The Duke of Hamilton nodded. "Lord Ross has jist mentioned the maitter. Maist serious indeed."

Clavers almost smiled at the Duke. Whit a hypocrite ye are, pretending ane thing and daing anither. Jist as weel I ken aboot yer secret preference for the Covenanting cause. Aloud he said, "Thank ye sir, I'm glad ye appreciate the problem. I hope the rest o their lordships will share yer concern for I bring news aboot yon traitor Renwick."

Now he had their full attention.

"I'm talking aboot the same man as disappeared aifter taking pairt in yon Lanark Declaration a while back. Naething's been seen or heard o him till the ither day when I learnt o his intention tae start the field-peaching again. And ye ken whit that means. Luk at the damage Richard Cameron did wi his open defiance, stravaiging the country, turning up here, there and ivverywhaur, inciting aw and sundry tae tak up arms against this lawful government. Nae content wi that he quoted the Bible as justification for sic treason, even decrying oorsels as instruments o the deil. If Renwick gets started unrest will follow as sure as day follows nicht. We need tae act at once."

"Cameron's deid twa years since," James Douglas cut in. "Why wud folk want tae listen tae anither madman? Aifter aw Clavers, ye're tasked wi keeping the south o the country in order and ye've tellt us often enough that resistance against the government has quietened doon. I trust ye havena been misleading us."

Clavers bristled. "As appointed sheriff I've worked hard throughoot ma area tae preserve his Majesty's peace and guid order as weel as administering proper justice."

"Oh ay," Queensberry muttered. "Clavers has aye been keen on justice. Or so he claims. Mind ye, I dae wonder if he's developed a new attitude in dealing wi they rebels. Mibbe marrying intae a notorious covenanting family has softened his thinking. Aifter aw, a fine wife's influence can nivver be discounted."

Clavers' face paled and tightened. For a moment he said nothing then strode towards Lord Queensberry's ornate chair. Queensberry saw him approach and leant back as if he expected Clavers to actually strike him. Instead an angry face leant close to Queensberry's great, florid one.

Almost eyeball to eyeball Clavers spoke his mind. "I ken fine whit ye're at, sir. I'm neither deaf nor a fool and weel aware o yer whispering. Ye dinna like me enjoying favour wi the Duke o York. Oh ay. Jealousy is a terrible thing, has ye suggesting tae his Grace's ear that my marriage is undermining my loyalty. No content wi that ye've been whispering that I'm nae above pocketing the fines it is my duty tae collect frae offenders. I've heard it aw. But so far it's been passed on frae ithers. Today is the first time ye've been man enough tae spit oot yer spitefu words tae ma face. I compliment ye, my Lord. Hae ye turned ower a new leaf?"

At the back of the room Mackenzie flapped his hands as if trying to warn Clavers to stop.

It was too late so he sat down with a thump.

Clavers turned from the red-faced Queensberry to stare long and hard at each Lord, his grey eyes no longer cold nor calculating but on fire with a deep anger.

No one spoke.

Queensberry's face grew even more red.

Clavers stepped back into the centre of the room. "Ay, tak a guid luk. Here I am bringing news that needs tae be acted on only tae find ye're intent on wasting time wi yer usual dirty games." He pointed an accusing finger at the gaping faces. "Yer conniving schemes disappoint me. Of course, I dinna hae the honour o belanging tae the House o Douglas, the same house as has seen fit tae indulge in treachery and treason on mair than ane occasion afore noo."

There was a quick intake of breath but Clavers kept going. "I'm no a major baron. Ma faither wis a simple laird but ma military rank and seat on this council is doon tae masel, ma honesty and guid service tae ma monarch. The laurel emblem o this Graham taks nae second place wi loyalty tae the highest in the land. The rest o ye wud dae weel tae consult yer ain conscience. Ken whit, ye micht find it wanting." He turned and walked from the room.

Behind him their lordships sat very still, listening to his angry footsteps ringing on the flagstone passage beyond.

The silence lasted several minutes before Queensberry lurched off his padded chair to dust down his embroidered waistcoat. He seemed almost pleased as he nodded to the rows of shocked faces. "When his Majesty hears aboot this unfortunate wee altercation he'll understaund only too weel that a man whae canna listen tae criticism or keep his temper is haurly fit tae be trusted wi administering the king's justice or keeping his secrets. Mind ye," Queensberry admitted, "Clavers is richt aboot yon scoundrel Renwick. We need tae discuss a way furrit. Aifter that I need tae draft a careful letter tae a certain important person in London."

John Graham's temper had barely cooled by the time he returned to the Glasgow garrison, but out of duty for one of his men he went straight to the hospital dormitory to see if Crichton's condition had improved.

"He's only said a word or twa," the surgeon explained. "Mair lying there staring at the ceiling and luking angry."

"I can imagine," Clavers nodded.

"It's taking time." The surgeon sounded defensive.

"I'm sure it is." Clavers touched the man's arm. "Withoot yer undoubted care and attention he micht no be here."

"Ay. We're daing oor best, sir. In truth some o the credit is doon tae Meg, the wummin as found him. She kens aboot herbs and often maks up ointments for the men's aches and pains. She's been maist attentive, coming in each day tae apply some special salve tae help his bones knit thegither. It's making a difference. Ye'll see hoo he's lying mair natural like altho he's still glowering at us. Weel, no at Meg. He seems tae calm doon when she appears."

"Dis he indeed." Clavers smiled. "This'll be a first. He's no a freendly man at the best o times. I'll gang in and see hoo he responds tae me."

Crichton's eyes were open. He stared at his master but said nothing.

Clavers smiled at the set face. "The surgeon says ye're improving, got yer speech back. That's guid news. Ye've had a hard time but I'm wondering if ye're able tae answer some questions aboot whit happened?"

"Ay," Crichton croaked. "Ah wis aboot tae arrest twa rebels. Ane said he wis frae Holland an ah heard him refer tae the ither as Renwick."

"Wis it they twa attacked ye?" Clavers asked.

"Naw. It came frae ahint. An awfy dunt. Ah dinna mind onythin aifter that."

"So there wis mair involved? They'll need tae be held tae account. Can ye mind whaur this happened? It certainly wisna whaur ye were found."

"A stable and blacksmith's shop, jist aff the High Street. Ah think it's cawed Greendyke. Ah followed the twa rebels frae an inn. That's whaur ah first saw them. They wur that suspicious ah went aifter them. When they reached the stable they stertit arguin aboot buyin a horse. The Renwick ane wisna on wi the idea, said mony a field-preachin place disna suit a horse, that walkin is easier oot on the moors." Crichton suddenly gasped, seemed to choke then flapped his hand and closed his eyes again.

"Nae maitter." Clavers leant close. "Ye've done weel tae mind as much. Yer information aboot Renwick is important. I've aready tellt the Privy Council tae act on it. But richt noo I'll awa and visit this stable and see whit I can find oot."

Clavers' horse trotted into Greendyke yard and stood obediently as his master dismounted. The commander looked round. Tidy place. Luks like a thriving business. He walked towards the open door of the blacksmith's shop where a big man in a leather apron was heating slim lengths of metal in his furnace. "Guid day." Clavers sounded polite, almost friendly.

The smith looked up, saw his grand visitor in the expensive black cloak and hat with a flickering white feather and laid down his tools. "Guid day sir."

"Fine place ye hae," Clavers remarked. "Busy I tak it?"

"Busy enoch," Ted nodded.

"And yer name sir?"

"Ted Williams sir."

"Weel Maister Williams, I commend yer ability tae draw in the customers. I tak it yer work is maistly local?"

"Ay." Ted sounded wary. "But why are ye askin, sir? We're licensed an hae a guid reputation fur oor service."

"I'm sure ye dae." Clavers smiled. "Of course it depends on the type o service."

"Ah dinna unnerstaund, sir."

"So ye say. But whit if I wis tae ask if twa strangers came here a wheen days ago asking aboot buying a horse?"

"Ye'd need tae ask the stable maister aboot that. He's nixt door."

Clavers nodded and strolled into the stable. A few minutes later Ted heard much the same routine being repeated before a scared looking stablemaster came out with the grand gentleman.

If he's nae carefu he'll gie us awa. Ted glared a warning at the stablemaster.

Clavers seemed to sense this and switched to a formal approach. "My name is John Graham, a government representative seeking information aboot a certain military captain's unfortunate attack which happened in the line o his official duty on these very premises only a few days ago. The man's in a bad way, richt bad, but recalls exactly whaur the attack happened. Whit hae ye tae say aboot that?"

"Neither masel nor ma freend here wud dream o mistreatin a customer let alane hurtin them in onyway. The captain ye mentioned must be mistaken. Naethin oot the ordinary has happened here. Certainly naethin tae bring the likes o yersel askin questions we canna answer."

"Is that so." Clavers pursed his lips. "And here's me thinking itherwise."

The two men stared at the commander who glared back, his piercing grey eyes searching for any sign of weakness.

None came.

Clavers shrugged. "So be it. I'll leave ye tae yer work. Guid day." He turned and walked back to his waiting horse.

Ted and the stablemaster watched their visitor mount up, signal to them, then trot out the yard.

"That wis close." The stablemaster was shaking. "Thank God he's awa."

"Fur noo. He's no feenished wi us," Ted replied. "Trust me."

Clavers went straight to the garrison captain to give orders about visiting the Greendyke, to search the stable and blacksmith's shop that evening. "I want ye tae check ivvery nook and cranny. Leave naething unturned. And see that ye question ivverybody aboot Captain Crichton's attack. If ye get nae satisfaction I expect ye tae gang again. And if need be, again. It's wonderfu whit extra persuasion can dae."

"Ay sir." The garrison captain looked annoyed but didn't dare argue with the likes of Claverhouse.

"Richt then." Clavers turned to go. "I'll leave ye tae yer work. I'll hear hoo the inspection goes when I'm next in toun."

That evening Lord Ross returned from the Privy Council meeting in Edinburgh. He was still smiling at the memory of Clavers' performance as he rode through the main garrison gate to be met by the captain who immediately complained about the commander's instructions.

"Ay weel." Lord Ross shook his head. "I'm mair interested in finding oot if there's ony whispers aboot the toun mentioning field-preaching and a certain Maister James Renwick."

"Whit aboot Commander Claverhoose? He wis awfy insistant."

"Jist leave him tae me." Lord Ross waved a dismissive hand. "Richt noo ma dinner is mair important. Does the cook ken I'm here?"

The captain saluted and headed for the garrison kitchen to do his master's bidding.

"Whit's up?" Jonas looked at Renwick's gloomy face. "Wur still alive an on oor way. Unner the circumstances ah find that remarkable. Back at yon stable ah thocht it wis the end. Whit mair dae ye want?"

"I am grateful," Renwick replied. "But the way it happened seems wrang."

"Ye'd best git aised tae it," Jonas replied. "Aince ye stert yer field-preachin ye'll git plenty mair lik this. The real world disna aye follow whit the Guid Book says."

Renwick didn't reply and they trotted on in silence till they reached the next village. "This is Bothwell," Renwick explained. "A sad place wi sad memories. Nae far alang we'll find Bothwell Brig."

Jonas blinked. "Ye mean – ?"

"Ay. Aifter yon terrible defeat we were left wi dark times aheid."

"Faither spoke aboot it. So did John Steel when he spent time wi us in Holland. He wis still angry hoo yon supposed leader ran awa. He'll nivver forgie Robert Hamilton fur whit he did. As fur seein him strut aboot in Groningen, moothin aff as if his opeenion maittered, weel ... It wis aw ah cud dae tae stoap John frae attackin the man."

Renwick sighed. "He certainly made his feelings braw clear and I did try tae help him see that Hamilton's had time tae regret whit taen place. Time tae work oot ither ways o furthering oor cause."

"Frae the safety o Holland," Jonas snapped. "Ah'm wi John Steel on this."

Renwick sighed again. "In that case we must agree tae disagree."

Neither spoke as they crossed the famous bridge, some of which had been repaired. The uneasy silence continued along the road which skirted a broad-leafed wood for some way before arriving at a signpost with Hamilton carved into it in large letters.

This seemed to encourage Renwick to speak again. "The wood we've passed belangs tae the Duke's estate. Mind ye, Duchess Anne is the ane controlling things. She's the mither and a fine lady wi sympathy for oor cause, much lik a guid few ithers aboot this toun. In fact," he hesitated, "cud we mibbe tak time tae visit ane o oor supporters? He's a guid freend and micht hae some information aboot the Societies and their whereaboots."

"If ye must but ah hope it disna turn oot lik yer last visit tae a freend."

"I canna guarantee onything." Renwick glared at Jonas. "As for back in Glesca – "

Jonas flushed. "We best say nae mair."

Once in Hamilton Renwick turned onto a paved street, past several well-appointed town houses then down a long track to a row of new-built stables with a large, stone-built inn just beyond. He pointed at the sign swinging above the door. "The *Palace Inn*, named aifter the Duke's grand hoose. The innkeeper here is a maist reliable man, he's helped me afore and nae doubt will again." He jumped down from his horse and tethered the beast to a large ring by the open door. "Bide here. I'll gang in and see whit's whit."

Jonas looked doubtful but sat still and waited.

A few moments later Renwick appeared with a round-faced, grey-haired man in a white apron. "This is Amos Heaps. A stalwart for the cause. He's willing tae try and find oot the information I'm aifter. It'll tak time so we must consider spending the nicht here."

Amos Heaps stepped forward and reached up to shake Jonas's hand. "Welcome. Ah unnerstaund ye're accompanyin Maister Renwick on his way tae stert his life's work."

Jonas returned the firm handshake. "No quite. Wur travellin thegither but ah'm goin on tae mak a special visit tae ma faither's folk at Wanlockheid in the Lowther Hills."

"That's a lang way yet," Amos said. "Onyway, in ye come." He nodded to a young boy standing in the doorway. "Ma grandson here will see tae the stablin o yer beasts. Ah dare say ye're ready fur a hot meal an mibbe a mug o ale?"

"Noo ye're talkin." Jonas jumped down, handed the reins to the boy and followed Amos into the inn, through a low-ceilinged room humming with customers' chatter and the clatter of knives on plates. Beyond this they were ushered into a quieter back room with a welcoming fire crackling away.

"Sit yersels doon. Baith o ye. We'll hae ye fed in nae time." Amos bustled away and left them to settle down and wait for the promised meal.

It was a good feeling to sit in such quiet privacy, feeling comfortable and safe for the first time in many hours.

A plate of rabbit pie and mixed vegetables followed by a rhubarb tart with a dollop of cream helped that feeling. Jonas enjoyed every bite. Now all would be perfect if he could just lie down, close his eyes and allow the past few hours to fade away.

"Ye luk tired sir," Amos suggested as he cleared away the plates. "A wee while langer by the fire an ye micht nod aff."

"Indeed," Jonas agreed. "That wis a grand meal. And grand tae be here. Wud it seem ungratefu tae think – "

"Aboot bed." Amos smiled. "Nae problem. Ah'll tak ye upstairs an show ye yer room."

Minutes later Jonas was stretched out on a comfortable bed and sound asleep while downstairs James Renwick and Amos Heaps spent long hours discussing what had happened since Renwick set out for Holland. It made grim listening and Renwick was left in no doubt about the challenge ahead.

"Ah've sent oot for the information ye're aifter," Amos finally said. "We shud hae news by mornin. Guid news ah hope."

"I'm grateful." Renwick stood up. "Wi the Lord's grace onything is possible." His words sounded almost desperate.

Amos seemed to catch the tone. "Ye're tired sir. A few hoors sleep will mak a difference. We've talked lang an covered mony a topic but noo it's time fur some rest." With that he led Renwick upstairs to the best room. "Guid nicht, sir." The old man smiled as the slight figure dropped to his knees for a final prayer. "Sleep weel." He closed the door quietly and tiptoed away to his own bed.

When Jonas woke next morning he stretched and enjoyed the comfort for a few more minutes before sitting up to check his surroundings, then remembered where he was and why. His next thought was Renwick. He sighed. That yin attracts trouble lik wasps roond a jam pot. Whitivver he's plannin he's a hard road aheid. He sighed again. Ah dinna want tae travel that road. He sat up and stared round at the clean, simply furnished room with its white-washed walls and wood floor gently smelling of the same lavender polish his mother used each week without fail. The jug and urn on a side-table by the window had a similar blue and white pattern to the one in his own room way back in Groningen. Ay. Aince ah've seen faither's folk ah'm fur back hame.

Downstairs he found Renwick already eating breakfast and

looking unusually cheerful. "Guid news ah tak it."

Renwick nodded. "Richt noo the Societies are gathering for some important meeting in Edinburgh. I must mak aw haste there. Amos has sent on word so I'll be expected. Nae need for me tae cairry on tae Lesmahagow." He hesitated and looked down at his plate of food. "Of course I'll see ye on yer way. Gie ye proper directions."

Jonas grinned. "Ah'm pleased fur ye. Ah ken hoo much this means tae ye; hoo ye've prepared fur it. Dinna worry aboot me, ah'm nae a bairn an ah've a guid tongue in ma heid tae ask directions."

Renwick seemed relieved. "If ye're shair I'll leave ye at the crossroads jist past the next village."

Immediately after breakfast the horses were brought round and Renwick thanked Amos for his hospitality. "And yer news. Ye've made my day." He almost hugged the old man.

"God speed sir. An tak care. Ye ken whit ah mean."

Renwick nodded, mounted his horse and trotted off leaving Jonas still standing there waiting to say his own thanks.

"He's a mite anxious." Jonas shook Amos's hands. "And a mite difficult whiles. But then so are we aw if the truth be tellt."

"If onybody can face whit's aheid it's that same man." Amos gave Jonas a knowing smile. "Enjoy yer family visit."

"Ah will," Jonas replied and smiled again at the prospect of parting from his serious, difficult companion and maybe having the chance of meeting up again with John Steel.

The road out of Glasgow seemed unusually busy with slow-moving carts taking up more space than usual. John Graham's sense of frustration increased as he tried to negotiate his way round these obstacles.

Once past Hamilton he glimpsed the open road. With a sigh of relief he encouraged his horse into a gallop. The beast seemed as pleased as he was and lunged forward. Galloping along with the cool air hitting his brow seemed to help with the planning of fresh orders for Lanark and beyond. After that fiasco back at Edinburgh nothing must be left to chance. His Privy Council colleagues must find no weakness in John Graham's methods of enforcing law and order.

Engrossed in his thoughts he paid little attention as he passed two riders trotting along quietly on two brown horses.

If only he'd known.

Up ahead the road split, one for the Clyde Valley then the town of Lanark, the other to the village of Larkhall and on to upper Clydesdale. Swerving to the left Clavers allowed himself a smile; soon he'd be issuing orders to Meiklejon the sheriff, enjoying the fat man's annoyed expression at having extra duties to undertake along with more reports to complete.

"Somebody's in a hurry." Jonas Hawthorn watched the fast-moving dark-cloaked figure turn his horse off to the left then nudged Renwick riding alongside. "Whaur dis that road go?"

"Alang the Clyde Valley then up tae Lanark," Renwick replied. "Guid orchards and fields in the valley. Lanark itsel is a busy market toun wi a garrison. That's likely whaur yon rider's going. Probably delivering some important message."

"Must be awfy important. As if his tail's on fire. He's near oot o sicht aready." Jonas sighed. "Jist sae lang as he's nae cairryin word aboot oor wee altercation in Glesca."

"Nae reason why he shud." Renwick shook his head. "Onyway, this is whaur we pairt. I tak that same road for a bit then on tae Edinburgh. Ye keep going past a few mair villages afore ye come tae Lesmahagow. Ye canna gang wrang."

"Lik ah said, ah've a guid tongue in ma heid." Jonas held out his hand. "We've come a lang way thegither an hud some strange experiences as weel as disagreements. But ye're a brave man, willin tae face whitivver, so gang weel an gang wi ma blessin."

Renwick blushed as he returned the handshake. "Thank ye for yer company and yer support. Sometimes I didna deserve it. May the Lord travel wi ye and keep ye safe." With that he wheeled his horse round and galloped away to follow the same road as John Graham had chosen only minutes before.

Jonas listened till the sound of clattering hooves faded away then reached forward to pat his horse's head. Nae mair worryin whit James Renwick micht say, nae mair feelin guilty ower ma lack o prayin, nae mair havin tae justify ma opeenion, nae mair arguin. Nae mair. He looked round and smiled. A great weight seemed to slip from his shoulders. Noo ah can jist please masel. He began to whistle.

On either side of the road the fields were full of crops or healthy looking beasts. As he rode along Jonas enjoyed peering over the hedges, making comparison with how it was done in Holland. Nae as guid, he decided. Nae as tidy. Still, each tae thur ain.

The next village was Larkhall, more of a long street with low, thatched houses on both sides, each built in the same style, same chimney poking above the straw, same number of tiny windows. He began to count the lines of dark-brown doors and gave up after seventy. Half-way along he passed a poor-looking tavern, a tiny shop, then came on a wide stretch of grass. Here the village seemed to come alive with lines of washing flapping in the wind. Groups of women talked while they laid out sheets to bleach or helped each other fold those that were dry and place them in big wicker baskets. Behind them children played with a ball or chased each other round a bench where old men sat smoking their clay pipes and gossiping as much as the women.

Jonas nodded to them and smiled as he trotted on towards more houses. He was wondering why everything here seemed the same when up ahead he saw a fenced off yard with a high metal gate. Inside he could hear the loud clang of a metal hammer. It struck a chord. One he didn't want. He shook his head and tried not to think about a red-jacketed military man standing in the door of another smiddy, aiming a pistol at his head, threatening him with God knows what. He shook his head again. It's ahint me noo. Stop behavin lik an eedjit. He egged the horse on and forced himself to whistle again.

And then he remembered something else. His hand slid inside his jacket, to search the deep, inner pocket. It was still there. The letter from Captain Lowis. Ay. An ah promised tae deliver it. He said the place wis near Hamilton. Mibbe ah shud turn roond an gang back tae ask Amos at yon tavern. He's bound tae ken.

He was about to wheel round when he saw a man on horseback at the far end of the long street. He peered at the shape, frowned, peered again, and kept staring as the man on a beautiful black horse trotted slowly towards him.

Shairly no.

The horse and rider drew closer.

Canna be.

A few more steps and it was.

"John. John Steel." Jonas stood up in his horse's stirrups and waved.

John pulled Juno's reins tight and stopped abruptly as he recognised the familiar voice. He stared at the figure in front of him and Sandy Peden's prediction pounded in his head; proof of the old man's prediction.

And then he hurried forward, leaning across to reach Jonas, clapping him on the back. "My God ah can haurly believe ma een. Ye're the last man ah expectit tae meet. Whaur did ye come frae?" Wisely he made no mention of Peden's words.

Jonas shook John's hand several times. "Aifter ye left ah had a notion aboot seein ma faither's folk. When Maister Renwick announced he wis ready tae set oot fur hame ah thocht why no gang wi him fur company."

"So he's back?" John frowned. "Whaur is he?"

"High tailin it fur Edinburgh tae meet up wi his precious Societies an stert his life's work."

"Is he noo." John's frown deepened. "An nae doubt meanin tae tak on the government lik anither that went afore him. That didna end weel."

"It'll no stoap him."

"Fine ah ken." John nodded. "But richt noo we'll forget aboot Maister Renwick an heid up the road tae ma farm. Ye must bide a day or twa an then if ye're willin ah'll see ye intae the Lowther Hills tae meet yer relatives."

"That wud be grand. But afore ah dae ah've a letter tae deliver. Somewhaur near Hamilton. Mibbe ye'll ken whaur it is." Jonas fished out the sealed envelope and read out, "John Hart, Shawtonhill by Glassford."

John nodded. "It's nae mair than ten miles frae here."

"Cud we go ther first? Ah owe the man as gied me the letter a favour." He went on to explain about the terrible storm at sea, the near sinking of the *Mary Rose*, his adventure in Rye, ending with his parting from Captain Lowis in Dublin

"Aifter aw that yer captain deserves a favour." John sounded impressed. "Ye say he's a Quaker? Folk aboot here dinna unnerstaund thur ways. But nivver mind, this ane soonds a fine man."

90

"He is. But mibbe ah'm stoapin ye frae somethin important?"

John shook his head. Now he'd no need to trail into the city, to see James McAvoy and ask if the two Jamiesons would keep an eye out for any strangers arriving by ship. Aloud he said, "Naethin as canna wait. The Glessart here we come."

"The Glessart?"

"It's jist a local name."

Jonas grinned. "Naethin here maks sense."

"Ye cud be richt," John agreed. "But noo ye're here – "

"Ah'd best git aised tae it."

The two friends trotted out of the long straggling village and began a slow climb towards open country.

Jonas enjoyed the journey along the Avon Valley towards Glassford. It was also good to catch up on all kinds of news, to tell John about the latest part of his journey, his near escapes, and sometimes interrupt their conversation by asking questions about the variety growing in the fields they passed, particularly the vast cabbage patches which seemed to compete with stretches of oat and barley and very healthy looking rows of turnips.

John turned off the road about a mile-and-a-half short of the market town of Strathaven, crossed a hump-backed bridge and began to follow a steep, twisted track which seemed to lead towards the little village above.

So far they'd more or less allowed the horses to walk along. Time had slipped past without them realising. It was early evening when they approached a small farm poised on the edge of the hill they'd just climbed and discover the name Shawtonhill carved into a heavy wooden gate which was closed.

"That wis easier than ah thocht." John jumped down, opened the gate and signalled for Jonas to follow.

A short path led them into a neat, well-swept courtyard. Facing them was a tall two-storeyed house of grey stone, woodwork fresh painted, windows clean and sparkling. A white-washed stable stood on one side of the yard. A large byre, also white-washed, and two small sheds filled the other side.

"Tidy place." Jonas looked round. "Naebody aboot tho. Nae even a dug tae bark at a stranger."

"Mibbe naebody's at hame. Byre an stable are shut. So's the ither doors. C'mon we'll soon find oot." John went up to the main house door and grabbed hold of a long metal bell-pull alongside the closed door.

A loud jangle filled the quiet then echoed round the yard but no one appeared.

"Try again," Jonas suggested.

John gave the bell an extra jerk while Jonas stepped back and stared up at the windows. "Thur's a face up there." He waved.

The face drew back and disappeared.

John frowned. "Ah dinna want tae pit ye aff but ah'm gettin a feelin wur nae welcome."

Jonas took out the captain's letter and held it up then they both stepped back and waited.

A few moments passed before they heard a heavy bolt slide back, a key turn, then a sneck click. Finally the door opened a crack and a pair of eyes peered out.

"Ah saw the name Shawtonhill on the gate back ther. Are ye John Hart? Cousin tae a Captain Edward Lowis frae the toun o Rye?" Jonas took a deep breath. "In the sooth o England?"

"Ay." The voice behind the door gasped.

"In that case," Jonas stepped forward and thrust the sealed envelope towards the tiny open space, "tak this. Ah'm jist the messenger, dain a favour fur the captain, an mean nae harm."

A work-worn hand reached out, took the letter then the door closed again.

"Is that it?" Jonas looked at John.

John shrugged. "Jist wait an see. The man in ther seems either suspicious or feart or baith."

Jonas thought of the visit he'd made with Renwick to the friend in the city, the white face, the frightened voice. He turned to John. "Ay. Somethin's nae richt."

"Lik ah said, jist wait."

They stood several minutes before the door swung open and an anxious looking man stood on the doorstep.

Jonas smiled at him. "My, but ye're lik the captain, same shape, same face. Ye huv tae be his cousin John Hart."

John Hart seemed pleased. "Apologies baith and thank ye fur this." He held up the open letter. "Tie yer beasts tae the rail by the stable-door then in ye come an tell me mair. Ye're maist welcome."

John and Jonas followed their host through a long, dark hall and into a big room with heavy curtains closed against the daylight. John Hart crossed the room and yanked the curtains back to reveal tapestry covered walls, a row of highly-polished hardback chairs against one wall, a long settee of woven cane beside a carved, wooden fireplace, three green armchairs placed at intervals across a matching green carpet while in the centre stood a round, inlaid table with what looked like a closed Bible carefully placed beside a silver candelabra and a glass vase filled with fresh flowers.

John Steel stared at the strange arrangement. "Is this yer guid room?"

"We use it for oor meetins," John Hart explained, "but sit yersels doon while I fetch ma wife. She'll want tae thank ye for takin sic trouble tae seek us oot."

John shook his head. "Naethin against yer meetins but ah'd be happier in anither room." He paused. "Yer kitchen wud be fine."

John Hart looked unsure and glanced at Jonas.

Jonas nodded. "It wud be mair freendly. No that wur meanin tae tak up much o yer time. Ah've reason tae be gratefu tae yer cousin. Very gratefu. When he heard ah wis fur Scotland he asked me tae tak this letter tae yersel. Ah'd nae idea whaur the village o Glassford micht be but aifter aw he'd done fur me it wis a sma request. So here ah am, task complete, an able tae continue ma journey wi a clear conscience."

"Indeed." John Hart smiled. "But no afore I offer ye a meal and ask if ye'll tell me a bit mair aboot ma far awa cousin. If ye prefer the kitchen the kitchen it is. Come thru." He turned and led them back along the hall and into a room with a welcoming feeling. The heavy rafters were hung with bunches of dried herbs interspersed with maturing legs of ham and several lidded baskets. The back wall was entirely taken up by an enormous dresser with an impressive display of lustre-ware jugs and large pewter plates. Two settles perched beside a black range where a joint of meat was speared and gently turning above the glowing embers of the fire while a heavy looking, ribbed pot hung on a swee at the side. In the middle of the room was a well-scrubbed table partially laid with brown and cream earthenware bowls and mugs, a pile of wooden platters and several horn-handled knives and spoons.

Jonas sniffed the sweet smell of lamb mixed with the scent of simmering vegetables and suddenly felt very hungry. "Smells guid."

A gentle voice said, "I hope ye'll find it acceptable."

Jonas hadn't noticed a woman sitting on a rocking chair by the window. She laid aside her sewing and stood up. "I'm Mirren Hart. Guid tae meet ye."

Jonas blushed. "An ye mistress." He stepped forward, took her hand and clicked his heels in the way his mother had taught him. "Jonas Hawthorn frae Holland. Here in Scotland tae visit ma faither's family at Wanlockheid."

The woman had the same anxious expression as her husband but she did smile. "Ye've still a way tae go."

"No afore we feed him." John Hart walked over to the side of the room and pulled a chair towards the table. "Sit yersel doon and share oor meal." He went back to fetch another before turning to John. "Are ye frae Holland as weel?"

John shook his head. "Logan Waterheid farm near Lesmahagow. Ma name's John Steel."

"John Steel. Nae the John Steel as fought at Bothwell Brig?"

"Hoo dae ye ken aboot that?"

"Yer fame gangs afore ye. Ane o ma Presbyterian neebors wis ther and tellt me aboot the battle, hoo he saw ane o the Covenantin captains fight his way aff the brig only tae be challenged by a mounted government leader. Somehoo he reached ower, cut the horse's traces and sent the great man tae the ground afore escapin. Ma neebor said it wis a Captain John Steel frae Lesmahagow."

"An ah'm payin fur it. Declared a rebel an on the run ivver since. Ma pair family huv suffered as weel."

John Hart frowned. "I'm sorry tae hear that. Lik yersel ma neebor hus tae hide when the government troopers come searchin the village. Man's hatred is an awfy thing. Ay, and us Quakers ken aboot that." He shook his head then smiled again. "But richt noo lets think aboot pleasant things and enjoy a meal thegither." He opened the kitchen door and called out, "Edward, Mary, Jonathan come doon for supper."

A moment later two boys appeared in the doorway, one holding the hand of a little fair-haired girl in a blue smock. Again Jonas and John couldn't miss the anxious expression in all three children.

John and Mirren Hart did their visitors proud with a meal to remember. Jonas found it difficult to mix eating as much as he'd like with answering so many questions; but he did his best telling them about Rye and the secret Quaker meeting; finally he described the *Mary Rose* and her near demise in the English Channel. This brought gasps of admiration and then comments about their relative's sea-going skill.

John Steel sat enjoying his meal, nodding and smiling at the family's obvious pleasure. He also saw how their worried expression still hovered. This made him ask, "Whit aboot yersels? Hae ye been here lang?"

"Aw ma life," John Hart replied. "It wis ma mither's sister as moved awa when she married William Lowis. He wis a sea captain as weel. At the time he sailed oot o the Broomielaw but it wis nae time afore he moved south for the chance tae captain bigger ships. We nivver saw them aifter that. It wis a peety. Ma mither and her sister wur richt close."

"If only she'd lived a bit langer," Mirren cut in. "Think whit this letter wud hae meant." She shook her head. "We only buried the auld lady twa days ago."

John Hart held up his hand as if to stop her. "The worst day o ma life and the maist frustratin."

"Sad ah'll grant ye," John said gently, "but shairly nae frustratin?"

"It wis." John Hart's fist clenched. He seemed close to tears. "The disrespect wis terrible and I wis useless against it."

No-one spoke as they all waited.

John Hart took a deep breath. "Some men claimin tae be Covenanters arrived at the graveyard. They climbed ontae the wall, and sat there shoutin lik banshees, threatenin tae stoap us lowerin the coffin intae the ground. Us Quakers are against violence but it wis touch and go when they stertit takin stanes aff the wall and flingin them in oor direction."

"It wisna aw bad," Mirren grasped her husband's arm. "Some o oor Presbyterian neebors heard the noise and ran doon frae the village tae try and help. Withoot them God kens whit micht hae happened. They saw oor attackers aff but no afore the deils threatened tae come back and deal wi us in oor ain hoose."

"Did they noo?" John Steel spoke quietly. "Covenanters ye say?"

Mirren nodded. "They kept pointin at us and shoutin, 'Death tae the unbelievers.'"

"Men lik that are the real unbelievers." John's voice rose. "Thur only loyalty is tae themsels an whit they can git oot o tormentin ithers fur nae guid reason. Wur they local men?"

"Naw." John Hart clenched his fist again. "Ma neebor thinks they mibbe come frae Strathaven. They've caused trouble in the toun afore. Noo they're spreadin their wings. Last week they went tae a farm on the ither side o the village, broke intae the hoose, attacked the farmer and his family, near wrecked the place then made aff wi money and a guid horse. Aw in the name o teachin they Quakers a lesson. Ma neebor said we micht be nixt."

John Steel frowned. "In that case ye need tae be prepared."

"I ken," John Hart sighed. "That's why – "

"Yer place wis shut up when we arrived. Why ye didna open the door." Jonas glanced at John. "Ah kent somethin wisna richt." Jonas jerked back in his seat as a stone hit the kitchen window and shattered one of the tiny panes of glass.

Mirren's hands flew to her mouth.

The three children sat as if frozen.

John Steel stood up. "Bide still while ah see whit's oot there." He ran into the hall and they heard his feet rattle upstairs. A minute later he was back. "Three men are staundin in yer yard facin the hoose, each wi a musket an a stave. They seem set on attack."

"They canna git in." John Hart sounded defiant. "The door's thick, bolted and locked. Ma lads shut yer horses in the stable. They're safe enoch."

"An then whit?" John Steel snapped. "Ye canna sit in here forivver."

"Mibbe they'll get fed up and gang awa," Mirren suggested.

"An come back anither day."

A second stone crashed through the window and landed at John Hart's feet.

"Only ane way tae deal wi this." John Steel glared at him. "An dinna tell me ye're against violence."

Hart flushed and looked away.

"Wi ye or withoot ye somethin needs tae be done."

Hart looked at the round pebble at his feet then at John. "Whit dae ye suggest?"

"We open the door."

"Please. No," Mirren pleaded. "The bairns."

"Will bide safe." John Steel spoke slowly and calmly. "Jist tak them upstairs while we sort oot the problem doon here."

Mirren stood up and herded the three white-faced children from the kitchen.

John waited till he heard their feet patter on the floor above then said, "We open the main door. Thur's three o them but they need tae come thru the space ane at a time. Jonas an masel staund ahint the door ready tae gie them a dunt on the heid wi somethin heavy. An rope. Hae ye ony in the hoose?"

"In the cellar." Hart disappeared and returned with a coiled length of hemp.

John nodded. "Licht a wee lantern an staund in the hall, waitin tae welcome yer uninvited guests. They'll see ye frae the wee licht, ken ye, an think it's jist yersel an yer family. That's whit we want." He looked round the kitchen. "If ye huvna ony heavy sticks ah'll use ma sword."

"No. Please." Hart looked even more scared. "Thur's twa scythe handles ahint the scullery door. They're made frae beech and richt heavy. Wud that dae?"

"Perfect." John signalled to Jonas who went off with Hart and returned with two lengths of solid beech.

"Hart." A voice roared outside. "Open up or else."

Another stone hit the window.

Hart took a little lantern from a shelf by the door, lit the tiny candle then led John and Jonas into the dark hall.

The voice roared again.

"Gettin impatient," John smiled. "An that maks a man careless." He pointed to a spot half-way along the hall. "Hart. Staund there. They'll see ye clear enoch while the rest o the place bides dark. Ah'll open the door an gie the first yin as comes in a guid dunt on the heid. Jonas will be waitin tae grab haud an pu the body tae the side while ah deal wi the second yin. Same fur number three. If ah hit them hard enoch it shud be nae problem."

"If ye dinna?" Hart stuttered.

"Nae fear." John laughed.

The voice roared again then came three musket shots.

John looked pleased. "They canna fire again till they re-load an by that time – " He signalled to Jonas who flattened himself against the wall while John drew back the top and bottom bolt, turned the big key, lifted the heavy sneck then yanked the door open.

Whoever was waiting outside didn't expect this. Nothing happened for a second then a dark shape appeared on the doorstep to stare at the figure standing halfway down the hall in a soft lantern glow. "Richt then Maister Quaker, ye've a wee lesson tae learn." The dark figure strode in.

John's leg shot out to trip him up.

"Whit the – " The man jerked forward. His musket hit the wall "Chriss." He crumpled as a heavy, scythe handle crunched against the back of his head.

Jonas leant down, grabbed the limp weight and pulled it to the side as a second figure barged in to meet the same fate.

The third figure seemed to sense something was wrong. He hesitated on the doorstep only to have a large hand grip his throat and pull him inside. Gasping for breath he tried to pull back as heavy beech hit his brow. He dropped with a loud groan then the hall was quiet again.

Half-way along the hall Hart stood as if frozen staring at the three still bodies.

"Thur nae deid," John hissed. "Dinna jist staund there. Tie them up afore they come roond."

Three would-be attackers opened their eyes to discover their roles had changed. Now they were captive in John Hart's kitchen, each lashed to a chair, unable to move. Heads pounding with a mixture of fear, anger and pain they had no idea how this had happened.

John Steel leant forward to study three angry but scared faces. He stopped at the middle one. "Ah ken ye." He glared at the scowling, ferret-like face with its cold eyes full of hatred. "Nisbet isn't it? Frae Stonehoose?"

"Ah ken ye as weel."

"So ye shud. We wur baith at Bothwell Brig. Ah mind ye fine in yon platoon frae Stonehoose. Bit o a troublemaker even then. Seems lik ye huvna chainged, attackin folk fur nae guid reason."

"Thur Quakers," Nisbet hissed, "wi evil ways that need tae be stoaped."

"It's the government hus evil ways nae the pair Quakers. They suffer lik oorsels."

"They dinna haud oor beliefs. They think different, behave different."

"An that justifies stravaigin the countryside, terrorisin folk in thur hames an stealin frae them?"

"Wur staundin up fur the truth o the Word, supportin the cause, adherin tae the Covenant by takin on ivvery enemy we meet. If they Quakers are nae wi us thur agin us." Nisbet looked defiant and spat. "Whit aboot yersel? Whit aboot the way ye behaved back at Bothwell when Sir Robert ordered yon baggage thief tae huv his ears cut aff? Ye didna like it did ye?"

"Whit are ye on aboot?"

"Ye ken fine whit ah mean. Insteid o challengin the great man ye stamped awa lik a bairn in a huff. Wisna yer best meenit wis it?" Nisbet laughed. "Ah saw ye, face lik a turkey but dain naethin, so dinna bother moothin aff tae me."

Suddenly John understood exactly what Nisbet meant. Suddenly he was back at Bothwell, the night before the battle, discovering what Sir Robert Hamilton was capable of, admitting his rage at the stupid self-obsessed man, remembering how he'd reacted by hurrying from the camp to sit alone on the edge of Duchess Anne's fine wooded estate for hours, trying to rationalise the madness around him.

If only came winging out of the past, fresh as the moment along with the thought of what he might have done to Sir Robert. He could almost hear the gentle snuffles of creatures close by in the undergrowth and then there had been that glimpse of a tiny, red ladybird marching across a dandelion leaf. He even remembered her five round, black spots. Most of all he remembered her unhesitating progress. She kent whit she wis aboot. He blinked. Ay. *If only.*

"Touched a raw nerve, eh?" Nisbet bared his teeth.

"No in the way ye think." John leant close, grasped the scrawny neck and squeezed till Nisbet's eyes bulged. "Ye deserve tae be whipped. If Richard Cameron or James Renwick kent whit ye wur dain they'd disown yer evil thochts. As fur yer an actions – "

"Cameron's deid a while back an Renwick's nae here. It's up tae the likes o us tae cairry on the cause. If that means dealin wi

Quakers so be it."

John looked as if he might strike Nisbet then turned to Jonas. "Tie somethin roond this ane's mooth afore he utters ony mair lies."

Jonas went through to the scullery and came back with a length of torn linen. Nisbet twisted his head back and forward then tried to bite Jonas as he forced part of the strip into his mouth.

John nodded. "Dae the same wi the ither twa, jist in case."

John Hart spoke for the first time. "Whit noo?"

"We put them in yer cellar an leave them tae rot. Naebody will ivver ken."

Jonas and Hart stared at John. They looked shocked but neither argued.

The three men, still lashed to their chairs were carried down to the cellar and left in the cold, damp darkness with their own thoughts, no way of moving or even speaking to each other and worst of all, feeling the weight of John Steel's threat.

Back in the kitchen Hart sat down at the table. His hands were shaking.

Jonas watched him for a moment then turned to John. "Did ye mean whit ye said?"

"Whit dae ye think? They kinda men are bullies. It's nae hard tae knock the stuffin oot them" John winked. "Jist as lang as they think the worst."

The thought of the three captives now in the farm cellar weighed heavily on John, Jonas, and Hart but nothing more was said till Hart suggested, "My wife and bairns must be hungry by noo. Shud ah caw them doon?"

John shook his head. "Tak up some bannocks an cheese an some watter. Best they bide whaur they are. We dinna want them gettin involved or seein onythin they shudna."

Hart gaped at him. "Ah thocht ye said – ?"

"Ah said it's nae hard tae fricht they kinda folk an that's whit's happenin in yer cellar richt noo. A nicht in the dark, hearin strange beasties scuttlin aboot close by, canna see onythin, mooths gagged, nae able tae move withoot a rope diggin in, feelin richt isolated as the cauld seeps intae thur bones, nae idea aboot time passin, an worst o aw wunnerin whit micht come nixt."

"Ay weel. When ye pit it lik that ah doubt if ah cud thole bein doon ther," Hart admitted. "Ah tak it ye're nae plannin ony mair violence?"

"Depends," John replied. "But rest easy, ah'll be surprised if they need onythin ither than a wee slap aboot the lugs tae remind them whae's in control."

Hart glanced at Jonas who shrugged but said nothing. "Richt then, ah'll see tae the wife an bairns then git somethin ready fur oorsels."

John nodded. "Stoap worryin man, it'll work oot fine. Jist be patient. Oor captives need a wheen mair hoors sufferin fur ma plan tae tak effect."

"John kens whit he's dain," Jonas joined in. "Lik he said, patience."

Hart looked uncertain but busied himself filling a basket with bannocks and cheese then muttered, "Mibbe a wee treat wud help." He took a small round fruit cake from a tin on a nearby shelf.

"Vera thing tae cheer them up." John went through to the scullery and came back with a pitcher of water. "They need this tae wash it aw doon. An dinna forget tae tell mistress Mirren that ivverythin is in haund, jist takin a bit langer than expectit."

Hart took the pitcher, swung the basket over his arm and scurried upstairs.

Jonas listened to the heavy boots rattling up the stairs. "Ah suspect he'd raither be up ther as weel."

"A nervous man. An wi guid cause," John replied. "It's nae easy livin wi constant harassment fur nae guid reason. Ah ken that masel. Hopefully aifter this he'll be left in peace."

Jonas frowned. "Whit if yer plan disna work?"

John laughed and shook is head. "Huv faith, young man. Huv faith."

When Hart came back downstairs he set out a decent spread for his visitors along with a jug of ale. Jonas and John tucked into the selection while Hart cut himself a hunk of bread, picked at it and only spoke when answering the few questions Jonas asked about farm life.

Once they'd eaten and the table was cleared John went over to the settle by the fire. "If ye dinna mind ah need an hoor or twa sleep. Ah want tae be fresh fur the mornin." He took off his jacket, lay down, then draped his jacket over himself.

Hart stood a moment as if surprised by John's behaviour then turned to Jonas. "Mibbe ah shud bank up the fire. Keep us warm thru the nicht." He stepped forward to add more logs and damp down the blaze with some coal dross from a pail beside the range. Satisfied with the way the flames changed to a gentle flicker he turned towards the figure stretched out on the settle. "Is that aricht fur ye Maister Steel?"

A soft snore was his only reply.

"We best baith dae the same," Jonas suggested.

"Ay." Hart pointed to the smaller settle opposite. "Wud that dae?"

"Ye huv it." Jonas lay down on the rag-rug close to the fading embers. "This spot will suit me fine."

Hart sat down on the smaller settle and watched his second visitor quickly fall asleep. For him it would be a long night.

Early next morning the three captives were carried up from the cellar to the kitchen and placed in a row. They sat there blinking in the sudden light, their expressions betraying the effect of so many hours in black isolation.

"Had enoch?" John asked.

Two of the men nodded.

Nisbet remained firm.

"Luks lik twa o yer freends huv seen sense." John smiled. "But whit aboot yersel, Nisbet? Still o the same mind? Mibbe ye'd raither be back doonstairs sittin in the dark? An dinna be expectin ony food or watter. But mibbe ah'm underestimatin ye. Mibbe a stalwart lik yersel is prepared tae bide doon ther till ye'r deid?"

Nisbet jerked his head back and forward and tried to utter a sound through his cloth muzzle.

"Here, let me help ye." John untied the strip of linen then stood back as Nisbet coughed and spluttered for several minutes. "Dis that feel better? Mind ye, if ah dinna git the richt answer – " He flapped the strip of cloth a few times.

Nisbet sat there like a landed fish, his mouth opening and shutting, eyes staring at the length of cloth then at John's expression.

"Weel?" The cloth flapped a little closer.

Defiance fading with every gasping breath he whispered,

"Whitivver."

"Aboot time." John gave him a friendly pat on the shoulder. "Noo jist suppose ah feel generous enoch tae set ye free?"

"Wur oot o here an awa."

"An ye'll promise tae leave this family an aw the ither Quakers in the Glessart alane?"

Nisbet stared at the floor. "If that's whit ye want."

"It is." John's voice rose. "No jist that. If ah happen tae hear a whisper aboot ony ither exploits – " He slapped Nisbet's back. "Lesmahagow's nae that far frae Stonehoose. Easy tae come wi some o ma freends an seek ye oot tae complete the punishment ah really hud in mind. Mibbe ye'd like a meenit tae think aboot it?"

"Nae need." The words came through gritted teeth.

John signalled to Jonas and Hart. "Ah think oor freends huv seen the error o thur evil ways. Mibbe it's time tae untie them an show whit guid, forgivin Christians we can be."

Once untied the three men struggled to stand. It took several minutes before they managed a single step.

"Richt." John pointed to the door. "Thru there, oot this hoose, across the yard an keep walkin. An mind yer promise."

"Whit aboot oor muskets?" Nisbet dared. "They cost plenty."

"An bide here alang wi the memory o yer bad behaviour."

John Hart, Jonas Hawthorn, and John Steel stood on the doorstep of Shawtonhill Farm and watched the three dispirited figures trail across the farmyard and out of sight.

John stepped back into the hall and called out, "It's safe noo Mistress Mirren. Yer veesitors are awa."

Later that morning John and Jonas trotted down the winding track from the village of Glassford. As they reached the road below Jonas turned and looked back up the hill. "Mind whit ye said aboot James Renwick disownin they men? Are ye shair aboot that?"

"Aboot as much as yersel," John admitted.

They glanced at each other then trotted on without another word.

Chapter Eight

John turned his horse off the road and onto a farm track. "Is this whaur ye bide?" Jonas pointed to a wooden sign. "It says Waterside. Ah thocht yer farm hud anither name."

"This ane belangs tae ma wife's family. We'll leave the horses there. Bein on the wrang side o the law means ah need tae keep the troopers guessin whaur ah micht be. That's why ma brither-in-law stables Juno fur me. He'll tak yer horse as weel, nae bother."

Gavin Weir appeared as soon as the horses clattered into the yard. He seemed relieved to see John. "Ye're back quicker than ah thocht. Did ye see Maister McAvoy lik ye wantit?"

"Nae need." John jumped down beside Gavin. "The man ah went tae see aboot appeared oot the blue. Ah'm on ma way intae toun an whae's ridin towards me frae Larkhall? Ah can haurly believe he's here. Meet Jonas Hawthorn. Aw the way frae Holland. He'll bide wi me a day or twa then gang on tae Wanlockheid tae see his faither's family."

"Ah'm Gavin Weir, John's brither-in-law fur ma sins." Gavin stepped forward to shake hands. "Pleased tae meet ye."

"Gled tae be here." Jonas leant down to return the firm handshake.

"Ye micht no be when ye hear that the platoons are nivver far awa these days. We hud them on the farm yesterday, again this aifternoon, turnin the place ower, pokin in ivvery corner, askin questions aboot whaur we'd been, whae we'd seen, whit wur we dain, tryin tae catch us oot. Mither's dementit wi mucky boots trailin across her kitchen."

"Wunner whit triggered this aff?"

"Folk say it's orders frae Claverhoose himsel. He even turned up at Westermains askin aboot yersel."

John frowned. "Airlie must be on his back again. The auld deil still seems determined on revenge against me."

"Ye shud hae run him thru when ye hud the chance at Bothwell Brig."

"Weel ah didna an nowt ah can dae aboot it noo," John snapped. "Huv the troopers been harassin Marion?"

"Up an doon at aw hoors pokin aboot. But thur's anither captain in chairge. No yon Crichton. Marion says this yin's nae sae bad."

"Nae lik Crichton tae miss oot tormentin folk. Wunner whaur he's got tae?"

"Accordin tae village talk he wis hurt bad tryin tae arrest twa rebels at some stable in the toun. They say ane o them wis Maister Renwick. Shairly no? Ye left him still studyin at some university in Holland."

John gave Jonas a warning glance. "Ah heard that he's back."

Gavin frowned. "Ah suppose that means the field-preachin sterts again. An then mair trouble."

"Mibbe so but richt noo ah'm mair concerned fur ma veesitor."

"Ah can ride on masel tae Wanlockheid," Jonas cut in.

"No ye'll no."

Before John could say any more a stout little woman wrapped in a grey shawl appeared with a young woman carrying a wicker basket. "Rachael Weir, John's mither-in-law." She nodded to Jonas then turned to the young woman. "This is Janet, ma son's wife."

Janet smiled. "Guid tae see ye, Maister Hawthorn. John tellt us hoo kind ye wur tae him in Holland." She smiled again then turned to John. "Ye'll nae like whit ah've tae say."

"Whit's wrang?"

"Troopers, that's whit. Richt noo it's ower dangerous tae bide here or at yer ain farm."

"Ah wis meanin tae gang hame."

"Ah dinna think sae." Janet's voice sharpened. "Ye best tak yer freend on the moor fur the nicht whaur ye can rest easy. Ah'll gang roond an tell Marion ye're back wi yer freend an meanin tae travel on tae Wanlockheid wi him."

"But – "

"But naethin. Marion kens the danger. The way Clavers spoke when he visited the farm left her in nae doubt he's determined tae git ye. So listen tae whit ah'm sayin. Huv a nicht on the moor. Nae worries aboot the law arrivin unexpected like. In the mornin Gavin can tak yer horses, haund them ower at the usual place by the broken tree an awa ye go." She held out the wicker basket. "Ye'll nae gang hungry wi this an we'll pack anither fur yer journey."

John shrugged and took the basket.

"Fur aince jist dae as ye're tellt." Rachael Weir flapped her hands at him. "Awa ye go an bide safe. It's been a while since ye wur declared a rebel wi a thoosand merks on yer heid. That kinda money can persuade some folk tae dae ill things lik gien awa yer whauraboots. Ah ken ye've been lucky so far but dinna tempt fate."

John signalled to Jonas to dismount. "Luks lik wur heidin across the moor."

"An then whit?"

"Ye'll see."

As soon as they crossed the last field before the moor John and Jonas were straight into the grey tendrils of a deepening mist.

John didn't hesitate.

In minutes Jonas could barely see John's bulky shape only a few feet in front of him. "Is this wise?" He sounded anxious.

"Nae worries. Ah ken whaur ah'm goin." John kept walking and Jonas had no option but stumble behind muttering to himself.

There was no let up and eventually he gave up being scared or angry, just wished he could see his way through this wet blanket of nothing, stop having to brush the water droplets from his lashes, stop gasping with the effort of trying to keep up with the relentless figure in front. John suddenly stopped.

"Whit's wrang?" Jonas collided with him.

"Wur on the edge o a steep bank. The bushes alang the tap here streetch aw the way tae the bottom. We need tae slide thru them so dig yer heels in tae slow doon."

Jonas grabbed at the wiry fronds to steady himself as he made his way down. When he emerged from the maze of tight broom and whin he'd reached the bottom of a long, narrow gorge. In front was a fast-flowing burn, close enough for his boots to be touching the edge of the bank.

Everything was clear again, large stones, rough pebbles, water, grass, heather, ferns, and the tall arms of whin bushes marching up the steep sides to meet the mist still swirling above. "Unbelievable," Jonas whispered. "Anither world."

"Thankfully a secret ane. But since ye're a freend ah'll share it wi ye." John jumped from stone to stone to the other side then followed the burn further into the narrow valley towards the sound of crashing water. And then in the fading daylight Jonas saw a little waterfall gushing from a rocky outcrop.

"Ower there." John pointed to the right of this waterfall, to a sheer rock face rising into the misty ceiling. More broom and tall ferns grew near the rock face. John disappeared behind them.

Jonas followed and found himself in the entrance to a long, narrow cave with a level floor. It didn't even feel damp or cold. Logs and kindling were neatly piled against the wall. Further in he could see a cooking pot, plates, mugs, while on a low ledge was a pile of folded blankets. He smiled. "Luks guid."

"An better aince the fire's lit." John began to set twists of straw among tiny kindlers, gradually adding a few thicker sticks before sparking his tinderbox in the centre. After a few tries the straw flared and lit the kindling that licked and danced. He watched and waited as the heat increased then laid a few logs on top. Now there was the promise of a proper fire.

"Richt. Let's see whit's in here." John unpacked the basket he'd carried through the mist and produced Janet Weir's offering of a small rabbit pie, a cheese, a pile of carefully wrapped bannocks, and a small flagon of ale.

They ate in silence then sat a long time enjoying the crackling fire, watching the moving shadows it cast on the cave wall, feeling at ease with each other, safe from anything likely to cause any ill.

It was only when Jonas broke the quiet to speak about James Renwick that their feeling of well-being began to slip away.

James Renwick decided to break his journey at a small farm near Kirk-o-Shotts. He was tired; it had been a long ride across rough, open country. Here he'd find friends, a meal, and time to rest. Edinburgh was still a distance away.

His welcome didn't disappoint. It almost felt as if he was expected when he met the farmer, John Shields.

"Guid tae see ye Maister Renwick. Hoo are ye?" Shields shook hands then ushered him inside. "Ye've been sairly missed since the Societies sent ye tae study in Holland. Ah heard ye've been ordained. Dis that mean ye're back tae bide, ready tae tak up the cause again?" Shields prattled on. "Leave yer horse tae me. Sit doon. Ma wife will see ye fed in nae time an then we can talk richt." He shook Renwick's hand again. "Guid tae see ye, sir. Mair than ah can say." He went off whistling leaving Renwick to finally sit down in the tiny kitchen and draw breath while Mistress Shields bustled back and forward preparing food for her unexpected guest.

After a good meal and a brief respite by the fire Renwick was interrupted when Shields ushered in the first of many visitors. News of his arrival seemed to have spread. A number of people had made the effort to come and see him for themselves, to ask if he was indeed James Renwick.

His nod brought more questions.

"Are ye an ordained minister noo? Are ye willin tae conduct a service fur us? We huvna seen a preacher since pair Maister Cargill wis captured an done awa wi. An whit aboot oor bairns? Thur's a wheen waitin tae be baptised."

Renwick listened patiently then nodded again. "It'll be a privilege."

"We cud hae a meetin the morn," Shields suggested. "Whit aboot ma barn? It's big enoch tae haud a guid crowd. Ay. The vera thing. Ah'll send oot word."

Next morning Shields' barn was packed by the faithful and the curious with many others clustered at the open door to listen. Renwick's slight figure stood in the middle of this crowd and smiled at the expectant faces. "If ivver I needed proof that the truth will prevail this is it. We micht be living thru a time o dark shadows and suffering but oor Lord is aye beside us, sharing ivvery step o the way. So lets bow oor heids in grateful prayer for the strength he gies us tae carry on." Then came his chosen theme from 2nd Kings, *'And he shall deliver you out of the hands of all your enemies.'*

With a promise like that he launched into a stout defence of his proposed resistance against King and government. His audience nodded at his biblical references, drank in his conviction, and began to sense that the cause might not be dead after all. Many stayed behind to press for another meeting the following day to spread the need for resistance as soon as possible.

This time the lonely spot known as Little Drumbeck was suggested as a safe place for a large crowd to gather in the open without the likelihood of troopers disturbing them.

It was a long, rough walk to the meeting place, similar to many more Renwick would endure in the future but today felt different. It was all new, the beginning of what he'd longed for.

The weather was kind with little wind and no rain as John Shields accompanied him through undulating mounds of heather and fern. For once Shields remained solemn and silent as if sensing the power and majesty this vast space might bring to the occasion.

Renwick too seemed to feel the influence, as if raw nature was reaching out to welcome and approve.

"This is grand," Renwick whispered as they arrived to greet the waiting congregation.

"Ay sir," Shields nodded. "A guid turn oot. Aw ready an willin tae listen."

Again Renwick prayed, and persuaded, and challenged in a way that held total attention. No one doubted a word. Everything seemed to be falling into place especially when he finished with the reminder from 2nd Corinthians, *'For we walk by faith and not by sight.'*

The numbers of people on the move and the talk afterwards about Renwick's two meetings did not go unnoticed. The news soon spread till it reached the Privy Council. Furious at this they took action.

The Laird of Dundas, who owned the land around Kirk-o-Shotts, was fined £50 as was the owner of Little Drumbeck. Both were then threatened with worse if there was a repeat performance. From now on all landowners would be held responsible for what happened on their land. Knowing or not knowing made no difference to the judgement.

Sir George Mackenzie, the King's Advocate, took it further: he had a notice printed condemning James Renwick as a traitor. Once this appeared in every town and village he'd become a marked man wherever he went.

It was barely daylight when Jonas woke to find the fire lit and the porridge pot bubbling away.

"Mornin." John handed him a steaming bowl. "Git that inside ye an we'll git on oor way."

Once they'd climbed out of the little gorge there was no sign of the earlier mist. Everything was clear in every direction. "That wis a queer thing last nicht," Jonas said. "Worse than the fog ah saw on the sea."

"It can be guid tae," John replied. "The way it comes an goes withoot rhyme nor reason tae wrap itsel roond whitivver it touches."

"Hoo's that guid?"

"Sometimes ah'm on the moor when troopers appear unexpectit like. Afore ah can even think aboot tryin tae run the mist micht rise frae the heather an come tae ma rescue. Within meenits ah'm oot o sicht in ma wet blanket. When this happens ah jist hunker doon an wait. The troopers dinna ken whit tae dae in the mist. Ah think thur feart, flounderin aboot, shoutin, makin the awfiest noise in case they lose ane anither. Whiles they pass that close ah cud reach oot an touch them an they've nae idea ah'm ther."

"But hoo dae ye find yer way? Last nicht ye walked alang as if ye cud see whaur ye whaur goin."

"Ah wis born here. Ah can sense the richt direction. It husna let me doon so far."

"Ah'm impressed."

"Nae need, it's aw doon tae respectin yer ither senses lik touch and listenin. But richt noo it's aw clear. We tak different care, keepin oor een peeled fur ony movement."

They walked on till they came to a birch wood. "Wis that ther yesterday?" Jonas asked.

"Ye walked thru it."

"An didna even ken. Ah've a lot tae learn."

"So huv we aw. But come on, we'll gang thru the wood here. It taks us oot above Westermains. Thur's a wee path doon tae the farm. Ah'd like a word wi Marion afore we leave."

Minutes later they were standing on the edge of the little birch wood staring down at the smoke rising from the farm chimney. John stepped forward then stopped abruptly. "See." He pointed beyond the farm to the end of the winding track. "Wur oot o luck."

A flash of red emerged from the beech avenue on the Lesmahagow road.

"Early on the go," John whispered. "Janet wis richt." He turned back among the trees. "Gavin will huv oor horses waitin fur us at the broken tree lik he said. Aifter that we can ride further intae the moor an bide weel awa frae the road."

It began to rain, a fine drizzle which grew into a steady downpour as John led the way across the moor. He glanced back at Jonas. "Less likely tae be seen in this."

"If ye say so." Jonas hunched down in the saddle and began to feel cold as well as wet.

With each passing mile their surroundings seemed to grow more desolate. No sign of any building, hardly any trees, only a collection of hillocks that all looked the same, covered in fern or heather or sodden grass while a few sheep munched on, heads down, not bothered by the lashing rain. None of it like the ordered landscape Jonas knew and loved. Here it seemed all about emptiness. As for the cold and wet and wind, it went on and on like some relentless punishment.

Eventually in the distance he made out the faint outline of several low buildings. Could this be the chance of some shelter from this watery world that seemed to be seeping into his bones?

John pointed towards the buildings. "Yon's Red Moss farm. We'll stop ther an ask if we can sit in the barn a while an rest the horses. Wi luck the farmer micht even gie us somethin tae eat."

A young man's face peered round the half-open door of a shed to watch two bedraggled figures on horseback appear from the rain-swept moor. They stopped in the farmyard and he called out, "Whit is it sirs?"

"As ye can see wur weary an soaked thru." John spoke first. "Wud ye alloo us a wee while in yer barn tae rest oor beasts an gie them a rub doon? The pair things must be chilled trampin thru this awfy weather. If ye've ony spare hay we'll gladly pay."

"Wait ther. Ah'll ask faither." The young man hurried across the yard and disappeared into the house.

A moment later an elderly man in a long overcoat appeared in the doorway. "Awfy weather sirs. Whaur are ye heidin?"

"Wanlockheid." Jonas answered this time. "Tae visit ma faither's folk."

"An they wud be?"

"Name's Hawthorn. A minin family."

The old man stepped into the rain and came closer. "Are they indeed?" He stared up at Jonas's face. "Ah micht be mistaken but ye luk raither familiar."

"Ah dinna think sae," Jonas replied.

"That's whaur ye're wrang. Ah ken that face. Nivver shairer. It's the vera spit o Tobias Hawthorn as became a preacher an left here years ago tae tak up a chairge in Holland."

Jonas gaped at the old man. "He's ma faither. Dae ye ken him?"

"Ma name's Hector Hawthorn." The old man wiped the rain from his face and smiled. "Oor faithers wur brithers. Tobias an me are cousins. We grew up thegither, peas in a pod ye micht say, intae mony a scrap afore he got serious an went awa tae study fur the ministry. Aifter that, weel ye ken yersel. Come in. Come in. Ye're richt welcome." He turned to the young man still standing in the doorway. "This is ma son Sam. He'll tak yer horses intae the barn an see tae them."

"Ah'll help him," John said. "Least ah can dae while ma freend an yersel git mair acquainted."

John and Jonas jumped down. Jonas handed the reins to John and happily allowed Hector Hawthorn to lead him indoors.

When John and Sam came into the farm kitchen they found Hector and Jonas in deep conversation while a tiny, red-faced woman bustled between the pots simmering on a glowing range and the kitchen table where a basket of vegetables, two loaves and a whole cheese sat beside a bowl of red apples.

"Mither's makin a meal fur ye," Sam whispered. "An luk at faither. He's mair excited than he's been in years. He often speaks aboot his preachin cousin. Ony letter that comes is read ower an ower again. He's richt prood o him altho he husna seen him since God kens when."

"Tobias Hawthorn is a fine man an weel respectit," John volunteered. "Nae lang ago ah wis in Holland an spent some time in his company. Ah'm John Steel by the way, frae Lesmahagow."

"Are ye indeed. Ah've heard aboot ye." Sam walked over to his father and tapped his shoulder. "Faither. Yer ither visitor is John Steel frae Lesmahagow." He turned to John. "Ah tak it ye're John Steel as wis captain o the Lesmahagow brigade at Bothwell Brig. They say ye've ended up a rebel wi a price on yer heid."

"Ye cud say that."

Hector pushed back his chair and stood up to shake John's hand. "Gled tae meet ye, sir. The cause wud be pairer withoot folk lik yersel. My, this is a special day indeed, bringin twa special veesitors. Ma cousin's lad aw the way frae Holland an a respectit rebel fur the cause. Please, sit yersel doon an share a meal wi us."

Mistress Hawthorn was about to ladle out bowls of soup when they heard heavy hooves clatter on the cobbled yard. She went white. "Whit if it's himsel?"

John stood up, grabbed Jonas's arm.

Hector pointed to a door behind him. "Gang intae the hall."

John nodded and pulled Jonas towards the door.

Hector waited till the door closed behind the two figures then quickly put the soup bowls back on the dresser shelf and the spoons in the nearest drawer.

John and Jonas leant against the wood-panelled wall and listened as their host opened the outside door. Next they heard a polite voice, one with a sharp edge as if used to issuing orders, one John recognised. He sighed. That's whae Mistress Hawthorn wis referrin tae. Himsel is nane ither than John Graham.

John Graham stepped into the farm kitchen and removed his dripping hat. "We're oot and aboot on the law's business in the worst o weathers."

"Which maks a man think aboot a bowl o hot soup an mibbe a bannock wi cheese." Mistress Hawthorn's voice was almost welcoming.

The polite voice laughed. "Indeed mistress. When we saw yer farm I minded yer hospitality tae us mair than aince and wondered if ye had ocht tae spare for the King's men. There's six o us. Each as hungry as the next. Wud ye manage a bite for us?"

"Indeed sir." Mistress Hawthorn spoke clearly enough for the two silent men in the hall to hear.

"Tak aff yer cloaks." Hector joined in. "Ah'll hing them by the fire then sit yersels doon while masel an ma son see tae yer horses."

The outside door banged. Quiet conversation came and went. Time passed. John and Jonas remained in the dark hall. Eventually the sound of several chairs scraped across the flagstone floor and the polite voice said, "Again, thank ye ma'am." The outside door banged then everything was quiet.

Jonas turned as if to make a move.

"Haud on," John stopped him.

Moments later the hall door opened and Sam whispered, "Thur awa."

In the kitchen Mistress Hawthorn was busy clearing the table. She smiled at Jonas and John. "They've eaten maist o the soup."

"An nae doubt enjoyed it," John replied. "Nae problem. An thanks tae yersel. Ye did weel wi Claverhoose. He didna suspect a thing."

Sam grinned. "He didna git the chance tae see yer horses either. Ah made sure the horses wur waitin at the hoose door when they came oot."

Hector turned to John. "Hoo did ye ken himsel wis the commander?"

"Him an me gang back a lang way. Aince heard nivver forgotten. Mind ye, ah'm surprised that he's oot here. He wis scourin aroond Lesmahagow the ither day. Travellin sae widely must mean somethin serious is up."

"Mibbe no," Mistress Hawthorn said. "He comes by here noo an again, especially when he's billeted at Moffat. Aye polite. Nivver causes ony bother. Quite the gentleman. Aye leaves a bit siller fur whitivver his men eat. No that ah'm taen in wi his fine gestures. Ah've heard whit he's capable o."

"Wise wummin," John smiled and turned back to Hector. "Whaur did they go?"

"Heidin fur Douglas ah'd guess. Weel awa by noo."

"Which means we'll nae be disturbed." Mistress Hawthorn opened the little oven door and took out a covered ashet. She laid it in the centre of the table and lifted the lid. "Roast ham wi barley, tatties an gravy. Will this dae insteid o soup? An whit aboot stewed apples wi some pastry?"

Supper was a lively affair with much laughter, questions and story after story from Jonas as he regaled his relatives with his father's life and work in Holland. Once or twice Hector seemed to hesitate, his eyes showing a sadness as he looked round the group at the table. Once or twice his wife and son seemed on the verge of saying something but a glance at Hector seemed to stop them and the moment passed.

John noticed this, but like a welcome guest he didn't pursue his curiosity.

Later when he and Jonas lay down beside the banked-up fire he stared up at the kitchen ceiling thinking about Hector's fleeting sadness. He'd seen that expression before and looks like that made him feel uneasy.

Next morning they were up early to continue their journey, pleased that the rainstorm had passed and happy with the full breakfast Mistress Hawthorn insisted on giving them.

Sam fetched the horses, well rubbed down and refreshed, then stood beside John as he checked his saddle bag while Jonas spent a few minutes saying thanks to his new uncle and aunt. "Ane thing ye dinna ken," he whispered. "Faither made nae mention but ah think it's best tae tell ye since yer freend Jonas is expectin tae meet his faither's family in Wanlockheid."

"He's lukin furrit tae it. Is somethin wrang?"

"It's the faither. Uncle Tobias's brither Gavin. He's in jail. He wis arrested, taen tae the Dumfries Tollbooth weeks ago an found guilty o subversion. He's locked up in the castle richt noo."

"Whit fur?" John asked.

"He wis caught comin back frae a field meetin wi three ithers. They say thur tae be sent abroad as slaves."

"Dear God," John frowned. "Shairly no?"

"At least it's nae a hangin. Faither's distraught aboot it. He insisted on ridin aw the way doon tae Dumfries and offerin tae pay fur Gavin's release. He nearly got arrested himsel and cam hame wi a face as if he'd seen a ghost. He did tell us whit happened but since then not a word."

John shrugged. "Last nicht ah did notice that somethin wis botherin yer faither but felt it wisna ma place tae ask ony questions. Leave it wi me. Ah'll warn Jonas tae expect a less than happy family when he reaches Wanlockheid."

Hector Hawthorn's guess was correct. John Graham led his little group towards the village of Douglas, to Douglas castle. Here he'd arranged to wait for the arrival of a number of rebel prisoners captured for various so-called offences against the crown. Most of them came from the Dumfries area and the Justiciary Court in that town had already dealt with them. Instead of the usual hanging it had been decided to send out another message, one of human trafficking. These condemned men were bound for the Americas, to be sold as slaves. Their value of £10 a head seemed attractive, but only if they survived the long and difficult sea journey. For several weeks they'd been shut in the vaults of Dumfries castle awaiting the necessary arrangements. Soon they'd be marched to the port of Leith, loaded on the *Lady Clare* and shut up in a dank, smelly hold with little to drink or eat and no exercise. By then the thought of a simple hanging would have its own attraction.

Not one to waste an opportunity John Graham had sent word to the Earl of Kellie at the Ayr courthouse to give out a similar judgement on any rebels coming before him. Already there was a good number available for transport. If both groups of prisoners came by Douglas they could then be escorted as one and delivered to the waiting ship with little trouble.

To make sure of complete safety Lord Ross's mounted troop of horse would join the marching caravan for the rest of the journey. They were billeted at Newmilns and could arrive quickly when required.

John Graham was pleased with this plan. It would be talked about, remind the rebels about other fates almost as terrible as death, and show how effective Graham of Claverhouse really was as a law enforcer. Ay, and the bonus micht be scuppering Queensberry's plans to undermine my standing at court. Clavers smiled to himself. Aifter this the Privy Council will be hard pressed tae cast doubt on my effort or commitment. He smiled again. And they'll see that I'm mair than fit for the auld deil.

John Graham and his men came off the moor and into a long, green valley where the land seemed fertile and well-tended with healthy cattle grazing and crops almost ready for cutting. Further along a winding road led to the huddle of smoking chimneys and thatched roofs of Douglas village. Beyond this stretched a patchwork of fields, a strip of tall pine trees then low hills, one after another into the horizon.

John Graham had ridden this way many times but never close to the castle. Now he turned right and trotted along the side of a large lake with two densely-wooded islands in the middle, past an ornate stable block by the water's edge then on to a broad gravel drive that led to the main building.

As they approached the tall archway he noted '*Jamais arriere*' carved into the central lintel. It was well-weathered, almost faint but still readable. He gave a wry smile before trotting on through to look round the cobbled courtyard like the stranger he was.

This was the first time he'd ventured into a Douglas stronghold. Why would he when none of that illustrious family had ever offered a hand of friendship?

Lanark garrison might have been a better choice to receive the two batches of expected prisoners. Or maybe bloody-mindedness was playing a part in using one of the Douglas properties while furthering his plan to undermine their constant conniving against this simple laird's son from Dundee.

As a castle it was solidly built, almost medieval in the thick walls and two large but unevenly shaped towers to the front. The blue and yellow Douglas flag fluttered above the ramparts of the larger one like a warning.

A line of low, slate-roofed buildings leant against one of the outer walls of the courtyard. But everything was strangely quiet, no sign of the usual activity required in the daily upkeep of such an important building.

On the opposite wall stood a massive, pillared entrance to the main living quarters. Behind the pillars was a heavily studded wooden door which was tight shut. Beside it hung a long metal bell chain.

John Graham edged his horse near enough to pull the chain and listen to a faint clang deep within.

Several minutes passed before a stocky, red-haired man in faded livery opened the door and glared out at six military riders who dared to allow their horses to stamp and snort within the well-brushed courtyard. "His lordship's nae at hame. We nivver receive ony veesitors when he's awa."

"Is that so." John Graham smiled politely. "And ye are?"

"George Gregor. Chief steward."

"Weel Maister Steward, ye need tae understand that we're nae visitors. We're here on important business for his Majesty wi authority tae mak use o this place as we see fit."

Gregor opened his mouth as if to argue then seemed to change his mind as he met the commander's grey eyes. "Ah'm only sayin."

"I ken only too weel whit ye're saying." The polite voice sharpened a little. "Jist mind that his lordship wud expect ye tae dae yer bit in assisting the crown. I tak it there's nae question aboot yer loyalty tae baith maister and his Majesty?"

Gregor blinked and shook his head.

"Richt. Ye can show willing by summoning some stable lad tae help ma sergeant luk aifter oor horses. Aifter that ye micht be guid enough tae conduct masel and ma men tae accommodation suitable for a day or twa. And while ye're at it tell yer cook that six hungry men have arrived and expect a decent meal withoot delay. Is it a problem?"

"No sir." Gregor gave a stiff bow and invited the group to dismount.

Chapter Nine

Jonas and John set out on the final stage of their journey. Behind them an almost tearful Hector stood at the entrance of his farmyard until they were out of sight.

It was a fine morning with a few bursts of sunlight. Jonas was in high spirits as they passed the tiny hamlet of Crawfordjohn and took the track towards the Duneaton Water.

John pointed to the wide, grassy area beside the river. "That's whaur ah heard Richard Cameron preach tae a huge crowd. They'd travelled miles tae hear him an didna seem disappointit in whit he said. He wis weel named the Lion o the Covenant, defiant as they come an determined tae face doon the government. Ah wis worried aboot whit micht happen. Ay, an it came tae pass. Only weeks later he wis deid. His mighty resistance at an end. Aifter that the law made mony a martyr tae the cause. A guid few hud done naethin ither than bein in the wrang place at the wrang time."

"Ye soond bitter," Jonas said. "Is it because o yer ain sufferin?"

"It's mair complicatit than that. Whit ah saw an experienced chainged hoo ah see things. Believe me, it's a tad different tae hoo ah thocht at the stert." He shook his head. "But enoch o this, ye must be excitit aboot meetin mair o yer relatives. Back ther ye certainly made Hector a happy man."

Jonas nodded. "It wis a big surprise findin ma faither's cousin lik that. He's a kind man. Ah enjoyed oor visit an bein able tae tell him aboot faither. Oor wee interruption wis excitin tae. They seem richt feart o this Claverhoose. Is he really that bad?"

"He's as wily as a fox an ruthless wi it, believes it's his mission tae rid this country o ivvery rebel against his beloved monarch. He scares the wits oot o maist he encounters altho ah must admit thur's somethin aboot him that demands respect as weel. The way he dealt wi me wis clever. Ah wis up afore him in court a while back an the way he strung me alang then pounced ... weel, ah didna see it comin. Trust me, ye want tae avoid John Graham o Claverhoose at aw costs." John gave Jonas a side-long glance.

"He's nae likely tae be at Wanlockheid. We shud be safe enoch. Ay, ah'm lukin furrit tae this visit."

"We'll see."

"Whit's that supposed tae mean?" Jonas sounded suspicious.

"Ye'll nae like it."

"So. Git on wi it."

"Sam tellt me that yer faither's brither, the yin ye're goin tae visit, wis caught attendin a field-meetin an taen tae Dumfries. He's been afore a judge an sentenced tae slavery in the Americas."

"Why did Hector no say?"

"Too upset. Husna gotten ower whit happened when he went doon tae Dumfries tae confront the law an offer tae pay fur yer uncle's release. The answer wis naw. He even tried tae argue an nearly ended up as a prisoner himsel. The thocht o his brither's sufferin seems tae huv shaken him that much he canna even speak aboot it. Sam thocht ye shud ken."

After this Jonas stared ahead and seemed unaware of the winding road which led them past vast, steep slopes with purple patches of heather and waving fronds of fern where many sheep lay or wandered at will below an ever-changing sky.

John let him be as they climbed the long hill which would take them out of one valley and into the deeper one which led into the Lowther hills. Here the road plunged into a long, dark pine wood with occasional clearings where trees had been cut down and stripped to become long smooth poles. Several were stacked as if ready for use. "Mine shafts ah expect," John broke their silence. "This is a minin area. No somethin ah'd care tae dae fur a livin."

Jonas looked round. "Nor me."

The height of the trees, their closeness to each other caught the light and turned it into a soft gloom which also seemed to soften the sound of the horses' hooves as they picked their way past the many rough stones. Once or twice a fat pigeon blustered off a branch and flapped past as if annoyed by this disturbance.

Gradually the quiet began to affect Jonas like the mist a couple of days before. He hunched down as if suspicious of the gloom on either side, ahead and behind. Or maybe the thought of his long journey to here, the dangers he'd faced, the uncertainty of it all was making him wonder if he should really be here at all.

It was a relief to finally step out of this darkness into open space again to see the sky in its rightful place above the valley. Better still they heard the gurgles of a fast-flowing burn almost by the side of the road.

They stopped to rest the horses and give them a drink. Jonas was much taken with the clear, sparkling water. He knelt down to scoop up some for himself. "It's sweet-tastin."

"An icy cauld." John took a mouthful then washed his face. "That's better."

So far they'd met one loaded cart slowly trundling in the opposite direction. There was no sign of any military activity. Maybe Claverhouse and his men were well-gone somewhere else. This seemed to lighten Jonas's mood. He began to whistle as they trotted along and the miles passed pleasantly enough till they saw the first of the low, straggling buildings that made up the little village of Leadhills.

"Is this it?" Jonas sat up straight.

"Naw," John replied. "Wanlockheid is farther alang by aboot anither mile, perched on the edge afore the road sweeps doon intae the Mennock Pass an on towards Thornhill an Moniave."

"That's whaur Renwick said he wis brocht up," Jonas said. "He came a lang way frae ther tae study an then…" He stopped and frowned. "Wunnerfu whit moves folk."

"Tell me aboot it," John nodded.

"Bein here's nae whit ah imagined," Jonas admitted.

"It nivver is. Ye best git aised tae it." John laughed. "Aince wur past this village, up yon hill an ower the tap yer destination awaits. No that ah ken much aboot it. In fact ah'm as curious as yersel."

They clicked the horses into a faster trot along the narrow main street.

Minutes later Jonas had his first sight of Wanlockhead, much like the village behind him, same scattering of low cottages, same thatched roofs held down by thick rope with heavy rocks dangling at the end, same tiny windows and low doors, same neat vegetable patch on one side or another while above and around them stretched the same wild countryside.

Back in Groningen Jonas lived in a spacious, brick-built house with decent-sized sparkling windows, a proper tiled roof and tall chimneys to send the smoke on its way. The front was bounded by a beautifully kept flower garden, a neat paved path and a metal gate to keep things private. Behind this fine house his father had made an enormous vegetable garden with many fruit trees and a wide grassy space for his mother to hang out washing, a long chicken run, even a small duck-pond. It was all so ordered, so right, so good. And then there was his father's grand church which regularly held more than a thousand worshippers. How could a man like Tobias Hawthorn ever have belonged to this strange place? The man he knew and loved was totally alien to this kind of existence. He blinked then blinked again. His good idea all those weeks ago had begun to feel like some terrible mistake.

John glanced at Jonas. "They twa villages are fur miners. They earn a pittance dain work ah'd hate, huv a pair existence compared tae ithers but ah'm shair it'll nae affect yer welcome." He turned off the road and began to follow a gravel track that wound past the higgledy-piggledy buildings.

As they passed the third house a man came out and stared at them. "Are ye lost?"

"The Hawthorn family," John replied. "Dae they bide nearby?"

The man pointed along the steep, sloping path. "Hoose at the bottom. The yin on the richt wi a shed tacked on an a goat in the field at the back. It's number three the lane. Ye canna gang wrang."

"Thank ye." John edged Juno on.

The slope was indeed steep, the path narrow, well overhung with grass plus a scattering of loose stones which forced both horses to pick their way with extra care.

At the bottom of the slope the ground became a level plateau before it dropped down again towards a little valley where a long, low stone building with a tall chimney belched out black smoke.

Jonas reined his horse back, forced it to stop.

John went on a little way before realising what had happened. He turned and glared back at Jonas. "Whit's up?"

Jonas didn't move.

"God's sake, ye've come aw this way tae see yer faither's family. They'll be delighted tae meet ye an hear aw aboot him. When ye gang back hame yer faither will be jist the same."

They stared at each other.

"Weel?"

Eventually Jonas shrugged and came on down the track.

Jonas dismounted then handed his horse's reins to John and walked towards number three the lane. Before he reached the little door it swung open and a worried looking woman peered out. "Whit is it?" She peered again, gasped, then turned and vanished inside.

Jonas stood there as if unsure what to do next.

A moment later a broad-shouldered young man appeared. This time John Steel gasped. The figure in the doorway was almost a mirror image of the one standing on the doorstep. They stared at each other then Jonas offered his hand. "Ah'm Jonas Hawthorn, Tobias's son, yer cousin frae Holland."

"And ah'm Jamie Hawthorn, Gavin's son, yer cousin frae Wanlockheid." The young man reached out to grab Jonas in a bear hug. "Welcome hame." He turned to the woman who now stood beside them. "Mither, this is Jonas. Aw the way frae Holland."

"So he said." She laughed. "Let go o him till ah welcome him masel."

John Steel watched this performance and called out, "Ye twa are lik peas in a pod. Nae doubt aboot it."

The woman looked past the two young men to the figure on horseback. "Ah tak it ye're wi Jonas?"

John nodded. "Jist here tae show him the way."

"Weel thank ye fur that. Come in and be welcome. Ah'm Helen Hawthorn."

The visitors followed Helen Hawthorn along a tiny dark hall and into a sparsely furnished, white-washed kitchen. She waved a hand at the lack of comfort. "We dinna hae much. Life hereaboots isna easy. A miner disna earn muckle in spite o lang hoors and nae lang ago we hud a big fine tae pay fur nae attendin the kirk. That meant sellin oor guid stuff. But nae maitter, ye're here and maist welcome tae share whit we huv. It's a peety ma man isna at hame. He'll be richt sorry tae miss yer arrival."

"We ken the truth," Jonas said gently. "Sam at the Red Moss farm tellt us."

Helen stared at him then burst into tears and sat down with a thump. "Ma Gavin's as guid as deid and naethin we can dae aboot it."

Jamie put his arms round his mother. "Ay thur is." He turned towards Jonas. "Wur waitin on word afore we mak a move."

Jonas looked puzzled.

"Since ye've heard aboot faither bein locked up in the Stane Jug at Dumfries castle ye likely ken he's been sentenced wi a wheen ithers tae slavery in the Americas. Strange as it seems that gies us hope."

"Hoo come?" Jonas looked more puzzled.

"The Americas means a ship is needed tae tak them ther. We believe it's docked at Leith which is a lang walk frae Dumfries. Onythin cud happen alang the way."

"But he'll be weel guarded." John added.

Jamie smiled. "Some o the routes are across wild and dangerous country."

"An open tae opportunities," John seemed to understand, "if ye ken which way the prisoners will come."

"Lik ah said, wur jist waitin on word. It shud come ony meenit."

As if on cue the outside door burst open and a tall dark-haired man hurried down the hall and into the kitchen. "Wur hopin they come by the Enterkin Pass. It's shorter an quicker an a richt climb which suits us jist fine. Ye best be ready."

"Are ye shair, Michael?" Jamie looked excited.

"Early hoors o the mornin maist like. They've jist aboot reached Thornhill by noo."

Jamie patted his mother's shoulder. "Did ye hear that?"

Helen Hawthorn looked up and seemed even more upset. "Yer faither wudna want ye takin sic a risk."

Jamie gave her another hug. "Thur's nae ither way."

"Ye need tae be carefu," John Steel interrupted. "Huv ye thocht aboot hoo many prisoners? Hoo many dragoons keepin them in order? Hoo many men willin tae attempt the rescue? Ah dinna doubt yer intention but ye need tae ken whit ye're up against."

Michael turned to John. "Dinna worry sir. We ken exactly whit's happenin. Claverhoose hus ordered the condemned prisoners frae the Stane Jug tae be marched tae Leith for transportation. They'll pass by here, then on tae Douglas an meet up wi himsel afore proceedin tae Edinburgh an then Leith."

"Ye're weel informed." John sounded impressed.

"Lik ye said, we huv tae be." Michael grinned. "A lieutenant wi hauf a platoon are leadin sixteen prisoners. We huv aw the names and ken that Gavin Hawthorn is amang them. As for oorsels, we've at least twenty willin tae gie it a go. Fifteen mounted troopers against twenty weel-armed men wi knowledge o the area seems lik guid odds tae me."

"Ah'll come," Jonas announced. "If ye'll huv me?"

Jamie and Michael gaped at him.

"Ah want tae," Jonas insisted then turned to John Steel. "Ah'm gratefu fur aw ye've done an yer company in deliverin me safely amang ma relatives. But this business has nowt tae dae wi ye. Onyway, ye've plenty tae worry aboot yersel so mibbe ye'd best think aboot heidin back hame an leave me tae whitivver."

John shook his head. "Ye dinna git rid o me that easy, especially if this wee plan micht dae some guid as weel as tweekin Claverhoose's tail."

Lieutenant Mulligan read the day's orders then looked at his captain. "When dis Commander Claverhouse expect us tae arrive?"

"Ye're tae mak the best possible time." Captain Simpson's impassive face stared over the pile of papers on his desk.

"Dis that mean ye dinna intend leadin us, sir?"

"Last nicht three Covenantin rebels broke oot the jail in Wigtown. The sheriff wants me there as a maitter o urgency. I canna be in twa places…"

"But surely the Commander's expectin ye?"

"Why wud he? He kens hoo things happen and things chainge. It's been five years since we defeated they Covenantin rebels at Bothwell Brig but folk doon here are still listenin tae ony renegade meenister as comes by moothin aboot resistance. Clavers unnerstaunds the need tae maintain law and order. King Charles himsel expects it. This is jist sic an occasion and since ye're nixt in command – " Captain Simpson glared at Mulligan's expression. "God sakes man, aw ye huv tae dae is tak sixteen prisoners frae here tae Douglas. Ye've patrolled the Lowther Hills often enough and ken the way. It's the month o July. The weather's fine. Ye'll huv the stalwart Sergeant Kelt as back up. Whit mair dae ye want?"

Mulligan saluted then rattled down the steep stairs to the courtyard where his new charges had just been led out to stand blinking in bright sunshine.

"Luk at them." Mulligan nodded to Sergeant Kelt who stepped forward to join him. "Weak as bairns wi mony a mile in front o them."

"Ah'm sure oor captain kens best," Kelt replied.

"Mibbe so," Mulligan snapped, "but the orders frae Clavers say he's expectin them tae walk aw the way tae Leith."

"An so they will, sir."

Mulligan shrugged. "At least oor responsibility is only as far as Douglas Castle. The quicker wur awa the quicker wur done."

Within an hour Sergeant Kelt had sixteen anxious prisoners tethered in four groups with mounted soldiers in front, behind, alongside.

"Step furrit." Sergeant Kelt's riding crop enforced his order and the strange procession slowly left the notorious Stane Jug prison to follow the banks of the Nith till they could cross the river by a narrow stone bridge. The news had spread. The streets of Dumfries were lined as pathetic figures trailed past within a tight cordon of mounted troopers who sat high and proud against the silent anger from so many staring eyes.

It seemed a long time before the town boundary was passed. Ahead lay the open road with fifteen miles to cover before the first official stop. Mulligan looked back at the line of prisoners and groaned. At this rate it'll be nicht afore we git there.

And so it was.

When the procession finally reached the village of Thornhill and Mulligan saw the sign for *The Drumlanrig* he smiled with relief. It was a fine inn, the largest and best for miles, ideal for the overnight stop. A meal and some ale would be waiting. This encouraged him to jump down from his horse and lead the prisoners into the wide courtyard where they stood shaking with exhaustion and nursing blistered heels.

Sergeant Kelt now advised the young lieutenant to feed the prisoners and warned about the physical effort required to tackle the terrain ahead. "A guid few will nivver mak it as far as Douglas if thur bellies are left empty. Dinna forget that each man is worth £10 on the slave market. But only if they reach thur destination. Whit's Claverhoose gonna say if less than sixteen bodies arrive? Him and thur lordships see this as an investment. They'll be less than pleased if it's shrinkin afore it's richt stertit."

Mulligan listened to the older man and delighted the local baker by ordering sixteen small loaves then asking the innkeeper to cut wedges of cheese to go with them. Buckets of water were carried into the yard along with several ladles so no one would go thirsty. Even use of the privies would be allowed under strict supervision.

Having authorised all this Mulligan left the sergeant to see that every detail was carried out and hurried indoors to enjoy a good supper, a few mugs of ale, and a soft bed for the night.

Sergeant Kelt was thorough and fair. Each prisoner received his proper ration, tethering ropes were loosened, the troopers understood when they were on guard duty and for how long. Only then did he follow the young lieutenant into the inn for a decent pie and a welcome mug of ale.

The first part of this forced march had been straight forward. The next stage would be different, with prisoners expected to stumble through bracken and climb steep gullies before tackling miles of open moor to Douglas Castle. Here Commander Claverhouse would add this collection to other captives arriving from Ayr and two other towns. Once checked and fed the prisoners would be rested overnight before the closely guarded caravan set out for Edinburgh's port of Leith where a ship was waiting to take the unfortunates on a long sea journey to the Americas.

Next morning platoon and prisoners were up and away just after daylight. Good progress was made over six easy miles to Durisdeer Mill where Lieutenant Mulligan turned onto a bridlepath instead of keeping to the road. This path led to the Enterkin Pass which was a more direct route but brought the need for extra care. Accidents could and did happen on the steep, stony path as it skirted the edge of the Enterkin burn racing from the heights to the gully below.

"A word, sir." Sergeant Kelt shook his head and began to edge his horse along the line of prisoners.

Mulligan heard the shout and turned as the determined looking sergeant arrived at his side.

"A meenit, sir."

"Whit is it? We need tae keep movin. Ye ken that weel enoch."

"Indeed sir. But ah need tae ask why wur goin this way? It wud be easier an safer tae bide on the road and gang by the Dalveen Pass."

"Yon way taks forivver. Think aboot it; oor Commander isnae the maist patient man. He'll be champin at the bit aready. Onyway, the sky's clear, we can see for miles, and thur's haurly ony wind tae haud us back as we climb. The weather's been grand for days. It'll be dry underfoot wi less chance o horses or men slippin or slidin. A bit extra care is worth the time saved."

"No afore ah re-arrange the walkin order." Sergeant Kelt shook his head again. "The path's haurly wider than a single horse. We need the men in ticht order ahint yin anither." Kelt began to untie the rope tethers, line the men in twos, rope round each waist but allowing enough spare to counter an unexpected stumble which might result in one prisoner pulling his partner over the edge. He then placed a mounted trooper between each group to ensure a steady pace and good order.

Satisfied at last he called out, "If ye lead sir, ah'll position masel at the rear."

Mulligan moved to the front and they began to climb the ever-narrowing path.

Most of the prisoners knew the area, were familiar with the route and understood the danger. Usually this wouldn't bother them but several weeks chained to a wall in a cold, damp prison with a mix of poor food, no fresh air and constant fear of what next had taken its toll on mind and body.

The pace grew slower. The mounted guards began to wonder if they'd ever reach the top of the ridge. They signalled back to the sergeant who called a brief halt. After that he repeated this every fifteen minutes and was pleased to see how it made a difference to the progress.

Gavin Hawthorn was one of those sixteen unfortunates. He'd always been a resolute, determined man. Not today. The past few weeks had been ordeal enough, never mind all that time to think and realise the truth. Caught and sentenced as a Covenanting rebel this forced march to a waiting ship was only the start. Next would come weeks locked in some dark, stinking hold. If he survived the journey his reward would be slavery. Each step now took him towards this fate, and had him asking whitivver made me think that transportation wis a kinder verdict than hangin?

The Via Dolorosa. The old name of the pass was from a time when suicides were trailed up on sledges to be left in no man's land.

Now it seemed even more appropriate.

Each time the prisoners were allowed a brief rest Gavin thought about stepping out from the narrow path, to feel the empty air and just let go.

At the next stop he shuffled close enough to feel the toe of his boot at the edge. From here the drop was sheer and long. An if ah dae? He glanced at his roped companion then pulled back to kick at a pebble.

He felt it move and looked down to study the white, oval shape; a piece of snow quartz formed deep in the earth below then pushed to the surface to lie there for just such a moment. The toe of his boot touched it again. He couldn't resist another kick. This time the pebble shot clear, held a second, then was gone. Ay. Mibbe. He had eased his foot beyond the grass when the cold metal of a sword hit his shoulder.

"Staund back that man."

He glanced behind.

"Did ye hear me?" The nearest mounted trooper's sword repeated its warning.

Gavin hung his head and obeyed.

As the line began to move off he dared to look up towards the topmost ridge. Not much further and they'd be tramping through thick fern and heather. He sighed. And then spied a familiar small brown shape fluttering way above in the clear air. A kestrel. In spite of himself he smiled and watched how the outstretched wings allowed this bird to rest on the upsurge of air while keeping its eyes fixed on some tiny spot below. He'd always admired such wonderful ability. He smiled again. Happy memories of another place, another time when he had a life, a future. *If only*, he thought. *If only.*

The unwilling line of feet and minds lurched on, forcing him to keep walking while his eyes remained on that hovering shape.

The procession was now at a snail's pace, approaching the steepest part of the climb where rocks like strange-shaped gargoyles stuck out above the bobbing heads of the mounted troopers. Behind them, if they dared to turn, they'd see the whole green swathe below where grazing cattle had become mere dots on a vast, patterned carpet.

The man in front of Gavin suddenly stopped. Gavin bumped

into him. The man behind did the same, almost knocking him over.

He twisted round to right himself and heard a single musket shot ring out.

The nearest mounted trooper toppled from his saddle and slipped over the edge with a long scream which grew faint as he fell through the air to the valley below.

"Ambush!" Sergeant Kelt stood up in his stirrups. "Aaaa…" The word became a gurgling gasp as a lead ball tore a hole in his chest and knocked him sidewards on his lunging horse. He hung a moment till sheer weight pulled him free to crash down then roll into empty space.

His riderless horse now stamped its feet and tried to force a way through the nearest group of prisoners. A man was trampled. The next in line saw the huge shape coming, tried to escape, and pulled his neighbour with him. Time seemed to stop as they both leapt upwards before disappearing head first in a series of terrified screams.

"Free the prisoners." A loud voice cut through the noise and confusion.

Gavin recognised that voice. He looked up to see James MacMichael, the Duke of Buccleuch's most senior fowler, leaning over the rocks with his musket levelled at Lieutenant Mulligan. Alongside him was a line of other familiar faces, each behind a well-aimed musket.

Gavin's heart sang. It sang even more when he saw his own son Jamie scrambling down towards him, knife unsheathed, ready to cut through his tethers.

Mulligan sat very still watching this prisoner being freed then half-pulled, half-carried towards two armed figures waiting on the path ahead. What was happening seemed to warn that his own life was a mere pawn in all this. One more shot rang out as if to confirm it. A third trooper fell from his horse and vanished. This seemed to terrify his horse. It reared up, metal hooves lashing out to try and create space.

John Steel was one of the men perched above. From here he could see clearly what was about to happen. Thrusting his musket against the man alongside he jumped from the rock, and slithered down the almost vertical slope of grass to land beside the champing beast and grab the reins and the sweating neck. The horse heaved and bucked, eyes rolling with frustration and fear but he hung on till the mixture of his own brute force and persuasion seemed to communicate itself. The movement grew less violent till the beast stood there snorting and shaking its head, but no longer the killing machine it would have been.

He now signalled to the prisoners who pressed against the rocks while he gently led the quivering creature past them, past the gaping soldiers, past the lieutenant, on up the path and away.

After this the troopers took their lead from the lieutenant who continued to sit perfectly still, saying nothing, offering no resistance. The ambush was complete. The path ahead was blocked by threatening figures. Behind was blocked. Overhead was the same. There was nowhere to go. Nowhere to turn.

Two other attackers came down to quickly cut the remaining prisoners free and lead them away from their guards.

Mulligan said nothing, didn't move other than scanning each rebel face as it passed. The man who'd jumped down to deal with the horse had surprised him. He'd seen him a long time ago. He thought about it. Ay. Ah mind fine. Ah wis alang wi Clavers when he went tae a farm near Lesmahagow. Yon man hud been afore the commander in court at Lanark. Ay. Clavers gied him a hefty fine an decided tae collect it himsel.

When the prisoners were safely away the attackers calmly retreated up the path and disappeared without another word.

Once clear of the pass John Steel offered Gavin Hawthorn the dead trooper's horse but he seemed too weak to ride alone so Jamie lifted his father onto his own horse and held him tight.

"Need a horse?" John offered the reins to another prisoner who was up and away with a happy wave.

MacMichael frowned as he watched the man disappear.

"Whit's wrang?" Jamie asked. "Ah'm happy tae git faither released. Yon man's ower the moon gettin awa on a horse. Whit's wrang wi that?"

"Of coorse ah'm gled fur him. Same as the ithers we freed. Ah'm annoyed aboot nae dain mair." MacMichael shook his head. "We shud huv feenished aff the troopers, ivvery last man afore we left."

"Naw, naw," Jamie argued. "It wis a rescue nae a slaughter."

"That's aw vera weel but think aboot it, oor faces huv been studied. Ivvery detail will be noted an repeated ower an ower again. Somebody's bound tae ken whae we are. They micht bide shtum at first but the promise o siller in thur haund will chainge that. An then we'll aw live tae regret this mistake."

"Weel ah'm gled hoo we did it," Jamie's voice rose. "The deaths that did tak place wur bad enoch."

"Please yersel. But ye're wrang. Jist mind ma words when ye git caught an end up swingin frae the gibbet in Edinburgh's Grassmarket." MacMichael shook his head and rode off.

"Cud he mibbe be richt?" Jonas turned to John.

"Maist likely. Frae ma experience sparin a man disna aye bring gratitude."

"Ye mean yon earl ye tellt me aboot? The yin at Bothwell Brig when ye hud the chance tae run him thru?"

"Ay. He's been on ma tail ivver since."

"C'mon." Jamie roared at them. "This isna the time nor the place." He spurred his horse and galloped off.

John and Jonas followed him.

Mulligan stayed put and issued no orders till he was sure the attackers were well away before calling out, "Walk on."

Slowly he led his shocked men out of the Enterkin Pass and onto the open moor. In the distance he could see a few figures running towards freedom. They'd easily be recaptured. There was no sign of the attackers or the other prisoners. Extra horses must have been brought to allow a quick getaway. Mulligan was impressed with the planning, the daring of it, how well informed these rebels seemed to be about every movement the government made. He was also worried about the consequences of this incident, was already trying to form a report for Commander Claverhouse.

If only. Ay. *If only.* He sighed as Sergeant Kelt's warning pounded in his head.

When the little group stopped outside number three the lane John shouted, "Grab whit ye need. Bring yer mither and then pit distance atween yersels and whit wis left back at the pass. This is the first place the authorities will come. Yer faither wis sentenced as a rebel. They'll expect ye wur involved in his rescue so ye're as guid as condemned. Yer mither will git short shrift tae." He turned to Jonas. "Ye as weel."

Three white faces gaped at him as if this was unexpected news.

The door opened. Helen Hawthorn gave a shriek and threw herself at her husband. After that no more could be said till she calmed down.

John tried again. This time they listened and quickly packed what they could. "Whaur dae ye suggest?" Jamie asked. "Whaur micht be safe?"

"Hoo lang's a piece o string?" John shook his head. "As ah ken weel masel. Havin a thoosand merks on ma heid maks life mair complicated and whiles mair unpleasant than ah'd like."

"Whit aboot oor Hector's farm at Redmoss? He'll help. He tried tae help faither aready."

John shook his head. "He's a relative. Suspect richt awa. His place will be searched. He'll be questioned within an inch o his life. Dae ye want tae subject him tae mair danger or even torture? The less he kens the better. Ah agree yer faither needs a place o shelter but nae aboot here. Only thing ah can think o is a hoose ah visited a while back. The folk ther are fur the cause. It's by Crawfordjohn. Mibbe we cud mak fur it an see whit's whit."

No-one questioned him. No-one argued. Minutes later Helen Hawthorn closed the door of her cottage for the last time, climbed up beside John Steel and they all set off as if John knew what he was doing, or even where to go.

Half-   way along the valley beyond Leadhills village the weather changed. A cold wind swept down off the hills along with driving rain. Ahead was the dense pine-wood John and Jonas had passed through the day before. Without a word they galloped towards it.

Once under the sheltering branches they dismounted and sat on a pile of stacked logs. Around them came constant pattering as heavy drops of water managed to slide past layer upon layer of tight needles and sink into the muddy ground or soak into the soft patches of green moss and lichen.

Gavin Hamilton hadn't uttered a sound since they'd left Wanlockhead; he slumped against his son. The trauma of his arrest and sentence followed by weeks of ill treatment and no hope had been bad enough. The sudden shock of release from all this had been wonderful but what might have been was still there, overwhelming his very being. Now his eyes were tight closed. Even through his thick jacket Jamie could feel him shiver as if struggling to pull back his self-control before it was too late. Rather than panic his mother Jamie said nothing and clung to the frail shape of his once stocky father and tried to will him the strength he'd need.

The wind eased and the heavy drumming noise of the rain quietened. "Time tae move." John helped Helen Hawthorn onto Juno's back again and signalled for the others to follow.

Jamie lifted his father again. By now Gavin's deteriorating condition was becoming obvious. This worried John with more miles to cover before there would be any chance of help or rest.

"Hing on," John whispered to Helen as he clicked Juno forward. "We'll git ther an dae the best fur yer man."

Once in the open the air seemed colder, more biting than before. They were all aware of it but said nothing as they trotted on through a constant drizzle.

A mile beyond the wood they turned onto a narrow track to the left, climbed a long slope, over the top, felt the wind pick up again as they hurried down the other side towards another wider valley and John's hope of shelter at Gilkerscleugh House.

When the outline of the house appeared through the gloom John wondered if this was wise. But whaur else? Whaur wud be safe tae rest? He'd only visited once before with his friend John Brown when they'd come to hear Richard Cameron preach to a large crowd by the Duneaton Water.

Anna Hamilton, the mistress of Gilkerscleugh, had welcomed them, as had her husband. It all seemed to be going well till Lucas Brotherstone had come downstairs to shock John. He'd gaped at Lucas, couldn't believe he was actually there instead of safe in Holland, out of harm's way, lecturing students in the Scots College in Utrecht. The last thing he'd expected or wanted was to find this vulnerable man accompanying a firebrand like Richard Cameron. What followed had become the stuff of nightmares which still haunted John. Maybe this too was a mistake?

– Ower late tae chainge ma plan. Onyway, ah dinna ken onywhaur else. He stopped by the white-painted wooden gate and stared at the grey stone building, three storeys at least, turreted in the Scottish style, imposing. The Hamiltons are wealthy, important folk an ah haurly ken them, yet here ah am aboot tae ask a favour an pit them at risk if they agree.

The big, studded door opened and a small woman in a white apron waved to the group.

John returned the wave, lifted Helen Hawthorn from Juno, opened the gate then led her towards the woman in the doorway. "Mistress Hamilton. Mibbe ye dinna mind me. Ah'm John Steel frae Lesmahagow bringin a few Covenanters in need o some assistance."

The woman smiled. "I mind ye fine, Maister Steel. Ye came here a while back wi John Brown tae hear Ritchie speak and ye met up wi anither meenister. A richt troubled young man."

"Indeed he wis," John agreed and turned to Helen Hawthorn. "May ah introduce Mistress Hawthorn frae Wanlockheid. The group by the gate are her family. Her husband wis a prisoner bein marched frae Dumfries tae Edinburgh and sentenced tae slavery in the Americas. Alang wi ither helpers they managed tae rescue him an a wheen ithers back at the Enterkin Pass. Ah wis ther an can vouch fur thur bravery an guid intention. As ye can guess thur noo on the run lest the likes o Claverhoose catches up wi them."

"Dear God." Anna Hamilton held out her hand to Helen Hawthorn. "And nae doubt sic a rescue wis done at great risk. Come in. Come in and be welcome."

Gavin Hawthorn was carried into the big, stone kitchen and laid on a settle by the fire.

"Faither's done in," Jamie explained. "Mither's fair worried aboot him. He spent weeks in the Stane Jug at Dumfries Castle."

"And it's taen its toll." Anna Hamilton looked at the chalk-white face with blue-rimmed lips. "A wee sleep in a warm, proper bed shud help. We'll cairry him upstairs." She turned to Helen Hawthorn. "While we dae this ye best gang wi ma maid Jessie, see tae drying yersel oot and getting fresh claes."

"Naw, naw," Helen protested. "Ah'll be fine. Ah need tae see tae Gavin."

"So ye will." Jessie stepped forward and held Helen's arm. "But first things first."

Jamie and Jonas lifted the limp figure and followed Anna Hamilton into the hall while Helen stood uncertain till the maid gently steered her through to another room.

Gavin was gently undressed, his soaking clothes changed for a linen gown before he was slipped between clean white sheets, in a proper bed for the first time in many weeks. He seemed unaware of anything, neither moving, nor speaking, nor opening his eyes as a soft quilt was tucked under his chin.

"It's been ower much," Jamie whispered.

"I can see that," Anna nodded. "We'll dae oor best and ye nivver ken." She busied herself placing hot bricks on either side of the still figure.

"He wis aye that determined fur the cause. But noo the fight's gone oot o him. Withoot yer help…" Jamie's words tailed off.

"The cause is dear tae ma heart," Anna replied, "and them as are pairt o it whiles gie aw they can. By the luks o yer faither he's ane o them. It's a privilege tae offer a bit help. I neither need nor want ony thanks. Noo awa doonstairs and dry yersel oot afore ye feel ill as weel. I'll bide here till yer mither is ready tae come up."

Gavin Hawthorn felt as if he'd reached the top of the pass. Somehow he'd managed to leave the dank darkness of that awful prison behind. Now he was walking through bracken and heather, heading for his own village, his own home, his own family. He looked up. The kestrel was still there, still hovering. He smiled. Nae lang noo. Ah'm nearly there. Ah'll be fine.

Helen and Jamie felt helpless as they sat beside the unconscious Gavin and listened to his gasping breath.

It was a long night before the rhythm grew quieter, then slower, then irregular, then so faint they almost missed the moment when it finally stopped.

They looked at each other then Helen leant forward to kiss the cold brow.

"If only ah'd been able tae rescue him earlier." Jamie's voice sounded harsh.

"Ye did yer best." Helen squeezed her son's fingers.

After that they sat on in silence till daylight began to creep through the cracks in the shutters, telling of a new day when they must tiptoe away to leave husband and father alone on his longest journey of all.

Late that afternoon the white sheet Gavin Hawthorn lay on was wrapped tightly round to become his shroud before he was placed in a hastily constructed box.

That done and a lid securely nailed in place he was carried downstairs on the shoulders of his son, his nephew, and a man he didn't know.

Helen and Anna were waiting by the outside door and stood aside as the coffin emerged into the fading light.

"We canna gang tae the graveyard," Anna's husband explained. "Best nae draw attention for aw oor sakes."

John, Jamie and Jonas had dug a deep trench at the far end of the garden, almost under the elegant branches of a young rowan tree. The significance of this was lost on no one. Good Presbyterians or not there was something reassuring about the myth of the rowan's ability to ward off evil spirits.

The simple wooden box was laid on the grass, a stout rope wrapped round either end before Jamie and Jonas lowered it into the dark space. "Ashes to ashes. Dust to dust." Robert Hamilton then said a brief prayer before a handful of soil was thrown on the box. Shovels of earth quickly followed till the space filled level with the ground again. Rolled up turf was replaced and patted down. Finally a small boulder was placed as a marker and the burial of Gavin Hawthorn was complete only hours after he'd arrived in this place.

Back in the warm kitchen Anna Hamilton offered fresh baked shortbread and a tiny glass of whisky. "In memory o a guid life freely gied for the cause. God bless ye, Gavin Hawthorn."

Everyone downed the spirit then an awkward silence prevailed till Anna spoke again. "When the nixt preacher comes by I'll git him tae gie a richt blessing. I've noted the proper name and date and whit Gavin suffered. Come the day we're aw waiting for it'll be recorded and his name added tae the martyrs' list."

"Thank ye." The words were a soft whisper as Helen stared at her empty glass for several minutes.

No one spoke. Everyone waited till she lifted her eyes and nodded to each face round the table. "But whit noo?" She stopped and stared at John Steel and repeated the question as if he might know the answer.

Chapter Ten

Once the runaway prisoners on foot were recaptured Lieutenant Mulligan and his men continued their journey, to meet the expected wrath of their commander at Douglas Castle.

The man himself saw them come by the edge of Stable Lake and was standing by the arched entrance as they trotted into the courtyard.

He stared at the handful of tied prisoners. "Whit's this?" The elegant eyebrows drew together. "I wis expecting sixteen men ready tae march on tae Leith." He waved a piece of paper. "Sixteen names listed here for transportation. Are they still locked up in Dumfries?"

Mulligan jumped down from his horse and saluted. "There wis an unfortunate incident durin the maist difficult pairt o the journey."

"And whaur wis that micht I ask?"

"The Enterkin Pass."

"And?" Clavers voice tightened.

"Maist o the prisoners wur rescued. We managed tae roond up a few but the rest are still at liberty." Mulligan coughed. "Three troopers wur killed as weel as twa prisoners."

"Indeed." This time the eyebrows almost disappeared into the dark, curly hairline. "In that case I need tae hear aw aboot it."

"I'll write oot a fu report sir."

"Naw, naw. I need it first haund afore that. Question and answer man tae man." The commander waved a hand at the miserable huddle in the middle of the courtyard. "Git the prisoners ye still huv locked up. See tae the men and beasts. Aifter that come upstairs tae masel." Clavers turned on his heel and left a red-faced Mulligan staring after him.

Having dealt with everything as ordered Mulligan climbed the twisted stair to the commander's private apartment with a heavy heart. Mibbe ma career's feenished. Wudna be a surprise aifter this. Whit a mess. And it's nae as if Clavers suffers fools gladly. Ah weel, here goes. He took a deep breath, rapped at the stout door and waited till it was opened by the commander's personal orderly.

The man looked the travel weary figure up and down. "Himsel is expectin ye. Come in."

Mulligan nodded and stepped inside to salute then stand awkwardly staring at the wooden floor, trying to avoid eye contact with his master.

"Come furrit man. Come furrit." The commander sounded firm but calm.

Mulligan took a few steps closer.

Clavers sat behind a long, trestle table piled with books and papers. He seemed to have been writing and laid down an ink spattered quill before turning to his servant. "On ye go Wattie. Nae need for yer lugs tae hear ony o this."

"As ye wish, Maister John."

Mulligan blinked at this implied familiarity then snapped to attention while the orderly withdrew and closed the door.

"At ease man. Nae need tae staund there lik a rigid poker." The voice sounded almost friendly, no sign of the famous temper that could erupt at any moment.

Mulligan looked even more uncomfortable as his commander leant back in the high-backed chair and studied him with a pair of cool grey eyes as sharp as any cat watching a mouse. Behind him, the quiet tick of a clock on the wall almost filled the room. Neither man moved, one watching the other, resisting the challenge to speak first. Eventually Mulligan surrendered. "Sir. Will I stairt ma report?"

The elegant mouth almost twitched but the eyes remained still.

"Sir?" Mulligan sounded desperate.

"Vera weel." Clavers nodded. "On ye go."

Mulligan began his tale of woe, trying to be as accurate as possible, covering every detail of every stage of the journey from Dumfries, describing the pass, how sheer it was, how narrow the path, how that had contributed to the ambush. "When we wur attacked we'd naewhaur tae go. Rebels aheid, ahint and lukin ower frae above, each wi a musket aimed at oor heids. The maist worryin thing is I still dinna unnerstaund hoo we nivver saw them comin nor heard a soond till they wur on us."

"Experienced hill men." Clavers seemed to accept this. "Hoo mony?"

"Mair than twenty. Weel armed and determined. I decided nae tae resist. It wis ower risky. Even so, three men wur shot, fell aff thur horses and..."

"Went doon the ravine?" Clavers frowned.

"Ay sir. Twa prisoners taen fricht and jumped aff the path."

"And went the same way?"

"Ay sir. I'm afraid ane o oor losses wis Sergeant Kelt."

"Weel, he'll be sairly missed. A thoroughly dependable man wi years o experience."

Mulligan nodded. "He advised me against the pass, suggested goin by Dalveen but I didna listen, thocht I kent better."

"Tempted tae save time?"

"Ay sir. I shud huv listened. Nae jist that, I didna realise hoo weel informed they dissenters are. They seem tae ken oor ivvery move, whaur wur goin and when."

"Ane thing ye got richt." Clavers' voice sharpened. "They rebels huv an impressive network. Better than oorsels. It's the bane o ma existence. Nae maitter whit we dae they're aye a step aheid, challenging oor attempts tae bring law and order in these difficult times."

Mulligan shuffled his feet uncomfortably. "The hale thing wis weel planned, even extra horses hidden nearby. That's hoo as mony prisoners got awa aifter they wur cut loose."

"So naething guid tae report?"

"No really sir, except ane o the attackers luked familiar, minded me o a man we dealt wi a while back. I had a guid luk when he jumped doon aff a rock tae steady a buckin horse that wis aboot tae send a few mair men ower the edge. Rebel or nae it wis a brave thing tae dae."

"Or foolhardy. Ye say he luked familiar?"

"Ay sir. Dark hair, weel built an broad shoodered, richt strong. I'm shair I recognised his face. I believe he's yon farmer frae Lesmahagow whae came afore ye a while back in the Lanark courthouse? The yin as wis tried and fined for makin a fool o Lieutenant Crichton when he slung him across the back o his horse and walked him doon the main street in front o the hale village? I wis ther at the trial in Lanark and hud a guid luk at him. Ay. And I wis alang wi ye when ye went tae the farm tae collect the beasts and money as a fine. If I mind richt ye wur pleased wi the quality o his stock and the way he paid up ivvery last merk withoot arguin."

Clavers stared past the lieutenant. He seemed lost for a moment then blinked. "Indeed, I mind it fine." He almost smiled. "Has tae be John Steel. Weel, weel that is interesting. A lad o pairts, it wud seem." The elegant lips pursed. "Ma freend Airlie will be mair than interested tae hear aboot this."

"Sir, are ye referrin tae the auld earl frae Strathmore?"

Clavers' smile broadened. "Tak care Mulligan. Auld. If Airlie hears that word he'll hae ye whipped. But ay. Jamie Ogilvie and Maister Steel had a wee altercation at Bothwell Brig. The great earl came aff worse. He's been aifter his tormentor ivver since."

"He'll be keen tae deal wi him then?"

"Mair than keen but I'm mair concerned aboot this so cawed rescue o as mony felons and the message it sends oot."

"So whit's tae be done?"

"Raither a lot. Needs must for aw oor sakes. As for the Privy Council, weel – " Clavers pursed his lips. "But first I want time tae digest yer story. Git it aw clear in ma heid afore deciding on oor response. Leave me alane for a while. Awa and git a bite tae eat. I'll gie ye a shout when I'm ready. Ay. And warn the men tae be ready for the aff the meenit I say."

"Ay sir." Mulligan almost stumbled from the room leaving his commander deep in thought.

Jonas Hawthorn and John Steel sat on a bench in the far corner of the Gilkerscleugh garden and stared at the gentle mound of fresh turf which covered Gavin Hawthorn. The remaining moments of the day mingled with gathering gloom, much like their mood.

Eventually Jonas said, "Whit noo?"

"Depends." John allowed the word to hang a moment. "Depends whit happens when the government hears aboot oor escapade. Depends hoo lang we huv afore hale platoons are sent oot tae scour ivvery corner o the countryside. Believe me, that's a given an micht happen sooner raither than later fur the great an the guid will see whit we did as ootricht rebellion an worthy o a fu scale hangin. Depends if they've ony idea whaur we micht be an it'll nae be for the want o askin. An whit aboot the Hamiltons? They've pit themsels at risk by takin us in. If word gits oot they'll be in as muckle danger as oorsels. Altho this is a lonely place thur's aye een watchin, an nae aye friendly een."

"Whit dae ye suggest?"

"Yer aunt an her son are worst aff. They darena gang back tae

141

Wanlockheid an be lik sittin ducks waitin tae be arrested. They canna gang tae the Red Moss farm either an land yer ither uncle's family in trouble. They need tae pit distance atween here an themsels if they want tae keep thur heids on thur shooders. As for yersel, ye need tae think aboot hame an safety an the chance tae leave aw this ahint."

Jonas nodded. "Comin here seemed lik a guid idea but noo – "

"Ye're in a richt pickle. Frae veesitor tae rebel afore ye even kent whit wis happenin. Aifter a lang an nae doubt difficult journey ye haurly hud time tae draw breath or enjoy a proper welcome afore bein drawn intae rescuin a man ye'd nivver even met."

"Naebody forced me. Ah offered tae dae it."

"An ended up amang men as attacked an killed government troopers as weel as releasin a wheen condemned prisoners. No that ah've ony richt tae criticise. Ah encouraged ye. Even came as weel. An taen pairt. If the truth be tellt wur a richt pair, allooin oor hearts tae rule oor heids. Speakin for masel, ah nivver seem tae learn, mair's the peety." John stood up. "Richt noo ah need time tae masel, tae think, tae mak up ma mind aboot whit's best. If onybody in the hoose asks aboot me tell them ah'm awa fur a walk and micht be a while." With that he left Jonas to wrestle with his own confusion and sense of despair.

John walked through deepening night towards the sound of the Duneaton Water. As he did, a skliff of the new moon appeared, a slender crescent, but bright enough when it slid in and out hazy clouds to light up patches of hill and moor beyond the grey shape of Gilkerscleugh House. None of this bothered John who was well used to finding his way by night where others might stumble or lose direction.

He reached the river bank and stopped to admire the flashes of moonlight reflected on the surging water below his feet. Something about the tiny sparkles held his attention and he sat down to watch.

Long minutes passed. Minutes he enjoyed till clouds closed over to shut out the glimmering moon and allow his thoughts and fears to come hammering in again.

Annoyed he stood up, moved too quickly, lost his balance and slid down the soft, sandy bank to land on a narrow curve of pebbles with the toes of his boots in the shallow water.

He bent to pick up a handful of little stones, held them tight then gave a shout as he hurled the lot across the river. Three reached the soft bank opposite and stuck there. Two made a splash and were gone below the ever-moving surface. Gritting his teeth he turned away, clambered back onto the bank, and stretched out on the dewy grass to stare up at the dark sky while his anger simmered away.

After Enterkin the Hawthorns had allowed him to take control and lead them to temporary safety. Now it hardly seemed worth the effort; just one more incident among all the others he'd wrestled with these past few years.

When John returned to Gilkerscleugh House he found everyone seated at the kitchen table. With them was an anxious-looking slim girl in muddy clothes.

Anna Hamilton stood up as he entered the room. "Guid mornin, Maister Steel. Come ower and meet Miss Elsie Spreul."

John stiffened at the surname but gave a friendly smile. "John Steel. Farmer frae Lesmahagow."

Elsie looked up but said nothing.

"Spreul's an uncommon name. Wud ye happen tae ken a John Spreul, as wis an apothecary in Glesca, Dovehill Street, richt at the top, near the corner wi the Auld Vennel?"

"He's ma uncle."

"Maist likely ye ken the pair soul is shut up in the Bass Rock prison in the Firth o Forth fur refusin tae pay a fine. No that he did onythin tae merit sic treatment."

"We've heard naethin aboot that." Anna Hamilton frowned. "Whit a terrible thing tae happen."

"Ah only ken because Maister Spreul wis arrestit in his shop alang wi ma freend Lucas Brotherstane."

"The young meenister as wis here a while back wi Richard Cameron?" Anna Hamilton's frown deepened. "It wisna lang aifter that Ritchie wis captured and killed."

"Ay. Ma freend wisna at Airds Moss that awfy day but it affected him badly. Ah persuaded him tae leave the country fur his ain safety an taen him tae Glesca hopin fur passage on a ship tae Holland. He wisna a guid sailor an went tae Maister Spreul's shop fur sea-sickness pills at the vera meenit troopers barged in wi an order tae

143

arrest John Spreul. Lucas stertit arguin wi them an they liftit him as weel. They wur baith taen tae Edinburgh, mairched in front o the Privy Cooncil nae less then sentenced tae the Bass Rock. It didna end weel fur ma freend but so far Maister Spreul seems tae be haudin oot against sic ill treatment. At least he wis last time ah saw him."

"Ye saw him?"

"Ah went tae the Bass Rock wi Mistress Spreul. Ah huv a freend in Glesca by the name o James McAvoy. He's a weel respectit goldsmith. His business alloos him contact wi folk aw ower the place. He jist happened tae ken Mistress Spreul an persuaded her tae tak me alang when she made a visit tae her man. Ye see she'd paid the prison governor fur the opportunity. She made oot ah wis her manservant. When we got there we discovered that Lucas wis aready deid." He hesitated. "Dinna ask. It's ower painfu."

"As is Miss Elsie's plight." Anna Hamilton seemed close to tears. "She had tae flee frae her post as teacher tae the bairns in the big hoose at Skirling by Biggar, forced tae leave durin the nicht tae avoid capture and torture and mibbe burnin as a witch."

"Shairly no?" John gaped at her.

"Oh ay. Some evil-minded folk taen ill against her. Jealous maist like. They spread rumours aboot her interest in herbs, said she made up potions fu o magic insteid o remedies for common ailments. Nae content wi that they stertit mentionin the deil and made some awfy suggestions. That did it. In nae time the hale thing got oot o hand and turned intae a witch hunt when a wheen villagers decided they shud attack the big hoose and git haud o Elsie. God kens whit micht hae happened nixt if somebody wi sense hudna warned the maister tae mak shair Elsie wis weel awa afore they arrived. She's ridden thru the nicht and here she is safe."

"Is she?" John sounded unsure. "Misguided folk will gang tae awfy lengths tae huv thur way."

"Aw she did wis learn aboot herbs and their uses. The maister at the big hoose saw the worth o helpin his servants bide weel. He hud a wee lass workin wi Elsie tae gaither the herbs she needed. He even set aside a special room for dryin them."

"Nane o that will maitter if her enemies git haud o her," John persisted. "Whit if they find oot she's here? Aifter aw, this is her hame. Mibbe she needs tae go further afield, somewhaur naebody kens onythin aboot whit happened."

"But I brocht her up. Her faither wis John Spreul's brither Joseph. He wis a neighbour in Crawfordjohn and worked as supervisor wi the minin company up at Wanlockheid. Her pair mither wis a frail, wee lass and gied her ain life when Elsie wis born. She wis haurly a day auld when her faither brocht her here and asked us tae help while he made suitable arrangements. Less than a week later he disappeared. John Spreul wis richt angry at his brither, tried tae find him, mak him face up tae his responsibility. But it wis nae use. We nivver saw him again. But Joseph's loss wis oor gain. Bringin up Elsie has been a privilege and her uncle didna forget her. He paid for the best o schoolin. In fact he's the yin as taught her whit she kens aboot herbs. Aw done wi proper study. Nae nonsense aboot spells or magic. She's a clever lass wi much tae offer."

"An richt noo needs tae bide safe."

"Indeed."

John sat down beside the terrified looking girl. "Jist suppose ah manage tae contact yer aunt, Mistress Spreul, an ask if ye can go ther fur a while. Hoo wud that be?"

Elsie glanced at Anna Hamilton then burst into tears.

"Dinna worry." Anna Hamilton pulled her close. "It'll aw work oot."

"So it will." John agreed. "If ye come tae ma farm near Lesmahagow ma wife an bairns will see ye safe while ah seek oot Mistress Spreul. Aifter that ah'll tak ye ther masel."

"Whit aboot us?" Jonas spoke up. "Ah've hud a word wi Jamie an aunt Helen an asked them baith tae come hame wi me."

"Tae Holland?" John sounded surprised. "Thur willin?"

"Why no? Whit's here fur them, bein chased frae pillar tae post, nivver kennin whit nixt, when they can huv a decent life elsewhaur? Ma mither an faither will be mair than happy tae welcome them."

"Richt then." John smiled. "Aw ah huv tae dae is deliver Miss Elsie tae her aunt then find a ship fur ye three. Jist as weel ah happen tae ken a man as can help." He smiled again. "Here's me worn oot spendin aw nicht ootside on ma ain, wrestlin wi this problem an gettin naewhaur when the answer wis richt here."

Everyone laughed and looked relieved.

Anna Hamilton's husband looked round the group at the kitchen table. "When ye leave here ye'll need tae be careful. Nae draw attention. Can I mak a suggestion?"

John nodded. "Ye've ivvery richt tae aifter whit ye've done fur us."

"I'm jist thinkin that a line o horses micht staund oot and attract the troopers that must be oot searchin for them involved at Enterkin. They micht come aifter ye. But a horse and cairt wi a family on the move – "

"Micht slip by." John smiled. "An mibbe ye jist happen tae huv a horse an cairt ye're willin tae lend?"

"Tae see ye aw safe I'd gladly gie it awa."

"That's generous," John said. "Whit aboot oor horses?"

"They can be stabled at ma farm on the ither side o the village. Horses come and go maist days wi folk passin thru on their way tae the Dalveen Pass. Naebody's likely tae notice."

John turned to Jonas. "Hoo aboot Maister Hamilton pleasin himsel whit he dis wi the horses? Whaur ye're goin disna require a horse." He turned back to Robert Hamilton. "Except ma Juno. She comes wi me. Ah'll tie her ahint the cairt."

"That's settled then. Come oot tae the big shed and see the cairt." Robert Hamilton led the group out to inspect their new transport.

An hour later a tearful Anna Hamilton watched the loaded cart leave Gilkerscleugh courtyard and plod through the village towards the Glasgow road. Jonas held the reins, Jamie and Helen Hawthorn sat alongside in the front while John and Elsie were in the back, partly covered by a tarpaulin. Juno obediently trotted behind.

"They'll be fine." Robert Hamilton reassured Anna. "So will oor wee Elsie. John Steel's richt, she's best awa frae here for the time bein."

The cart made slow progress and met no one till it reached the cut off for the village of Douglas where a sudden flurry of red came galloping off the narrow track and onto the road.

John ducked down and pulled the tarpaulin over Elsie and himself. "Bide doon and bide still. The less the troopers see the better."

As the horses approached they slowed to a trot to pass the slow-moving cart then broke into a gallop again.

John waited till the sound of the metal hooves faded before pulling back the tarpaulin. "Maister Hamilton wis richt. The hunt is up but a family on a cairt isna worth anither luk." He sat back and smiled. "Ay. We'll be fine."

The cart trundled on for a while then Elsie grasped John's arm and whispered, "Ah'm gled ye're willin tae help me. Really ah am. But mibbe ye dae think ah'm a witch."

"Why wud ah?" John shook his head. "Thur's nae sic a thing as a witch ither than in folk's heids. Ma ain wife an her mither often work wi herbs. Mony's a time ah've seen the benefit they bring. Tae tell the truth ah think accusations aboot magic are aised tae settle auld scores, or mibbe it's sheer badness, or plain stupidity whaur eedjits alloo themsels tae be led lik sheep by folk as shud ken better an end up dain some terrible things. Whit happened tae ye wis bad but it's come tae nowt. Ye're on yer way tae bide wi a fine lady. She'll see ye richt. Afore ye ken it ye'll be as free as a bird."

Elsie's eyes filled with tears. "It's jist…Ah didna want ye tae think – "

"An ah'm nae. Neither are the ither three sittin up front so stoap worryin."

While the cart crawled along Jonas told Jamie and his mother about life in Holland, described his father's church, the work he did in the town of Groningen, how his grandfather farmed, his mother's skill of making cheese, how he missed it all.

"Whit a language," John added. "But he's richt, it's a grand place tae be."

"Ye've been then?" Jamie asked.

"Ay. Ah found the Dutch freendly, God fearin folk. Ma only problem wis the young meenister ah wis there wi; a man o fixed ideas aboot oor Kirk's future. Mibbe ye've heard o him. James Renwick. Him an me fell oot an ah cam hame early. He's back noo tae stert up the field-preachin again an boost resistance against the government."

Jonas gave John a quick glance but said nothing

"Ye dinna soond vera approvin." Jamie looked from one to the other.

John shrugged. "He reminds me o anither young preacher,

Richard Cameron. He hud the same ideas."

"Cameron." Jamie took a quick breath then shook his head.

After that no-one spoke till they'd almost reached Lesmahagow.

"Nearly ther." John broke the silence.

"If ye say so." Jonas sounded weary as they approached a huddle of tiny cottages.

"Ah'm tellin ye," John retaliated. "Jist past they hooses turn left ontae the auld drovers' road. That way we dinna need tae gang thru the village itsel."

Before they reached the turn off Jonas saw another a flurry of red coming towards them. He signalled to John then stopped the cart rather than cutting across in front of the horses.

Once again John and Elsie ducked under the tarpaulin. Once again the mounted platoon slowed down but passed with scarcely a glance before picking up speed.

"Mair troopers on the hunt." John peered over the edge of the tarpaulin at the disappearing cloud of dust. "Jist as weel wur heidin in the opposite direction."

"Jist as weel wur on a cairt which isna worth a glance," Jonas said. "Maister Hamilton wis richt."

"Ay." John grinned. "We'll be fine."

Young Johnnie Steel ran into the kitchen of Westermains farm and pulled at his mother's apron. "Ah've jist seen a cairt turnin aff the road an comin up the track tae the farm."

Marion looked annoyed and stopped rolling the dough to top the casserole for dinner. "Dinna tell me they troopers are comin back? They wur here yesterday."

"Naw. It's nae them. Jist a cairt wi three folk sittin up front. Nivver saw it afore. Come an ah'll show ye."

Marion banged down the rolling pin and followed Johnnie into the yard.

"See." He pointed. "Dae ye ken them?"

Marion studied the approaching strangers and shook her head. "Nae idea."

The cart came closer. A dark-haired young man held the reins. Beside him sat a woman wrapped in a thick woollen shawl. Her face was weary and sad. Next to her another young man had his arm round her as if for extra strength and protection.

Marion and Johnnie moved to stand in the middle of the entrance. "Guid day. This is Westermains farm. Can ah help ye?"

"Ye must be Mistress Steel?" The young driver pulled on the reins and stopped the cart. "Pleased tae meet ye. Ah'm Jonas Hawthorn alang wi ma aunt Helen an cousin Jamie."

Marion gaped at him. "Are ye the Jonas frae Holland?"

"Ay." Jonas smiled. "The ither twa are frae Wanlockheid."

"Ma John tellt me aboot ye but nae the ither twa. He'll be surprised tae ken ye're here."

"No ah'll no." John Steel stood up in the back of the cart. "It's me bringin them."

Marion squealed, ran forward and reached up to grab John's hand. He leant over and kissed her brow. "Easy lass. It's jist me. Naethin tae worry aboot." He kissed her again then turned to help Elsie to her feet. "Let me introduce Miss Elsie Spreul."

Marion smiled at the young girl's anxious face, smiled again at the other three then stood there looking awkward.

John jumped down, gave her a tight hug. "Ah'll explain later."

"Ye'd better." Marion whispered then turned to her unexpected visitors. "Weel this is a pleasant surprise." She ruffled Johnnie's hair. "This young man's excited tae see ye."

The three Hawthorns nodded, smiled at the child then climbed down and waited while Jonas lifted Elsie to join them.

"Richt then, in ye come an be welcome." Marion led them all into the farmhouse.

Helen Hawthorn stood in the warm, comfortable kitchen and thought of her own tiny space at Wanlockhead. She looked at the rolled-out dough on the table, smelled the meat casserole standing ready, the kind of preparations she'd make herself, part of a family's normal routine. *If only,* she thought and fought back tears before turning to Marion Steel. "Ah see we've come at a busy meenit. Can ah gie ye a haund?"

Marion leant forward as if sensing the need to deflect the older woman's pain. "That's kind o ye. Ay. If ye feenish rollin oot the dough then cover the meat in the casserole ah'll stert on the soup. That way we'll eat sooner raither than later." She handed Helen Hawthorn the rolling pin.

"Ah'll show the ithers roond the place," John suggested. "Jonas micht be interestit tae see hoo we dae things here compared tae his farm in Holland." He bent down to lift Johnnie on his shoulders. "An ye can help. Whaur's yer brither an sister?"

"Oot the back playin wi the dug."

"Richt, we'll gang an see them first. They'll want tae meet oor veesitors." He turned to Elsie who was hanging back by the door. "Mibbe ye'd raither bide in here?"

Elsie nodded and pointed to the vegetables piled at the end of the kitchen table. "Bit o choppin needed?"

Marion smiled. "Ay. Thank ye. Mak a stert wi that lot then ah'll gang oot tae the well fur watter." She opened a drawer in the big dresser and took out two aprons. "Here, baith o ye. Ye need tae luk the pairt."

Helen and Elsie laughed, laid their shawls on the settle by the fire and tied on the aprons. Within minutes the three women were working together and the initial formality began to disappear.

Over a good meal the three Hawthorns told Marion their story and their plans. Shocked and intrigued she listened, nodded sympathetically, and listened again as the strange and terrible events were explained.

Finally John said, "In a day or two ah'll tak Jonas, Jamie an Mistress Hawthorn intae Glesca and find Maister Middleton, the ship owner whae helped Lucas a while back. Wi luk we'll hae them on thur way tae Holland withoot ony problem." He smiled across the table at Elsie. "Miss Elsie will be goin tae her aunt aince ah find whaur she bides these days. Ah'll visit Maister McAvoy first an ask the best way tae gang aboot it. He hus a guid network. Somebody's likely tae ken whaur Mistress Spreul can be found. Meanwhile we need tae tak guid care o the lass. She hud a bad time."

"I've tellt Mistress Steel whit happened," Elsie cut in.

"An ah'm ashamed tae hear o folk no jist thinkin sic terrible things but actin on them." Marion reached across the table to touch Elsie's hand. "Happy tae huv ye here, ma dear."

Elsie flushed and looked down at her plate.

Now Marion tackled John. "Ye'll nae ken this but ma brither Gavin heard somethin aboot ye in the tavern the ither nicht. A trooper wis sayin ye'd been recognised as ane o the attackers at

Enterkin, said Claverhoose hus ordered them doon that way tae help search fur ye as weel as the ither rebels. Ah didna see hoo that wis possible but noo ah ken better."

John shrugged. "A platoon passed us jist afore the village. Suits me fine if thur oot searchin the Lowther Hills insteid o prowlin aboot roond here."

Marion's voice rose. "Weel, ah dinna like the way ye're drawin attention tae yersel."

"It's nae worse than afore," John smiled. "As lang as ah tak care."

"That's whit ye aye say." She gave him a hard stare and said no more.

Chapter Eleven

Captain John Crichton looked annoyed, or maybe more desperate as the garrison surgeon shook his head. "I gied ye a guid luk ower and in ma opeenion ye're still nae fit for duty."

"Hoo no?" Crichton snapped. "Ah've a platoon waitin and rebels tae catch. Nae doubt Commander Claverhouse is gettin impatient at ma absence."

The surgeon laughed. "Ye cudna ride a hunner yards withoot losing yer balance. Jist content yersel. Yer commander left money tae see ye weel luked aifter. He said naething aboot hurrying back tae yer post. Ye're maist fortunate wi a maister as cares for his men's welfare enough tae dig deep in his ain pocket. Ma advice is tak a walk, enjoy some fresh air, test yer legs. Dae it ivvery day and I'll check ye again nixt week." He turned away to continue his round.

Crichton swore and flopped back down on his bunk. At first he'd been barely conscious, drifting in and out of strange dreams and terrifyingly lucid moments which had him staring death in the face along with constant pain. This gradually became long hours and days, staring at the cracks on the low ceiling, nothing else to do but follow the strange patterns they made or wondering what had really happened that awful day when his attempt to arrest two rebels had backfired so spectacularly. He still resented the garrison surgeon telling him he was lucky to be alive.

A mix of frustration and anger forced him upright to sit on the edge of his bunk to pull on his new boots. They felt stiff and unyielding, like his replacement uniform hanging on the wall nearby. The commander had paid for them, which made Crichton uneasy for he suspected that Clavers didn't hold him in such worth. Mibbe it wis the name ah gied him. James Renwick. He seemed excited enoch aboot it. He pulled on the tight jacket. At least ah luk the pairt. Richt. He lurched down the long dormitory into the dark corridor which led to the inner courtyard where lines of men were marching back and forth to familiar commands.

Once in the courtyard he stopped, leant against the rough, cold wall and tried to face down growing anxiety. It would be so easy to turn round and creep back to his bunk. This was a new sensation for a man usually so full of confidence. Jist dae it. He stepped forward, unsteady as he walked through the outer gate and into the city again.

Forcing one foot after another gradually achieved a rhythm. He began to feel stronger as he went down the hill to join the High Street, following his nose which led him towards Greendyke stable and smiddy with the chance to demand some answers face to face; better still, the chance of revenge for all his suffering. Ay, he consoled himself, ah dinna haud back frae dain ma duty. Ay. Naebody can say itherwise.

The High Street was busy with loaded carts, carriages and handbarrows while a motley collection of men and women made the best they could with whatever space was left. Being too weak to push his way through the crowd made progress slow. Several times he was glad to slip into an open close, away from the throng till he eased his gasping breath.

Half-way along he passed the *Crooked Man Inn* and glared at the swinging sign, the tiny, sparkling windows and persuasively open door. That's whaur it stertit. Whaur ah saw they twa rebels. He stopped and tried to pull up a picture of the two faces of the young men he'd known were trouble yet had to be followed, be challenged, if necessary arrested or even shot.

He walked on, preparing himself for the encounter to come once he reached Greendyke.

Lying in his bunk he'd dreamt about it, tried to analyse and grasp at least some of the knowledge about his attackers. Aw they ither times ah didna need tae luk for the culprit. It wis aye John Steel. Nae this time. Nivver seen either o they twa buggers afore. An it wisna them as felled me. No when ah hud them staundin richt in front o me wi terrified faces. Ay, it came frae ahint. An sic force. Hud tae be the blacksmith. Ay. An ah mind somebody sayin the name Ted as ah fell. Hoo cud ah forget? When ah see his face an hear him dare tae deny – Weel, ah ken whit tae dae. Ay. Ah'm lukin furrit tae that. Crichton squared his shoulders, tried to ignore the growing pain across his back and turned into Greendyke Lane.

Ahead stood the open gate and the stone building at the back of a gravelly yard with the blacksmith's shop and stable as he remembered. Noo for some answers. He walked up to the open door of the smiddy and watched a big man in a torn leather apron bend over an anvil to begin shoeing a pony. Once the job was done and the owner led the beast away he waited a minute till the smith turned back into the hot, dark space. The man was replacing his tools on a rack along a side wall when Crichton came up behind to say, "Weel met, Ted."

The man straightened then slowly turned. "Naw. Name's Rab. Can ah help ye?"

"Whaur's Ted?"

"Nae idea. Ah've taen ower here."

Crichton gaped.

"Ted gied up weeks ago. Ane day here nixt day gone. Tellt naebody. Didna even pay his rent. Ma brither heard aboot it frae the landlord an tipped me the wink. Ah jumped at the chance. Been a guid move."

"Whit aboot nixt door?"

"Same. A new man taen ower." The smith peered at Crichton's obvious disappointment. "Ted an the stablemaister are lang gone." He glanced at the fine uniform. "Ah tak it the maitter micht be serious?"

"It is. Somethin the law is keen tae deal wi."

"That serious? Weel, ah'll keep ma ears open. Ye nivver ken whit ah micht hear. If ah dae ah'll let ye ken. In that case whaur dae ah find ye?"

"Main toun garrison. Ask for Captain Crichton."

The smith shook his head as he watched the trooper walk through the gate and away. As if ah'd tell sic an arsehole onythin.

Weary and disappointed Crichton went back down the High Street. Now it seemed more of a distance than before, his feet heavier and less willing with every step.

By the time he reached the *Crooked Man* he was exhausted. He hadn't expected the stable and smiddy to offer nothing. Feeling sorry for himself he wandered inside, sat down at one of the vacant tables and called for a jug of ale.

In a quiet corner, beyond the bar counter Alex Jamieson sat contemplating his next move in the everlasting chess game he played with his brother Pete. He glanced up and recognised the captain's hunched figure only a few feet away. The last time he'd been that close he'd been pushing Crichton's unconscious body feet first down the steep bank to the river Clyde. *If only*, he thought. If only ye hudna got tangled up in the weeds at the bottom. He sighed. An here ye are again lik the proverbial bad penny. Win some lose some ah suppose. He lifted an ornately carved bishop and moved the ivory piece across the chequered board. Brither Pete will huv a problem wi this. He sat back to sip his glass of best port and continue to watch the trooper.

Hoo dae ah solve this? Crichton tormented himself yet again. Claverhoose said he'd deal wi it an bring ma attackers tae justice. Aw he's done is fricht the smith an the stablemaister intae runnin awa an leavin me wi nae chance o gettin ony revenge. He mulled over the little he knew once more. It stertit here. Mibbe the innkeeper minds somethin. Worth askin. He left his seat and went over to the counter where the innkeeper was busy dunking mugs and glasses in a pail of hot water. He rapped on the counter top. "Dae ye mind me?"

The innkeeper barely looked up. "Shud ah?"

"Aboot a month ago ah wis in here, hud somethin tae eat. Ah wis sittin ower there." He pointed to the exact table.

"And?"

"Twa young travellers, ane fair, ane dark haired, came in and sat close by, hud somethin tae eat as weel then left in a hurry. Mibbe ye mind me gettin up and followin them oot?"

"Is that so? Weel, whitivver yer game or whitivver ye're aifter ah canna help ye. Aw kinds come in here. A hale month is lik the dim an distant past." The innkeeper lifted a piece of grey muslin from the counter and began wiping the glasses.

Crichton gave up and returned to his seat. A snout, that's whit ah need. Some low life willin tae ferret oot the smith. Aifter that ah ken whit tae dae. He shook his head. Whit an eedjit nae thinkin this afore. The sergeant at the garrison must ken somebody willin tae sneak aboot fur a bit siller. He turned and called for another jug of ale and considered this possibility.

When Crichton left the inn Alex Jamieson followed him into the street and waited till the red-jacketed figure merged with the crowd. That yin's trouble an if need be he'll be dealt wi. Ay. An richt this time. He went back inside to wait for his brother Pete to join him.

Crichton did ask the sergeant where he might find a good snout. At first the sergeant seemed reluctant but mention of Claverhouse seemed to persuade him to give over a couple of names and where to find them. This encouraged Crichton who duly went to the specified place, left his request and the promise of earning good money.

Whoever they were seemed to think better of making any contact. Nothing happened so he was forced back to the sergeant. "Ye must ken ithers. Whit aboot yins as come aboot the garrison?"

"Ah'm nae at liberty tae mention the likes o that. Onyway, ah dinna deal wi they kinda snouts direct. These are difficult an dangerous times. Ye ken that yersel. They kinda folk are kept weel unner wraps. They need tae be protectit fur thur ain safety. If ye want ony mair ye'll need tae speak tae the garrison commander."

Undeterred, Crichton sought out the commander who refused point blank; Clavers name made no difference this time. "I canna divulge hoo we gaither oor information."

"But shairly?"

"Luk here sir," the garrison commander eyed Crichton with obvious dislike. "I'm sorry ye wur attacked. But ye're here oot o courtesy tae yer maister John Graham. He paid for yer treatment and yer medicine and asked us tae tak guid care o ye. That we've done and gled tae see ye weel on yer way tae a guid recovery. As for providing assistance wi some personal investigation. No sir. That's best left tae the richt authority. Dae I mak masel clear?"

Thrown back on his own resources Crichton resorted to walking the same route to Greendyke and standing in the open gate to stare at the smiddy and stable for a while before retreating for a welcome sit down at the *Crooked Man*.

He ordered a mug of ale then tried another approach. "Ah'm lukin for some help in findin a freend ah've lost touch wi."

The innkeeper handed over the ale but said nothing.

"Mibbe ye ken somebody aboot here, a customer mibbe, as cud ask aboot on ma behalf? Thur's guid money in it."

"Maks nae difference. Ah serve ma customers, bide polite an pass the time o day, naethin mair. Hoo wud ah ken ocht aboot sic a person? If it's ale or wine or spirits or even a bite tae eat ah'm yer man, nane better. This is a law-abidin inn wi a proper license. It's weel respectit which is mair than can be said fur mony a place aboot here. That means ah need tae keep ma nose clean. Dis that answer yer question?"

This time Pete Jamieson was hunched over his chess board and heard every word. *Alex is richt. Yon's trouble an needs watchin.*

Crichton returned to the garrison in a bad mood which wasn't improved when he found the sergeant waiting for him. "Whaur huv ye been? The captain wants a word. Some message arrived fur ye."

"Whit aboot?"

"Hoo wud ah ken? Ah'm only repeatin whit ah wis tellt."

Crichton brushed past the sergeant and hurried upstairs to the captain's private quarters. He knocked politely and waited till he heard, "Enter."

He walked in and stood to attention in front of the captain's battered old desk covered with piles of paper relating to the day-to-day running of the garrison. "Sir."

"Stand easy man." The captain leant forward and held out a letter sealed with a laurel leaf emblem.

Crichton took the letter, stared at the familiar leaf pattern in the wax seal then at the captain. "It's frae ma commander."

"Open it man." The captain frowned. "I'm as curious as yersel." He slid a little knife towards the edge of the desk. "Here."

Crichton slit the fold and opened out the thick piece of paper to read a spidery scrawl. He read it again then looked up. "Ma commander requires ma presence at Douglas Castle as a maitter o some urgency."

"Dis he mention the nature o this urgency?"

"No sir. But it must be serious. This is the first time I've hud a written summons. He asks the loan o a horse tae git me ther as quickly as possible."

"Douglas is a fair distance awa. Are ye fit tae ride as far? The surgeon's report states ye need a guid few weeks yet afore taking up duty again."

"Ah'll be fine." Crichton slipped the letter in his pocket and stood to attention again. "If ye'll alloo me a horse ah can leave in the mornin?"

"Nivver let it be said that this garrison hindered John Graham's work for the country."

"Thank ye sir." Crichton saluted and left.

The captain watched the door close behind the trooper and shook his head.

Crichton's spirits rose. Clavers still needed him. Had said so. Sore back, throbbing head, frequent dizzy spells would soon disappear once he had some real work to do. He went back to the hospital dormitory, stretched out on his bunk and stared up at the cracks on the ceiling, the cracks with their patterns which somehow had helped him work his way back from the darkest depths; this time he could see himself back to normal, leading his platoon, enforcing the law, showing those rebels the price of defiance.

After breakfast Crichton collected the promised horse from the stable and led it into the covered courtyard. As he lifted himself into the saddle the sudden movement made his head spin and the ache in his back seemed to surge right down his legs forcing him to lean forward and grip the reins before he fell off. He gritted his teeth, straightened again and edged the horse towards the open gate. When he saw the busy street and remembered how difficult it had been just to walk through the crowd he hesitated. Git on wi it, he told himself. Ye've done it mony's a time. He clicked the horse forward and winced as the surge of pain reminded him that riding a horse took more effort than he'd realised.

The Jamieson brothers were worried by Crichton's re-appearance and the way he seemed determined to find some answer to his attack. Alex had been especially annoyed when he heard what Pete had seen and heard. "Jist suppose oor freend gits somebody willin tae luk fur the smith an the stablemaister. An jist suppose thur found. They baith ken us an saw whit we did. If oor freend's willin tae pay them the promise o siller's awfy guid at loosenin tongues."

"In that case we best feenish the maitter afore that can happen."

"Ay. Ah wis thinkin the same. Fur a stert ah'll gang by the garrison in the mornin an see whit's whit." Alex did exactly that and was waiting in a close-mouth opposite the garrison when Crichton rode out the gate and began to pick his way along the busy street towards the main road out of the city.

A pair of sharp eyes studied the rider, the way he sat, the tense expression, the grey pallor, the clenched hands holding the reins. Ye dinna luk fit tae be in chairge o yon beast. Ah wunner whaur ye're aff tae? He crossed the road to the garrison for a quick word with one of the men and discovered that Crichton was bound for Douglas, summoned at short notice by Claverhouse himself.

"When's he comin back?" Alex pressed.

The man laughed. "Back. Ah doubt it. He's far frae weel. Be lucky tae mak it the length o Douglas nivver mind think aboot ridin aw the way back here. No that we want him onyway. Mair trouble than he's worth an aye complainin."

Alex returned to the *Crooked Man*, to his chessboard, and a celebratory glass of best port.

Crichton felt more in control once he was on the open road, away from the crowded streets. He nodded to himself and tried to pretend he wasn't already feeling weary. *Ah'll be fine.* And so he was till the rain began, cold, driving, stinging his cheeks and brow and gradually soaking into his thick jacket. He hunched down to protect himself, reined the horse back to a steady walk.

Head bowed he leant further over. That felt better. He eased down till his face was almost touching the beast's mane. This way the rain bounced off the skip of his helmet, clear of his eyes and stinging cheeks. *If only*, he thought. *If only ma heid wisna sae sair. If only ah didna feel sae dizzy. If only the pain in ma back wud ease aff. If only ah cud tak a rest. Mibbe lie doon fur a meenit. Dinna be daft.* He shook his head. *Ah canna dae that. Keep goin.* He straightened a little but this made his back pain worse, made the urge to lie down more persuasive. *Mibbe a wee rest against this strong neck wud gie me some support.* He tried it. *Ay. Jist fur a meenit or twa.* Experienced rider as he was these thoughts seemed perfectly natural. Eyes closed he gave in and lay against the horse while it walked on through the driving rain.

Gus McPhail was on his way back from Glasgow, his cart loaded with orders to be delivered that day. He hated the rain but was well used to it and tried to cheer himself up with loud whistling. And then up ahead he saw a figure slumped across a horse. The horse was barely moving. Gus easily drew abreast and reached over to grab the reins and bring the beast to a halt.

He jumped down then froze. That figure was a soldier. Worse than that, he was familiar. A man Gus had good reason to hate. "Chris' sake, it's Crichton. Hauf deid by the luk o him." He studied the still shape. Ay. Ye shot ma best freend an partner John Brown an laughed while ye did it. Same when ye blasted the face aff young David Steel at Skellyhill farm in front o his wife an wean. Nae doubt thur's a wheen ithers if the truth be tellt. As fur ma freend John Steel, ye've a lot tae answer ther, harassin him at ivvery turn an abusin his pair wife wi yer threats. Deil incarnate, that's whit ye are. Ay. An here's me wi the vera chance. Naebody wud blame me. No even masel. He reached inside his heavy coat for the small pistol he always carried. Richt thru the heid shud dae it. Nice an close. Nice an neat an nae fear o missin.

An then whit? a small voice asked. Tak care. This is a trooper. Protectit by law.

Whae'd ivver ken? he argued. Naebody's aboot tae see or hear onythin. An aince he's deid...

Ah, but thur's shair tae be a fuss when he's found, the voice whispered. Questions will be asked. Whae will the law come aifter but them as travel this road ivvery day?

He thought about it. Ay, ah suppose so. Whit wud ah say if asked? Wud ah be believed? Wud ah end up deid masel?

He loosened his grip on the pistol. If ah tak the bugger and haund him ower the law micht be pleased wi ma act o kindness in rescuin ane o thur ain. Mibbe ah'd git a thank ye. Mibbe they'd stoap harassin me as much aifter that. Ay. That wud be guid, Micht be worth ma while presentin masel as a potential freend. He stood there staring at the unconscious, hated face. Aw the same, it's temptin tae jist dae it. His fingers gripped the pistol, felt for the trigger. Weel? He hesitated then shook his head and withdrew an empty hand from his inner coat pocket.

"Richt." He pulled Crichton from the horse, balanced the heavy body across his shoulders and staggered back to the cart. "In ye go." He tipped the figure over the back-board of the cart then jumped up to pull an edge of tarpaulin over. "Best keep the rain aff an mak it luk as if ah'm concerned fur yer welfare."

He tied the horse to the back rail of the cart and returned to his driving seat. Noo fur the billet in Lesmahagow an deliver this bugger intae his freends haund's afore ah chainge ma mind.

Captain Dominic McCann was leading his patrol out of Lesmahagow to begin their routine inspection of local farms.

Claverhouse had sent strict instructions that this had to be done each day, at varying times with a special look out being kept for any sign of strangers. McCann had little taste for such work, hated the harassment it caused and felt ashamed at the looks they received as they prowled through every corner of each farm. Obedient as he was he tried to do it as humanely as possible. Not that it seemed to make any difference to the hate he felt.

He was about to turn into one of the farm tracks when he saw a cart coming towards him with the driver waving as if to attract attention.

"Yon's McPhail the carrier," one of his men said. "Seems tae want somethin."

The platoon waited till the cart came close.

McPhail pointed to the back of his cart. "Ah found ane o yer men a wheen miles back, lyin across his horse, seems hauf-deid. Ah put him unner a tarpaulin tae keep the rain aff. His horse is tied ahint ma cairt."

McCann edged his horse to the back of the cart, leant over to lift the tarpaulin and gasped at the rigid figure. "It's Crichton. Captain Crichton. He's supposed tae be in Glesca recoverin frae bein attacked while arrestin twa rebels. Whit's he dain oot here?"

"Nae idea," McPhail replied. "Aw ah ken is ah found him on the main road frae the toun. Much as ah tried he wudna utter a word. He's cauld as ice an far frae weel, an needin a doctor as soon as."

"Lucky ye came on him," McCann nodded. "Cud ye mibbe gang on tae the village? We're billeted in the hoose ahint the inn by the kirk square."

"Nae bother."

The platoon turned and followed Gus McPhail's cart back the way they'd come. Crichton was quickly lifted from the cart and carried indoors before McPhail was thanked again for his act of kindness and allowed to continue his deliveries.

Once he finished his day's work Gus decided to avoid going back through the village. Word would be out by now. Everyone must know about Crichton. Worse than that, what would they say? He'd been worrying about this all day. The last thing he wanted was the chance of any confrontation or awkward questions.

On the edge of the village he turned off the road onto an old drovers' track which was little used and the cart began to lurch along the rough path. Ay, best bide oot the way. He began to whistle then jumped when a voice called out from among the trees, "Evenin, Gus."

He stopped the cart and turned to see a familiar figure sitting on a large stone beside a line of old beech trees. "Oh. It's yersel Gavin. Whit are ye dain oot here?" He smiled. At least Gavin seemed friendly.

Gavin Weir smiled up at Gus then pointed to a bulging sack lying at his feet. "Mither sent me oot here tae gaither a wheen beechnuts. Aince dried thur guid alang wi kindlins fur the fire. Jist huvin a wee rest an hopin this rain will stoap afore ah walk back hame."

"Ah canna dae ocht aboot the rain but jump up. Ah'll be passin yer farm road-end."

"Thanks." Gavin lifted the sack and heaved it into the back of the empty cart. "Much obliged." He climbed up beside Gus. "Ah believe ye've hud a day an a hauf the day."

Gus stiffened. "The news is oot then?"

"Somethin lik that disna gang unnoticed."

"Ay weel. Ah'm still no shair aboot whit ah did."

"Because it wis Crichton?"

"Whae else? Yon's the last man ah'd want tae meet let alane help in ony way." Gus stared ahead. "Ah did think aboot puttin a bullet in his heid."

"Naebody wud blame ye."

"Mibbe so. But ah didna dae it. Noo ah'm worried whit folk will think. Hus onybody said ocht?"

"Jist surprised that ye saw fit tae rescue him aifter the pain he's caused yersel. The loss o yer freend John Broon must still be gey raw."

"Ay. That ah canna forgie. An ah thocht aboot a wheen ithers foreby. But ah still cudna bring masel tae – "

"Be like him."

"That's ane way o puttin it."

Gavin nodded.

Dominic McCann organised what he could to make Crichton comfortable, giving up his room and bed, stripping him from sodden clothes and putting him into clean, dry linen before wrapping the icy body in soft, warm blankets backed up by quickly heated bricks.

McCann's sergeant shook his head at all this effort. "Ah ken yon carrier said git a doctor. Is it worth the bother? The nearest yin is ten mile awa in Lanark. By the time ane o us rides there, finds the man, an brings him back it'll be ower late. Jist luk. Ah suspect he wis far frae weel tae stert wi. God kens whit the eedjit wis thinkin ridin oot in his condition. An aince the cauld rain got a grip, weel – "

McCann held up the letter he'd found in the captain's inside pocket when he hung the wet jacket up to dry. "He wis daing his duty. The commander wrote and summoned him tae Douglas withoot delay."

"But the man wisna able."

"Crichton dis whit Clavers says withoot question. If his commander says jump he jumps nae maitter hoo high or difficult. He has mony a fault lik nae respect for the likes o us as works wi him nivver mind his determination tae force surrender on his so-cawed enemies. Cruelty at ony price is pairt o his nature but loyalty tae his maister is nivver in doubt. Claverhoose will be expectin him and needs be tellt whit's happened. I'll write a quick message, and send a rider tae Douglas, and anither tae Lanark for a doctor, jist in case. Bide here. Keep an eye on the patient. Ony chainge gie me a shout."

McCann rattled downstairs determined to do his best for a man he'd learnt to despise. Or maybe it was shock at seeing how the powerful could be reduced to utter helplessness.

Within minutes he'd scribbled a message for John Graham and sent a dispatch rider off for Douglas and another for Lanark to summon a doctor. He then went over to the inn and asked if one of the serving girls could be spared to help with nursing Crichton. Keen to keep things sweet with the military the innkeeper called Jessie McPhail from the kitchen where she was chopping vegetables for soup. "Jessie, Captain McCann's here needin yer help. Can ye spare a wee while?"

Jessie appeared at the kitchen door. "Whit's wrang?"

McCann stepped forward. "Ane o oor troopers has been brocht in, far frae weel. We've done oor best tae mak him comfortable but a wummin's touch wud mak a difference."

Jessie already knew who the trooper was. She also knew he'd been brought in by her own brother. *God kens whit oor Gus wis thinkin aboot, rescuin yon rat.* However, she just smiled and said, "Ah'll dae ma best."

Once in the military kitchen she quickly filled a pot with water and swung it over the hottest part of the range then ran back to the inn to collect some muslin cloth and sprigs of lavender.

McCann helped her carry the heated water upstairs along with a large china bowl and watched as she sat it on a table beside the bed, filled it with water then scattered some lavender across the surface to let it steep a moment.

She turned to the captain. "If ye've ocht needin attention ah'll manage fine frae noo on." She dipped the muslin in the water, squeezed out the excess then leant over Crichton's still figure to gently wipe the brow and cheeks.

"If ye're sure I'll gang doon and gie the men new orders. They've waited lang enoch and it's time they were oot on the day's inspection. I'll be back in nae time."

"Nae worries." Jessie smiled and moved the blankets aside to begin wiping the exposed arms and hands.

Jessie continued wiping Crichton's cold skin till she heard McCann's boots hit the bottom step then stopped to study her patient. "Weel, Captain High an Michty, things are different noo. Here ye are, helpless as a bairn an nae a peep oot o ye. Must be a first. When ah think aboot aw they times ye sat in the front room o the inn boastin aboot whit ye'd done tae they pair rebels, hoo they'd suffered, and whit ye'd dae nixt if ye got the chance. An the way ye behaved tae masel, time aifter time grabbin haud o ma waist, puin me ontae yer knee an expectin me tae smile as if ye wur dain me a favour. Weel noo's the meenit fur pay back. Lang overdue if the truth be tellt. Ma brither Gus hudna the guts tae dae whit's richt but ah huv." She lifted a plump pillow from the side table. "An the vera thing is jist handy." She bent over the unconscious figure with the pillow. "Ye'll nae even feel a thing, mair's the peety."

"Whit are ye dain, mistress?" McCann came up behind Jessie.

She froze for a second then turned with a smile. "Ah wis aboot tae lift him. His breathin soonds terrible. Thocht it micht help if he wis mair upricht wi anither pillow. He's a bit heavy. Cud ye help me?"

"Ye jist had tae gie me a shout." McCann moved to the side of the bed and raised Crichton while Jessie carefully placed the pillow behind the patient.

"Thank ye sir. Noo that ye're here ah'll gang back tae the inn fur a wee while. Wur aye busy at this time o day. If he wakens up let me ken. Ah'll be richt back."

McCann watched her leave the room, looked back at the still figure in the bed then shook his head and whispered, "Ah think ye've jist been raither lucky. Anither meenit. Ay. Ye near reaped as ye sow."

When John Graham received McCann's letter he told the rider to wait while he drafted a reply ordering the captain to come to Douglas in place of Crichton.

That evening McCann arrived as requested and Claverhouse wasted no time in explaining what had happened at Enterkin. "And noo we need tae scour the moors afore the runaways mak guid their escape. Lieutenant Mulligan will dae a sweep roond by Cumnock and Muirkirk while ye tak men frae here and dae the same up by Crawfordjohn. Ye'll mibbe box in ane or twa. It's worth a try."

Early next morning two lines of mounted troopers set out to do their master's bidding and hopefully have some success.

Late that evening, after weary miles of riding, McCann's platoon had turned to make their way back to Douglas when they almost stumbled on three men sheltering in a deep hollow, overhung by deep heather. They must have been asleep for the troopers had them before they could react. It was an easy capture and none of them offered an explanation as to why they were there.

"Richt, tie them up," McCann ordered, "and hing them across the horses. We'll be quicker that way than tryin tae walk them back."

His men were happy to do this and relieved to return with something to show for their efforts.

When John Graham saw the three men he seemed pleased at first then frowned. "A big group o prisoners were delivered frae Ayr while ye wur awa and are locked up in the castle dungeon. They've aw been sentenced for transportation tae the Americas. A boat's waitin for them at Leith. Are they three amang the Enterkin escapees?"

"I dinna think sae," McCann replied. "They seem ower weel

dressed. I assumed they were locals up tae nae guid."

Clavers frowned. "In that case they need tae gang afore a magistrate afore we dae onything. Tae dae things richt we need tae keep them separate. Tak them tae the Tolbooth in Douglas whaur they can be sentenced in the morning."

When McCann arrived at the Tolbooth the jailer shook his head. "We've enoch nair-dae-weels waitin in oor strong room fur the magistrate withoot addin ony rebels tae the mix."

"I'm here on John Graham's orders," McCann insisted.

"Commander Claverhoose, ye say. Weel, since it's him. Whit aboot the storeroom at the back o the buildin? It's hauf fu o boxes and bags o supplies. Aw the same, thur micht be space fur three bodies."

"Perfect," McCann nodded. "It's only for ane nicht."

The three prisoners were untied from the horses, marched into the Tolbooth and locked up in the back storeroom. McCann and his men returned to the castle while the jailer checked his other prisoners in the strong room and ordered his assistant to see about feeding them. "Cut up a loaf or twa. Thin slices mind ye. Nae need tae be ower generous. Ane piece each alang wi a bowl o gruel is mair than plenty. Aifter that mak sure awthin's secure. We want nae mistakes fur the magistrate tae find fault wi in the mornin, especially when thur's as mony waitin tae be dealt wi."

The three prisoners sat down on stacked bags of flour and stared at each other. "So much fur escapin aifter Enterkin." John Gemmel groaned and flapped his hands. "They mibbe dinna ken we wur amang them as escaped but it'll mak nae difference, we'll jist be added tae the list fur the Americas."

Andrew Easton, who was sitting alongside, nodded. "Ah suppose sae."

Peter Miller, the third prisoner, shook his head. "Nae way. We've landed lucky."

"Hoo come?" Gemmel asked. "Whit's lucky aboot this?"

"A way oot, that's whit. Ye forget ah belang tae Douglas."

"Whit's that got tae dae wi onythin?"

"Ivverythin." Miller began to move the bags of flour closest to the wall. "Jist watch, or better still gie me a haund tae move stuff back frae this corner."

The other two did as he asked and within minutes they'd cleared a small space.

"Noo whit?" Gemmel asked.

Miller didn't reply. He knelt down and began to examine the joints in the flagstones then pointed at the one nearest to the corner. "If we can jist loosen that yin it shud lift. He took off his thick leather belt and forced the edge of the heavy metal buckle into the narrow groove. After several attempts he managed to push it further in and the stone itself appeared to rise a fraction. The other two leant down and held it steady till Miller managed to push the buckle right through. His strong fingers now gripped the depth of the flagstone and almost lifted it clear. "Richt, grab haud an we'll lift the hale thing oot."

Excited by now the other two obeyed and the three men soon had the flagstone out and sitting alongside a dark hole.

"Weel ah nivver." Gemmel and Easton gaped at Miller as he sat back and and wiped his face.

He gave them both a grin. "Nice surprise eh, an jist whit wur aifter. This is the stert o a tunnel. It runs frae here, unner the road opposite tae the kirk. It comes oot on the far edge o the graveyard. It'll be a ticht fit. We'll need tae crawl alang. Yon jailer disna ken aboot it itherwise we wudna be in here."

"Hoo did ye ken?" Gemmel asked.

"Ma grandfaither helped dig it. He tellt me whaur it wis an made me swear tae bide schtum. In they days whaeivver wis in chairge o the Tolbooth seemed tae think thur micht be a need fur some kind o escape route."

"It's needed noo," Gemmel laughed. "Thank God ye ken aboot it. Aifter ye." He waved Miller forward.

It was a tight fit but the three determined men eventually made it to the end of the tunnel and scrabbled out behind a thick, jaggy gorse bush at the farthest end of the kirk graveyard. By now it was dark. No one seemed to be about. No one saw them as they hurried towards the moor, with every intention of not being caught again.

Come morning the jailer's assistant went to the back storeroom and unlocked the door to find no prisoners, only one dark space where a flagstone should have sat. He gaped then ran for his master who joined him and demanded, "Did ye ken aboot this?"

"Hoo cud ah?" the man replied.

"Ye belang tae this village."

"Mibbe so, but ah've nivver heard aboot sic a thing. Onyway, shud it no be in the plans fur the buildin?"

"Plans. Whit plans?" the jailer snapped. "Ah've nivver seen nor heard aboot ony plans."

"Whitivver. It's nae lukin guid."

"Tell me aboot it," the jailer groaned. "Whit's the magistrate gonna say when he arrives? Or Claverhoose fur that maitter?"

To the jailer's surprise John Graham laughed out loud then pointed at him. "And naebody kent? I find that raither strange."

"We hud nae idea," the jailer insisted.

"Doon ye go then and see whaur this wee escape tunnel micht lead."

The jailer glanced at his assistant.

"Naw, naw yersel," Claverhouse ordered. "On ye go."

The jailer obeyed and pushed his bulky body into the tight-fitting hole then disappeared.

Claverhouse sat down on one of the flour sacks while the jailer's assistant stood biting his nails.

Now well into the tunnel the jailer was crawling along the narrowest, pitch-black space with his shoulders scuffing past soft earth, loosening it, making it slide off and patter on the soles of his boots. As if this wasn't bad enough above him the tunnel height rose and fell, sometimes to what felt like mere inches, making him terrified his every movement might cause the whole thing to give way and bury him. The damp, stale smell and lack of air didn't help but a mix of fear and the will to survive kept him gasping along till he saw a tiny circle of daylight ahead. Suddenly it was no effort. Minutes later his face poked out, then his shoulders cleared the tight space. Nearly free. One more push and he shot forward to scrabble past a thick gorse bush like some demented, earth-covered mole.

Beyond the jaggy thorns he lay on the wet grass, relieved to have escaped, to be out in the open, gasping in fresh air. "Nivver again," he vowed and stumbled back to Claverhouse with the news.

"Whit kept ye?" The commander smiled at the dirt covered apparition. "Ye were that lang I began tae think ye'd escaped yersel or been buried alive."

"Neither sir. It wis a ticht fit. Ah needed tae crawl richt slow and wi great care or ah wud hae been buried. The tunnel comes oot beyond the graveyard, ahint a thick, jaggy gorse bush which hides the entrance. It's jist above the field that slopes doon tae the wee burn at the bottom. It's nae owerluked by ony hooses so it's fine and secret."

"Richt." Claverhouse nodded. "Git yersel cleaned up then order a cairt load o earth tae fill in baith ends o the tunnel. That shud dae it. Frae noo on see that ye stack aw yer supplies and boxes at that parteeclar end o the storeroom. And," his voice hardened, "mak shair naething lik this happens again." Claverhouse smiled. "Jist tae try and help ye I've sent word tae the magistrate that he's needed at Lanark first. That shud gie ye plenty time tae mak sure awthing is in a fit and proper state tae receive the man. And," the commander lowered his voice, "there's nae need tae mention onything aboot the wee tunnel escapade and the loss o three prisoners. Itherwise yer post here micht be raither short-lived."

"No a word." The jailer bowed and sighed with relief.

Lieutenant Mulligan and Captain McCann rode out together on a widespread search of the moor beyond Douglas. Between them they captured another two runaways although the three who'd escaped from the Douglas Tolbooth managed to elude them.

Meanwhile Claverhouse was busy preparing a report he'd deliver personally to the Privy Council, warning how things seemed to be changing for the worse. To sweeten the pill he'd take the load of prisoners bound for the Americas as proof of transportation being able to finance further law and order without over-straining the government purse. He hoped the sight of so many rebels being dragged through the centre of Edinburgh would scare the wits out of Queensberry and his self-satisfied cronies, and make them admit the value of Clavers' contribution instead of always conspiring against him. Maybe after this they'd listen to his proposals for the next move needed to counter growing resistance in the south of Scotland.

As soon as Mulligan and McCann returned to the castle John

Graham sent for them both. "I intend setting oot in the morning for Edinburgh wi a convoy o prisoners."

"Dae ye need us?" both men asked.

"Quite the opposite. Arrangements for supervision alang the way is weel taen care o. Yer work is around here. Ye're daing weel thegither. Mibbe send word tae Jamie Ogilvie doon at Ayr and ask for his assistance tae mak a three-pronged attack o the hale area. The great earl enjoys a chase and mibbe this micht squeeze oot a few mair runaways or would-be rebels or baith. I'll be back in a week or twa depending on the Privy Council and whit they decide for the future."

"Whit aboot Lesmahagow and Clydesdale?" McCann dared. "I left ma sergeant in charge. Will the platoon continue the routine inspections or gang further afield?"

"Nae worries." John Graham nodded. "Bennet is a perfectly capable man wi years o experience. He'll huv nae problem organising rotas, supervising the men, and making ony necessary decisions till Crichton is on the mend."

"Crichton micht no recover, sir. He wis at death's door when I left."

"If that happens the captain will be sair missed."

McCann almost said, for aw the wrang reasons, then clamped his teeth together as Clavers flapped a ringed hand at him. "When Crichton recovers, and I dae believe he will, he can tak ower again frae Bennet. He's done it afore and kens the Lesmahagow district lik the back o his hand. No much is likely tae escape his attention. Ye see, I've learnt that John Steel wis tae the fore at Enterkin and Crichton is mair than keen tae catch that parteecular felon."

"Really?" McCann looked surprised.

"Oh ay. In the thick o the action. Mulligan himsel recognised him. In ma opeenion that man seems tae be getting a bit above himsel, spreading his wings far and wide and becoming a richt nuisance. Mibbe it's time tae up oor efforts and catch the deil aince and for aw. Lik I said, it's aye been Crichton's ambition. Him and Steel hae history so leaving Crichton in Lesmahagow, close by Steel's farm micht jist provide the richt opportunity. I'll send Sergeant Bennet official word o his responsibilities afore I leave."

McCann bowed and didn't argue.

John Crichton's eyes opened. He blinked, blinked again then stared up at the low white ceiling. The cracked patterns he'd had as company during his many weeks of pain were gone. He closed his eyes and felt anxious. He opened his eyes again and slowly looked round the room. This isna the garrison hospital. So whaur am ah? Whit am ah dain here?

"Woken up then?"

He turned his head towards the voice and recognised his platoon sergeant.

Sergeant Bennet loomed over Crichton and nodded at the captain's confused expression. "Ye've been oot o this world fur days. Near deid if the truth be tellt. Ye wur brocht in by a carrier whae found ye unconscious, soaked tae the skin, and slumped ower yer horse on the road oot o Glesca."

Crichton stared up at the round, honest face. "Bennet?"

"Ay. Ah'm in chairge here. Been tellt tae luk aifter ye an see ye mak a guid recovery."

"And then whit?" Crichton croaked.

"Ye're back as platoon captain lik afore, patrollin this district wi special instructions frae the commander tae luk oot fur yer freend John Steel. Claverhoose sent me official word. Captain McCann is bein kept at Douglas Castle meantime. Somethin tae dae wi roundin up extra rebels. Noo first things first. Hoo aboot a bite tae eat?"

Crichton nodded.

"Richt. Ah'll run doon tae the inn and tell ane o the lassies tae bring ye some broth." Bennet turned and hurried away to spread the news that Crichton was now awake and needed help with washing and feeding.

Jessie McPhail refused to attend Crichton again. No amount of persuasion or threats from the innkeeper would move her. Finally the man's wife reluctantly agreed to take over.

"On yer ain heid be it," Jessie snapped then flounced back into the kitchen and banged the door shut.

Sergeant Bennet returned to Crichton and found the captain had managed to sit up. His recovery seemed well and truly underway.

Chapter Twelve

The Hawthorns talked long and sounded anxious about their next step, asking more questions about how John might help them find a ship bound for Holland, wanting to know who might he approach, how long would it take. John did his best to reassure them but it was some time since he'd spoken with any ship's captain let alone one sympathetic to the cause. Time had moved on. There was no guarantee if this plan would work let alone go as smoothly as he said. As for Elsie Spreul, he'd need to find where her aunt lived but he suspected this might be easier than finding a ship owner willing to take three runaways.

It was almost midnight before Helen and Elsie admitted they'd had enough and allowed Marion to lead them through to bed in the spare room. Once the two women had gone Jonas and Jamie seemed happy enough to stop talking and lie down beside the fire. At last John and Marion could go to bed themselves.

Marion lifted the lamp from the kitchen table and signed for John to follow.

Once down the hall to their own room she surprised him by pushing him inside, snapping the door shut, and pointing towards the bed. John stepped forward only to have his eager smile disappear when she placed the lamp on the blanket kist then turned her no nonsense face towards him. "Richt, ah ken whit ye said aready but tell me again. The hale thing frae stert tae feenish aboot oor veesitors."

They sat together at the top of the bed. John said nothing at first then slowly began to explain how the past few weeks had unravelled. It took a long time. Whatever he said seemed to lead to more questions about the why and the wherefore. And when Marion burst out with, "Will ye nivver learn?" he could only shrug and shake his head.

Eventually it all proved too much. Marion's eyes closed and she slumped against his chest. Now she lay in his arms, silent at last apart from a few gentle snores.

John sighed, glad that the grilling had stopped but well-aware that she hadn't finished with him yet.

Moonlight crept through the cracks in the shutters to send slivers of light across the patchwork quilt at the foot of the bed. Their pale glimmer reminded him of that night he'd recently spent on the bank of the Duneaton Water, watching the moon slip in and out of racing clouds while he tried to sort out so many thoughts and fears after his fateful involvement in the Enterkin Pass rescue.

It hadn't worked out too well, that he did know.

Aince ah see Jonas an the ither twa Hawthorns safely on a boat an awa, an then see young Elsie safe wi her aunt, whit then? Thur's nae reason why that canna happen an ah'll be gled fur them. An here's me left dodgin the government withoot ony end in sicht.

The bedroom door opened and his son Johnnie's little shadow stood in the space. "Da. Ah can hear hooves comin up the track frae the road. Ah ken it's the middle o the nicht but it micht be – "

"Troopers." John jumped out of bed leaving Marion to roll over and squeal with fright. She squealed again as the word troopers registered and followed him down the hall and into the kitchen where Jamie and Jonas were stretched out on the rag-rug in front of the glowing embers of the fire.

"Up ye git." John bent down to shake them both. "Troopers. We need tae hide."

Jamie and Jonas gaped at him.

"C'mon." John pulled them upright. "This way."

They stumbled into the dark hall where John tore jackets and coats from a long, hanging rack. Next moment a wooden panel swung towards them.

"Git in." John pushed them into a tiny space and squashed in beside them while Marion pushed the panel back in place. There was a loud click; on the other side they could hear a pile of coats and jackets being hung up again.

Johnnie appeared beside his mother and held out a lighted candle. "Whit aboot the twa ladies?"

"Ay. Clever lad. Ah'll see tae them. Noo dae me a favour. Keep an ee oot in case William an wee Isabel wake up wi the noise o the troopers. We dinna want them giein onythin awa as micht hurt Pa."

Johnnie nodded.

"Whit wud ah dae withoot ye." She kissed his upturned brow, took the candle and hurried through to the spare room where

Helen Hawthorn and Elsie Spreul shared a bed.

As she opened the door both women sat up, terrified eyes stared at the guttering flame.

"Whit's wrang?" Helen whispered.

"Troopers," Marion replied, "tryin tae catch us oot. The men are hidden ahint a panel in the hall an shud be safe enoch. In a meenit ah'll huv tae open the ootside door an let the troopers in. They'll insist on searchin thru the hoose. Aifter that thur's the byre, the stable, an God kens whit else. Likely they'll want tae ken whae ye are an whit ye're dain here. Helen, ye're ma aunt frae Hamilton here on a wee visit. Elsie is yer dochter. Ither than that say nowt."

Both women blinked and nodded as a loud hammering began on the outside door.

Marion took a deep breath, lifted the heavy bar across the door, turned the key then jumped back as the door burst open and a helmeted trooper marched into her hall.

She held the candle in front of her, shielding the flame from the sudden gust of cold air. "Whit's this aboot? Frichtin folk fur nae guid reason in the middle o the nicht."

"Nae guid reason," Sergeant Bennet snapped. "Whit aboot a wantit rebel on the run and mibbe hidin here? And nae jist ony rebel but a man whae the great and the guid are vera keen tae git haud o." He smiled. "Of coorse we baith ken whae that micht be."

"Thur's nae rebel here, on the run or itherwise."

Bennet took a step closer. "And whit aboot yer guid man? Is Maister Steel nae a wantit felon wi 1000 merks on his heid?"

"John Steel isna here. Ah huvna seen him in months as nae doubt yer spies and maisters are aware. God sakes, we can haurly chainge oor claes withoot ye kennin the vera meenit." She glared at his red face. "Onyway, whaur's Captain McCann? He's a man wi better manners that disna arrive at sic an ungodly hoor, makin a noise an fuss as terrifies ma bairns."

Sergeant Bennet flushed. "McCann's awa on important business. Ah'm in chairge, wi official permission tae search this hoose and ootbuildings at ony time ah choose, includin the middle o the nicht. But rest assured ah've nae intention o terrifyin ony bairns."

"Git on wi it then." Marion turned and marched into the kitchen and began building up the fire again. "The sooner ye stert the sooner ye'll feenish."

Bennet stood in the doorway watching her for a moment then waved his men forward to begin the search they'd done so many times before.

In a few minutes they were back. "Twa boys and a wee bairn in ane room. Twa wummin we huvna seen afore in anither. The bed in the big room is empty."

"Of coorse it is," Marion said. "It's mine. An afore ye ask the twa wummin are relatives frae Hamilton here on a wee visit. Ah tak it that's nae against the law?"

"Mind yer tongue maam," Bennet frowned. "Whit aboot the ither buildings? Mibbe Maister Steel's hidin oot ther thinkin he's safe?" He turned back to the troopers crowding the hall. "Ivvery ootbuilding, ivvery corner and watch oot for yon collie dug. It's nipped a wheen as got ower close."

"Here." Marion held out a lantern she'd lit. "This'll help ye see thur's naethin untoward aboot this farm."

One of the troopers took the lantern and led the way as the platoon spread through the courtyard, poking into corners, disturbing the cows in the byre, sticking sword points into the hay in the stable, alarming the sheep in the back pen, even setting the hens into a loud cackle before returning to report, "Nae sign o Maister Steel or ony ither fugitive."

"Whit did ah tell ye?" Marion sounded defiant. "Ye're wastin yer time an effort wi aw this nonsense."

"So ye say." Bennet smiled. "But trust me, Maister Steel's days o freedom are numbered. Aince Captain Crichton is back on the job it'll aw chainge."

"Crichton?" Marion's voice almost trembled. "Whaur is he?"

"Recoverin at oor billet in the village aifter an incident in Glesca. He wis sair hurt but on the mend noo. Ye'll soon huv the pleesure o seein him again, maist likely ivvery day, for he's awfy keen tae catch up wi yer man."

Marion stood on the doorstep watching while the troopers re-mounted and clattered out the courtyard. As the sound faded into the distance she walked through the archway and a few yards down the track, staring into the night trying to make sure they were up on the road heading back to the village. It was too dark to make out any movement in the distance but gradually everything seemed to settle again. She was about to turn back to the house when an owl hooted close by. She jumped and suddenly was shaking at the thought of what might have happened. *If only,* she thought, if only they troopers hud kent hoo close they wur. Still trembling with fright she hurried back indoors.

Rain began before the platoon reached the end of the track. Once they turned onto the shale road it was driving into their faces, cold, stinging, and persistent. Hunkered down they endured an unpleasant gallop back to the village.

Once in the stable the horses took priority over the men. Each beast must be unsaddled, tack wiped and put away, wet backs and legs dried and rubbed down, and finally hay given before any of the men could see to themselves.

The commander's rules were strict and each man knew better than disobey. It didn't stop them complaining or feeling resentful after such a miserable outing. As they finished their tasks more than one man rounded on their sergeant. "Whit wis that aw aboot? Soaked tae the skin, near frozen tae death in the middle o a cauld nicht, chasin aifter a man we'll nivver catch?"

Bennet didn't seem in the least surprised at the men's anger. "Ah ken that. Ye ken that. We aw ken that. But orders are orders. Commander Claverhoose maks them and wants us tae search at aw hoors, includin durin the nicht. While ah'm in chairge that's hoo it is. If ony o ye feel lik arguin ye ken whit tae dae. And dinna forget aboot him upstairs in oor billet, snug in a warm bed, gettin the best o attention tae mak sure he recovers frae his near-death experience."

"Whit's that tae dae wi onythin?"

"Ivverythin. Jist wait till Crichton's fit enoch tae be in chairge. He's obsessed wi Maister Steel."

"Obsessed?"

Bennet nodded. "Him and John Steel gang back a lang way. Nane o it guid for Crichton. Steel hus bestit the captain an made a fool o him mair than aince. The aulder he gits the worse he gits wantin revenge. A bit lik the earl whae's aifter Maister Steel as weel. He micht be important but he's as much a pig-heided eedjit as Crichton. Rain, hail or shine the captain will huv ye oot scourin the moor nicht and day, pryin here and ther, annoyin aw kinds o

176

folk as hate us aready. Trust me, ah ken whit ah'm talkin aboot."

Marion quickly took down the coats and jackets from the hanging rack then opened the panel in the hall. "Oot ye come."

Three red-faced men stumbled out and stood gasping with relief to be out of that tiny, airless space.

"It's a guid hidey hole," John said. "But nae meant fur three."

"Tell me aboot it." Jamie wiped his sweating brow. "Mind ye, ah'd happily dae it again raither than end up captive. Ah saw whit happened tae ma faither."

"Ah think this is a warnin tae see ye on yer way afore they beggars decide tae pay us anither visit." He turned to Marion. "Did they notice Juno?"

"If they did they nivver said."

"If Crichton or McCann hud been here they wud hae recognised her an kent ah wisna far awa."

Marion smiled. "Thank yer lucky stars yon sergeant isna sae quick on the uptake."

"Ay. But ah best tak the beast back tae Waterside jist in case."

Jonas shook his head at John. "It's beyond me hoo ye pit up wi this. Comin here seemed lik a guid idea but when ah think hoo ma life wis back in Holland it feels lik time tae – "

"Gang hame." John was about to say more when Helen Hawthorn appeared in the hall. She was crying.

Marion hurried towards her and put her arms round. "The troopers are awa. Ye're safe."

Helen shook herself free. "It's no me. It's Elsie. Ane o the troopers whispered somethin in her ear that upset her."

"Did he dae onythin else?" John asked.

"Naw. But it hud her shakin, wi tears runnin doon her cheeks. Ah tried tae calm her doon but it wis nae use. The mair she shook the worse she got. An then she jist up an runs alang the hall. Ah tried tae follow but ah'm ower slow. Last ah saw wis her openin the ootside door an disappearin. She's in her nicht-shift an bare feet."

Marion gaped at Helen. "Ah nivver heard nor saw ony sign o Elsie when ah wis staundin by the courtyard entrance watchin the troopers leave. Dear God why did ye nae shout oot or somethin?"

Helen began to cry again.

"Leave the auld wummin be. Ye're makin things worse." John

ran forward to open the outer door. "Aw naw. Luk at the rain." He grabbed his jacket. "We need tae find her."

Elsie's bare feet made no sound as she ran across the cobbled courtyard. Fifty yards away Marion was staring in the opposite direction unaware of the ghost-like figure disappearing behind the stable, past the byre and across the rough ground that led to the moor.

Sharp stones and heather roots scratched and cut her toes but she felt nothing. Nor could she see anything other than faint shapes in the dark. Not that she cared where she might run so long as she kept moving, anything to escape from that trooper's whisper which seemed to be following her.

Soon the ground began to rise. It was harder to keep up the pace. By the time she reached the first ridge of the moor she was forced to a stumbling walk. But at least she was still moving. And then the rain grew heavier with large drops trickling across her brow and filling her eyes. Not that she minded. She lifted her face and welcomed their coldness, sensed a feeling of cleansing, smiled as more raindrops coursed down her burning cheeks.

By now her hair was soaked, clamped to her scalp and her thin cotton shift stuck to her body. None of it mattered. She could still hear those words, so soft, sounding almost kind, "My ye're bonnie." *If only,* she thought, if only they three words had nivver existed. If only they cud be washed awa.

The cold air and cold rain began to have an effect, sapping her strength till it was more and more difficult to keep going. She stumbled, stopped, steadied herself, managed a few more steps then simply sat down where she was and allowed the deepening chill to take her into a strange quietness where nothing seemed to matter anymore.

Only days ago she'd been happy, gainfully employed at Skirling House near Biggar, well-thought of by Sir Andrew Hislop, her employer, who appreciated her knowledge and ability with herbs and their uses. Her salves and mixtures had already benefited the whole household. With Sir Andrew's approval she'd treated two of the villagers, one for a stomach disorder, the other for constant headaches. Both had reported improvement.

After this success he'd given her extra time to develop a herb garden and ordered the gardener to lay everything out exactly as the young lady required. "Whitivver she asks jist dae it."

Malcolm the gardener had nodded, seemed happy enough to follow instructions. All went well till that morning when Elsie had gone into the room behind the laundry which had been set aside as a drying space for the herbs. Bunches of them tied with soft string, hung in rows from the low rafters, all labelled and dated, awaiting use.

She'd been reaching up for a few stalks of Colt's Foot to boil with honey to ease the cook's shortness of breath when a pair of rough hands gripped her waist and spun her round to stare into Malcolm's brown, weather-beaten face.

"Let go. Whit are ye dain?" She glared at a man with a wife, three children and a strange look in his eye.

He edged closer, hands tightening their grip as he whispered, "My ye're bonnie."

She squirmed, tried to pull away as his stubbly beard grazed her cheek. "Git awa. Dae ye hear me?" Her clenched fists rose, ready to strike but a large hand held both wrists as he deftly kicked her feet away then allowed his heavy body to follow as she fell.

His rank breath was as strong as his ability to pin her down and hold her still as a long tongue like a flicking snake forced its way into her mouth, sliding along her teeth, all the way to the back before flipping up to begin tickling the roof of her mouth. Shock was now terror, enough to make her retch. It made no difference. The tongue continued, forcing her to swallow the bile as an exploring hand joined in, tracing a route across her breasts, squeezing each one as it went. Back it came, repeating the squeeze while the other hand lifted her clear of the floor to yank up her skirt and petticoats then pull off her drawers in one well-practiced movement.

She tried to keep her legs tight together but a pair of powerful, determined knees soon forced them apart.

Even though her mouth was still full of vibrating tongue she managed a scream of sorts. In desperation she tried again, choked and passed out till a searing, burning thump within her body brought her back to her senses.

Now Malcolm seemed part of her, moving in some sort of ghastly rhythm that had her bare bottom bouncing against the earthen floor. Arms tight round her waist, his vice-like grip made sure of no escape as he thrust faster and faster, each one more painful than the last till suddenly the pulsing softened. With it came a horrible wave of warm wetness that seeped down her legs as they lay locked together and unmoving for several minutes before the hardness came back, stronger than ever, the push slower and deeper, more powerful this time.

Eyes tight closed she prayed please, someone, anyone. Please. Make this stop. Please. Someone. Anyone. Please. The words hammered in her head till it almost burst with rage and terror. Most of all was disgust at her own helplessness.

Not far away there was a shout then feet running away. Malcolm seemed to hear. He hesitated then pulled clear to release his grip round her waist.

Free of his weight she dared open her eyes. He was standing up, fastening his breeches, straightening his tousled hair, wiping his sweating brow, and still smiling at her. "My ye're bonnie." With that he turned and left.

Minutes later the scullery maid, who'd raised the alarm, arrived with the cook. There was no doubt what had happened.

Sir Andrew Hislop sat at his mahogany desk in his grand library giving a careful third reading of a letter delivered that morning. As a sympathiser of the Covenanting cause he'd turned a deaf ear to any whispers of open-air meetings that might have taken place on his estate; he'd even been fined for his own church absence on two occasions. His most daring involvement was allowing any passing preacher to shelter in one of the bothies and make sure they had a decent meal before they left. This letter would stop all that.

From now on the Privy Council was declaring each and every landowner would be responsible for any illicit field-preaching discovered to have taken place on their land. Not only that, Sir Andrew was now responsible for his tenants' proper adherence to the crown. Ignorance of any misdemeanors would be no excuse.

He was sitting worrying about this when his cook burst into the room. He stared at her flustered face. "Can ye no see I'm busy, Meg? Whitivver it is, come back later."

"It canna wait, sir. It's Miss Elsie. She's near deid. Ye need tae come."

"Whit's wrang?"

"The gardener's hud his way wi her. She's sair hurt."

"Malcolm? Malcolm Wilson?" Sir Andrew dropped the letter and jumped up from his chair. "Whaur is she?"

"This way." Meg turned and ran from the room with her employer close on her heels.

When they arrived in the herb room Sir Andrew gasped at the bundle on the floor, curled up as if trying to disappear.

"We canna git a word oot her," Meg explained.

"So hoo dae ye ken whit happened?"

Meg pointed to the scullery maid crouching beside the still figure. "Annie saw Malcolm in here astride Miss Elsie. He hud his breeches doon gien her laldy. Annie screamed fur him tae stoap but he kept goin. Thank God she hud enoch sense tae run fur help. Malcolm must huv guessed whit Annie wis aboot an taen aff afore she brocht me back wi her."

"Whaur is he noo?"

"Nae idea. Miss Elsie is oor concern."

"Indeed. See if ye can lift her intae the hoose then dae yer best. I'll seek oot the culprit."

"An deal wi him," Meg shouted as Sir Andrew strode down the gravel path towards the gate for the vegetable garden.

Malcolm Wilson was sitting on an upturned bucket at the open door of his toolshed. He puffed at a clay pipe, seemingly unconcerned as his master banged to a halt in front of him.

"Whit's the meaning o this?" Sir Andrew roared. "Miss Elsie o aw folk."

Malcolm smiled. "She wis askin fur it. If ye mind richt ye tellt me tae dae whitivver the young lady asked."

Sir Andrew gaped at him. "Ye dinna deny whit ye did?"

"Why wud ah? Lik ah said, she asked fur it. Ah jist obleeged."

"Enoch," Sir Andrew almost stuttered, "frae whit ah've seen ye near killed the pair lassie. As for asking for it, hoo dare ye even suggest sic a thing." He stepped forward as if to strike his gardener then stopped. "Ye're despicable. Deserve tae be flogged and locked up for a lang time."

Malcolm blinked at Sir Andrew. "Is that so, sir. Weel jist listen. That young lady's a clever ane, puttin me unner her spell afore askin me. Hoo cud a pair, simple man lik masel resist sic magic?"

"She did nae sic thing," Sir Andrew roared again. "Frae noo on ye're oot o here and if ye ivver dare tae show face again I'll nae be responsible for whit happens."

"Ye mean ah've lost ma job?"

"By richts I shud haund ye ower tae a magistrate."

"Are ye tellin me ah'm dismissed aifter aw they years o guid service?"

"Indeed. And conseeder yersel lucky. "

Malcolm tapped his pipe out on a stone by his feet. "If that's hoo ye feel thur's nae point in arguin." He stood up. "Lik ah said, she charmed me then asked fur it." With that he walked off and left Sir Andrew staring after him.

"As if I huvna enough tae worry aboot." Sir Andrew turned and walked slowly back to the house.

Elsie swam in and out of consciousness as Meg and Annie struggled to carry her into the big house, up the steep stairs and finally lay her down on her own bed in her own tiny room.

"Whit noo?" Annie whispered.

"We dae whit we can tae mak things better fur the pair soul. Run an fetch me a pair o big, strong scissors. Thur's a pair in the kitchen dresser drawer. An bring a bowl o warm watter, twa big towels an a square o muslin. We'll need a wee drap lavender oil as weel. Ah've a bottle in ma room that Elsie made up fur me. An mind nae a word tae onybody."

Annie hurried back with everything then watched as Meg swiftly cut Elsie from her clothes before sliding one of the towels under the shivering body. "Richt." She pointed at the dark bottle of lavender oil. "Pit ten draps in the watter. We dinna want it ower strong." She dipped the muslin cloth into the water, swished it back and forward then began a long, gentle sponging first of Elsie's face then methodically worked her way all the way to her toes, squeezing scented droplets into every crevice to remove any trace and lingering smell left by Malcolm Wilson. This done she spread the second towel to cover the scratches and blue weals on the lower body and legs. "Whit a mess." Meg shook her head. "A man. Naw. An animal. An a bad yin at that."

Sir Andrew knocked softly at the door then stepped in to see what was being done for the unconscious girl. He winced at the white face and the tight-shut, red-rimmed eyes. "A bad business. But Miss Elsie is safe noo. I've dismissed Wilson, forbade him tae set foot on ma land again."

"Is that aw?" Meg sounded annoyed. "It's the law he's needin."

"I'm thinking aboot Miss Elsie's reputation. We dinna want word getting oot. God kens whit micht be said."

"That's aw vera weel sir. But sendin fur a magistrate wud mak shair Wilson gits his due punishment. Gie a man lik that an inch he'll tak a mile." Meg sniffed. "An trust me he will." She sniffed again. "Ah'm jist sayin ye micht live tae regret bein sae easy on him."

Sir Andrew stiffened. "My concern is weel meant."

"Ah ken, sir." Meg turned to lift the pile of cut clothes then handed it to Annie. "They need tae be burned. Ivvery last scrap. We want naethin left. Intae the big range an mak shair they flare up. An mind – "

"Nae a word." Annie nodded and ran off with the bundle of cloth.

Meg gave Sir Andrew a hard stare. "If ye dinna mind me sayin, sir, ah'd git a doctor tae luk at Miss Elsie. Jist in case."

Sir Andrew frowned. "If it becomes necessary I shall. But we'll wait a day or twa. Gie things a chance tae settle doon."

Meg's eyebrows rose but she said nothing.

"It's for the best. Discretion has its place as weel." He took the key from the door and handed it to Meg. "I'd be grateful if ye'd keep an ee on the young lady. Itherwise keep the door locked. Noo I think we best alloo her some quiet. Sleep can work wonders."

"As ye wish." Meg took the key. "An rest assured it's nae problem tae luk aifter her." She lifted the patchwork quilt from the bottom of the bed, tucked it round the silent figure then obediently followed her master from the room, locked the door and returned to her kitchen with an angry face.

Sir Andrew stood a moment in the dark hallway then went back to his library, to sit at his mahogany desk and feel uneasy about how he'd dealt with Malcolm Wilson.

A full moon rose to flood the land and light up Elsie Spreul's dark little room. She woke with a start and blinked at the window where twelve twinkling panes of glass were at odds with their usual blackness. How odd. She thought about it, wondered what the garden beyond might look like, bathed in silver instead of the warmer light of day. It was a formal garden, Sir Andrew's pride and joy, with criss-crossing lines of low hedges, everything pristine with no weeds to mar the curves and angles of an intricate pattern. High stone walls had been built to protect from frost and wind and keep it exactly as the master demanded. The central path of fine, red gravel led in a straight line to an ornate metal gate which opened into the vast vegetable garden much needed to help feed a large household. Beyond this a new garden had been created, as fine a herb garden as anyone could wish for, where orderly rows of herbs flourished and allowed Elsie to dry and prepare all kinds of remedies, simple and complex to aid the many ills of body and mind. She thought of the good achieved so far then remembered something else. Something which brought terrible panic as she heard that whisper, "My ye're bonnie." She forced herself to take a slow breath, in through the nose out by the mouth; again and again till eventually it worked and those awful words began to fade. Uncle John had taught her how to do this. He'd also recognised her talent and keenness to learn the ways of the apothecary. He'd been a good teacher, Elsie a good student, happy to listen and discover how careful use of such knowledge could put most ills right.

Ay. So it can. She sat up, the sudden movement making her gasp with pain. Whit if? She glanced at the dark outline of her locked wooden medicine box sitting on the table by the window. This box held a collection of special salves and potions and infusions not regularly used. Mixtures that she stored with special care and attention. Uncle John had been insistent on the need for this extra care as well as always being prepared to deal with the unexpected. She smiled and thought of his wonderful shop in Glasgow where clients would come for advice about their ailments and leave with the right medicine. Glass jars and deep drawers were full of dried herbs and stalks and roots, easily accessible unlike the special mixtures and potions and infusions, which were always locked away. "Just in case," as Uncle John would whisper. "Better safe than sorry."

Within that box nearby nestled two tiny glass vials, each filled with an infusion of angelica, wormwood and pennyroyal leaf. A few drops of each could trigger off a woman's absent bleeding, help regulate her menstruation. Mixed together they had the power to dislodge an unwanted foetus or even remove a stillborn before it killed the mother. Tiny new seeds from the likes of Malcolm Wilson would be no problem.

Struggling out of bed she limped over to the table, took out the little key she always hid at the back of the drawer, then opened the box. There in the centre were the two vials filled with the answer she sought.

She lifted both, held them to the bright moonlight. Ane or twa? She replaced them and thought about that, then unstoppered the first vial and swallowed the vile tasting liquid in one gulp. She reached for the second then hesitated. "Aye act wi caution. Nivver exceed the richt dose." Uncle John's often repeated instructions rang in her head. She nodded and lowered the box lid.

Box re-locked, key hidden again she stumbled back to bed and flopped down to await what should happen next.

She lay for what seemed a long time before the first muscle cramp. A gentle warning. The second lasted a little longer. She clenched her fists and willed the next to come. And it did. Again and again, each one fiercer than the last till it became a tight belt of pain circling her stomach, strong as steel. Next came contractions. She gasped and gritted her teeth. No way back now and no regrets as a flow of blood began.

Aware of a seeping mess spreading below her, she lay very still, allowed it to soak through the thick soft towel, into the sheets, probably even the mattress. And then the pain eased then stopped. It must be over. Completely exhausted but relieved she finally fell asleep.

Early in the morning Meg unlocked the door and was surprised to find Elsie sitting on a tiny stool by the window. She had the patchwork quilt draped over her shoulders.

Meg glanced from the still figure to the empty bed. Even in the faint light she could see a large patch of dull red covered much of the once white sheet. "Oh." She looked back at Elsie then noticed the discarded shift lying beside the bed. It too was well soaked with the tell-tale dark stain. "Ah see ye kent whit tae dae."

"Dinna think bad o me but ah cudna jist tak ma chances. Ah hud tae – "

"Mak shair." Elsie smiled. "An so ye huv. Thank God ye hud the means. Weel done. Noo ye ken naethin else can happen an the

185

memory o yon awfy man can be pit tae the back o yer mind."

"Ah hope sae." Elsie's voice trembled. "Ah'm sorry but the bed's in a mess."

"A price worth payin fur peace o mind. We'll burn the lot."

"Whit aboot the mattress?"

"That tae. Nae problem. It's fu o straw. Annie will help me tak it oot the back by the midden an mak a big bonfire. She's as concerned as masel tae see ye richt. As fur yersel, ye need tae huv a warm soak in a richt bath, weel scented tae gie ye the fresh start ye deserve. Ah'll git it ready then gie ye a shout. Ah'll set it up in ma ain room. Ye'll be private enoch ther. Naebody tae disturb ye fur the less onybody else kens the better."

Three days passed. Sir Andrew was relieved to see how Elsie seemed almost herself, if a little pale. Neither made any mention of what had happened although he did ask if a visit from a doctor might be advisable.

"No need," was the curt answer.

From the look on her face he asked no questions and did not press the matter. After all, he'd heard nothing of Malcolm Wilson. Hopefully he'd hear no more.

A week later he was proved wrong when a strange rumour began to circulate through the village. Not just strange but dangerous. When Sir Andrew heard what was being said he remembered Meg's warning about Malcolm Wilson and wished he'd listened.

By the time one of the villagers came demanding a word he knew he'd handled the man all wrong.

The elderly woman came straight to the point. "Thur sayin Miss Elsie's a witch, workin wi magic potions which alloos her tae huv her way wi ony man she chooses. Malcolm Wilson hus been tellin ony as will listen that she mesmerised him then forced him intae dain the deil's will ower an ower again. Ye ken hoo gullible folk can be. A guid few are believin him an agreein when he says that she shud be taen frae the big hoose and dunked in the village pond tae test if she's a witch."

Sir Andrew stared in stunned silence.

"If ah wur ye, sir, ah'd dae somethin quick tae mak shair the young lady's safe. Itherwise – "

"Indeed I will."

"Aifter the guid she did fur me an did it sae kindly ah cudna staund back an nae warn ye."

Sir Andrew sent for Elsie, quickly explained the danger she was in and suggested she should return to her guardians, the Hamiltons at Crawfordjohn, at once. "We'll gang doon tae the stable, git the best horse oot. Aince ye pit a wheen miles atween yersel and here ye'll be safe enough. Aifter aw this nastiness dies doon we can think aboot ye coming back."

Elsie shook her head. "Aince awa ah'd prefer tae bide awa. It wud be best for us baith and nae mair bother."

An hour later she was away, galloping past Biggar and heading across the open moor to Crawfordjohn.

Elsie Spreul's horse had barely reached the turn off from the main road when the usual quiet of Skirling House was broken. A large stone rattled against one of the mullioned windows of Sir Andrew's fine library and made him jump. He'd been sitting at his desk, trying to make sense of what had happened. How he'd handled Wilson was bothering him, challenging his judgement. Maybe his answer was the Italian pistol lying on the desk, ready primed.

A second rattle at the window had him lifting the pistol to go downstairs and find a scared looking Meg standing in the big hallway.

"It's them, sir. Lik they said. Come fur Miss Elsie. Thank God she's awa an hauf-way hame by noo."

"Hoo dae ye ken aboot that?"

"Yon auld wummin tellt us afore she left. We aw ken sir. An wur ready tae see they dafties aff if need be."

"Thank ye. I micht need yer support." Sir Andrew opened the front door and stood on the top step to see about a dozen villagers milling about on the wide, gravel path below. From the angry sounds and faces they seemed to be in an ill mood. Several carried thick, wooden staves, one was swinging a length of coiled rope while Wilson marched up and down in front, waving a short sword, and encouraging them to chant, "The witch. The witch. Bring oot the witch!"

Sir Andrew held up his hand for quiet. It made no difference. He was forced to stand there for several minutes listening to the racket. Eventually he roared, "Nae witch lives here. Ye've come tae the wrang hoose. Dae ye hear? Nae witch lives here."

The noise stopped. Wilson now stood on the bottom step. "Ay thur is. Miss Elsie Spreul. Bring her oot or wur comin in."

Meg appeared beside Sir Andrew. "No ye're no. Ye're wastin yer time. Miss Elsie's nae here." She went half-way down the steps to defy Wilson. "Ye're a lyin rat Malcolm Wilson. Makin up awfy tales when ye ken fu weel whit really happened, whit ye did tae a defenceless lassie, hain yer way wi her, ridin the pair soul till she wis nearly deid. An dinna deny it. Ah saw the result. Ye shud think black burnin shame an no be staundin here wi yer lyin threats."

Wilson jumped up a step and swung his sword at Meg.

"Nae further." She held out her arm to stop him, met the edge of the sword's swing and screamed as blood spurted from her torn sleeve.

"Enough!" Sir Andrew came down to stand beside Meg who seemed more angry than hurt.

Eyes bulging, Wilson took another step closer.

"Enough, I said." Sir Andrew levelled his pistol. "Anither step and I shoot."

"Is that so." Wilson bared his teeth. "Ah dinna think sae. A peely-wally laird lik ye is mair lik a moose than a man." He pointed his sword at Sir Andrew's chest. "Weel?"

Whatever else he said was drowned by a blast from the pistol.

A cloud of white smoke enveloped his burly figure for a moment before he re-appeared tumbling backwards down the five bottom steps to lie crumpled on the fine raked, gravel path.

The crowd gasped, took a few steps back and stood as if unsure what to do.

Before any decision could be made Sir Andrew's manservant Ben appeared beside his master holding a heavy musket. "Oot o here the lot o ye afore onybody else gits hurt."

One of the men stepped towards the twisted shape at the foot of the steps. "Whit aboot Malcolm? He's deid wi a big hole in his chest."

"Nae mair than he deserves." Ben swung the musket towards the man. "Naebody asked him tae come here threatenin tae run his maister thru wi a sword, nivver mind the lies he's been spoutin aboot an innocent wee lass. When the sheriff comes, an he will, us as ken the truth will be tellin him that Wilson wisna alane."

The word sheriff seemed to make up the crowd's mind. Without another word they turned away and trailed back down the long gravel path.

"Thank ye." A white-faced Sir Andrew turned to his two servants. "Withoot yer help this micht hae ended raither different."

"Ah dinna think sae," Meg snapped. "The bugger threatened ye. Mair or less asked tae be shot. Ye hud nae choice. We jist backed ye up against the ither villagers. An we will again when the sheriff arrives."

Ben laid down the heavy musket and ran down to examine the body. "Definitely deid. Will ah move him somewhaur oot o sicht? His family will need tae be tellt."

"Ay. First things first. Put the body in the toolshed. Mind and lock the door, then bring me the key, jist in case. Ay. That wud be best. Aifter that find the kitchen boy and send him up tae the library tae wait while I write a letter tae Mistress Wilson stating that I'm willing tae pay for her man's funeral but only if she agrees tae confirm the truth o this maitter. I'll send for the sheriff but I suspect it'll mean a magistrate as weel."

"Lik ah said sir, ye've naethin tae fear," Meg insisted. "Whaeivver comes askin questions he'll git the truth."

"Meg's richt," Ben agreed. "But regardin the letter for Mistress Wilson, shud ah gang wi the kitchen boy when he delivers it. Jist tae mak shair thur's nae mair trouble?"

"That micht be better," Sir Andrew nodded.

"Nae problem, sir." Ben bowed as he always did, went back up the steps to lift the musket then disappeared inside the house.

"A bad business." Sir Andrew stood staring at Wilson's body. "I nivver thocht it wud come tae this."

"Ah dare say, sir," Meg sniffed. "Dinna say ah didna warn ye. Noo if ye'll excuse me, ah'll awa an see tae ma cut arm afore ah stert cookin yer dinner."

The Hamiltons were shocked enough when they heard the witch accusations. Elsie decided there was no need to add to their grief by mentioning Malcolm Wilson. He would remain her secret, pushed to the back of her mind and allowed to disappear like Meg had suggested. And she did manage this till that trooper whispered, "My ye're bonnie," and sent her back into a madness which took her out on the moor in the dark and the driving rain to sit and become ever more wet and chilled till finally numbness took over.

189

Chapter Thirteen

"Whit a nicht." John peered into a growing storm. "Atween the dark an this drivin rain ah can haurly see whaur ah'm goin. If Miss Elsie's only wearin a thin shift she's in trouble. God kens whit made her run aff lik that, withoot a word tae onybody, in a strange place, in the middle o the nicht."

"Soonds lik madness tae me," Jamie replied as he and Jonas trudged along behind John.

"Ay," Jonas said, "ah've hud some bad times masel but nivver been driven lik that."

"Count yersel lucky," John said between gritted teeth. "But richt noo we need tae find her afore the cauld an wet dis her real harm. She didna pass Marion, an she's no in the byre, the stable, an the sheds so she must be somewhaur on the moor. We'll try a bit further; up the hill by the wee birch wood."

They trudged on in silence, climbing the steep path to the first ridge of the moor. By the time they reached it they were soaked and cold themselves.

"We'll gang tae the edge o the wood then turn. Ah canna see her managin ony further. She husna been awa that lang." Head down John plodded on till they passed the dripping birch trees. "Richt, that'll dae." He made to turn when only a few feet away he saw the white shape, curled up as if asleep on a comfortable bed instead of rough heather. "Got ye." He bent, scooped up the cold, wet figure and began running back down the way they'd come, leaving Jonas and Jamie to slither and slip as they tried to keep up.

An unconscious Elsie was handed over to Marion and Helen, stripped from her sodden shift, rubbed all over with a thick towel then put to bed, surrounded by hot bricks and tucked under extra blankets.

"Luk at her," Marion whispered. "Pair lassie. Whitivver brocht this on hus near killed her." She hurried away and quickly came back with a large bowl, a steaming kettle, and a small basket filled with what looked like crinkly, dry leaves. "We'll sprinkle some o they dried herbs in this bowl, pour ower the hot watter then wait a meenit fur them tae tak effect afore stertin tae sponge her doon wi a saft cloth. Addin some chamomile, feverfew an lavender will dae a lot o guid tae ease ony discomfort within an withoot."

"Ah've aised lavender but nivver onythin else," Helen admitted. "Ye seem weel versed in whit's needed. Ah've often thocht it wud be guid tae learn but ah've nae idea whit tae gaither let alane hoo tae aise them."

"It's nae difficult. Ma mither showed me, same as her mither. We've aye done it. Aince Miss Elsie opens her een ah'll try an persuade her tae tak a spoonfu o ma special mixture. By the luks o her she's on the verge o fever." Marion took a small dark bottle from her apron pocket. "The mixture's in wi some honey an easy tae slide ower."

"Ye made this up yersel?" Helen looked impressed. "Whit's in it or is it a secret?"

"Not at aw. Dried valerian, skullcap an mistletoe ground intae a fine powder. Mind ye, ah'm aye carefu wi the balance, keepin it even, yin alang wi the ither. Aifter that ah jist heat them in guid clean watter then leave it aw tae settle owernicht afore strainin the liquid thru a muslin cloth an intae a bottle wi honey sittin at the bottom."

"Soonds complicated."

"Naw, naw ye jist tak yer time an bide carefu." Marion hesitated. "Ah dinna usually talk aboot it. Folk are keen enoch fur help when they need it but thur superstitious as weel, if ye ken whit ah mean? Ah believe Miss Elsie kens a lot aboot herbs an worked wi them in the big hoose whaur she wis employed. Likely she hud tae be carefu as weel."

"An luk whit happened. Named fur a witch."

"Ay that wis worse than terrible but ah've a feelin thur's mair tae it than that."

"Whit dae ye mean?"

Marion frowned. "We'll mibbe find oot when she comes tae. Or mibbe no." She trailed her fingers through the floating leaves then sniffed the rising perfume. "The watter's ready. We best git stertit."

By midday Elsie's temperature was down, her face less flushed, her breathing easier and the shivering had almost stopped. Her two carers sat by the bed and felt their long hours of constant care was making a difference.

John took Jonas and Jamie with him when he led his precious Juno to Waterside farm for safe keeping, away from the prying eyes of troopers. He also wanted to ask his brother-in-law Gavin about contacting Gus McPhail, the carrier, as soon as possible.

The Weirs were keen to hear what had happened since they last saw John but horrified to learn about Enterkin and the loss of Jamie's father.

"Whit if ye wur seen? Mibbe even recognised?" Gavin frowned at John. "Ye need tae stoap drawin attention. Ane o they days – "

"It'll aw be ower an we can luk back an be gled."

"So ye say. But richt noo things are gettin worse. If we want tae survive we need tae – "

"Bide ane step aheid," John smiled, "which means ah've they twa tae sort oot wi passage tae Holland an then find a safe hoose fur a wee lass we brocht back wi us frae Gilkerscleugh Hoose."

"Mibbe we cud help wi the wee lass?" Gavin's wife Janet suggested.

"That's kind o ye but ah made a promise."

"Ye nivver stoap, dae ye?" Janet shook her head.

"As it turned oot ah hudna muckle option. But tae git back tae Gus McPhail, ah wis thinkin we cud travel intae Glesca on his cairt. He often gies folk a lift. It shudna draw attention."

Gavin frowned again at John. "If that's whit ye want ah'll gang intae the village an wait fur him comin back wi his deliveries then let ye ken whit he says."

"Fine. He's richt helpfu so it shudna be a problem. Richt noo ah'll awa oot tae the stable fur a meenit an mak sure Juno's aricht afore we leave." John nodded to Jonas and Jamie. "Back in a tick."

Once John left the room Gavin turned to the two visitors. "Ah ken John's dain his best tae help ye." He nodded towards Jamie. "Goin abroad wi the chance o a fresh stert soonds sensible." Now he turned to Jonas. "An it's great ye're in a position tae help yer cousin mak that stert. An dinna git me wrang, ah wish ye baith weel, but findin passage oot the country micht nae be sae easy at the meenit. As fur John, weel, whiles he taks on mair than he shud, if ye git ma meanin?"

Jamie and Jonas looked uncomfortable. "He insists. He's nae the easiest man tae argue wi."

"Ay weel, that's true. Jist try an mak shair he disna tak mair risks than he shud."

As they made their way along the track from Waterside Jonas repeated what Gavin had said. "Ah dinna think he's best pleased wi us twa."

John laughed. "Dinna mind him. He worries ower much. He means weel. But whitivver ah decide ah decide fur masel. Ah said ah wantit tae help ye so nae worries. Mind ye, richt noo ah'm wunnerin if tryin tae seek oot Miss Elsie's aunt is the richt thing tae dae while the wee lass is sae poorly."

"Mibbe we shud aw wait an see hoo she dis?" Jamie suggested. "Dinna forget ma mither agreed tae come wi us tae Holland an richt noo she's helpin yer wife wi the nursin."

"Ay weel. We'll see. But hingin aboot here isna a guid idea. Nae wi as mony troopers searchin here an ther at aw hoors o the day an nicht. That's whit's botherin Gavin an hud him speakin oot lik that." John pointed off to the right. "That way. Withoot the horse we'll gang back by the birch wood. It's quicker."

They walked on in silence till they reached the wood which was perched high above Westermains farm. They'd just stepped out from the tree shelter when John suddenly stopped and stared.

"It wis only hoors ago." Jonas sighed. "An thur back."

John reversed into the shadows. "Ay, an nowt we can dae aboot it but wait here an watch. It's the name o the game."

"Game?" Jonas looked puzzled. "Whit game?"

"Cat an moose." John smiled and leant against a tree trunk. "When the cat's awa the moose will play. The law's the cat. Ah'm the moose."

Jonas shrugged and looked at Jamie.

Jamie nodded. "John's richt. That's whit happened tae ma faither except that parteeclar moose wis caught an it didna end weel."

Jonas stared from one to the other. "Ah dinna unnerstaund, an ken whit, ah dinna want tae. Ah feel fur ye, whit ye've been thru, whit's happenin, whit's ahint it. But ye need tae luk at it frae ma point o view. Back in Holland – "

"Ye dae things different," John said, "an if ah'm honest mibbe ye dae it better."

Jonas opened his mouth as if to reply then nodded and shrugged again before sitting down on a pile of stones to watch the soldiers below go through their routine inspection of the farm yet again.

Sergeant Bennet marched into the back bedroom of Westermains and stopped short at the sight of an unconscious Elsie Spreul tucked up in a small truckle bed. "Whit's up wi her? Bit sudden is it no?"

"An doon tae yer men." Marion followed him into the room. "Durin yer last visit ane o yer troopers frichted her that sair she ran ontae the moor in aw yon rain. We hud an awfy job findin her. She wis oot there in her shift, lyin on a patch o heather, soaked tae the skin, near frozen tae death. She husna opened her een yit."

"Ma men are weel disciplined. They wudna."

"Is that so?" Helen Hawthorn looked up from her seat beside the little bed. "Ah wis ther an saw ane o yer men whisper in the lass's ear. Aifter that thur wis nae reasonin wi her."

"In that case ah need a word." Sergeant Bennet glared at Helen. "Come wi me and point oot the culprit."

Helen looked scared and glanced at Marion.

Marion nodded and stood aside to let them pass into the hall and out into the farmyard.

Sergeant Bennet marched into the centre of the farmyard and roared. "Ivvery man back here and line up."

The men returned and one asked, "Whit's wrang?"

Sergeant Bennet ignored the question and turned to Helen. "Weel?"

"That yin." She pointed towards a young man in the middle of the line-up.

"Richt. Ivverybody back tae work except Meikle." The sergeant waited till his men had resumed their search then signalled the young man to step forward. "Ah've hud a complaint aboot ye."

"Sir." Meikle stiffened.

"This wummin says ye frichted a young lass durin oor last inspection. Is that true?"

Meikle's face grew red. "Ah nivver touched her. Ah jist tellt her she wis richt bonnie."

"Naethin else?"

"Naw sir. Ah wudna dare."

Sergeant Bennet turned to Helen Hawthorn. "Ther ye are. As ah thocht, a fuss aboot naethin. Git back indoors an keep sic tittle-tattle tae yersel in future. Whitivver's wrang wi yon lass hus nowt tae dae wi ma men." He turned back to his trooper. "Awa ye go and frae noo on dinna speak tae they farm-folk unless ye huv permission. Ony inspection taks place wi yer mooth ticht shut. Unnerstood?"

Meikle saluted and scuttled off with obvious relief.

"Whit happened?" Marion asked as soon as Helen returned.

"The young trooper said he tellt Miss Elsie she wis richt bonnie but naethin else."

"An that wis enoch tae set her aff. Weel, weel." Marion lowered her voice to a soft whisper. "Did ye notice onythin when we sponged her doon?"

Helen flushed. "Bruises on baith inside legs." She stopped and looked away. "They kinda marks made me think somethin bad happened tae yon wee lass."

Marion nodded. "Seems lik the witch story is only pairt o it. Mair's the peety."

Elsie Spreul slowly opened her eyes and looked up to see a white-painted ceiling in place of the dark, swirling sky of before. She blinked. Ay. A ceiling. She thought about this then moved her toes. They felt warm and comfortable, no longer gripped by the icy power she'd welcomed and allowed to hold her still. She blinked again. "Whaur am ah?"

A soft voice said, "Ye're in bed in Westermains farm. It's me, Marion Steel beside ye. Naethin tae worry aboot."

Elsie felt a hand gently squeeze hers in an encouraging sort of way but still nothing made sense. "Whit happened?" Her whisper was faint, barely there yet none the less insistent.

"Ye've nae been weel." The hand squeezed again. "But ye're safe noo." Marion continued to hold the girl's limp hand till the dark-rimmed eyes seemed willing to accept her answer. She gave another gentle squeeze and spoke again. "Ye've nae been weel an need a wee drap medicine tae help ye feel better. Ah've the vera thing here. A wee spoonfu o somethin special. Will ye trust me an tak it?"

Elsie hesitated then her lips parted enough for Marion's spoon to slide over her tongue. The sweetness of honey only just disguised the bitter herb taste. Her eyes widened as she coughed and stared up at Marion.

"It'll dae ye nae harm only guid. Ah promise. Nae worries. Jist alloo yersel tae let go. Mibbe huv a wee sleep. Ye'll like that. Aifterwards ye'll feel better. Much better." Marion's voice rose and fell in a gentle rhythm.

Elsie's eyes closed. Her head slid sidewards on the pillow as she appeared to obey.

"That's it," Marion continued, "ye're perfectly safe. Naethin here will hurt ye. Naethin tae worry aboot." Now she took a damp herb-infused cloth and spread it across Elsie's brow. "That's it. Jist alloo yersel tae let go." Her voice came more slowly, each word softer than the next. "Ye're perfectly safe. Naethin tae worry aboot."

The room remained quiet as Marion sat watching and waiting till the tense lines on the girl's face smoothed away. She smiled and turned to a round-eyed Helen by her side. "She'll sleep weel enoch noo. When she wakens ah'll gie her anither spoon o the mixture."

"Ah've nivver seen the like," Helen admitted. "Ye hud her dain jist whit ye wantit. Ah'm shair it wis aw fur the best." She hesitated. "But ithers micht see it different."

"Ay weel." Marion nodded. "An whae's tae tell them?"

"Nae me." Helen leant forward to tuck the edge of the patchwork quilt under the sleeping girl's chin.

The next time Elsie opened her eyes Marion was relieved to see less pain staring out from them. She leant forward and said, "Feelin better?"

These two words chimed. And that voice. Elsie blinked. Of course, it was the same one she'd heard before she fell asleep. That voice had whispered, "Jist let it go." It hadn't made sense. Why should it? But in spite of herself she'd obeyed. Even now she didn't know why. It still didn't make sense. And yet?

She sighed and watched Marion Steel take a small, dark bottle from her apron pocket and give it a gentle shake before lifting a horn spoon from the bedside table. Spoon? Dark bottle? Ay. They gang thegither. Ay. Ah mind a bitter-sweet mixture sittin on ma tongue afore ah fell asleep. Ay. It wis Marion as gave me it. Ay. And then she whispered yon strange words aboot lettin go and feelin better. Ay. And ah dae feel better.

As Marion turned towards the bed she saw Elsie watching her. Their eyes met and neither said a word as a moment of understanding passed between them before they both smiled.

Chapter Fourteen

James Renwick ran through the gathering dusk as if his life depended on it. Well he might, for not far behind came the harsh clang of metal hooves on a gravelly track.

Swerving past close-growing tree trunks he forced a way through tangles of undergrowth as trailing lengths of brambles tried to catch hold.

The past two hours had gone well. A good crowd had turned out to hear him preach on the edge of Cambusnethan estate. Word had been widely passed and many were persuaded to make the effort and find out what this defiant young minister might say. Each person came at a risk. If caught it could mean a fine, imprisonment, even a pistol to the head and no questions asked.

Renwick was well prepared and didn't disappoint, mixing the power of the Word to good effect as he reinforced his condemnation of a rogue king backed up by a corrupt government. His congregation heard the challenge to resist, to show how God's truth could sweep away this evil. Shocked into listening they paid attention and were almost lost in its meaning till a runner arrived shouting, "Troopers. Git awa sir. The law kens whaur ye are."

Everyone moved at once, scattering in all directions.

Thomas Houston ran beside his friend Renwick, heading towards the top of the slope. From there they should have a clear view down to the River Clyde where a small rowboat would wait to take them across. Except the ferryman wasn't due till midnight which was still a few hours away. Meanwhile they needed to find a hiding place before the soldiers caught up with them.

Houston hesitated at the top of the ridge and pointed. "Luk. Haufway doon. Aff tae the left. An auld hay-shed. It's beside the track leading tae yon farm by the river. Dae ye see it? Ahint the drystane dyke." He pointed again. "Jist whit we need. A grand clump o thick broom bushes, thick enoch for us twa tae disappear. C'mon." He began to slither down the steep slope.

As they passed the ramshackle shed Renwick looked at the stacks of hay. "Whit aboot in there?"

"Naw, naw." Houston kept running. "If the troopers come oot

at the top o the slope they'll see the shed and want tae check it oot. If they dae they'll be that busy poking aboot the hay they'll nivver notice the broom."

Renwick had no reason to doubt for basic fieldcraft was still beyond him, although he was doing his best to learn.

Once over the rough stone wall they jumped in among the broom bushes, pushing into the centre before collapsing in an exhausted heap.

Lieutenant Colonel Winram was not in a good mood. Today had demanded far too much physical effort when he preferred his desk and papers where he could show his strategic prowess instead of galloping here and there on the off chance that a tip-off might prove worthwhile.

He'd already dented his fine helmet against low-hanging branches which hadn't improved his mood.

At the top of the hill Winram stopped his horse, checked the area below and fixed on the old hayshed. "That micht be worth a luk." He began to lead his men down the slope towards the old building.

The door was torn open and he studied the piled-up hay. "Richt." He drew his sword and signalled. The troopers obeyed and dismounted to begin stabbing into the hay.

Nothing happened. No screams.

"Mibbe a roasting is the answer." Winram snapped at his sergeant. "Git oot yer tinderbox and dae the needfu."

"Whit aboot the farmer?" the sergeant dared. "He'll be left withoot feedin fur his beasts."

"Nae doubt." Winram's tight little mouth formed a line like a rat-trap. "And whit aboot oor duty tae the law? Git on wi it."

The first few strands of straw stuttered and seemed reluctant to light. The sergeant tried again. This time he achieved a few wisps of smoke. "Richt. Needs must." He crumpled up the receipt for last night's stabling, lit it then thrust it deep into the straw.

At first he thought he'd failed again then a huge flame shot out to singe his face and fill the space above.

He leapt backwards and fell over while the horses reared with fright. Taken by surprise the men struggled to control the beasts as the sudden heat and flames grew fierce, rising higher and higher, roaring like some ill-intentioned monster. Finally the shaky roof fell in and the whole building seemed to implode, scattering multi-coloured sparks high into the darkening sky.

This hardly seemed to satisfy Winram who now turned towards the farm. "We micht huv mair success there."

A woman who'd witnessed the incident from an upstairs window of the nearby farm wept as she watched the long line of troopers wheel round and begin to trot towards her house. Whit huv we done tae deserve this? She wiped her eyes and hurried downstairs to give her husband the news that his precious store of hay had disappeared while he sat dozing and enjoying a pipe after a long day's work.

In a minute a loud rap at the door would announce the arrival of a military invasion to tramp through every corner of the house along with question after question, possibly even abuse when the so-called law enforcers heard the farmer and his wife insist they'd seen nothing of any rebel, heard nothing.

"That wis a vile thing tae dae." Houston peered through the fronds of broom and studied the black, smoking skeleton of the shed. "And the heat. We were near burned oorsels."

"Indeed." Renwick nodded. "And the Lord disna luk wi favour on sic an action."

"Pair farmer. He's done naethin and luk whit he's lost."

Renwick reached inside his jacket and took out a small cloth pouch. "There's four guilders here. It's aw I huv left frae ma time in Holland. Mibbe it'll gang some way tae mak amends. I'll leave the pouch on the farm doorstep on oor way by."

"But if that's the last o yer money?"

"Nae worries. The Lord nivver asks mair than he's aready given. Onyway, I ken he'll provide. He aye does."

Houston's eyebrows rose but he said nothing.

Renwick didn't seem to notice and lay back with his head resting on his leather bag. "Whit wi the sermon and the excitement o the chase thru yon wood I'd like a bit quiet." With that he closed his eyes and seemed to fall asleep with no effort.

Houston studied the pale face with the calm expression. Folk say he's wise beyond his years. Ay weel, mibbe. He shook his head and began to wonder how well he really knew this strange young man.

The military commander barked an order, then came a loud

banging on the farmhouse door. This was followed by a long silence before the sound of hooves came past the smoking shed. This time Houston dared to stand up and check if the soldiers really were leaving.

He sighed with relief and sat down again. Renwick was still asleep as if nothing had ever been amiss. Houston watched him for a few minutes. *Luk at him. Nae a quiver, nae sign o fear, or even worry, and here's me scared witless. Hoo dis he dae it?*

Now that everything was quiet he became aware of tiny sounds around his feet. He looked down at the carpet of dried leaves but saw nothing. This had him imagining whose tiny feet might be scratching or burrowing. Thinking about this seemed to calm him down until a green frond directly above bent with the weight of a landing bird and made him glance up. A fat, black shape gently swayed above his head, studied him with a bright yellow eye then lost interest and flapped into the air again. *If only*, he wished. *If only I cud dae that and flee awa.*

He thought again about the farmer and felt doubly sorry. *And whit aboot the law? Back there at Cambusnethan they hud near captured Renwick in the middle o his sermon. If they'd got haud, he'd be on his way tae the Tollbooth at Hamilton, no lying here dreaming aboot his next sermon. And he's guid at it. His fame as a preacher is weel deserved. Nane better. Nae wonder he attracts sic big crowds. And the way he condemns baith King and government. That seems tae hit hame and fire up the folk.*

Houston was right, the Privy Council were determined to stop this rebel fanatic with his message of subversion. New laws had been passed against field-preaching along with harsher penalties for anyone caught attending such an event. Many people had already suffered, some more than others, yet Renwick kept going, and seemed prepared to accept it was a price worth paying.

From this meeting at Cambusnethan Renwick had arranged to visit Logan House beyond Lesmahagow to stay with his friend and supporter Wylie McVey. Houston was wary of this. He remembered what had happened last time when Renwick drafted a declaration against King and state while McVey made sure that a crowd of supporters would travel with him to Lanark and help pin the offending paper on the Mercat Cross. The result had reverberated throughout the country, extra patrols had scoured here and there, arrests had been made, and one man hanged while Lanark itself suffered a heavy fine for not resisting this rebellious act. And Renwick hadn't yet become an ordained minister. Now that he had full spiritual authority what might he be planning?

Renwick and Houston left the clump of broom and made their way past the silent farmhouse where Renwick left his guilders beside the doorstep before they moved on to the next bend in the river.

All around were open fields which would be too exposed to cross in daylight but thanks to heavy clouds making the growing dusk even darker it seemed no problem.

When they reached the spot where they were supposed to meet the ferryman they saw that the curve of the river had formed a narrow shingle below a steep bank with a grassy overhang. Pleased with this find they jumped down and settled against the wall of soft soil. They began to relax and listen to the quiet surge of the deeper water and the gentle trickle over tiny stones at the shingle edge.

There was no movement on the opposite bank but neither felt impatient nor doubted that the faint shape of the tiny boat tied on the far bank would soon make its way towards them.

Exhaustion gradually took over. Houston closed his eyes, was almost asleep when a soft, muffled sound disturbed this pleasant feeling. Opening his eyes he stared round, saw nothing but his ears were telling him different as the sound of something steady, quiet, and heavy seemed to come closer. Now he could feel a slight tremor in the overhang. He glanced up as several lumps of soil hit his brow.

Only yards away two troopers were guiding their horses along the stretch of river nearest to the Cambusnethan estate.

"Winram and his daft ideas," one of the troopers growled. "It's aw vera weel fur the likes o the commander eatin a fine dinner an sittin by a warm fire while us twa are oot in the dark patrollin this damned riverbank on the off chance that yon rebel preacher's still hingin aboot, waitin tae be caught."

The horses stopped directly above Renwick and Houston. The weight of beast and man pushed into the soft grass, the overhang seemed to move and several lumps of soil rattled down to the stony shingle.

"Step back afore ye sink in." The first trooper pulled on his horse's reins.

Both reversed back a few feet then stopped when the first trooper pointed across the wide stretch of river. "Cud that wee shape ower ther be a boat?"

"Ah think sae," the second trooper agreed, "an afore ye ask, it's on the ither side. Oor orders are tae check alang this bank. Onyway, it's maist likely fur fishermen aifter salmon."

"If ye say so," the first trooper laughed. "Walk on. We've a mile or twa tae cover yit."

Houston waited till the soft sound of the hooves on grass faded away before he stood up and peered into the dark. "They're weel awa. Thank guidness. That wis close."

"We were nivver in ony danger." Renwick smiled and stood up. "Ye need tae trust mair, ma freend."

Houston turned to answer when he saw the shape of the tiny boat slowly edging towards them. "Hoo did that happen?" He stepped towards the water's edge.

"Evenin sirs." A soft voice spoke as the boat's prow scraped onto the stones. "Rab Mitchell at yer service." A small, stocky figure jumped from the boat and held out a hand in welcome. "Ah'm a bit late but ah saw yon twa troopers on the prowl an thocht it best tae wait till they moved on. Nae point in drawin attention."

"Indeed," Houston agreed. "Can we go noo?"

"Nae problem. Step aboard ma wee skiff. Twa meenits an ye'll be on the ither side."

Mitchell was as good as his word then they were out the boat helping to pull it onto the bank.

"Whit noo?" Houston asked.

"Ah'm yer guide," Mitchell replied. "Jist follow me an dinna hing back. Ah'm takin ye tae Dalserf manse. The meenister's nae at hame but his hoosekeeper's expectin ye wi a bed ready an somethin tae eat if ye're hungry."

"Hoo come?" Renwick sounded surprised. "I wisna aware o special arrangements ither than a wee skiff tae cross the river."

"Yer freend Maister McVey sent word tae the meenister, maist parteeclar. He also arranged fur twa horses tae be ready come mornin. Mak the nixt bit o yer journey tae Logan Hoose a bit easier."

"And we're maist grateful," Renwick replied. "Lead on."

The walk to Dalserf Manse seemed to take forever, or maybe Renwick and Houston's earlier exertions were catching up on them. They certainly seemed relieved when Mitchell said, "Nearly ther," then turned away from the riverbank to follow a tree-lined path, past a graveyard then on towards the dark outline of a church beside a cluster of houses. "Yon's the manse." He pointed to a flickering candle in a window nearby.

The door opened. A woman holding a storm lantern stood in the space. "In ye come an welcome."

The door clicked shut as soon as they stepped over the threshold.

"This way." They were led along a narrow passage and into a warm room where two oil lamps glowed at either end of a large square table in the middle of the room. A black-leaded range took up most of the near wall, its fire-basket glowing with carefully arranged lumps of peat. Beyond this everything else remained lost in deep shadow

The woman placed her lantern on the table then turned to introduce herself. "Ah'm Mary Mowat, sister tae the rascal as brocht ye here. Me an ma man Andra luk aifter the Reverend. He's awa visitin his auld mither in the toun. She disna keep weel. Ma Andra taen him in the trap yesterday aifternoon. They baith send thur apologies an hope awthin's tae yer likin."

Renwick made a polite bow. "We're real pleased tae be here and thank ye for sic generous hospitality."

"Ye're in safe haunds so ah'll awa." Mitchell spoke suddenly. "Come mornin ah'll huv yer horses ready." He ducked into the shadows and was gone before Renwick or Houston could thank him.

"Nivver heed," Mistress Mowat said. "It's jist his way. But he means weel."

"And he did weel by us," Renwick said. "We must say so in the morning."

"He'll like that." Mistress Mowat smiled. "Noo, whit aboot a bite tae eat? Ah can offer ye stew an dumplins."

Both men nodded.

"Richt then." She opened the oven door at the side of the range, wrapped a thick towel round her hands before lifting out a round metal pot which she placed on the table. "Platters are ahint ye on the dresser, spoons as weel. Fetch them ower while ah cut some hunks o fresh-baked bread."

Within a minute a pile of thick bread filled a basket beside two wooden platters now brimming with meat, vegetables and topped with a large dumpling.

Houston leant forward to sniff the appetising smell. He lifted his spoon then remembered and laid it down again.

"Ay." Renwick frowned. "First things first." He began to say grace and give thanks for their deliverance from the troopers.

"Amen tae that," Mistress Mowat added then smiled at the two hungry expressions. "When did ye last eat?"

"Afore first licht this morning," Houston replied. "Bannocks and cheese wi a mug o spring watter courtesy o a farmworker on the Cambusnethan estate."

"Time ye hud somethin mair substantial inside ye then. Aifter that yer beds are made up and waitin."

James Renwick lay on a soft bed, covered by a thick blanket and a hot stone-pig tucked in at his back. This was real comfort compared to the past few weeks when he'd attended meeting after meeting, sleeping rough or in a barn, sometimes forced to travel under cover of darkness to avoid the government patrols that seemed to be everywhere.

He thought about the sermon back at Cambusnethan when the troopers had appeared and forced him to flee. Instead of worrying how they knew where to come he had been concerned about disappointing his congregation.

Since the day he'd parted from John Steel and Jonas Hawthorn on the Glasgow Road Renwick had been to the capital and presented his credentials to the Societies. They'd welcomed him and been delighted to have their student back as an ordained minister. Word was sent out to all members inviting them to a formal meeting where he'd be officially appointed as their official voice to carry the cause forward against this renegade government.

So far he'd done well. Wherever he travelled people came, and listened, and seemed heartened by his challenging message and determination to succeed. The size of the crowds increased with each meeting. It also created its own problem as the law upped the patrols in their effort to capture him. So far he'd managed to remain one step ahead but life on the run was testing his nerves and physical stamina; and of course the weather hadn't been kind either.

Mibbe I cud tak time oot at Logan House and build up my strength again. Ay. And use the time tae prepare anither declaration against King and government. Wylie McVey certainly thinks it's time we had anither yin. Time the hale country taen notice and condemned sic cruelty being meted oot in the name o the law.

As for some o the meenisters. Whit are they up tae? Instead o supporting me they've been questioning my ordination because it taen place in anither country wi foreign meenisters daing the needful. They've been tellt braw plain it wis properly done according tae Kirk law but they jist shake their heids. And it's nae as if I huvna reminded them aboot oor way furrit being mair important than ony differences we micht huv. If only we cud work thegither. Ay. Jist think whit we micht achieve. Still, the Lord nivver promised me an easy road.

He slipped out of bed and crossed the bare wooden floor to stare out the tiny attic window. The first strands of dawn were beginning to show. As yet he hadn't slept.

Mibbe I'm demanding ower muckle frae ithers, dismissing ony criticism when I shud listen. This reminded him of John Steel and their last argument about Robert Hamilton, the erstwhile leader back at Bothwell Bridge. *"Whit dis he ken aboot leadin? Naethin."* John's words still rang in Renwick's head. And of course I jist shook ma heid. Nae wonder he stormed aff wi sic ill-feeling. Mibbe I shud gang in by his farm on my way tae Logan House and see hoo he feels noo.

He thought about Jonas Hawthorn, his companion all the way back to Scotland, the sea voyage, the terrible storm. Ay. And the Lord guided us and kept us safe. Ay. And he saw us thru that last bit o the journey as weel. Whit a nightmare, yet here I am and grateful.

Now he wondered if Jonas had reached the relatives he was so keen to visit. And then he was back worrying about that interrupted sermon, planning how he might return to Cambusnethan and finish what he'd started.

Each thought swirled in his head, demanding attention, till the next one forced its way in.

Eventually exhausted, he slept deeply for an hour before Mistress Mowat knocked on the bedroom door to waken him.

"Mornin." Mitchell was waiting for Renwick at the foot of the stairs. "Ah've brocht the horses frae the stable. Thur tethered in the big shed ahint the hoose. The less onybody sees the better."

"Thank ye," Renwick replied. "I agree aboot the need tae be discreet. With that in mind cud I ask that ye show us a quiet way tae Crossford. Frae there we can climb the Nethan Gorge, pass Craignethan Castle then oot thru Blackwood Estate and on tae Lesmahagow. It'll save time and be safer than jist following the road."

"Naewhaur's safe these days."

"We'll gie it a go onyway. And aboot last nicht – " Renwick hesitated. "We didna thank ye."

Mitchell shook his head. "It wud be a pair day if ah didna help ye on yer way. Ye've a hard enoch road in front o ye."

"Nae mair than I can cope wi. The Lord nivver asks mair than he gies himself."

"If ye say so." Mitchell smiled. "Noo whit aboot breakfast?"

Renwick nodded and opened the kitchen door to find Houston at the big table enjoying a large plate heaped with ham and eggs and sliced mushrooms.

"Morning." Houston waved his fork. "I hope ye're hungry. Thanks tae Mistress Mowat there's a grand breakfast."

Mary Mowat hurried forward with a bowl of porridge. "Sit doon an enjoy then ah'll bring ham an eggs same as yer freend. Ye need tae keep yer strength up."

Rab Mitchell walked beside the two horses, guiding them towards the riverbank. "Aifter whit ye said ah think this way is best. It's a kennin langer but avoids the main road an comes oot whaur the Nethan meets the Clyde. The stert o the gorge is close by."

"Perfect." Renwick seemed content as they ambled through the rising mist.

Two dairy-maids had just finished the morning milking. They were herding the cows back to the riverbank when two horses and riders and a familiar figure came towards them.

"Whae's that wi Rab Mitchell?" one maid asked.

"The young, fair-heided yin's Renwick the rebel preacher. The ither is his freend."

"Hoo dae ye ken?"

"Ah wis at Cambusnethan yesterday an saw them baith afore the troopers arrived."

"Ye mean ye went tae yon illegal field-preachin meetin folk wur whisperin aboot?"

"Whit if ah did?"

"Ye micht huv been arrested or worse"

"The troopers werena interestit in the likes o me, it wis the preacher they wur aifter."

"So whit's he dain walkin past us the noo?" The first dairy-maid nodded towards the two riders who politely returned her nod.

"Dinna be daft," the other replied. "He got clean awa. He aye dis."

The first dairy-maid frowned. "Is that so."

Later that day a line of mounted troopers were seen trotting along the same stretch of riverbank before heading into the little village of Dalserf to knock on every door and ask if anyone had seen a certain preacher and his companion.

When the two dairymaids met for evening milking one said, "This has been a sad day."

"Hoo come?" The other looked puzzled.

"Trust seems tae huv deed a death."

"Hoo come?" the other repeated.

"Weel, ah wis jist thinkin aboot they troopers appearin sae sudden, as if somebody had seen fit tae tell them whae'd been seen aboot here."

"Why wud they nae appear? It's whit they dae."

"Why indeed?"

After that a long silence grew between the two women.

"This is whaur we pairt." Rab Mitchell pointed to a narrow path which disappeared into a wooded hillside. "It's a kennin steep so tak yer time. Micht be a kindness tae lead yer horses, at least fur the first bit."

"Thank ye." Renwick and Houston jumped down beside their guide.

"Ye've been a Godsend." Renwick shook his hand.

"Weel that's a first." Mitchell grinned. "On ye go an tak care." He turned and walked away before any more could be said.

The first part of the climb was indeed steep, with boulder after boulder almost blocking the path which meant persuading the horses to squeeze through each narrow space. Fortunately the path didn't hug the cliff edge so both men felt relatively safe as they pushed on, often having to lift low-hanging branches aside.

Far below they could hear fast running water as the Nethan tumbled down to meet and merge with the Clyde. Where they were it was only bird song and the sound of metal hooves clicking against rough stone.

Neither spoke, both concentrating on achieving a steady rhythm to suit the horses. This seemed to work. Slowly and surely they reached a small clearing where the path widened and began to level out.

"We deserve a few meenits rest." Houston led his horse to a thick patch of grass then sat down beside the beast. "I wis raither nervous aboot this climb but it's turned oot fine. Jist fine. And whit a bonny spot."

Renwick nodded and joined him. "And nae mony folk come this way. The climb seems tae put them aff which maks it safer for us twa."

They sat enjoying the dappled patterns among the ash and elm and birch. After a few minutes there were glimpses of small fluttering shapes along with a variety of chirps as some of the woodland residents began to show themselves, hopping from branch to branch, coming closer as if to check out the intruders.

"Is that a wee wren?" Houston pointed towards a tiny brown bird pecking among the fallen leaves and patches of moss. She seemed unafraid, throwing up bits of bark close by Houston's boot. This happened several times then, head on one side, a diamond like eye seemed to glare up at the giant before the dot of brown scuttled under a trailing bramble and disappeared.

Renwick laughed. "Ay, it's a wren. Sma and defiant. A bit like oorsels. Which reminds me, we must press on and nae sit here indulging oorsels like gentlemen o leisure."

The second part of the climb grew less steep as the path wandered through the wood till it reached the top where they could look back over the treetops and admire the full length of the gorge.

"Ay," Houston sighed. "Like I said, jist fine."

A few steps more and the grey shape of half-ruined Craignethan Castle appeared on the edge of the treeline.

Renwick pointed. "It wis a fine fortress in its time but nae mair. Left empty for years till Andrew Hay, the lawyer, bocht it frae Duchess Anne Hamilton and built himsel a fine hoose in the outer courtyard. He's a supporter o the cause but discreet aboot it. Being a man o the law helps. He's weel acquaint wi the complexities and kens hoo tae mak them work for his ain advantage. Mibbe biding oot here in sic a quiet spot helps as weel."

"Ye're weel informed," Houston said.

"I need tae be," Renwick replied. "Richt. On we go. Jist beyond the castle we'll find open fields again and then tak the road tae Blackwood. I'd like tae gang thru the estate and stop at the big hoose."

Houston frowned. "Whit for? Ye said we shud press on."

"I want tae leave word aboot the maister, William Laurie. Pair man's locked up in Edinburgh, even been sentenced tae execution at the Mercat Cross mair than aince, reprieved then kept locked up in the Tolbooth. His health has suffered and noo the Privy Council are pretending sympathy by offering freedom provided he pays £600 Scots as a guarantee o guid behaviour in the future."

"Is he able tae pay that kind o money?" Houston asked.

Renwick nodded. "I believe so. And ivvery credit tae the man for stout support ower mony years. The least I can dae is warn his hoosekeeper tae expect her maister's return afore lang."

Renwick jumped down from his horse and handed Houston the reins. "Wait here while I leave word aboot Maister Laurie." He crossed the circle of raked gravel then up three marble steps to the heavily studded front door. He pulled the long metal bell chain making it clang long and loud.

No one responded.

He waited a moment on the top step then pulled the chain again.

The door remained shut.

He shrugged. "I'll gang round the back. Bound tae be somebody there."

As Renwick rounded the corner of the big house he saw a woman bending over sheets spread on an expanse of grass which was obviously used as a bleaching green. "Guid day." He went towards her and took off his cap.

"Whit is it?" The woman jumped and spun round to face him. "Whit dae ye want?"

"Naething ither than leave a message aboot Maister Laurie. My name is James Renwick."

"Did ye say Renwick?"

Renwick smiled and nodded.

"James Renwick the preacher?"

Renwick smiled and nodded again.

"Weel ah nivver." The woman's suspicious look vanished. "Yer fame gangs afore ye. Come awa in an gie me yer news. Ah'm Amy Gowan, hoosekeeper tae Maister Laurie, an happy tae offer ye a bite tae eat if ye're minded?"

"Why thank ye." Renwick bowed. "I hae a freend waiting at the front. May I?"

"Nae problem. Ye're baith welcome."

Renwick and Houston sat in the huge kitchen of Blackwood House enjoying an unexpected and welcome hot meal of braised rabbit with fine shredded cabbage and sweet onions. In front of them sat a tall jug of cider and a newly cut loaf.

Renwick had already passed on the information to the housekeeper who was delighted with the news.

"It shudna tak lang," Renwick explained. "Aince he pays the siller he'll be free tae come hame."

"An ivverythin will be ready tae welcome him. Whit a time he's hud." Amy Gowan nodded. "But whit aboot yersel? Are ye meanin tae preach aboot here? Ah've heard naethin. Usually we git a whisper aboot things lik that. Mind ye, nae preacher's come by fur a lang while."

"I'm on my way to Logan House beyond Lesmahagow. My last meeting was at Cambusnethan wi a guid turn oot. Unfortunately the law heard aboot it and came chasing aifter me. I wis lucky tae escape."

"Thur's aye somebody willin tae tell tales fur money." Amy Gowan shook her head. "That's whit maks ivverythin sae dangerous. If only we hud the auld days back insteid o this mess wur strugglin thru. Richt noo a wheen bairns in the village are still no baptised. That wud nivver huv happened afore. The parents keep hopin a meenister will appear an dae the needfu. They cud gang tae the curate but naebody wants that. Ma ain dochter wud like tae be mairried but canna bring hersel tae ask the curate. It's a peety. Ye see her young man's gotten the chance o a job in the toun but he'll need tae leave her here till sic times."

"Mibbe I cud help?" Renwick suggested. "Mibbe the villagers wud alloo me tae baptise their bairns. As for yer dochter. Wud she be interested? I've conducted several wedding ceremonies on the open moor."

"Ye're the answer tae a prayer so ye are." Amy Gowan grasped Renwick's hand. "Jist gie me an hoor or twa an ye'll be swamped wi requests. Tell ye whit, ye cud aise the chapel at the side o the hoose. The maister held services ther a while back when travellin preachers wur on the go."

Houston leant forward and whispered to Renwick, "Ye said we needed tae press on."

"And whit is mair pressing than the Lord's work?"

"Of course ye must." Houston flushed. "I wis only thinking aboot yersel. Ye've crammed sic a lot intae these past weeks wi aw they crowds coming tae hear ye preach and aye asking for mair."

Renwick frowned. "There's nae need for concern. In fact I see oor arrival here as nae jist opportune but essential."

James Renwick stood in the Blackwood House chapel. Around him every seat was taken, every space filled, even the corridor beyond was packed. Most of the village seemed to have come to see and hear.

In front of him was a line of babies and young children with parents trying to keep them quiet. Behind them stood a pleased looking young couple holding hands.

This would be Renwick's first indoor service since leaving Holland, a strange phenomenon after all those wild areas and open air he'd grown accustomed to.

Happy anticipation almost bounced off the walls as Renwick bowed his head for a short prayer before looking up to smile at his waiting congregation. "Peace be wi us aw as we come before the Lord in oor weakness and oor need." He waited, let the words sink in, then called the first family to come forward.

Eight baptisms took place, followed by a joyful wedding ceremony, followed by a rousing sermon on the need to hold firm to the cause.

Finally Renwick raised his arms and held them wide as if pulling everyone towards him. "My friends this has indeed been a special occasion. A real privilege. Tak heart in it and as ye gang hame carry this thocht wi ye. Richt noo the hosts o evil exert their rage and malice against us. But fear not for Christ displays superior power and is oor guardian." After that he walked through the crowd and stood at the door to shake every hand on the way out.

Once again Renwick and Houston enjoyed a comfortable bed in a proper room. This time Renwick fell asleep a happy man and slept soundly.

Early next morning Renwick and Houston set out on their last lap to Logan House. They cut across the estate fields then joined the long avenue which was used as a back entrance. They'd almost reached the bottom, ready to turn onto the Strathaven road when they heard a heavy cart lumbering on the road.

"Mibbe we shud wait under the trees till it passes." Houston sounded anxious. "Jist in case."

"Whitivver." Renwick was in too good a mood to argue.

As the cart drew closer to the estate entrance Houston counted the occupants. "Four passengers and the driver. The back is weel loaded."

Renwick paid little attention. He was still thinking about yesterday's success and didn't see two of the passengers who were well known to him.

John Steel was one of those passengers and noticed the two riders waiting in the shadows of the trees. He took another look then stared, blinked, stared again. "God sakes." It was out before he could stop himself. "Yon's Renwick."

Jonas who was sitting beside him stiffened. "Whit? Whaur?"

"Ower tae the left. They twa riders waitin unner the trees, near the bottom o the estate avenue. Ane o them is James Renwick."

Jonas turned and gaped. "So it is. Shud we stoap?"

"Naw." John kept his voice low. "An nae a word. Richt noo oor priority is findin three safe passages tae Holland. Nae harm tae Maister Renwick but thur's nae room fur ony distraction."

"Whit dae ye mean?"

"We've enoch problems withoot addin the likes o him tae the mix."

The cart trundled past the estate entrance and on to the village where it would join the Glasgow road. The two riders waited till it was out of sight then trotted from the estate and headed in the opposite direction.

Having spied Renwick John now knew he'd made the right decision. The troopers coming to the farm at all hours were dangerous enough and reason enough to move but the thought of having Renwick to contend with…well. Renwick attracted trouble.

John had been worried about how to deal with his visitors, especially after the promise he'd given. He'd discussed it all with Marion who'd agreed the situation was putting them all in danger.

That thought had focused his mind. He'd wrestled with possible consequences all night. Come first light they were still there, still tormenting him.

"Enoch's enoch." He'd sat up abruptly and woke Marion. "Time tae move." Jumping out of bed he'd hurried through to the kitchen where Jonas and Jamie were still sleeping on the rag-rug beside the range.

He shook them.

Both jerked up and looked alarmed. "Is it troopers again?"

"Nae this time but ah've been gien the maitter a lot o thocht. Yon wee hidey hole in the hall isna big enough fur three if they troopers come back, an they will."

"Ay, a guid chance," Jonas agreed. "An nae a guid thocht. Whit dae ye suggest?"

"Ye dinna hing aboot here ony langer in case the law gits haud o ye. That way ye lose yer chance tae mak ony journey nivver mind the big yin tae Holland."

"Dae ye mean set oot richt noo?" Jonas rubbed his eyes and sounded excited.

"Ay, an ah'll help ye best ah can."

Jamie stood up. "If that's the case ah'd best wake mither an tell her."

When Helen appeared she seemed far from happy or excited.

John noticed and asked her, "Is this really whit ye want? Ye're welcome here. We can say ye're an aunt come tae bide wi us."

Helen shook her head. "Whit's aheid hus tae be better than whit we've left ahint. Ah ken thur's nae way back tae Wanlockheid. We need tae move on. Onyway, it's whit Jamie wants. He hus aw his life in front o him; ah want the best fur him, an nae doubt a new life in Holland will turn oot fine fur masel as weel. It jist seems a bit dauntin."

Jamie's arms went round his mother. "Of course ye'll be fine. Onyway, ah'm nae goin withoot ye."

She'd kissed his brow and turned to John. "That's settled then."

John nodded. "Richt. Breakfast first then aff we go."

Within an hour brief farewells had been made. Marion shook hands with the two young men and gave Helen a big hug before the three would-be travellers followed John away from Westermains, over the hill, through the birch wood to Waterside farm where they'd met Gus McPhail and his cart to begin what could be a long and dangerous journey.

Gus McPhail's cart turned onto the Glasgow road and John glanced at the three figures sitting beside him. Thur's nae ither way. Ay. An the quicker the better.

Chapter Fifteen

Mirren Spreul stood in Meikle Gowan kirkyard and wept with grief and frustration. A small group of mourners stood at a discreet distance as if wishing to pay respect yet trying to avoid drawing attention. After all, one had to be careful these days for Mirren's sister-in-law Helen was too well known, too at odds with the great and the good and the powerful.

Sometime ago Helen's husband John had been snared by the law. As a well-respected apothecary and successful businessman he'd become a lucrative target, accused of rebel activity, arrested, and taken before the Privy Council who'd made the most of a trumped up charge by offering him the choice of paying £500 as a fine or facing imprisonment in the dreaded Bass Rock prison.

John Spreul would have none of it. He'd raged at his accusers and demanded an apology.

None was forthcoming.

He'd stood his ground. "Dinna expect me tae pay oot guid money for something I nivver did."

Their lordships then had him shipped out to that bare rock in the Firth of Forth until such time as he might change his mind.

His businesses at home and beyond were now at risk from that same Privy Council and Helen Spreul had been left to try and protect their assets as best she could. Treading a fine line between keeping the law at bay while avoiding accusation of preventing the course of justice was a dangerous game but there seemed little choice.

First of all she diverted their two ships, which plied between Rotterdam and Leith, and arranged for them both to dock in Dublin. That way ships, captains, and valuable cargo were protected from the grasping reach of the Scottish government.

She'd then arranged onward transport through a variety of routes, using little boats able to slip into smaller, less used harbours which made goods difficult to track let alone confiscate. This move quickly established Helen as the equal of her able husband and one to respect.

Nor was John Spreul left to his fate. She paid the Bass Rock governor to bend the rules, allow occasional visits, even permit John to keep the three laying hens she'd brought in a wicker basket. The garrison governor was rather taken with this feisty, good-looking woman and enjoyed their sparring each time she negotiated a little more consideration for her husband.

But now she was dead, an unexpected and sudden victim of fever which felled her in days. Mirren shivered. Little wonder. Pair soul wis worn oot. Ower mony problems week aifter week wi nae let up. Aw that responsibility. She shivered again. And noo I'm tasked wi cairrying on. She could still hear Helen's last whisper. "Ye're the guardian and the beneficiary. Ye ken whit that means."

Only too weel. Mirren watched shovelfuls of earth filling in the gaping hole at her feet then turned to glance at Helen Spreul's secretary Matthew Neilson, dutifully waiting a few steps behind. Luk at him. Same anxious expression since his mistress's last breath, as if he kens hoo useless I am. Will he bide on? Or jist excuse himsel and leave. I hope no. She stared at the length of turf now being rolled across the rectangle of soil and burst into tears.

Matthew stepped forward, gripped her elbow and gently guided her along the gravel path towards the kirkyard gate, away from this sad quiet and back to the bustling street.

A short, well-built man stood at the entrance as if waiting for them.

Mirren felt Matthew's fingers tighten but he said nothing.

As they drew level the man smiled. "Mistress Spreul? Mirren Spreul?"

"Ay," Matthew answered for her.

The man held out a small packet, tied with fine string, and sealed with red wax.

Mirren stared but made no move.

Matthew reached out his hand but the man shook his head.

Matthew stopped and whispered, "Tak it maam. It luks important."

Mirren obeyed. The man smiled again, nodded and walked away as Mirren slipped the little packet into the deepest pocket of her mourning coat.

Matthew waited till the man disappeared among the crowd then escorted Mirren to their horse and trap tethered beyond the gate.

Neither spoke during the drive back to Helen Spreul's house on the corner of Claythorn Street, close to a small farm with well-cared for cows whose milk was sold daily across the city, especially to wealthy merchants and those willing to pay extra for quality. Helen had been brought up here and had been glad to return after her husband's imprisonment.

Matthew unlocked the front door and ushered Mirren inside. The front door closed behind them and Mirren could wait no longer. "Whit wis that aboot?"

"Nae idea." Matthew shrugged. "Ither than the man as handed ye the packet is Pete Jamieson. Him and his brither, weel their fame gangs afore them wi guid reason. Whit they ken and whit they git up tae is best nae thocht aboot."

"Ye're scaring me. Noo that Helen's awa cud it be some sort o warning tae masel?"

"Best no jump tae conclusions. Gang intae the study and open the packet while I pour oot a glass o brandy tae calm yer nerves."

"And ane for yersel," Mirren said. "Ye deserve it."

Mirren took the packet from her coat pocket and laid it on the leather-topped desk. She hesitated then took the tiny dagger Helen had always used for opening correspondence, slid the blade under the seal then cut through the fine string and opened the little packet. Inside was a carefully folded sheet of best quality paper. "Richt." She laid it flat on the desk and began to read.

Mistress Spreul,

My name is James McAvoy. I had the privilege o considering masel a friend o yer sister-in-law Helen Spreul, a fine and capable lady whae bravely faced mony difficulties, nane o them o her ain making. She did weel but worried lest she wudna aye be here tae safeguard her family's interests. She spoke tae me aboot it, tellt me she'd made provision, that yersel wis her beneficiary. She also suggested that if the time came ye micht appreciate a word or twa aboot the way furrit. That is why I'm sending this invitation tae meet and speak privately.

Since I am raither elderly it wud be a kindness if ye'd consider coming tae my hoose on the High Street. Ye'll be welcome at ony time.

Sincerely,
James McAvoy

Mirren was reading the letter for the second time when Matthew appeared with her glass of brandy. She offered it to him. "Read and tell me whit ye think."

Matthew lifted the paper, went to the window, and read every word slowly and carefully before turning to face Mirren. "Guid news maam. An invite like this is jist whit ye need." For the first time in days his anxious expression seemed to lift.

"So whae is this James McAvoy?" Mirren asked. "I've heard the name but ken nocht aboot the man."

"He's a wealthy goldsmith and investor in mony a business. Weel respected as an honest man which means he's nae freend o yon rascals in the Privy Council. If my mistress trusted him so shud ye."

"I'll visit in the morning." Mirren sounded relieved. "And ye'll come tae?" She hesitated. "If ye're willing? And mair important, if ye're willing tae bide on and help me?"

"Pleasure maam." Matthew lifted his glass of brandy as if making a toast. "Thank ye."

Next morning Mirren and Matthew presented themselves outside the three-storey, sandstone building half-way up the High Street.

"Grand place." Mirren studied the golden facade, finished off with two sets of marble pillars on either side of a massive black door. On the wall was a well-polished brass plate inscribed with the name James McAvoy Goldsmith. "Ay, very grand." She watched as Matthew grabbed the long bell chain and yanked at it.

A bell clanged inside then the door opened.

A girl in a pristine starched apron and a shiny black dress with a fine lace collar stared at the two strangers.

"Mirren Spreul and her secretary tae see Maister McAvoy."

The girl curtsied. "Come in. Ah wis tellt tae expect ye." She led them across a vast black and white tiled floor to stop in front of a long, carved table piled with papers. A young man sitting at the table looked up and smiled as the girl said, "Mirren Spreul an her secretary fur the maister."

"I'm William McAvoy." The young man stood up and held out his hand in welcome. "My grandfaither will be delighted that ye've come. Please, follow me."

They went up a marble staircase at the far end of the hall and stopped beside a set of double doors. William McAvoy opened one of the doors and waved the visitors forward.

Mirren gasped as she stepped into a beautifully proportioned room painted in the softest shade of grey, enhanced by three elegant windows overlooking the busy street. An intricately patterned carpet in many shades of grey covered most of the floor and spoke of great wealth, impeccable taste and comfort. Opposite the windows was an ornately carved fireplace of white marble. A gleaming candelabra sat at either end of the broad mantelpiece. Even in daylight twelve candles twinkled along it with the gentle flames from a log fire adding warmth and life to the quiet room. Close by the fire, in a carved, padded chair, sat an old man wrapped in a red, tapestry cloak trimmed with thick black fur. The lined face smiled at Mirren. "Welcome Mistress Spreul. Ye'll hae guessed that this pair rickle o banes is James McAvoy. Thank ye for responding tae my invite and coming sae prompt like." He glanced at Matthew then looked enquiringly at Mirren.

"This is Matthew Neilson. He wis Helen's secretary. Kens the business and the problems better than ivver I will. He has kindly agreed tae bide on and work wi me. Let me reassure ye he has ma complete trust."

"In that case sit doon, baith o ye." McAvoy turned and signalled to his grandson. "Send up some refreshment for oor visitors and a selection o the cook's new biscuits."

William nodded and withdrew leaving Mirren and Matthew to begin a long conversation with their host.

Recognising that rider among the shadowy trees had shocked John Steel more than he cared to admit but he tried to concentrate on what lay ahead and ignore feeling guilty for neither acknowledging the man nor stopping for a word. He frowned and gritted his teeth but the thought of Renwick refused to go away. Why's Renwick back here sae quick? Jonas tellt me that he last saw him high-tailin it fur Edinburgh. Reportin back tae the Societies wis aw he cud think aboot, the chance tae stert the work he believes is his destiny. Whittiver he is, he's a brave yin. As fur the stramash he means tae cause, that's anither maitter.

He shook his head and sighed. The quicker ah huv a word wi James McAvoy the better. He'll ken whae's best tae ask aboot suitable ships. If he's nae sure the twa Jamieson brithers will soon find oot.

Difficult times tho, wi the law tichtenin its grip ivverywhaur.

He glanced at Helen Hawthorn sitting quietly beside her son Jamie. Yer man's deid, ye've hud tae flee frae yer hame, an noo ye're aboot tae cross the sea tae anither country, tae stert a new life wi relatives ye dinna even ken. Whitivver it is, it isna richt.

Gus glanced at the other three passengers. Like John they seemed to be wrapped in their own thoughts, just as unwilling to talk. Ah weel. Curious as he was about the three strangers he shrugged and settled down to a wearisome journey into the city.

When the hedgerows grew less and the first straggling buildings began to appear John turned to Gus. "Sorry if ah huvna been much company. At the meenit ah've a lot tae think aboot."

"Ye wurna ony company at aw," Gus replied. "But nivver mind, ah forgie ye."

"In that case, can ye suggest somewhaur ah can tak ma three veesitors tae wait while ah gang on masel fur a quiet word wi James McAvoy?"

"That serious?" Gus's eyes widened.

John nodded. "Somewhaur they can be private, enjoy a bite tae eat, and bide safe."

"Safe?"

John lowered his voice. "Ye've four felons sittin aside ye. The troopers are aifter them same as masel."

"Even the mistress there?"

"Ay. An the pair soul lost her husband as weel."

"Soonds terrible."

"It wis."

"An somehoo ye got involved." Gus shook his head. "When will ye learn aboot lukin oot mair fur yersel an lettin ithers hing as they grow?"

"Wheesht man. Git back tae ma question."

"Ah'm jist sayin. An nae doubt ah'll huv tae say it again." Gus shrugged. "But in answer tae yer question ah'd tak yer freends tae the *Burnt Barns* tavern, jist aff the Gallowgate. It wis built on the site o a terrible fire at a farm a while back. The farmer decided he'd be better

220

aff buildin a wee tavern an chaingin himsel intae an innkeeper. In memory o whit happened he named it the *Burnt Barns*. He's done weel. It's a clean place an weel run. We gang past the end o Saint Mungo's Lane. The inn's only a step ahint it. The innkeeper's Davie Davidson. Ah ken him weel. Tell him ah sent ye. He'll see tae yer veesitors withoot askin ony awkward questions or speakin aboot them aifterwards." Gus frowned. "Can ah jist say ah wis beginnin tae think ye'd nae mair use fur me. Nivver a word fur weeks. Nae like ye."

John stiffened. "Dinna be daft man. Ye ken ah'm beholden tae ye, as wis ma faither. Ye're as guid a freend as ah've ivver hud."

Gus looked away and smiled. "Jist so's ah ken."

John led the three Hawthorns into the *Burnt Barns* inn. It was a busy place, noisy with loud voices, clattering plates, and clinking glasses. John squeezed through the crowd to the serving counter and asked for Davie Davidson.

"He's ower there." The man he spoke to pointed to a tall, thin man, wearing a huge, starched apron and balancing an enormous tray of plates on his shoulder.

"Maister Davidson." John stepped forward and signalled.

The man acknowledged, finished serving his customers then turned to John.

"Gus McPhail sent me."

"Ah. So whit can I dae for ye?"

"Ah'm lukin for a private room whaur three freends can enjoy a meal withoot ony disturbance while ah gang intae toun on business."

"Richt noo the only private room is upstairs. It's raither wee but ye said three folk so it shudna be a problem. Wud ye like tae see it?"

They followed Davidson up a narrow wooden stair and into a tiny room almost filled by a table and four chairs. It looked and smelled clean, the window sparkled. Now that they were above the bustle and noise it seemed almost quiet. It certainly seemed private.

"The vera thing." John smiled at Davidson then turned to the Hawthorns and lowered his voice. "Mak yersels comfortable, order whit ye want tae eat. While ye're eatin ah'll gang on masel an see aboot a way furrit."

Jonas and Jamie seemed about to argue.

John treated them both to a hard stare. "It's easier on ma ain. But dinna worry. Ah'll dae ma best."

"Ah ken ye will," Helen spoke up.

"That's settled then." John offered Davidson two silver merks. "If this disna cover ivverythin ah'll pay the rest when ah come back. Noo if ye'll excuse me."

A few minutes later John Steel turned off the Gallowgate onto the High Street, heading for James McAvoy's fine house.

He crossed the busy street and up to the front door without noticing that a pair of hostile eyes had spotted him.

God's sake. That's Maister Steel. Ay, the vera yin as gied me a hard time at the Glessart aboot a month ago. Stopped me an twa ithers frae teachin yon Quaker farmer a lesson. Ower mony o they kind in yon village, spreadin thur queer ideas an ways. An yit Steel attacked us when we'd guid reason tae mak the eedjit see the errors o his ways. Bugger caught me oot an made a richt fool o me so he did. Nae somethin ah'm likely tae forget or forgie.

Giles Nisbet watched as John Steel pulled the bell chain and was almost immediately admitted by some serving girl. Hoo come he's welcome intae sic a posh hoose? Nisbet crossed the street, stood at the front door and read the brass sign saying James McAvoy Goldsmith. He read it again. But Steel's a named rebel, a wantit man wi 1000 merks on his heid. So hoo come? He frowned. Whit's he dain mixin wi the great an the guid? An why are sic folk allooin this tae happen? The law micht be interestit tae hear aboot this. Ay. A wee walk up tae the garrison an a word in the captain's lug micht dae the trick. Git ma ain back on Steel an mak some money at the same time. He turned and walked away whistling to himself.

"Weel, weel Maister Steel." William McAvoy abandoned the paper he was working on, stood up, and held out a hand in welcome. "Whit a nice surprise. Grandfaither wis jist wondering aboot ye the ither day."

John smiled as they shook hands. "Ah raither think the Maister finds me a trial."

"Quite the opposite I assure ye. Come and I'll tak ye up tae see him."

"Weel John, ye're back." James McAvoy's lined face lit up with pleasure.

John hurried over to the figure sitting by the fire in his favourite chair. "Grand tae see ye, sir. It's been a wee while."

"Indeed it has." The old man shook John's hand. "And much will have happened nae doubt."

"Ye cud say that." John grinned.

"So, sit yersel doon. I'm aw ears." James McAvoy sat back and began to listen, sometimes smiling, sometimes frowning, then shaking his head as what he heard grew more serious.

Finally John said, "An noo ah've promised the Hawthorns that ah'll see them on a safe berth oot the country."

"Which is becoming raither difficult these days." James McAvoy pursed his lips. "But not insurmountable. In fact." He pursed his lips again. "Dae ye mind Helen Spreul?"

"Ay. She's a fine lady."

"Sadly she passed awa a few days ago. Taken by a fever."

"Oh." John shook his head and thought about Helen Spreul, the journey they'd made together to the Bass Rock prison, how determined she'd been to do right by her husband.

James McAvoy watched John's face. "Her sister-in-law Mirren is the official beneficiary and has taken ower the business. Fortunately Mirren's secretary is staying on. He has a grand grasp o the problems so that shud mak a difference."

"Ah certainly wish her weel but hoo dis that relate tae ma problem ither than ah need tae tell her aboot Miss Elsie? Ah'm hopin she'll alloo the lass tae come an bide wi her. At least fur a while. Aifter whit's happened she's best somewhaur naebody kens her."

"Let me me explain. John Spreul did a lot o business wi Holland. He had twa ships sailing back and furrit and making guid money. When the Privy Council locked him up they thocht they'd naething else tae dae but confiscate baith ships and cargo and share the lot amang themsels. Helen must hae seen that coming. On the nixt trip back the ships sailed for Dublin. They've been daing that ivver since. She even hired a wheen fishing boats. Each taks some o the cargo tae different Scottish ports. And nivver the same yin twice. Their lordships are still trying tae work oot a way o catching her oot."

"And?" John persisted.

"Helen asked me tae keep an ee oot if onything went wrang. Neither o us were thinking it micht be her death. In fact it wis the last thing on oor minds. When it happened I felt obliged tae hae a word wi her sister-in-law, Mirren Spreul, as the beneficiary. I invited her tae visit me. She came yesterday wi her secretary. We had a lang talk. She's certainly a Spreul and naebody's fool. She sees the benefit o whit Helen set up. Indeed, she hopes tae build on its success. Dublin tae Rotterdam will bide a regular route for baith ships. If yer freends can get across tae Ireland I'm sure Mirren wud consider gieing them onward travel. That wud be safer than trying tae gain three berths frae Glasgow. At the meenit ivverything is closely scrutinised. Each ship must gie the port authorities a full passenger list as weel as the reason for the journey. The hale thing needs tae be approved afore the captain gets clearance tae set sail. Nae doubt yer three freends wud draw attention unless some captain's willing tae see them secretly ferried doon the Clyde and join his ship at the tail o the bank."

There was a sudden clang of the outside bell along with a loud hammering on the front door.

James McAvoy sat upright then turned and pointed to a tall bookcase at the far end of the room. "Soonds like unwelcome visitors. Mibbe best ye bide oot o sicht."

"Whaur?"

"There's a row o wee carved roses alang the top shelf o yon bookcase. Press the third ane frae the richt."

John hesitated.

James McAvoy's stare was warning enough. John crossed the room, pressed the carved rose then jumped back as the front of the bookcase swung out.

"Step in. There's a handle on the other side tae pull it shut again."

By now they could both hear William's protests as a rough voice demanded, "Whaur's the maister?" This was followed by the sound of heavy boots stamping across the tiled floor of the hall and the same voice ordering, "Bide whaur ye are. Ah'll find the maister masel." A pair of feet began to climb the curved staircase.

The bookcase door clicked shut as a burly trooper burst into James McAvoy's quiet sitting room.

"Whit's the meaning o this?" James McAvoy turned and glared at the intruder.

The trooper snapped to attention. "Sergeant Grant, sir. Ma garrison captain hus information that a certain rebel wis seen enterin this hoose."

"Has he indeed. Weel I think yer captain must be severely misinformed. We hae many visitors in the course o a day but this is a law-abiding hoose and vera particular whae comes and goes with or withoot an invitation."

"So ye say." The sergeant stepped closer. "Ma orders are tae search these premises frae tap tae bottom and mak an arrest if necessary."

"May I ask which rebel ye're aifter? And why wud he come intae my hoose?"

"Name's John Steel. Ken naethin aboot the man ither than he's on the run wi 1000 merks on his heid."

"Whit a way tae live." James McAvoy waved his hand at the sergeant. "Feel free tae go onywhaur ye choose. Ye'll find nae John Steel here."

Half-an-hour of intense searching began. Every room, corner, cellar, even the outhouse was inspected as six fully armed troopers were let loose across the house.

Finally the sergeant returned to James McAvoy's sitting room.

"Naething?" James McAvoy sounded sarcastic.

"Indeed." The sergeant flushed. "Ye wud appear tae be tellin the truth."

"But ye didna believe me did ye?"

The sergeant's face grew redder. "Sir. Ah hud ma orders."

"Of course." The old man's voice sharpened. "Jist so lang as yer captain has the guid grace tae send me a personal apology for this unwarranted upset and invasion."

"Ah'll tell him." The sergeant saluted and marched back downstairs to join his men. A moment later the front door banged shut and the big house grew quiet again.

James McAvoy rang the little hand bell he kept on the table by his chair and called out, "All clear."

John turned the inner handle and the front of the bookcase swung forward allowing him to step back into the room.

James McAvoy smiled. "I hope yer incarceration didna inconvenience ye ower much."

"Not at aw. It wis the best hidey hole ah've ivver been in."

James McAvoy smiled again. "We aim tae please."

"An ye did. Sad thing is, whaeivver saw me kens me yit ah nivver noticed. An luk at the bother it brocht ye."

"Weel, naething came o it. Noo, whit aboot yer freends? Ye said they're waiting at the *Burnt Barns* inn."

"Ay. An expectin me tae appear wi word aboot a ship. Frae whit ye've said it'll tak a day or twa tae sort things oot. Ah believe the inn hus rooms tae let. Ah'll ask aboot that an see whit the innkeeper can dae fur us."

"They canna bide in sic a public place. Nae aifter this." James McAvoy shook his head. "Ye best bring them here."

"Thur's three o them."

"Maks nae difference."

"Whit if the troopers come back?"

James McAvoy shook his head again. "Unlikely. Whit's jist happened cud mak this the safest place in the toun."

"Only if ye're shair."

"Whit did I jist say?"

John looked relieved. "Shud ah gang an fetch them?"

"Naw, naw. Bide whaur ye are. I'll send William tae the *Crooked Man* howf tae tell the twa Jamiesons. They'll dae the needful in case yer informant is still hinging aboot waiting for anither chance."

The *Burnt Barns* was a busy place, deservedly so with a reputation for good food and decent ale. Davie Davidson was glad of this although he was beginning to resent how relentless his life had become. Since early morning he'd been back and forward, brushing the backyard, laying fires in the main rooms, supervising the cleaning, checking the meat and vegetable orders, giving the cook instructions plus trying to find time to check the beer barrels. And all before he started serving customers. "A meenit. Jist a meenit tae sit doon or even draw breath." He was still muttering to himself when he came out the kitchen with yet another tray of steaming food and almost bumped into two figures standing in the middle of the hall.

"Ah'll be richt back, sirs." He bustled into the main dining-room, served his customers then hurried back to greet the two now waiting at the foot of the stairs.

As he came closer he recognised both faces and stopped short.

"Ye ken us then?" Alex Jamieson grinned at Davidson's reaction.

"Ay." Davidson gave a stiff nod. "Welcome tae the *Burnt Barns*. Are ye lukin for a meal or mibbe a sit doon wi some ale? As ye can see it's aw go in here but ah'm sure ah can find ye a corner."

"On this occasion wur jist aifter three o yer customers."

"Ah want nae trouble, sirs."

"An ye'll git nane," Pete Jamieson joined in. "Wur here tae collect the three folk in yer private room upstairs."

"As ah said, ah want nae trouble."

Pete's voice sharpened. "An ah said thur's nane. Wur only here because the man as gied ye twa merks tae cover his freends meal hus been delayed elsewhaur. He wants them tae join him an asked us tae act as a guide."

"Quite so." Davidson glanced at the heavy-looking wicker basket Pete Jamieson was carrying but asked no questions as he led the brothers up the narrow stairs.

"Whae's this?" Helen Hawthorn looked scared as the door opened and Davidson ushered in the Jamiesons.

Pete took off his cap. "Nae worries. Us twa are the Jamieson brithers, freends o John Steel. He sent us."

"Whit fur? Whit's wrang? Whaur is he?" Jonas and Jamie pushed back their chairs and stood up.

"Nae far awa. At the hoose o anither freend." Alex turned to Davidson who was still standing in the doorway. "Thank ye. Noo, gie us a few meenits tae oorsels."

"Nae problem." Davidson stepped back and closed the door.

Alex waited till the innkeeper's feet rattled downstairs. "As ah said, John Steel is at the hoose o a guid freend."

"So whit's the problem?" Jonas looked suspicious.

"When he left here earlier somebody saw him an recognised him. That somebody didna wish him weel an went tae the toun garrison an gied Steel's name as a listed rebel on the run. The captain sent a squad o troopers oot tae find him."

"Did they?" Helen seemed close to tears.

"Nae way. He's safe but keepin his heid doon an bidin oot o

sicht. That's why us twa are here. Tae show ye the way. But afore we go we've a wee suggestion." Pete lifted the basket onto the table and pulled out a heavy woollen cloak. "Ah've brocht ane fur each o ye."

"Why?" Helen frowned.

"We unnerstaund ye three are on the run, same as John. The less ye're seen the better so we'd like ye each tae pit on a cloak, wi the hood up, afore ye walk oot o here wi us."

"Is it far tae this hoose? It soonds dangerous." Helen twisted the fringes of her shawl and looked even more worried.

"Nae far. An ye'll be safe enoch. Wur jist makin shair." He offered Helen one of the cloaks. "Richt Mistress, if ye pit this on an come wi me we'll stroll alang thegither as nice as ye like an naebody will gie us a second glance."

"Whit aboot the ither twa?" Helen hesitated.

"They wait a few meenits then pit on a cloak an walk wi ma brither."

"If ye say so." Helen Hawthorn took Pete's arm and allowed him to guide her downstairs where Davidson was waiting in the hall. "If onybody asks we wurna here, same fur the three travellers. Ah've left a basket sittin on the table upstairs. If it's ony use tae ye feel free." Pete slipped a merk into the innkeeper's hand.

"Nae need Maister Jamieson." Davidson handed back the coin.

Pete nodded to Davidson, pocketed the coin then led Helen out to the street. Together, like many a couple, they made their way along the crowded Gallowgate, past the junction with the High Street and into a tiny close just beyond. This led them to a cobbled yard which was barred by a high metal gate secured by a heavy-looking padlock.

"Whit noo?" Helen whispered.

Pete grinned. "We open it." He took a large key from his pocket, turned it in the lock and the gate swung forward. "See, nae problem. In ye go, mistress, wur nearly there." He led Helen across the yard and up three steps to a large, black door. He pushed it open.

Helen found herself in a large, well-lit kitchen where a stout woman and a young girl were bustling about preparing a meal.

"Welcome tae a guid freend's hoose."

Helen smiled with relief when she saw John standing beside a young man at the far side of the room. "It's yersel then. Thank guidness. Can ah sit doon a meenit an git ma breath back aifter aw this excitement?"

"Here." Pete led her to a chair beside an enormous cooking range with its coals glowing red to keep a large casserole bubbling away on top.

Helen sat a moment watching the busy women then turned to John. "So." She sounded almost accusing. "Whit's aw this aboot?"

Before John could answer the outside door opened again and two hooded figures came in along with Alex Jamieson.

John signalled his thanks to the Jamiesons.

"Nae bother." The brothers flapped a dismissive hand. "Gled tae help. If the maister wants onythin else he kens whaur we are." They turned as if to leave.

"Here. Dinna forget this." The stout woman hurried over and handed a small parcel to each man. "Cheese an onion. Yer favourite."

"Thanks Jessie." Pete grinned and waved at the Hawthorns. "We'll leave ye tae it."

With that they both slipped outside and closed the door.

"Hoo dae ye ken they twa?" Jonas asked. "They seem a richt pair o characters."

John grinned. "They are. An the vera men ye want lukin aifter yer back. Ah've kent them a while an been gled o them mony a time."

"An whae's this maister?"

"Name's James McAvoy. This is his hoose. He's a goldsmith an a weel respectit man." He turned to the young man by his side. "Let me introduce his grandson William. He'll tak ye upstairs tae meet the man himsel."

The Hawthorns left the busy kitchen and followed John and William into the main hall.

"Oh my," Helen gasped at the size and the grandeur. "Luk at that marble flair." She studied the pale-blue walls, the line of slim pillars marching towards an enormous, black front door, the elegant furniture, the gold-framed pictures of beautifully-painted landscapes lining one wall, and the curved staircase along the other.

"Nivver seen the like."

John laughed. "Ah wis impressed the first time ah visited. But the man himsel is mair important. He's a guid freend. But on ye come an meet him fur yersel."

William McAvoy opened the double doors at the top of the stairs and ushered everyone into his grandfather's sitting-room.

James McAvoy sat by a crackling fire. He looked as if he was half-asleep but immediately stood up when William announced his visitors. "Come in. Come in. Welcome. I hope ye'll alloo me tae offer the hospitality o this hoose fur a day or twa." He shook hands with each of the group then indicated a half-circle of chairs by the fire. "Please, sit yersels doon."

"Thank ye." Helen was the first to sit. "But whit are we dain here?"

"Ye're here because o ma freend John Steel. He tellt me aboot ye. He also mentioned Elsie Spreul."

"Miss Elsie?" Helen looked surprised.

"Ay. John and masel are acquaint wi the Spreuls. Mibbe ye dinna ken but Maister Spreul is shut up in prison richt noo. His wife Helen had been running the business on his behalf. It includes twa ships which gang back and furrit tae Holland."

"Ships?" Jonas leant forward.

James McAvoy held up a hand. "There's mair tae it. Unfortunately Helen Spreul passed awa last week. Her sister-in-law Mirren is the beneficiary. John came here tae ask me whaur Helen wis as he wants tae tak Miss Elsie tae her for safety. When we spoke I tellt him aboot Mirren and hoo she means tae keep the business going. John had aready explained hoo ye're luking for passage tae Holland. Since Spreul ships sail there regular we're hoping Mirren Spreul micht be a help tae ye. Only thing is they sail oot o Dublin."

"Ah ken John must speak wi Mirren Spreul aboot her niece first. But kennin him he'll pit a word in fur us as weel?" Jonas looked hopeful.

"Ah hope this Mirren agrees tae luk aifter Miss Elsie," Helen Hawthorn cut in. "Pair lass hud the awfiest accusations made against her by folk wishing her harm. It wis ower much an she taen terrible ill. Ah helped John's wife nurse her an saw hoo bad she wis."

James McAvoy nodded. "John tellt me she's still too poorly tae travel. Mibbe jist as weel. It gies him time tae sort things oot for the best wi Mirren. She seems a kind and sensible lass so it shudna be a problem. And rest assured yer problem will be mentioned as weel."

"Ah dinna mean ony offence but ye're takin on an awfy lot fur folk ye dinna ken," Helen persisted.

"And none taken dear lady. I'll try tae explain. It aw started a lang time ago when I had reason tae be grateful tae John's faither. He kent naething aboot me yet offered help in resolving an unfortunate predicament. I've nivver forgotten his kindness and generosity. Later on I wis able tae offer Robert Steel some advice on a business maitter which worked oot weel. We met back and furrit and became freends. Noo I try tae dae the same for his son John."

Helen flushed. "Ah jist wantit tae be shair."

"Whit aboot this Mirren Spreul?" Jonas butted in again.

James McAvoy smiled. "I've invited her tae come here the morn. I'm hoping we can discuss the hale maitter. But richt noo lets think aboot eating. My cook shud hae a meal ready by noo." He turned to his grandson. "William, gang doon and ask Jessie if it's convenient tae serve up."

The Hawthorns sat in the grandest dining-room they'd ever seen and ate a delicious meal from delicate china plates. Using silver cutlery, being waited on, and offered the finest wines and ale was certainly a first and left them uncertain how to react. However, James McAvoy behaved so naturally that gradually they began to relax and even enjoy the experience.

After the meal they returned to the sitting-room where Jonas entertained them with his journey from Holland with James Renwick. "Mind ye," he admitted, "he wisna the easiest companion."

"Whit way?" Jamie Hawthorn asked.

"Some o his opeenions are a bit extreme. An aince he maks up his mind thur's nae shiftin."

"Tell me aboot it," John said. "He's a guid man tho."

"Ay." Jonas nodded. "But whiles hard tae pit up wi."

"He's certainly making a name for himself richt noo," James McAvoy joined in. "The Privy Council are desperate tae stop his field-preaching. Apparently he's attracting large crowds whaurivver he goes. I suspect their lordships sense growing rebellion in the air."

John frowned. "Ay. That's whit Renwick wants. Meantime ivverbody's unner suspicion an the hardship gits worse. Mind ye the incident at the Enterkin Pass didna help either. Claverhoose an ithers huv been scourin the hills, roundin up a guid few innocent folk."

"No jist that." James McAvoy sounded bitter. "I heard that some pair souls were shot on the spot wi nae questions asked. The rule o law seems abandoned these days."

The clock on the mantelpiece chimed like a reminder to call a halt before McAvoy said any more.

William glanced at his grandfather. "Is it mibbe time tae think aboot bed?"

James McAvoy nodded.

"Richt then." William turned a small wooden handle by the edge of the marble fireplace then stood as if expecting something to happen.

A minute later two manservants opened the door and bowed. They carried a tiny candle-lamp in each hand.

Jonas looked at the two men then at William. "Ye turned yon wee haundle on the wall an they twa jist appear. Hoo come?"

"The handle is connected tae a wire that runs aw the way doonstairs tae ring a bell in the kitchen. The staff hear it and ken tae come."

"But hoo did they ken whaur tae come?"

"There's a row o bells in the kitchen. Each wi a label. The ane I rang says sitting-room."

"Weel ah nivver." Jonas looked impressed. "An they ken tae bring lamps as weel?"

"Naw, naw." William laughed. "It's nae that clever. Jist common sense. It's late. We hae guests mibbe ready for bed." William turned to the two servants. "Show Maister Steel and his twa freends tae their rooms. I tak it ivverything is ready?"

Both men nodded.

William took one of the lamps. "Mistress Hawthorn I'll show ye whaur tae go. It's jist a step alang frae here."

James McAvoy stood up. "Guid nicht ma freends. Thank ye for a maist pleasant evening." He sat back down as they all left the room.

William led Helen into a large bedroom. He sat the tiny lamp on a table by the window, closed the shutters then lit an oil lamp on a chest of drawers beside a large bed. "I'll leave ye noo maam. Sleep weel." He bowed politely, stepped into the corridor and the door clicked behind him.

Helen stood a few minutes then lifted the oil lamp and began to explore the room. The washstand in the corner delighted her, so practical yet elegant with a large bowl and pitcher of finest china set in the centre. She held the lamp closer and touched the polished surface then traced the decorated circle of hand-painted roses along each china edge. On a tiny shelf stood a matching soap dish with a lid. She lifted it and sniffed the faint scent of wild roses. An luk at they towels. She counted a neat pile of six white fluffy towels on a low shelf. Ivverythin in its place. Ivverythin as it shud be. If ah wis a lady ah'd expect this. She smiled. Mibbe ah can jist pretend.

She continued to explore, opened the big double wardrobe, approved the cedar smell of moth repellent and the neat click of the latch as she closed both doors again. She moved on to a long, mirrored dressing-table filling the space in front of the window shutters. A silver-backed hairbrush and comb were laid out ready to use, along with a covered powder dish and a bowl of pot-pourri decorated with pink roses, same as a little bottle of what had to be perfume. She smiled again. Hus tae be. She pulled off the stopper. It was delicate and obviously expensive. Hoo the ither hauf lives. An luk at the size o that bed wi a fancy cover draped ower it.

She thought about her own tiny wood-lined room back at Wanlockhead. Ay, weel. Her lip trembled as she carried the lamp back to the table, took off her shoes and tiptoed over to the bed. It stood higher than expected forcing her to jump up, ruffling the pink cover as she landed. She lay down and felt a warm softness wrap round her. A chainge frae ma worn oot blankets an hard sheets. But aw the same. She stared up at the dark ceiling. Her eyes filled with tears. If only ah wis at hame. The salty tears spilt onto her cheeks. *If only.*

Chapter Sixteen

"Guid morning, Mistress Spreul and yersel Maister Neilson," William McAvoy welcomed Mirren and Matthew as they were ushered across the hall towards him.

Mirren smiled. "I must confess tae being curious at a second invite sae soon. I tak it yer maister has guid reason?"

"Maister McAvoy wis indulgin me, mistress." John stepped forward. "Ma name is John Steel an ah'm maist anxious for a word wi ye."

"Really? Hae we met afore?"

"Not at aw. But necessity maks me reach oot tae ye aboot yer niece Elsie."

"Elsie. Whitivver for?" Mirren frowned. "As far as I'm aware she lives happily wi the Hamiltons at Gilkerscleugh Hoose in Crawfordjohn."

"Nae mair ah'm afraid. She hud tae leave ther raither sudden like."

Mirren looked shocked. "But the Hamiltons are kindness itself. They've luked aifter her, brocht her up since her mother died and ma brither disappeared insteid o facing his responsibilities as the bairn's father."

"It wisna the Hamiltons. Lik ye say thur kindness itsel." John glanced at Matthew.

"It's a bit delicate."

This created an uncomfortable silence.

William stepped forward. "Mibbe ye twa wud prefer tae speak privately in the dining-room while I tak Maister Neilson upstairs for a word wi grandfather?"

Mirren shook her head. "Ye can speak freely. Matthew has ma full confidence."

"In that case." William opened the door to the dining-room. "I'll wait oot here and see that ye're nae disturbed."

Mirren's face grew chalk-white as John told her about Skirling House and what had happened there. She sat down with a thump when she heard how ill the girl had become.

"Miss Elsie didna confide in me," John admitted. "Nae aboot the gardener huvin his way wi her an hurtin her real sair. Ma wife nursed her and managed tae git at the truth. Speakin wi ma Marion seemed tae help. Bein accused as a witch wis bad enoch but when ill-meanin folk came aifter her she'd nae option but flee. She went frae the big hoose at Skirling tae Gilkerscleugh. That's whaur ah met her. The Hamiltons thocht she wud be safe wi them but ah warned them aboot folk back at Skirling mibbe realisin whaur she wis an comin aifter her. Ah suggested she come awa wi me an ma freends. They only agreed because ah promised tae find Mistress Helen Spreul an unite her wi Miss Elsie. Ah taen the lass hame wi me an she seemed nae bad at aw till a platoon raided oor farm. Masel an the twa lads managed tae hide while the mither pretended tae be a veesitor."

Matthew opened his mouth as if to say something then stopped.

John hesitated then continued, "It wis this lady as heard ane o the troopers say somethin tae Miss Elsie. Nixt thing she flew oot the hoose an disappeared. It wis a stormy nicht. By the time we found her she wis soaked tae the skin an deid tae the world. We cairried her back an did oor best but it wis hoors afore she opened her een. An a lang time aifter till she spoke a word."

"Dear God." Mirren burst into tears.

"She's recoverin noo. Better ivvery day. But whit happened seems tae huv affected her mair than she's lettin on. Mibbe bein wi her ain folk wud help. Ah certainly believe she's best as far awa as possible frae whit happened. Whaur naebody kens aboot her past. A proper fresh stert. Ah wis hopin tae approach Mistress Helen but sadly that's nae possible."

"Whitivver it takes." Mirren wiped her eyes. "It's the least Elsie deserves."

"Ah left her at ma farm. Dinna worry, she's bein weel luked aifter."

"I dinna doubt it. So whaur is yer farm?"

"Aboot thirty miles frae here, nae far frae the village o Lesmahagow. Aince ma wife thinks she's ready tae travel ah cud bring her tae ye."

Mirren looked at Matthew. "We cud tak the horse and trap and fetch her?"

Matthew nodded.

"That's settled then." Mirren leant over to shake John's hand.

"Thank ye." John looked relieved. "Thur's anither maitter ah need tae mention."

"Is whit ye've tellt me nae enoch?" Mirren sounded anxious.

This time John looked directly at Matthew who'd said nothing so far. "The twa Spreul ships. Nooadays they sail atween Dublin an Rotterdam an nivver come near a Scottish port?"

Matthew blinked. "Ay. It wis a smart move that Mistress Helen made tae protect the family interests frae the conniving lords on the Privy Council. Are ye interested in this arrangement?"

"Indeed. Ah've three freends needin passage tae Holland kinda urgent like."

"Dae ye mean at odds wi the law? On the run?" Matthew frowned. "Is it a maitter o rebellion or jist straightfurrit crime?"

John laughed. "Rebellion. But let me explain."

"Guid grief Maister Steel." Mirren Spreul shook her head as John finished his story. "Ye git yersel involved in some awfy goins on."

"Ye cud say that. But whit aboot ma question?"

"Weel, it jist happens that the *Nightingale* is berthed in Dublin, aboot tae be loaded for her next trip. Whit if yer freends were on yin o the wee boats we aise tae carry stuff frae here tae Dublin?"

John leant forward. "It soonds lik an answer tae a prayer."

"Haurly that Maister Steel." Mirren turned to Matthew. "Am I richt that a fishing boat is due oot o Ayr on oor behalf?"

"Ay." Matthew nodded. "In twa days wi tweed bales and whiskey barrels. But we'd need tae ask the skipper aboot passengers."

Next morning Pete Jamieson came into the McAvoy dining-room while breakfast was being served. James McAvoy, at the head of the table, looked up. "Morning Pete. I hope naething urgent brings ye here sae early?"

"Jist an update fur John." Pete came forward to stand beside John. "Dae ye ken onybody by the name o Nisbet?"

"Giles Nisbet. Comes frae Stonehoose. Hud a run in wi him ower his harassin o a Quaker family."

Jonas looked across the table at John. "Ye certainly got the better o that yin. Made him luk a richt fool. Ah can still see his face as he walked awa wi his tail atween his legs ."

"He must be nursin his wrath," Pete said. "Nisbet spotted John when makin his way frae the *Burnt Barns* tae here. The bugger followed ahint, an taen note which hoose he went intae. Aifter that the garrison captain wis hearin aboot it. Nixt thing the troopers arrived tae cause bother fur the maister."

"Ye nivver said." Jonas looked accusing.

"It was unfortunate but nothing came of it." James McAvoy sounded firm

Jonas gave John another suspicious look. "Hoo dis Pete ken aw this?"

John grinned. "He hus his ways."

Pete grinned. "An that's fur me tae ken an ye tae guess. But tae be serious. The captain hus tellt this Nisbet tae keep an ee oot fur John. It seems that the great an the guid are keen tae git haud o him. Claverhoose himsel wis mentioned."

"Enterkin Pass. Must be." Jonas looked alarmed. "It's comin aifter us."

"But ye're aboot tae leave the country." John frowned at Jonas. "At least ye will as soon as Mistress Mirren's secretary sorts things oot."

"While we sit aboot waitin." Jonas sounded impatient.

"Guid food and a bit rest will build ye up for the journey aheid." James McAvoy joined in. "Tak it while ye can and try tae be patient. Jist mind tae bide safe indoors till Matthew Nielson returns."

Matthew was hardly through the front door of McAvoy's grand house when John was beside him. "Weel. Did ye manage tae find a skipper willin tae help?"

"It didna work oot at Ayr. The skipper says it's ower risky. Even in sic a busy harbour yer travellers micht be noticed. These days the law has aw kinds o een and ears hinging aboot, luking for a chance tae pick up ony kind o information that micht be worth a bit siller. That parteeclar skipper is a guid man and sympathetic tae the Spreuls. But I didna want tae press him. I did explain the urgency and asked if he'd ony suggestions."

"And?"

"He said a mair oot the way harbour micht dae. Somewhaur lik Dunure, a few miles further doon the coast. It seemed worth a go so I went there and had a walk aboot the harbour. A wheen wee boats were at anchor and lucky enoch I got intae conversation wi yin o the skippers. It taen a wee while afore I broached the subject.

At first he shook his heid but the mention o a guid fee seemed tae swing his mind especially when I offered payment up front. Onyway, he agreed tae my request as lang as it's aw done discreet. Only thing is we need tae abide by the tides nae the clock. High tide is late the morn so he wants us tae arrive jist afore then and be ready tae leave as it turns. Late evening shud work fine wi less folk aboot.

It'll tak a while tae reach Dunure so we need tae be awa afore daylicht. I've hired a cart and twa horses and sent word tae a stable ootside Kilmarnock. They'll hae twa fresh horses ready for the second stage o the journey."

"Whit aboot the cost?" John frowned. "It soonds lik ye're runnin up a hefty bill."

"I've spoken wi Mistress Mirren. She says consider it her thanks on behalf o Miss Elsie."

Jonas and Jamie shook Matthew's hand and looked excited. John simply smiled and glanced at Helen who caught his gaze and quickly looked away.

Before daylight the little group of would be travellers left the backyard of James McAvoy's grand house in Glasgow and set our for Dunure. James himself, well wrapped in a thick dressing-gown, shook each hand then stood on the back step to wish them God's speed.

John saluted the old man then edged the horses forward towards the empty main street.

The light grew brighter. Soon the streets would fill up and the noise of the town take over. No one seemed interested in the steady trundling cart heading out of town with its load of silent passengers.

Once on the open road there was still no inclination to talk. John tried once or twice, but everyone seemed pre-occupied with their own thoughts. At Kilmarnock, when the horses were changed, the only conversation was with the stable lads.

And so it went on, with quiet hours slowly passing towards noon, then afternoon, then evening, as the cart passed one weary mile after another.

Helen Hawthorn sat beside John Steel while the cart rumbled

along. She shivered and pulled her woollen cloak tight. "Aw they roads an rough tracks. Ah'm fair worn oot an we huvna reached the boat."

"It's nae much further." John pointed to the angular shape of a castle perched on the headland. "See. Dunure castle. It sits ahint the village."

"Disna luk awfy freendly." Helen peered at it.

"It belangs tae the Kennedys o Ayrshire. Ah believe thur dukes noo an bide in a posh hoose somewhaur else. In past times ane o them roastit an abbot on a spit tae try an mak him gie up land."

"An did he?"

"He lastit twa hoors then agreed. Or so they say. But nivver mind, here's the sign fur Dunure an that's whit wur aifter." John slowly steered the two horses off to the right and began to ease them down a steep track towards the village and its harbour.

On their left was a long terrace of white-painted houses, so white they stood out in the half-dark of late evening. On the other side a rough stone wall stretched all the way to a high outcrop of jaggy rocks which warned him to be careful.

The air was still, so still a mist hovered above as if unsure whether to stay where it was or drift down from the high cliff behind.

"Is this it?" Jonas and Jamie crawled out from the tarpaulin where they'd been sleeping.

"Ay." Matthew, who'd been riding alongside, now trotted ahead till he reached the rocks. He jumped down and began to lead his horse along a stony path and onto the harbour itself. He stopped at the edge of the wall and studied a selection of small fishing boats, skiffs and rowing boats, each held by long ropes trailing out from metal rings set into the thick stones. Here they sat, nestled in the calm water of a tide about to turn.

Along one side of the square-shaped harbour were rows of stacked lobster pots, ready with bait for the next trip out while in front of them sat a row of empty wooden barrels, waiting for the next catch coming in when a cluster of girls in sack-cloth aprons would gut the silver fish and fill each barrel to the brim, all the time singing to a common rhythm which helped their skilled hands and sharp knives slice and chop without a break.

Matthew walked half-way along the edge of the wall then called out, "Edgar?"

The burly shape of a man stood up in the middle of the nearest boat. "Ay. Ye're cuttin it fine. The tide's aboot ready."

Matthew turned and signalled to John who helped Helen down from her high seat. "The boat's waitin. It wud seem that ivverythin is in order." He began to guide her towards Matthew's silhouette.

"Ah hope sae." Helen held tight to his arm. "But ah'm feart. Ah've nivver seen the sea or been onywhaur near it. Noo ah'm aboot tae sail on it."

"Ye'll be fine," John said. "Jist think, this is the stert o yer new life."

"That's whit's botherin me."

"Not at aw. Lik ah said, ye'll be fine." John squeezed her arm.

"Ye said three passengers. Is that richt?" Paul Edgar came up the steep harbour steps to meet Matthew and the travellers.

"Ay. This is them."

Edgar seemed to sense Helen's fear and stepped forward to reassure her. "Ma name's Paul Edgar, skipper o the *Lily-Jane*. She's a grand wee vessel. Ah've plenty experience an mony a sea mile ahint me, enoch tae promise ye a safe landin in Dublin."

Helen hung onto John. "Whit noo?"

"We board ma boat an aff we go." Edgar turned to Jonas and Jamie now standing beside Helen. "The breeze is aff the land so we shudna be held back. If it bides steady we'll be slippin intae Dublin harbour by breakfast time the morn." He took Helen's hand and edged her towards the steep steps. "Lean on me if ye need tae, tak ane step then anither an we'll be on ma boat before ye ken it."

A few minutes later Helen was sitting on a pile of rope, staring up from the deck of the *Lily-Jane* at John Steel staring down at her from the harbour wall.

"Doon ye come," Edgar waved to Jonas and Jamie. "The tide's aboot tae turn."

"Ah'm nae vera guid wi words but thank ye." Jonas shook John's hand. "Mibbe see ye again."

"Ay." John smiled at the eager face. "Ah'll miss ye."

"Mither an masel are beholdin tae ye." Jamie also shook John's hand.

John flushed. "Ay weel. Tak care. Bide safe. An enjoy yer new life."

Jonas and Jamie scrambled down the steps, almost tripping

before landing on the boat deck.

Matthew followed them with two baskets of their belongings then retreated back up to the top of the steps.

No one spoke as Edgar loosened the tethering rope and cast off. They all watched as he took a long boat-hook and pushed his boat backwards, away from the wall, and into the middle of the harbour where it swung round, creating ripples which widened and merged, bringing the flat surface to life as the boat seemed to slide towards the harbour entrance. There the current took over, pulling the boat into a narrow channel beyond and on towards the open sea.

It all happened silently and quickly. The turning tide took the *Lily-Jane* into the dusky night while three figures stood on her deck, facing the land they were leaving.

John seemed to guess Helen's expression, her eyes full of tears. He took off his bonnet and waved it above his head and shouted, "Ye'll be fine." Matthew did the same. The three figures waved back and shouted something which was carried away in the wind as the sail unfurled then swelled to speed the boat forward. After that there was nothing; even the twinkling lantern at the back of the boat was gone.

John listened to the soft swish of incoming waves, and turned to Matthew. "The mistress seemed a bit reluctant tae go. An she's nae alane. Mony a yin hus done it afore her, been forced tae flee. An fur whit?" His voice grew harsh.

Matthew shrugged. "Dinna ask me. It's aw I can dae tae try and keep things richt for the Spreuls. They've been guid tae me thru the years. Noo that the maister's locked up I need tae luk aifter his interests and keep the family as safe as I can, especially since we've lost Mistress Helen."

"Ye dae it raither weel," John replied. "Withoot yer expertise Mistress Mirren wud be lost. Luk hoo ye organised this trip tae Dublin. It wudna huv happened withoot ye."

"Ay, mibbe. But richt noo I'm thinking aboot aw they miles back tae Glesca."

John walked over to the waiting cart, climbed up, and took the reins. "Nae sooner said." He turned the cart round and coaxed the horses back up the slope to the narrow track above.

A few minutes later he began to whistle.

"Ye've cheered up," Matthew said as he rode alongside the cart.

"Ay. Ah've jist been thinkin. Frae noo on thur's three less tae worry aboot. Whit's nae tae like?"

They both laughed as the cart lurched on through the darkening night.

"I thocht ye said we're heading for Logan Hoose." Thomas Houston pointed to the carved sign at the end of a farm track. "This ane says Westermains."

Renwick nodded. "We've still a mile or twa afore reaching Logan Hoose but I'd like tae stop by here a few meenits. Ye see – " He paused. "Hae ye heard o John Steel?"

Houston frowned. "Ay. He brocht back a report aboot yer imminent ordination tae the Societies. They were fair excited aboot it but raither surprised hoo he'd come hame earlier than expected. They were a bit shocked aboot his opinion o Robert Hamilton and his work for us in Holland."

Renwick flushed. "Ay weel." He paused again. "Dinna get me wrang, John wis a loyal and maist helpful freend."

Houston laughed. "But ye didna aye agree?"

"Indeed. The last time we spoke harsh words were exchanged. I'll nae gang intae it ither than admit I wisna as careful as I micht hae been."

Houston pursed his lips. "And?"

"John Steel refused tae bide in Holland anither meenit. He did promise tae deliver ma report but itherwise we were at odds. I've thocht lang and hard aboot it and wud like tae try and mak things better atween us, if I can. This is whaur he bides so if ye dinna mind?"

"If it'll mak ye feel better."

Marion Steel was surprised to see James Renwick and a companion rattle into the farm courtyard. Johnnie and William came up behind and grabbed her hand. She turned and gave them her special 'say nothing' look before stepping towards the lead horse. "Guid day Maister Renwick. Whit can we dae fur ye?"

"Wud John be aboot?"

"He's awa in the toun helpin some freends escape frae the troopers. Nae doubt ye heard aboot the Enterkin Pass rescue. Weel John wis involved alang wi the folk he's noo tryin tae help. The government is desperate tae git haud o them."

"Brave indeed."

Marion frowned. "As weel as makin life mair difficult fur himsel. When John cam back frae Holland he tellt me he'd bide back frae ony further involvement in the cause an whit happens? It aw sterts again."

"But shairly we must dae oor bit?" Renwick said. "Sacrifices…"

"Are gettin mair an mair difficult tae tak." Marion's face tightened. "We're jist ordinary folk Maister Renwick, tryin tae live an ordinary life. Nae lik yersel, dedicated, committed, ordained, specially chosen an expectit tae tak ony risk fur the cause."

"Let it go," Houston whispered, "ye're getting naewhaur."

Renwick nodded. "I'm sorry maam. The last thing I want is tae upset or anger ye. Believe me, I appreciate the difficulties ye've suffered for standing oot against this ill-intentioned king and government. Times are difficult, sometimes even unbearable for us aw. Nae less for masel. With or withoot support I must keep my promise tae the Lord. John Steel is a fine freend and I'd feel better for a quiet word wi him. I'm on my way tae Logan Hoose. We'll be there for a wee while. When John comes hame wud ye mibbe tell him I'd appreciate seeing him again?"

Marion nodded but her expression didn't change. "If it's Logan Hoose ye're heidin fur ye best avoid the road past the village an tak the moors. The government patrols are oot aroond here at aw hoors."

"Thank ye." Renwick signalled to Houston and turned his horse round.

Marion watched the two riders trot through the archway, past the byre and the outhouses then start the long climb up the narrow path to the moor. Nae hairm tae ye Maister Renwick, but ye're trouble if ivver ah saw it. Trouble ah cud weel dae withoot.

John and Matthew found the return journey through a long night exhausting. By the time they returned the cart and horses to the stable on the Gallowgate they were also very hungry.

"Ah need tae eat," John announced. "Some food afore ah think aboot onythin else."

Matthew nodded. "Whaur dae ye suggest?"

"We pass *The Crooked Man* on oor way tae McAvoy's hoose. Will that dae?"

"It's nae yin ah'd choose."

"Whit way? It's a hame frae hame tae the Jamiesons."

"And has some odd craiturs wandering oot and in."

"Lik oorsels." John laughed as he stopped at the inn door. "C'mon. Live dangerously." He ducked under the swinging sign and led Matthew through a narrow hall into a badly-lit room. Surrounded by babbling voices they peered through the smokey fug and sniffed the welcome smell of food.

"Ower there." John pointed. "In yon corner. A bench wi a table."

"Drink or food or baith?" A girl appeared as they sat down.

"Baith," John replied. "Whit huv ye?"

"At this time o day it's aye stew wi roastit vegetables."

"Perfect. An a jug o ale each."

"Twa meenits." The girl disappeared and returned almost immediately with two bowls of stew covered by large hunks of bread. "That dae?" She disappeared again and came back with two jugs of ale and a large plate of mixed vegetables.

John and Matthew tucked in to the first meal they'd had in hours.

"Better than ah thocht," Matthew admitted.

John nodded and kept on eating.

Not far away a pair of eyes, still hostile, still full of resentment, peered at the two hungry travellers.

Weel ah nivver. That yin's Steel. Anither chance tae git even. An this time ah'll mak shair by dain it masel. Giles Nisbet leant forward and pulled a slim blade from his high boot. Place is haufdaurk an fu o smoke. Whae's tae see whit happens? He smiled to himself. At that distance ah canna miss. Ay. Quick, silent an lethal. Steel fur a Steel. Cudna be better.

Two tables away another pair of eyes were fixed on Giles Nisbet. Alex Jamieson was in his usual corner sitting by the ongoing game of chess he played with his brother. He'd seen John and Matthew come in, noted where they sat but let them be. Right now he needed to work out which piece to move otherwise his brother Pete might be about to win this game which they'd been battling over for days.

He might be thinking about chess but innate caution had him glancing up every few minutes, noting anything worth a second look. His gaze hovered on a gangly figure sitting close by. Somethin aboot that yin isna richt. Ay. Worth the watchin. He laid down his chess-piece and paid more attention as the man leant forward to pull something from his high boot then sit up straight again. Mmm a knife. That's nae vera freendly. An the way he's turnin yon blade roond an roond in his fingers he's nae stranger tae it. So whit's he up tae?

Alex stared past the figure and saw John, bent over his bowl of stew. He stiffened. Chriss he's in direct line. Hus tae be. Jist as weel ah didna gang ower earlier tae talk, itherwise ah'd nivver huv noticed.

Alex kept watching as he slipped his own perfectly-balanced blade from his coat sleeve and held the smooth handle hard against the palm of his hand. Richt ma man. Ready when ye are. His index finger lay along the spine of the blade.

Nisbet gently pushed back his chair, slowly stood up and looked round. No one seemed to pay any attention. He looked round again. Still no reaction. Ay. Nae problem. He crooked his arm, began to draw it back.

Behind him Alex Jamieson mirrored Nisbet's actions, then carried through with a quick flick.

Nisbet gasped as Alex's blade sank into his back. Eyes bulging he dropped his knife, collapsed and banged his brow on the table-top while his own blade glanced off his jug of ale to rattle on the floor. Spreadeagled across the table he became a man who'd overdone his ale.

In the half-dark the serving girl didn't notice the knife handle sticking out from Nisbet's back. She squeezed past his table and shook her head.

Alex stepped forward, grabbed Nisbet by the armpits and nodded to the innkeeper who'd seen what had happened. A door into a back corridor was flung open. "Naewhaur near here Alex. Mak shair." He held the door while Nisbet's feet were trailed into the dark space beyond.

Once outside Alex threw the limp body across his shoulder and half-ran through several closes and vennels till he reached a back-court midden. Here he simply let go, allowed the weight to hit the mud at the edge of the stinking rubbish. He bent over to pull out his blade and watch Nisbet's blood spurt then seep into the dirt. Perhaps he'd be found before it was too late. Perhaps not.

John finished his stew and leant back on the bench to savour the last of his ale. Matthew did the same and they were sitting in quiet contentment when Alex Jamieson appeared at their table. "Back then. Git yer travellers awa aricht?"

"We did." John nodded. "Taen a while comin back in the cart."

"Ah've been in ma ain wee world ower there." He pointed through the half-light of the busy room. "Studyin ma chess board. Huv ye been in lang?"

"Lang enoch tae enjoy a guid meal."

"Ye'll be feelin better then. Will ye be heidin fur the maister noo?"

"Ay. Ah'd like a word afore ah gang on hame."

"Ah'll come wi ye," Alex said. "Ah've a key fur the back gate. Since yer face seems tae be weel kent it micht be better that way raither than ringin the front-door bell."

Matthew stood up. "In that case I'll git on ma way and report back tae Mistress Mirren."

"Gie her this if she still means tae come tae ma farm." John took a small piece of crumpled paper from his jacket pocket and wrote down directions. "Tell her she best wait a wee while tae mak shair Miss Elsie's weel enoch tae travel."

"Thank ye." Matthew nodded to them both then headed for the door.

John and Alex turned into the narrow close leading to James McAvoy's backyard. Alex produced his key, opened the gate then turned to John. "Afore we gang in can ah jist say somethin?"

"If ye must."

"Ye shud pay mair attention tae yer ain safety."

John frowned. "If ye're referrin tae the ither nicht whit happened came aboot because ah wis a tad pre-occupied. Itherwise yon Nisbet wud nivver huv got the chance. Ah'm sorry fur the bother it caused the Maister. It's the last thing ah want."

"Fur yer ain sake, John."

"Ye mean in case Nisbet hus anither go?"

"He'll nae be botherin ye."

John opened his mouth as if to reply then seemed to change his mind.

Alex grinned at John's expression. "Ah wis jist sayin."

Pete Jamieson was less than pleased when his brother told him about Nisbet. "Wud a dunt on the heid no been enoch?"

"Aifter whit he did, naw. Jist suppose they troopers hud found John Steel in the maister's hoose. Whit then?"

"Ay weel." Pete shrugged. "If ye pit it that way."

"Ye luk tired, John." James McAvoy pointed to a chair by the fire. "Come and sit down. I'll ring for some refreshment then ye can tell me hoo things went wi yer freends."

"Nae need, sir. Matthew an me taen time tae eat. As fur ma freends, nae problem. They micht be in Dublin by noo. The trail tae Dunure an back wis a bit wearisome but naethin tae complain aboot."

"Glad tae hear it. Dare I ask aboot Mistress Hawthorn?"

"Nae keen on the journey or whaur she's goin but she didna let on."

"I suspected as much. Here's hoping the welcome waiting in Holland will mak a difference and help her settle." James McAvoy leant forward in his seat. "Noo whit aboot yersel?"

"Back hame. In a wee while Mistress Mirren will come oot tae ma farm for her niece. Aince Miss Elsie is safely settled wi her auntie ah mean tae bide oot o sicht an keep ma nose clean. Ma mither aye said flee low an flee lang. Mibbe it's aboot time ah paid attention tae her words."

James McAvoy smiled. "Until the next thing comes alang tae stir yer conscience. I doubt if ye'll chainge. But promise me ye'll pay mair attention tae yer ain safety."

"That's whit Alex said a few meenits ago. Ah thocht he meant Giles Nisbet as sent they troopers tae harass yersel. But he said ah didna need nae tae worry aboot Nisbet."

"Did he noo?" James McAvoy raised his eyebrows.

John stiffened. "That's whit ah thocht."

Neither spoke for a few minutes then the old man flapped his hand. "Alex maks a guid freend."

"An a bad enemy." John pursed his lips and looked away.

There was another awkward silence before James McAvoy said, "Yer carrier freend comes by ivvery time he's in toun. I had William tell him we expected ye here later the day. Is that aricht?"

"Perfect." John smiled. "Ye guessed ma thochts are fur hame."

"In that case – " James McAvoy rang the little handbell on the table beside his chair. When William appeared he said, "John's freend the carrier is likely tae appear at the door afore lang. Tell him tae wait for his passenger."

An hour later John was sitting beside Gus McPhail as the cart trundled past the city boundary. His bonnet was pulled down over his face, his jacket pocket weighed down with a bag of 1000 merks. James McAvoy had insisted he take it. John patted his pocket. "Maister McAvoy gied me a bit mair o ma inheritance."

"Did he noo?" Gus grinned. "Worth bangin ye on the heid then?"

"Ah suppose so."

"Och, nivver mind me." Gus reached over and touched John's arm. "Only jokin. Ah'm mair concerned aboot the toll aw this is takin on ye. Ye luk done in. Tell ye whit, why no crawl unner the hap at the back an huv a sleep?"

A moment later John was sound asleep, out of sight and comfortable. He only woke when Gus turned off the road to lurch up a farm track. "Whit's up?" John's face appeared. "Are we here aready?"

"Aready. Ther's a laugh." Gus looked over his shoulder. "Ye've slept nearly aw the way. Lik ah said, ye luk done in. Afore ye ask ah'm goin intae Waterside. Ah often deliver ther. Ony unfreendly een watchin will think naethin o it. If ah heid up tae Westermains, weel – "

"Is it that bad?"

"Ye've hud a taste o it yersel. Een an ears ivverywhaur as weel as troopers chargin up an doon at aw hoors makin a nuisance o themsels. In ma experience a bit siller slipped intae a man's haund can chainge the vera yin ye aye conseedered a freend."

Rachael Weir was waiting in the farmyard when the cart arrived and looked relieved to see John's face peering over the side of the cart. "Gled tae see ye. Yer freends are safely awa then?"

"Nae bother." John jumped down and gave her a hug while Gus turned the cart then steered the horse towards the close entrance. "Must git on. Tak care. An mind if ye need me ye ken whaur ah am."

A few minutes later the cart was back on the road heading for the village.

"Whit noo, John?" Rachael looked worried. "As far as ah can see the law's gettin mair determined tae catch mair rebels. Ye need tae think aboot bidin quiet an nae drawin attention."

"Ah mean tae be as quiet as the proverbial moose. Frae noo on it's Marion, an the bairns, an naethin else."

"So ye say." Rachael gave him a hard stare. "Ye forget hoo weel ah ken ye."

John flushed. "Ah'm gonnae try. But richt noo hoo's ma Juno?"

"As fine as when ye left her."

"Ah dinna doubt it but ah'll jist tak a meenit wi her afore heidin hame. Thanks fur lukin aifter her sae weel."

"She's safer here. This way the troopers dinna git the chance tae guess when ye're at hame Oot o sicht an oot o mind. On ye go. Huv yer meenit an then git hame tae yer wife an bairns." Rachael waited while John hurried across the yard and disappeared inside the stable. "Him an that horse." She shook her head again and went indoors.

John climbed the long hill towards the little birch wood. From there he'd be able to see any movement around the farm, make sure no trap was set up and waiting.

The grass on either side of the path swished by his legs. It was growing well, almost ready to cut. Ay, whitivver happens nature keeps goin. Somehow this felt reassuring, especially when among the swaying fronds he noticed crowds of dandelions with their bright yellow heads all tightly shut in the evening light. At least they ken whit thur dain. Nae like some ah cud mention. This thought of his own silliness brought another smile as he ploughed up the steep hill.

Once through the little birch wood he stood for a moment to

check there was no sign of any red jackets. Thank God. Bluidy pests. He grinned. At least ah've a guid hidey hole in the hoose when needed an ma ain secret cave when things git mair difficult. They huvna caught me yit. He grinned again. They can search an harass as much as they like but that's aw they can dae. Since faither husna been declared deid Marion an the bairns are entitled tae bide at Westermains. Ay. Jist as lang. His smile slipped then he patted his pocket and felt the weight of the bag of merks. If push comes tae shove thur's enoch siller tae help. He nodded. Ay, ah'm luckier than ah deserve.

He watched the lazy smoke spiralling from the kitchen chimney, the quiet courtyard, the few cows in the buttercup-field near the byre, the sheep busy munching along the tree-lined banks of the burn, the hens scratching and scraping out their own personal dust holes. *If only,* he wished. If only it cud aye be lik this. Normal.

He hurried down the steep path to the house and peered in the little kitchen window. Marion was busy mixing something in a bowl, Miss Elsie and Bella were sitting on the rag-rug by the range building a tower with wooden blocks. Jist as it shud be. He smiled and tapped on the window.

Marion turned, dropped the wooden spoon and was out beside him in seconds to hug and hold him.

Bella jumped at her father and demanded, "Whaur huv ye been?"

John laughed. "Awa tae luk at the sea."

"Whit's that?"

"A lot o watter."

Bella seemed to lose interest and slipped down to return to the wooden blocks and hand one to Elsie.

"Hoo are ye?" John asked as he watched Elsie add to the wooden tower.

"Better ivvery day, Maister Steel. Thanks tae Marion here."

"Weel, that's guid tae hear. Ah've some news fur yersel as weel. Guid and bad, but mair guid than bad." He told her about her uncle locked up on the Bass Rock, his wife's death, her aunt Mirren taking over the business and then ended with, "She cud dae wi help fur the apothecary side o things. She disna ken whit herbs tae order or whit tae dae wi them. It's a terrible problem fur Maister Spreul hus a grand reputation. Mirren is keen tae keep this goin an whae better than yersel wi the knowledge an expertise tae save this pairt o the business. Aifter aw, ye learnt maist o it frae yer uncle himsel. Hoo dae ye feel aboot takin it on?"

"Dis Mirren really think I'm able?"

John smiled. "Fairly soon Mistress Mirren means tae come here an ask ye hersel. Ah'm tellin ye noo so ye can think aboot it. An mind, let it be yer ain decision. Only whit ye want yersel."

Elsie nodded. "It wud be a big responsibility."

"That's whit ah thocht so tak yer time." He turned to Marion. "Whaur's ma lads?"

"Up on the moor tryin tae trap rabbits. They haurly ivver git ony but they enjoy wanderin aboot bein weans lik they shud be. Fly is wi them so thur safe enoch."

John sat down on the settle by the fire and felt more relaxed than he had for weeks. "Guid tae be hame."

Marion smiled at his weary face. "An guid tae huv ye."

John started to say, "Frae noo on – " when the kitchen door burst open and his two sons ran in shouting, "Ma. We saw a crowd o men up ahint Nutberry Hill marchin aboot wi muskets. They wur even firin them. It luks serious. Twa men on horses wur watchin. Ane wis yon man as cam by the ither day askin aboot Pa."

"Wis he a fair-haired young man?" John spoke up and astounded the two boys who gaped at him then ran to his side.

"Whaur did ye come frae?" Johnnie demanded. "Are ye back tae bide?"

"Ah hope so." John put his arms round them both and held them tight. "But richt noo tell me ivverythin ye saw." He looked across the room to Marion who shrugged and mouthed the word Renwick. He turned back to the two eager faces. "Richt. Frae the stert."

His face tensed as he listened. Any sliver of hope melted away. That young man could only be James Renwick. No doubt planning something. Whit noo? He groaned. Whit noo?

The End

251

Historical figures in *Broken Times*

John Steel of Loganwaterhead Farm Bonnet laird with three farms. Lived near Lesmahagow. Fought at the Battles of Drumclog and Bothwell Bridge. Declared a rebel with 1000 merks on his head for capture dead or alive. All his property was confiscated; he spent the next ten years on the run but was never caught. After what was known as the Glorious Revolution, when William of Orange became King, he accepted a Captaincy in the Cameronian Regiment in 1689 to oversee the ousting of English curates without bloodshed. Buried in Lesmahagow Old Parish Churchyard under a plain thruchstane. Date unknown but after 1707.

Marion Steel, wife of John Steel of Loganwaterhead Farm Dates unverified. After Bothwell Bridge she was named as a rebel's wife, thrown out of her farm and forced to live rough on the moor with her young family. Bravely endured ill treatment from government troops. Eventually dared to return to the farm.

David Steel , Cousin of John Steel Lived at Netherskellyhill farm near Lesmahagow. Fought at Drumclog and Bothwell Bridge. Fugitive till 1686 when he was caught and shot.

Lieutenant John Crichton or Creichton Dates not verified. Served in His Majesty's Regiment of Dragoons. He did rise to the rank of captain. Well known for his brutality to prisoners or any rebel on the run. One infamous incident involves the shooting of David Steel of Nether Skellyhill farm on 20th December 1686. Imprisoned in the Edinburgh Tolbooth after the change of government in 1690. He is remembered in Jonathan Swift's book in 1731 titled 'Memoirs of Lieutenant John Creichton' where the account of his exploits are somewhat at odds with recorded fact.

John Graham of Claverhouse, Viscount Dundee 1648-1689 Faithful supporter of Stuart Kings who relied heavily on his ability to keep order in the South of Scotland. One of the most successful Scottish soldiers of his time. Considered a ruthless opponent by Covenanters, he earned the title of Bluidy Clavers. Administered justice throughout Southern Scotland, captain of King's Royal Regiment, member of Scottish Privy Council, created Viscount in 1688. Killed at the Battle of Killiekrankie 17th June 1689 where his men won the battle.

Lady Jean Cochrane Married John Graham on 9th May 1684. Granddaughter of Lord Dundonald. She was 16 years younger than her husband. It was a love match not an arranged marriage as her family were strong Covenanting supporters. The immediate family were much against the marriage but her grandfather gave his consent. Members of Scottish Privy Council made mischief of this match to do down Graham at every turn. After Graham's death in 1689 she survived him only another 7 years before dying herself after an accident while staying in Utrecht. She was brought back to Scotland and is buried in Kilsyth.

John Spreul, Apothecary Wealthy business man arrested on the false charge of being at the Battle of Bothwell Bridge. He refused to confess and demanded an apology from the Privy Council. Given a fine of £500 which he refused to pay, he was sent to the Bass Rock till he would pay. He was there for years but still refused. Eventually the order was given for his cell door to be left open. Spreul took the hint and left. By this time he'd lost his businesses but he somehow started again and became an important merchant once again. A very determined man and clever apothecary.

Helen Spreul Wife of John Spreul who supported him during his imprisonment on the Bass Rock. She visited him on several occasions but never managed to persuade him to pay the fine of £500. She died before he was released.

George Mackenzie of Rosehaugh 1636-1691 King's Advocate. Main member of Scottish Privy Council. Sentenced many Covenanters to transportation, imprisonment, or death. After what was known as the Glorious Revolution in 1689 he wrote two books justifying his actions. A power-hungry man.

John Maitland, 1st Duke of Lauderdale 1610-1682 Secretary of State for Scotland. One of King Charles II's advisers. Another power-hungry, unethical man prone to plotting against colleagues. Fierce prosecutor of Covenanters.

Thomas Dalyell of the Binns 1602-1685 Long serving Royalist. Earlier in his career he awas Lieutenant General in the Russian army. Very individual, fierce, uncompromising, eccentric character. Given special privilege of raising regiment known as the Royal Scots Greys, which he paid for from his own purse. Determined persecutor of Covenanters. Member of Scottish Privy Council.

Reverend Alexander Peden One of the most significant Covenanter ministers. Inspirational preacher. Outed from his parish at New Luce in Wigtonshire, he spent most of his life living rough and taking secret religious meetings. Famous for wearing a leather mask. Credited with second sight and described as Peden the prophet.

Ambushed in June 1672, he was sent to the Bass Rock for four years then ordered aboard the *St Michael* for transportation to America. The ship put in at Gravesend in England where the captain set all the prisoners free. Returned home then wandered between Scotland and Northern Ireland. Died at his brother's house 26th January 1686 aged sixty. After burial troops dug up the corpse with the intention of staging a hanging. The local laird intervened and the corpse was buried at foot of the gallows. It was subsequently dug up again and buried in Cumnock.

Reverend Donald Cargill 1610-1681 One of the main ministers and rebel preachers of the Covenant. Minister of Barony Church Glasgow till 1662 when he was expelled for refusing to celebrate the king's birthday. Fought at Bothwell Bridge. Long career of rebel preaching. Colleague and stout supporter of Richard Cameron. After Cameron's death he published a paper excommunicating king and government. As a result, a 5000 merks reward was posted for his capture. He was caught at Covington Mill near Biggar on 12th July 1681, tried and hanged in Edinburgh Grassmarket 27th July 1681.

Reverend Richard Cameron 1648-1680 Radical Covenanter. Ordained in Holland before returning to Scotland to try and revive resistance against the government. Known as the Lion of the Covenant. A great preacher and fearless adversary. Drew up the Sanquhar Declaration denouncing the king. A 5000 merks reward for his capture dead or alive, was posted. Four weeks later he was killed during a skirmish at Airds Moss near Cumnock. A short but meaningful ministry. The 26th or Cameronian Regiment was named in his memory.

Reverend James Renwick 1662-1688 One of the most inspiring Covenanting ministers. Last martyr, at age of 26. Supporter of Richard Cameron and Donald Cargill. Ordained in Holland which caused problems when he returned to Scotland. He was involved in the Lanark Declaration 12th January 1682 and 2nd

Sanquhar Declaration 28th May 1685.

Sir Robert Hamilton of Preston and Fingalton A poor leader of the Covenanters at Bothwell Bridge. Almost first to leave the field and flee to the safety of Holland. In Holland he met and befriended James Renwick then encouraged Renwick to return to Scotland and begin field preaching. Returned to Scotland after 1689.

Logan House A remote farmhouse beyond Lesmahagow where Covenanters met after the death of Richard Cameron to form the Societies with an allegiance to field preaching. This meeting took place on 15th December 1681 and led to the publication of the Lanark Declaration in January 1682. They remained active till 1689.

James Ogilvie Earl of Airlie and Strathmore Stout royalist supporter. Cavalry leader at Bothwell Bridge. During the final stage of the battle he tried to capture John Steel. John Steel fought back, knocked Airlie off his horse then escaped. Airlie then tried to hunt down Steel, unsuccessfulyl. In revenge he claimed the Steel farm and land.

Lord George Douglas 1st Earl of Dumbarton, 3rd son of William, 1st Marquis of Douglas. Served in the French army then was recalled to Britain by Charles II who made him Earl of Dumbarton. When James VII came to the throne he was made commander-in-chief of the Scottish forces. An adversary of John Graham.

Andrew Bruce of Earlshall. Dates not verified. Military man on the Loyalist side, led troops at Airds Moss to kill Richard Cameron. Appointed Claverhouse's lieutenant in 1682. Very active in pursuing Covenanters throughout the south of Scotland.

Bibliography

I gained insight into this period from:

- W.H.Carslaw *The Life and Letters of James Renwick*
- Nicholas Culpeper, *Culpeper's Complete Herbal*
- Elizabeth Foyster & Christopher A. Whatley, *A History of Everyday Life in Scotland 1600-1800*
- Maurice Grant, *The Lion of the Covenant; No King But Christ; Preacher to the Remnant*
- John Greenshields *Private Papers*
- James King Hewison, *The Covenanters*
- John Howie, *The Scots Worthies*
- Dr. Mark Jardine, *Jardine's Book of Martyrs*
- Magnus Linklater & Christian Hesketh, *For King and Conscience*
- Dane Love, *The Covenanter Encyclopaedia*
- Rosalind K. Marshall, *The Days of Duchess Anne*
- Thomas McCrie, *The Bass Rock*
- David S. Ross, *The Killing Time*
- Andrew Murray Scott, *Bonnie Dundee*
- Ann Shukman, *Bishops and Covenanters*
- Charles Sanford Terry, *John Graham of Claverhouse Viscount of Dundee 1648-1689*
- J.H. Thomson, *The Martyr Graves of Scotland*
- Robert Watson, *Peden:Prophet of the Covenant*
- Ian Whyte *Agriculture and Society in Seventeenth Century Scotland*
- *The Laird and Farmer, by a Native of that Country* (published by Ecco)
- Robert McLeish (Archivist of Lesmahagow Historical Association), Newsletters (*Scottish Covenanter Memorial Association*).

About the Author
Ethyl Smith

As an illustrator ah interpretit ither fowk's wirds. Bit thru time ah stertit aisin ma ain. An the mair ah scrieved the mair ah wantit tae. Aince retired ah wis aff lik a whippet. First cam Strathclyde, than a course wi Janice Galloway at Faber. She recommendit me fur a Maister's at Stirling whaur ah got intae 17th Century Scotland wi its boorach o religion an politics.

Thur wis mony a happenin nearaboot ma hame makin it a skoosh tae howk oot the man tae cairry ma story; a bonnet laird cawed John Steel, a Covenantin rebel, 10 years on the run yit nivver caucht.

Findin oot mair hud me stravaigin thru moors an hills, veesitin unco places lik the Bass Rock, scourin papers, letters, academic buiks, speirin here an ther afore aisin whit ah'd lairnt in fiction.

Early on ah jaloosed hoo Scots leid brocht credence. Ah testit it wi short stories, got intae anthologies, an wun a wheen compeetitions. The best yin gied doon a storm at the National Library.

2014 brocht a big smile whan Thunderpoint published ma first buik. Wur noo on nummer four as weel as aisin speakin events tae pruive hoo history aye touches us.

Ethyl Smith is a graduate of the University of Strathclyde Novel Writing course and the Stirling University MLitt Creative Writing course. Smith has had numerous short stories published in a range of publications, including *Scottish Field*, *Spilling Ink*, *Stirling Collective Anthology*, *Mistaken Identities Anthology* (edited by James Robertson) and *Gutter Magazine*.

Ethyl was also a finalist in the Twice Dragons Pen competition, with the story recorded for BBC Radio Scotland, and a Finalist in the Wigtown Book Festival Short Story Competition.

Also from Ethyl Smith
Changed Times

ISBN: 978-1-910946-09-1 (eBook)
ISBN: 978-1-910946-08-4 (Paperback)

1679 – The Killing Times: Charles II is on the throne, the Episcopacy has been restored, and southern Scotland is in ferment.

The King is demanding superiority over all things spiritual and temporal and rebellious Ministers are being ousted from their parishes for refusing to bend the knee.

When John Steel steps in to help one such Minister in his home village of Lesmahagow he finds himself caught up in events that reverberate not just through the parish, but throughout the whole of southern Scotland.

From the Battle of Drumclog to the Battle of Bothwell Bridge, John's platoon of farmers and villagers find themselves in the heart of the action over that fateful summer where the people fight the King for their religion, their freedom, and their lives.

Set amid the tumult and intrigue of Scotland's Killing Times, John Steele's story powerfully reflects the changes that took place across 17th century Scotland, and stunningly brings this period of history to life.

'Smith writes with a fine ear for Scots speech, and with a sensitive awareness to the different ways in which history intrudes upon the lives of men and women, soldiers and civilians, adults and children' – James Robertson

Dark Times
Ethyl Smith

ISBN: 978-1-910946-26-8 (Kindle)
ISBN: 978-1-910946-24-4 (Paperback)

The summer of 1679 is a dark one for the Covenanters, routed by government troops at the Battle of Bothwell Brig. John Steel is on the run, hunted for his part in the battle by the vindictive Earl of Airlie. And life is no easier for the hapless Sandy Gillon, curate of Lesmahagow Kirk, in the Earl's sights for aiding John Steel's escape.

Outlawed and hounded, the surviving rebels have no choice but to take to the hills and moors to evade capture and deportation. And as a hard winter approaches, Marion Steel discovers she's pregnant with her third child.

Dark Times is the second part of Ethyl Smith's sweeping *Times* series that follows the lives of ordinary people in extraordinary times.

"What really sets Smith's novel apart, however, is her superb use of Scots dialogue. From the educated Scots of the gentry and nobility to the broader brogues of everyday folk, the dialogue sparkles and demands to be read out loud." – Shirley Whiteside (The National)

Desperate Times
Ethyl Smith

ISBN: 978-1-910946-47-3 (Kindle)
ISBN: 978-1-910946-46-6 (Paperback)

July 1680: Richard Cameron is dead, and John Steel and Lucas Brotherstone have only just escaped capture by government forces. The net widens to arrest anyone suspected of Covenanter sympathies, and the army becomes ever more brutal in its suppression of the rebels.

To have any hope of survival Lucas Brotherstone must escape to Holland, and John Steel is determined to make this happen.

Desperate Times is the third historical novel in Ethyl Smith's series, following *Changed Times* and *Dark Times*, about the lives of ordinary people in extraordinary times.

'Smith writes with a fine ear for Scots speech, and with a sensitive awareness to the different ways in which history intrudes upon the lives of men and women, soldiers and civilians, adults and children' - James Robertson

Also from ThunderPoint
The Bogeyman Chronicles
Craig Watson
ISBN: 978-1-910946-11-4 (eBook)
ISBN: 978-1-910946-10-7 (Paperback)

In 14th Century Scotland, amidst the wars of independence, hatred, murder and betrayal are commonplace. People are driven to extraordinary lengths to survive, whilst those with power exercise it with cruel pleasure.

Royal Prince Alexander Stewart, son of King Robert II and plagued by rumours of his illegitimacy, becomes infamous as the Wolf of Badenoch, while young Andrew Christie commits an unforgivable sin and lay Brother Brodie Affleck in the Restenneth Priory pieces together the mystery that links them all together.

From the horror of the times and the changing fortunes of the characters, the legend of the Bogeyman is born and Craig Watson cleverly weaves together the disparate lives of the characters into a compelling historical mystery that will keep you gripped throughout.

Over 80 years the lives of three men are inextricably entwined, and through their hatreds, murders and betrayals the legend of Christie Cleek, the bogeyman, is born.

'The Bogeyman Chronicles haunted our imagination long after we finished it' – iScot Magazine

The False Men
Mhairead MacLeod

ISBN: 978-1-910946-27-5 (eBook)
ISBN: 978-1-910946-25-1 (Paperback)

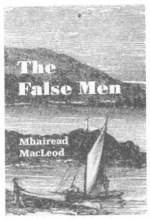

North Uist, Outer Hebrides, 1848

Jess MacKay has led a privileged life as the daughter of a local landowner, sheltered from the harsher aspects of life. Courted by the eligible Patrick Cooper, the Laird's new commissioner, Jess's future is mapped out, until Lachlan Macdonald arrives on North Uist, amid rumours of forced evictions on islands just to the south.

As the uncompromising brutality of the Clearances reaches the islands, and Jess sees her friends ripped from their homes, she must decide where her heart, and her loyalties, truly lie.

Set against the evocative backdrop of the Hebrides and inspired by a true story, *The False Men* is a compelling tale of love in a turbulent past that resonates with the upheavals of the modern world.

'...an engaging tale of powerlessness, love and disillusionment in the context of the type of injustice that, sadly, continues to this day' – Anne Goodwin

The Summer Stance
Lorn Macintyre

ISBN: 978-1-910946-58-9 (Paperback)
ISBN: 978-1-910946-59-6 (Kindle)

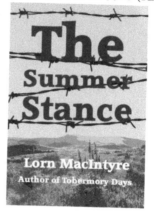

Abhainn na Croise, the river of the cross, where the otters swim and the Scottish Travellers camped for generations, working on the land, repairing whatever was broken, and welcomed back each year by the area's settled residents.

Those days are long gone, but Dòmhnall Macdonald, raised in a Glasgow tower block, yearns for the old ways and the freedom they represent. When his grandmother falls ill, Dòmhnall determines to take her back to the Abhainn na Croise one last time - but times have changed too much.

Instead of the welcome of old, the returning Travellers are met with suspicion, hostility and violence - and Dòmhnall becomes a hunted man.

Set in the timeless Scottish landscape, Lorn Macintyre's latest novel is an intimate portrait of a misunderstood way of life and a fast disappearing part of Scottish culture.

'The Summer Stance is about racial prejudice; the loss of the Gaelic oral tradition; and the destruction of the Scottish landscape, its historic sites and its wildlife through indiscriminate development.'